LOVE UNSCRIPTED

Love Series Romance Collection

SANDI LYNN

Sandi Lynn Romance, LLC

Love Unscripted
Love Series Romance Collection
copyright © 2025 Sandi Lynn
Publisher: Sandi Lynn Romance, LLC

All rights reserved. No part of this publication may be reproduced, distributed, or transmitted in any form or by any means, including photocopying, recording, or other electronic or mechanical methods, without the publisher's prior written permission.
This is a work of fiction. Names, characters, places, and incidents are the products of the author's imagination or are used factiously. Any resemblance to actual events, locales, or persons, living or dead, is entirely coincidental.

Love In Between

LOVE SERIES, BOOK ONE

Love In Between

(Love Series, Book One)

New York Times, USA Today & Wall Street Journal Bestselling Author
SANDI LYNN

Music Acknowlegement

Clouds
Music and Lyrics by Letters and Lights

I want to take this opportunity to thank Eric Knudsen of the band Letters and Lights for graciously allowing me to use the lyrics to his song "Clouds" in Love In Between.
You can connect with Letters and Lights on Facebook:
https://www.facebook.com/lettersandlights
https://twitter.com/letters_lights

Mission Statement

Sandi Lynn Romance

Providing readers with romance novels that will whisk them away to another world and from the daily grind of life – one book at a time.

Prologue

LILY

"You're the most beautiful bride I've ever seen."

"You have to say that. You're my mom." I smiled.

I stared at my white A-line strapless dress, embellished with rhinestone flowers that cascaded asymmetrically over the bodice, as I ran my hands down my sides. I turned my head to make sure my cathedral bridal veil was placed perfectly amongst my elegant curly updo.

"I can't believe you're finally getting married!" Giselle smiled.

"You're picture-perfect, Lily Gilmore," Gretchen spoke as she snapped a picture with her phone.

I was so nervous, and my hands were beginning to sweat. I couldn't believe this day had finally arrived. The past year of planning the perfect wedding was torturous but exciting. Hunter stood by my side and agreed with everything that I liked. I think he just wanted to keep the peace or didn't care. He didn't want a big wedding. He wanted to run off to Vegas and get married at one of those drive-by chapels. I've always dreamed of a big wedding, and he understood, so he nixed the idea of Vegas. Plus, my mother would have killed us both if we eloped.

People were gathered in the church, waiting for the ceremony to begin.

"Lily, where's your sister?"

"I'm not sure, Mom. She said she had to go get something and would be right back."

"She's your maid of honor and needs to be here. The ceremony is about to start."

I sighed and headed out of the dressing room. I walked down the long hallway that connected to a small kitchen. I figured she probably went out behind the church to have a cigarette, so I proceeded through the kitchen and stopped when I heard a noise coming from one of the rooms off to the side. I placed my hand on the knob and slowly turned it as I opened the door. Nothing had prepared me for what I saw.

I pulled the door shut and ran out of the church. My heart was racing, and my stomach felt sick. I heard my mother's voice following me from behind. I stopped when she called my name in a panic. I put my hand on my head and paced in circles. My breathing was rapid, and I looked up and saw Hunter standing there, looking at me and my sister standing behind him. Tears began to stream down my face as he slowly started walking towards me. I put my hand up before he took three steps.

"Don't you dare come near me, you bastard!" I screamed.

"Lily? Hunter? What the hell is going on?" my mother asked.

I stood there, pointing my finger. "Why don't you ask that cheating bastard over there and his dirty whore standing behind him?!" I spat.

My mother turned her head and looked at my sister, Brynn. She stood there, shaking her head, as she stared at them. By this time, a crowd had emerged from the church and gathered around to see the commotion. How my mother looked at Brynn and Hunter gave me the feeling that she knew what was going on between them.

"Lily, please, let me——" Hunter started to say.

"Don't you ever say a fucking word to me again!" I screamed, cutting him off.

Feeling about as small as an ant, I stood there and raised my arms. "Well, it looks like there isn't going to be a wedding today, folks! Unless my whore of a sister over there wants to marry this cheating bastard!" I yelled as I pointed to Hunter.

"Lily! That's enough!" my mother commanded.

I looked at her with disgrace and slowly walked towards her. "You knew, didn't you? You knew they were screwing behind my back!"

She stared at me with a look of guilt. She didn't have to say a word. Her reaction said it all. I shook my head as I looked at my sister, who was crying on the church steps.

"Why are you crying? Isn't this what you wanted? You can have him, baby sister, because you were made for each other!"

I ripped off my veil and threw it on the ground as I turned on my heels and stomped away. Giselle and Gretchen followed behind, and we took the limo back to their hotel room.

Stepping into the hotel room, I immediately sat on the edge of the bed. The only tears that fell were the ones outside the church. I was still in shock until Giselle sat beside me and told me it was okay to cry. I broke down as she held me. Gretchen walked over and sat on the other side as we hugged.

"It's going to be okay, Lily," Gretchen whispered.

"How could he do this to me?" I sobbed.

"He's an asshole, and it's better that you found out now," Giselle said.

"She's right, honey. It's better now than five years from now," Gretchen spoke.

I sniffled, and Giselle handed me some tissues.

"What are you going to do now?" Gretchen asked.

"Gretchen!" Giselle scolded.

"It's okay. I don't know what I'm going to do. I can't go back home, and I can't face my family. I can't believe my mother knew about Hunter and Brynn. How could she keep that from me after what my father did to her?"

"I don't know, sweetie. It's pretty fucked up that she knew, and your sister, my God, why would she do that to you?"

"I feel like I'm going to be sick," I said as I sprang from the bed and into the bathroom, shutting the door behind me.

~

I stayed in the hotel room for an entire week. I didn't get out of bed except to use the bathroom. I kept my phone off and instructed Giselle and Gretchen not to let anyone know where I was staying. They went out and bought me a new cell phone so that we could keep in touch because they needed to get back to California for their jobs. I ordered room service when I felt like it, but I mostly stared at the ceiling, thinking about how much my life sucked. I cried until it felt like my eyes were going to fall out. I couldn't understand why Hunter would do that to me. Oh, wait, yes, I did. It's because he's a man, and that's what men do. They're cheating, lying bastards who can't commit to one woman. Are all men like that? I started to believe they were. Then, there was my sister.

~

It was Wednesday, and I knew my mother would be at her charity meeting and my sister would have lunch with her friends. It was something they did every Wednesday. As the cab pulled up to the house, I stared at it for a minute through the window.

"Miss, are you getting out?" the driver asked.

I looked at him, and it took me a minute to register what he'd asked.

"Yeah, I'm sorry."

I paid him the cab fare, climbed out of the cab, and stood in front of the long, winding driveway that led to the only house I'd known my entire life.

I slowly entered, making sure no one was home. I couldn't face my family, not after what they'd done to me. I quickly went upstairs to my room, grabbed my suitcases from the closet, and threw only the necessities inside. I needed to do this quickly before someone came home. I grabbed a handful of clothes from my closet. My makeup, bras, underwear, and shoes. I had two suitcases packed and ready to go. I opened the top drawer of my desk, pulled out my bank book, and stood in the doorway, looking at the room that had been mine my entire life. I headed down the stairs with my suitcases. As I approached the front door, it opened, and my mother walked in. She froze when she saw me, and tears filled her eyes.

"Lily, my baby, I was so worried about you. Where have you been?"

I gave her a stern look and instantly felt sick to my stomach.

"It doesn't matter where I've been. The only thing that matters is I'm gone and out of this family forever. What you did to me by not telling me about Brynn and Hunter is unforgivable. You helped me plan my wedding, knowing he was fucking my little sister. You were going to let me marry a cheater and a liar. What kind of mother are you?!" I started to cry.

"Lily, please. You have to understand that I was trying to protect you, and he promised me that it was over," she said as she walked towards me with her arms out.

"Don't you dare take another step!" I snapped. "I'm nothing like you, and I won't live my life like you either."

I walked out the front door, stopped, and turned around, staring at my mother as she stood there, crying.

"This family is dead to me. Tell my little sister I hope she and Hunter live happily ever after. Have a nice life, Mother." I threw my suitcases in the back of my Explorer, climbed in, and started it. My mother ran out of the house after me as I began to back out of the driveway.

"Please, Lily. I'm sorry. Please don't do this to us. You're going to regret it."

"The only thing I regret is ever being a part of this lying, cheating family!" I spat as I peeled out of the driveway and headed as far away from this place as I could. I only knew that I couldn't stay in Seattle anymore. It was time for me to disappear and start a new life.

I DROVE for about three hours until my gas light came on. I had reached Portland, Oregon. I pulled into a gas station and opened my purse to get my credit card. I froze when I saw the two tickets to Aruba, which was supposed to be my honeymoon. We were supposed to leave tomorrow because Hunter couldn't get two weeks off the day after the wedding. I filled the Explorer with gas and drove to a mini outdoor mall. I took out my camera and took pictures of every place I stopped because I wanted to make a scrapbook of the journey to my new life. I took photos of the shops, signs, and people around.

It was a beautiful, warm, sunny day, and I noticed a café with tables that sat outside. I wasn't hungry, but it had been several hours since I'd eaten. I sat at an open table and placed my order with the waitress. As I looked around, taking in the fresh air, I noticed a couple sitting a few tables over, holding hands and laughing. The guy was hot. There was no doubt about that, and his girlfriend was beautiful. Something about his smile struck me in more places than one. They looked happy, and I could see they were very much in love. I grabbed my camera and snapped a picture of them.

I ate lunch, had a couple of glasses of iced tea, and reached for my purse to pay the bill. As I reached inside and grabbed my wallet, the airline tickets fell out and onto the cement. I reached down, picked them up, and held them in my hand, staring at them in disgust. After I left some money on the table, I had an idea. Walking over to the happy couple that I'd been watching since I sat down, I approached them.

"Hi. I know this is weird, but I have two airline tickets to Aruba. The flight leaves tomorrow, and I want you to have them."

They both looked at me like I was crazy.

"You aren't going?" the woman asked in confusion.

"No, something came up, so my fiancé and I couldn't go. I don't want them to go to waste, and I can't get a refund. The two of you look like you would enjoy Aruba together."

She looked at him, and they both looked at me. "Let me pay you for the tickets," the guy said as he reached into his pocket to pull out his wallet.

"No. Please take them. I don't want your money. Just promise me that you'll have a good time," I said as I put the tickets on the table and started to walk away.

"Wait!" the girl yelled. "Thank you." She smiled.

"Consider it a gift, and just pay it forward someday." I smiled as I walked back to my Explorer.

Chapter One

ONE YEAR LATER

LILY

Inserting the key into the lock, I unlocked the door. I slowly turned the handle and lightly pushed the door open as I stepped inside my new apartment. Setting down my suitcases, I took a deep breath. I flipped the light switch on the wall next to the door and looked around. The furniture that I ordered online had arrived, and it was scattered all over the room. I rented this apartment based on the pictures showcased on the internet. Walking around, I inspected my new home. The light gray walls and white moldings gave the place a classic look. The eggplant color couch and loveseat I bought matched perfectly, as did the glass coffee table and end tables. I walked down the hall and into my bedroom. Flipping the light switch, I stared at the empty space as the bedroom set was being delivered tomorrow. It was late, and I was exhausted since I drove fourteen hours straight from Portland to Santa Monica. My Explorer was filled with boxes, but they would have to wait until the morning. At that moment, I just wanted to feel the comfort of my new couch.

I spent the last year in Portland when my car broke down, and it took two weeks to get repaired. I guess you could say the place grew on me, and I really didn't have any other place to go. I rented an apartment, took a job as a freelance photographer for the local newspaper, and was a substitute teacher for a few months at one of the local elementary schools. I ended up in Santa Monica because the local newspaper shut down, and my gig as a substitute teacher ended when the regular teacher came back from maternity leave.

Giselle called me one day and said that her Aunt Chris, the principal of an elementary school in Santa Monica, was looking for a long-term substitute teacher and that I should call her. So I did, and that's how I ended up here.

The twins Giselle and Gretchen lived in Santa Monica, and I was excited to be living near them again. We'd been best friends for as long as I could remember. I met them when I was six years old when they moved into the house next door. Their father was an investment banker, and their mother was a model in her younger days. Giselle and Gretchen followed in their mother's footsteps. With their five-foot ten-inch height and size six bodies, they were made to be models. I was envious of their deep brown eyes and their long, straight brown hair. Our mothers used to call us the three musketeers because we were inseparable. We did everything together, and were always there when the other needed us. The twins were my rock, and no matter what exotic place their job took them to, we talked almost every day.

I opened my eyes and was startled by the music I heard coming through the wall. I grabbed my phone and looked at the time. It was three o'clock in the morning. I had been sleeping for about two hours, which had become the norm for me since I caught Hunter and Brynn together in the church. My mind was on permanent rewind, and every time I closed my eyes, that scene played over and over again.

I got up from the couch, grabbed my purse, and walked to the bathroom. I wanted to wash my face, but I forgot that all my towels and washcloths were packed away in one of the boxes that sat in the Explorer. I took the brush out of my purse and ran it through my long, blonde hair. I searched for a rubber band and pulled my hair into a high ponytail. As I looked at myself in the mirror, I couldn't help but notice the bags underneath my blue-gray eyes. I needed a shower, so I put on my shoes, grabbed my keys, and headed to the Explorer.

As I stepped out into the hallway of my apartment, I stood there and stared at the door from which the blaring music was coming. Shaking my head, I rolled my eyes and headed to my SUV for the box that was labeled BATHROOM.

I lifted the box out of the Explorer and carried it to the apartment building door. Inserting the key, the door opened, and I stumbled back, nearly falling over.

"Hey there. I'm sorry. I didn't see you," a good-looking man apologized.

He looked at me and then at the box on the ground. "Are you moving in?" he asked as he looked at his watch.

"Yes. I just got here a few hours ago and haven't had a chance to get the boxes from my truck."

"It's nice to meet you. I'm Sam," he said as he held out his hand.

"Hi, I'm Lily. It's nice to meet you, too."

"Let me grab that box for you." He offered as he bent down to pick it up.

"No, that's alright. I've got it," I said.

"Don't be ridiculous. Let me carry the box for you since I almost knocked you on your ass with the door." He smiled.

It was the middle of the night, and I was arguing with a hot guy over a box.

"Fine. My apartment's right there," I spoke as I pointed to my door.

Sam looked at me and smiled. "Well, look at that. It looks like we're neighbors."

I opened the door for him as he stepped inside my apartment and set the box down on the floor.

"So, you're the one playing the loud music at three a.m.?" I asked.

"Sorry about that," he spoke as he shrugged his shoulders. "I'll tell Lucky to keep it down."

"I'd appreciate it. Thanks for the help with the box."

I spent the next hour unpacking the box and putting away the towels. I organized all my bathroom items and then took a hot, relaxing bubble bath. My hands began to wander as it had been a while since my battery-operated boyfriend and I had a date. As soon as I was finished, I climbed out of the tub, wrapped a towel around me, and walked into the living room where my suitcases were. Opening my larger suitcase, I pulled out a pair of jean shorts and a navy-blue tank top. I grabbed my phone from the couch and looked at the time. It was six a.m. Giselle and Gretchen were coming over to help me unpack around eight, and the bedroom set was being delivered between nine and eleven. I blow-dried my hair, then put it back up in a high ponytail. After putting on some light makeup, I decided to go for coffee before starting my day.

I stepped out of my apartment at the same time Sam did his. We both looked at each other.

"Don't you ever sleep?" He smiled.

"I should be asking you the same thing." I smiled back.

Sam was hot, there was no question about it. He stood around six feet tall with a great muscular body, sandy brown hair, and brown eyes. He definitely fit the Santa Monica image.

"Where are you off to so early in the morning?" he asked.

"I'm off to find some much needed caffeine," I replied as I stepped out of the building door, and he followed behind me.

"Me too. I went to make some coffee, but the bag was empty. I hate it when Luke doesn't tell me we're out of coffee."

"Luke?" I asked.

"Yeah, he's my BF and roommate. Hey, would you like to go get some coffee together?" he asked with a smile.

I studied him for a few moments. Sam seemed like a really nice guy, and he was gay, so I didn't have to worry about him hitting on me.

"Sure, I'll go with you, but we have to make it quick. My girlfriends are coming over to help me unpack."

I hopped into his truck, and we drove down the road to a coffee house called Brewster's. As we walked inside, Sam was instantly greeted by the girl behind the counter.

"Morning, Sam. Who's your friend?" she asked as she was wiping down the counter.

"Morning, Jamie. This is Lily. She just moved in next door. Lily, this is my cousin, Jamie. She owns this lovely coffee house."

Jamie wiped her hands dry and held it out to me as I gently shook it.

"It's nice to meet you, Lily. Are you new in town?"

"Yes. I just moved here from Portland last night."

"Great. Welcome to Santa Monica and to Brewster's. What can I get you?" she asked.

"I'll just have a large black coffee." I smiled.

I looked over at Sam and found him staring at me.

"What?"

"That's how Luke drinks his coffee. I don't understand how you can drink it without sugar or cream. We argue about it all the time."

"Everyone has different coffee tastes," Jamie said.

"Let me pay for your coffee," I said to Sam.

"It's on the house." Jamie smiled as she handed us our coffees. "Cheap-ass Sam over here never pays. Consider it a welcome to Santa Monica gift."

"Thanks, Jamie!" Sam smiled as he grabbed a bag of coffee from the shelf. "I'm taking a bag home. I owe you!"

Jamie rolled her eyes. "He owes me every week." She laughed.

"Thank you, Jamie. It was nice to meet you." I smiled as I held up my coffee cup.

"It was nice to meet you too! Make sure to stop by occasionally and say hi."

I walked out of Brewster's and climbed into the truck. "Your cousin is really nice."

"Yeah, she's more like my sister. She came to live with my family and me when she was eight. Her mom and dad were drug dealers, and they were sent to prison."

"Are they still in prison?" I asked.

"Yeah. Twenty years later and they're still there. She hasn't seen them in all these years either."

We arrived back at the apartment building, and I climbed out of the truck. I walked over to my Explorer and set my coffee cup on the hood. Sam followed me.

"Let me give you a hand with those boxes."

"That's alright, Sam. Go enjoy your coffee. I can handle this."

He walked over to the back of the Explorer. "Nah, come on, Lily. Let me help. It's the neighborly thing to do."

I sighed and unwillingly opened the hatch. Sam smiled, grabbed a box, and headed towards the apartment building. I stepped ahead of him so that I could hold open the door. Before I got up to the door, it swung open, and a guy stood there, staring at me.

"Luke, you're just in time. Hold this box," Sam said as he handed it to him.

"What are you doing?" Luke asked. "I woke up, and you were gone. By the way, there's no coffee left."

"Yeah, I know. I just picked some up at Brewster's. I have the bag in my truck. By the way, this is Lily. She's our new next-door neighbor."

"Hey," he spoke as he quickly looked away.

"Hey," I replied.

I couldn't help but stare at him as he stood in the doorway—all six feet of him—in ripped jeans and a gray muscle shirt. He was barefoot, and his short, brown hair was messy. He was definitely one of the hottest men that I'd ever seen. You could tell he worked out by the muscles and definition in his arms and shoulders. He had a Celtic cross tattooed on his left bicep, with wings behind it. Thank God he was gay. I felt somewhat uncomfortable because Luke didn't seem as friendly as Sam.

"Lily, go unlock your apartment door so we can get these boxes in there," Sam said.

As I walked past Luke, I caught him staring at me. The minute I looked at him, he turned away. As I unlocked and opened the door, I stepped outside and held the building door open so that Luke could set the box down in my apartment. After setting it down, he walked away and inside his apartment. He shut the door behind him without saying a word.

"What's his problem?" I asked Sam.

"Just ignore him. He's not much of a morning person."

I couldn't shake the feeling that he seemed familiar to me, but I knew it wasn't possible. He just had one of those faces. As Sam and I were bringing in the last of the boxes, Giselle and Gretchen pulled up. I hadn't seen them in over three months. I set the box down and ran over to them as they climbed out of the car. I hugged Gretchen first and then Giselle.

"I'm so happy you moved to Santa Monica," Giselle shrieked as she hugged me tight.

"Me too." My eyes began to swell with tears.

"Who's the hot guy walking towards us?" Gretchen smiled as she pushed her hair back behind her ear.

"Hello, ladies." Sam smiled.

"Sam, this is Giselle, and this is Gretchen. They're my two best friends."

"It's a pleasure to meet the both of you," he spoke as he held out his hand to each of them.

"Sam lives next door, and he's been helping me bring the boxes in."

"We also went out for coffee this morning," he blurted out.

Giselle looked at me and smiled. "Did you hear that, Gretchen? Lily went out for coffee with a guy."

"I sure did, sis!" Gretchen smiled at me.

I turned and looked at Sam. "Don't listen to them. Thank you for your help. I appreciate it."

"No problem. If you need anything, just knock on my door or wall." He smiled.

I grabbed Gretchen and Giselle's hands and led them into my new apartment.

Chapter Two

LILY

"So, Lily, tell us about Sam from next door and what's going on between the two of you," Gretchen smirked as she ran her hand along my new couch.

"Nothing's going on between us!" I exclaimed. "He helped me bring in my boxes. That's all."

"But you went out for coffee with him," Giselle said.

"Correction, we went and grabbed a coffee to go. Besides, he's gay."

"Shut up! He can't be," Gretchen moaned.

"Yes, he is. He has a boyfriend named Luke," I said as I started unpacking the box for the kitchen.

"What a shame," Giselle said. "He seems like a nice guy and would be perfect for you."

"First of all, I'm not on the market. I'm done with men, remember? And second of all, you've known him all of ten seconds. How do you know that he'd be perfect for me?"

"We can tell," Giselle and Gretchen spoke at the same time.

I rolled my eyes. "Come on, help me arrange this furniture." I smiled.

We moved the living room furniture around until it was perfectly placed. My bedroom furniture had been delivered, and most of my boxes were unpacked.

"What's this?" Giselle asked as she held the box labeled SCRAPBOOK.

"Those are just some photos I took when I left Seattle. I was going to make a scrapbook dedicated to the start of my new life. But since I ended up staying in Portland, there isn't much in there. Just put it in my closet. I'll go through it someday."

"Oh, okay," she said as she headed to the bedroom. She came back out a few minutes later, holding my guitar.

"Aren't you going to keep this out?"

I looked at her and then at the guitar.

"Yeah, I almost forgot about that. I put it in the closet so it didn't get damaged while I unpacked and moved things around. Just find a corner in the bedroom and set it there."

"I'm starving!" Gretchen blurted out.

"Me too." Giselle sighed.

I looked at the clock, and it was already six p.m. I realized I hadn't eaten a thing all day.

"Let's order a pizza and a salad," I said.

"Sounds good. Where are your menus?" Gretchen asked.

"Considering I moved in last night, I don't have any menus." I laughed.

"I have an idea. Why don't you go next door and see if Sam has any pizza menus?" Giselle winked.

"I have an idea. Why don't you do a search on your phone?"

Giselle rolled her eyes, and there was a knock on the door. I looked through the peephole to find Sam standing on the other side. Opening the door, I was surprised to see him standing there, holding two pizzas and a large brown bag.

"Sam, what's all this?" I asked as I pointed to the pizzas.

"I thought you ladies would like something to eat since you've been working hard all day." He smiled.

"Come in. Thank you." I smiled. "You didn't have to do that."

"You're a lifesaver!" Gretchen said as she walked over and kissed him on the cheek. "We're starving."

"That was very nice of you to think of us, Sam. Let me get my wallet. How much do I owe you?"

"Nothing. It's on me. Consider it a housewarming gift," he said.

"Thank you, and please join us," I insisted.

"Don't mind if I do." He grinned.

I took some plates from the cabinet, grabbed some forks from the drawer, and sat next to Sam at the table. Gretchen had already torn into the breadsticks while Giselle opened the salad. Sam grabbed a slice of pizza from the box, put it on my plate, and then smiled at me.

"Thank you," I whispered.

"You're welcome," he whispered back.

"You could have invited Luke to come over."

"I already asked him, but he refused. I told him we'd be in the company of three beautiful women and great food, so it was his loss."

"And what did he say to that?" I laughed.

"He said he's good and just for me to come alone."

I got up and grabbed the bottle of wine Giselle and Gretchen had brought. I took the wine glasses from the cabinet and set them on the table. Sam stood up, opened the bottle, and poured each of us a glass. He held up his glass for a toast.

"To my new neighbor, Lily. May we become great friends and share many good times."

We all smiled and clanked our glasses. "Thank you, Sam."

We talked for a few hours about our careers. Sam was an architect and worked for a well-known company called Glassman and Fillmore. I shared my love of photography and the fact that I had a teaching degree, which was the reason that brought me to Santa Monica. Gretchen and Giselle talked about their modeling careers and the exotic places they had been. It was late, so Gretchen and Giselle called it a night. I hugged them goodbye, and Sam walked them to their car.

As I was cleaning up the kitchen, a text message came through from Gretchen.

"I'm in love with Sam. Why does he have to be gay?"

I smiled and shook my head as I replied.

"All the good ones usually are."

I finished cleaning up and looked at the clock. It was now two forty-five a.m. I turned the lights off and walked into the bathroom. Turning on the shower, I undressed and stepped inside. It was a long day, and all I wanted to do was stay under the stream of hot water forever. After dragging myself out of the shower, I put on my pajamas and looked at the guitar sitting in the corner of my bedroom. Walking over to it, I picked it up. I sat down on the edge of the bed and started strumming a few chords. Memories of my father came to my mind, and I began to play the song he used to sing to me as a child. When I was done playing, I looked at the clock again. It was four a.m. I returned the guitar to its stand and climbed into my new bed. I prayed to God to please let me sleep peacefully.

～

MY EYES FLEW open from the nightmare I had. I glanced at the clock; it was six, and I had only slept two hours. As I tossed and turned, I knew there was no way I was going back to sleep. My mind was racing because I began my teaching job tomorrow. I loved kids and being a teacher, but I also loved photography and wanted to make that my career.

Being twenty-six years old, I was still undecided on what I wanted to do with my life. I thought I had it figured out with Hunter. My life was all planned out. We would get married, have a couple of kids, and live in a house with a white picket fence. I would pursue a career in photography while tutoring kids on the side. He would come home from work, and we'd eat the meal I had prepared. Was I just desperate to find some normalcy in my life?

I climbed out of bed and put on a cute little floral print sundress I bought back in Portland. I dragged my ass to the kitchen for some coffee.

"Shit, I forgot to buy coffee." I sighed.

I wondered if Sam was awake. I walked over to the wall and pressed my ear up against it. Since I didn't know the layout of his apartment, I took a chance and lightly knocked. I smiled when there was a knock back. Walking next door, I knocked on the door. I gasped when it opened, and Luke was standing there in a pair of navy blue pajama bottoms that sat just below his hips. Instantly, I became nervous and started fidgeting.

"Can I help you with something?" he asked as he stared at me.

"Um, hi. I was wondering if Sam was around," I replied nervously.

"No, Sam isn't here."

There was a tone in his voice that suggested I was bothering him.

"Oh, I'll catch him later then." I turned my back and started to walk to my apartment.

"Wait. Was there something you needed?" he asked.

I turned around and looked at him. Even though he was rude, he was sure as hell the sexiest man that I'd ever seen.

"I was just going to ask if I could borrow some coffee. I forgot to buy some yesterday, and being the caffeine addict that I am, I need some quickly."

The corners of his mouth curved into a small smile. "Come on in," he said as he stepped aside.

As I stepped inside his apartment, I was shocked at its size. I guess being the end apartment had its advantages.

"What do you take in your coffee?" Luke asked as he opened the refrigerator.

"I drink it black. But it's okay. I'll borrow some and make it at my place."

"You said you needed coffee quick, and I have some made, so take this cup and drink it," he growled.

"Okay." I nervously took the cup from him.

I looked around his apartment as I took a sip of coffee. It was spotless, and everything was in its place. The dark brown leather furniture complimented the beige walls where a 65-inch TV was displayed. I was very uncomfortable but couldn't leave until I finished my coffee for fear Luke would yell at me.

"You're one of the very few people I know who take their coffee black," Luke said out of nowhere as he poured himself a cup and sipped it.

I sat down on the stool in front of the island. Luke was leaning up against the counter with his coffee across from me. My eyes couldn't help but wander to his perfectly defined six-pack and sculpted V-line. He worked out; there was no doubt about it. I think it was time for my battery-operated boyfriend and me to get reacquainted. I couldn't help but notice the scar that went from his right hip and around to his back.

"Is there something wrong with me?" he asked.

Instantly, my eyes darted up to his. "No, why would you ask that?"

"I don't know. It's just the way you were staring at me."

I wanted to die. I got lost in his body, and he caught me. I was so humiliated at that moment. I had to think of something quick.

"I'm sorry. I wasn't staring at you. I was thinking about something."

"Thinking about what?" he asked as he leaned over the island.

Out of the corner of my eye, I saw an acoustic guitar sitting by the TV. "Who plays the guitar?" I asked to change the subject quickly.

"I do," Luke said.

"Cool," I replied.

He walked over to his guitar, grabbed it, and held it out to me. I stared at him in confusion.

"Here. Play that song you were playing last night," he said.

"You heard that?"

"Yeah. See my couch right there? That's where your bedroom is."

"Oh, I'm sorry if I disturbed you."

"You didn't. I was up anyway. Now, why don't you play that song?"

I took the guitar from his hand and set it on my lap. I positioned my fingers on the strings and began to play. He grabbed my empty coffee cup and filled it back up. He set the cup before me as I strummed the song he wanted to hear.

"Who taught you how to play?" he asked as he leaned against the island.

"My father," I answered as I strummed the last chord.

"What song is that?"

"A song he used to sing to me. It's called 'Little Girl of Mine'."

He looked at me blankly, and I handed his guitar back to him.

"Your turn." I smiled.

"No. I'm not playing right now," he growled and walked back into the kitchen.

I didn't know what to say or think. One minute, he was being nice, and the next, he acted as if I was bothering him. He was like a woman with severe PMS. I got up from the stool.

"Thanks for the coffee, and tell Sam I stopped by," I said with an attitude.

He didn't say a word. He just stared out the kitchen window with his hands pressed against the counter. When I opened the door to walk out, Sam was standing there.

"Hey, Lily. Good morning," he said with a confused look on his face.

"Tell your friend there he needs to learn some manners regarding women," I snarled.

I walked back to my apartment, and Sam followed behind me.

"What the hell happened?"

"He's just rude, Sam."

Sam walked over to me and placed his hands on my shoulders. "Listen. Luke's a great guy once you get to know him. He's had a rough year, and I'm trying to help him."

"Yeah, well, so have I, but I'm not rude to people."

"Trust me when I say to cut him some slack. He's probably just nervous around you because you're so beautiful." He smiled.

I looked at him with a perplexed expression.

"I want to ask you something. Can you give me Gretchen's phone number?"

I looked at him again and shook my head as I put my hands up in front of him.

"Wait–wait–wait. Why do you want Gretchen's phone number?"

Sam twisted his face. "I want to ask her out on a date."

"A date?" I asked totally confused.

"Do you have a problem if I go out on a date with your best friend?" he asked, giving me a weird look.

"You're gay. Why would you want to date Gretchen? What about Luke? I don't think he'd appreciate his boyfriend going on a date with a woman."

Sam took a step back and put his hands up. "Whoa, wait a minute. You think I'm gay?!" He laughed.

A horrified look swept across my face. "Aren't you?"

"You thought Luke and I were a couple?!" he said, still laughing.

"Oh, my, God." I turned away in humiliation.

Sam grabbed me and hugged me. "You're so cute, Lily. I haven't had a good laugh in a long time."

I stood there with my nose pressed against his chest as I patted him on the back. "I'm glad I could amuse you."

"Now, about that phone number." He smiled.

"Hand me your phone," I said as I held out my hand. I keyed in my phone number, Gretchen's phone, and Giselle's phone. "Just in case you ever need to get a hold of me when I'm not home."

Sam smiled as he took his phone from me. A few moments later, my phone went off. I walked over to the counter, picked it up, and saw that I had a text message.

"Now you have my number if you ever want to talk."

I looked at him and smiled. "Get out of here and go call Gretchen. She thinks you're hot, but don't tell her I said that."

Sam winked at me and laughed as he left my apartment.

Chapter Three

LUKE

I was sitting on the couch when Sam came through the door and started in on me.

"What the hell's your problem, Luke?"

I looked at him as I took a sip of my coffee. "What the hell are you talking about, Sam?"

"You know what I'm talking about. Why do you have to be such an asshole to Lily?"

"I have no idea what you're talking about," I said as I got up and walked to my bedroom.

Sam followed behind me. "Bullshit! You know exactly what I'm talking about."

"Leave me alone, Sam," I warned.

He left my room and went into the bathroom, mumbling. I opened my drawer and noticed it was almost empty. Looking over to the corner of my bedroom, I saw my laundry basket was heaping with dirty clothes. I couldn't remember the last time I did laundry. I picked up some clothes lying on the floor and shoved them into the basket. Picking up the basket, I set it by the front door while I went to the refrigerator and grabbed a bottle of water. Sam came out of the bathroom just as I was walking out the door.

"By the way, Lily thought you were gay!" he shouted.

I stopped and put the laundry basket down. Turning around, I looked at Sam. "What do you mean she thought I was gay?"

"What part of 'she thought you were gay' do you not understand?" He smirked.

I rolled my eyes, shut the door, picked up the laundry basket, and headed down the hall to the laundry room. As I approached the doorway, I saw Lily putting clothes into the washer. She saw me and stopped.

"Hi. Do you need to use this?" she asked, pointing to the washer.

"Yeah, but it's fine. I can do laundry another time," I replied.

I couldn't stop thinking about how I was an asshole to her this morning and how she must have mentioned it to Sam. Otherwise, he wouldn't have gone off on me as he did.

"You can throw some of your clothes in with mine. We can split the cost." she offered.

"Didn't you just move in yesterday?" I asked.

"A couple of days ago."

"If you just moved here, why are you already doing laundry?"

She looked at me with anger in her eyes. "I didn't do—hell, just forget it. It's all yours," she said as she took her things out of the washer and stormed out of the laundry room.

I didn't say anything wrong, so I didn't know why she got so upset. But it didn't matter anyway. I didn't care. I threw my clothes into the washer, started them, and returned to my apartment. Charley came running to me as I opened the door, and I picked her up.

"Uncle Luke, look what my mom bought me!" she said as she showed me her silver butterfly bracelet.

"Wow, that's beautiful." I smiled and kissed her on her head.

"She bought it for me as a present for my first day of school tomorrow."

"That's really pretty, peanut," I said as I put her down. "Where's your mom?" I asked as I didn't see her around the apartment.

"She went to the store. She asked Uncle Sammy if he could keep an eye on me until you came back from doing laundry."

My sister, Maddie, was a single mom, and Charlene, or Charley as we called her, was her nine-year-old daughter. They lived in one of the apartments upstairs. Her so-called dad, who denied he was the father from the start until a paternity test proved Charley was his, came around every couple of years. He didn't pay child support and never called her on her birthday, Christmas, or Easter. He's nothing but a deadbeat dad, and I wished my sister would get him to sign over his parental rights. He wasn't a good influence on Charley, and I wouldn't stand by and let him ruin her life.

"Hey, Charley. Why don't you take your crayons and paper to the dining table and color me a pretty picture? I need to talk to your Uncle Luke for a minute," Sam said.

I walked to the refrigerator and grabbed a beer. I took off the cap and flung it at him. He caught it in his hand like he always did. I swear that boy should have been a baseball player. I think he missed his calling in life. I walked over to the couch, sat, and put my feet on the coffee table.

"I realized something today, and I want you to know about it," Sam said.

"Yeah? What did you realize, Sam?" I asked, staring at the TV.

"I remember while growing up, my sister would come home crying because some boys were being mean to her."

I looked over at him as I took a drink of my beer. "Yeah, and what's your point?"

"I remember my mom telling her the only reason they were mean to her was because they liked her, and they didn't know how to express it because they were scared."

"Is there a point in telling me this story, Sam?" I asked.

"Yes, Luke, there is. My point is that I think you have an attraction to Lily, and that's why you're acting like you are towards her."

"Jesus Christ, Sam. Do you listen to yourself? You have no idea what you're talking about!" I spat as I got up from the couch.

"Luke, it's been a year since Callie—"

"Stop! Don't you ever say her name again!" I yelled.

Suddenly, I felt someone tugging on my jeans. "Uncle Luke, why are you yelling?"

I looked at Sam and shook my head. I bent down and placed my hands on Charley's shoulders.

"I'm not yelling, peanut. I just raised my voice by accident. I'm sorry."

"Mommy always says to use your inside voice when you're indoors."

"I know, and I will. I promise. Now, go back over there and finish coloring that pretty picture." I smiled as I kissed the top of her head.

"Look, man, I'm sorry I upset you, but Lily's a real nice girl, and she doesn't deserve to be treated rudely. She's never done anything to you."

I stared at him, sat on the couch, and threw back my beer. "You act like you've known her your whole life when it's only been two days. Do you want to date her or something? Are you trying to get my approval?" I asked.

"No, I'm not trying to get your approval, and I don't need it either. If I wanted to date Lily, I would ask her on a date, but I'm really into her friend, Gretchen."

I took the last sip of my beer as Maddie walked through the door. I got up from the couch and kissed her on the cheek.

"Hey, sis, do you need any help?"

"Nope, I already took the bags upstairs." She smiled.

We both walked over to the table where Charley was coloring and looked at her picture.

"That's a pretty picture, Charley. Can I have it?" I asked.

"Sorry, Uncle Luke. This picture is for my new teacher tomorrow." She smiled.

"Ah, well, she's one lucky teacher to get such a pretty picture," I said.

Maddie and Charley cleaned up the crayons and paper, then

walked out the door. Charley stopped in the hallway and turned to look at me.

"Uncle Luke, will you come over before I go to school tomorrow morning?"

"You bet I will, peanut." I smiled at her as she waved goodbye.

I loved that little girl more than anything in my life.

∼

LATER THAT EVENING, Lucky came over, and we headed to Bernie's. It was the bar my sister worked at during the day and some evenings, but it was also where the boys and I played a little music. We could draw in quite a crowd when Bernie, the owner, told people when we were playing. We weren't playing tonight. We had a few drinks and shot some pool.

I'd known Lucky and Sam since my first year at college. The three of us were roommates. Lucky's a womanizer. He always had been, and he always would be. His real name is Thomas, but we started calling him Lucky when he scored with the hottest chick on our college campus. He knew the right things to say to a woman, and they always fell under his spell. After a few games of pool and a few beers, I was calling it a night. Lucky invited a few girls to the apartment to play his version of strip poker.

We arrived back at the apartment, and Lucky got out the cards. It was him, Sam, and two other girls playing. The third girl didn't want to play, and neither did I. I walked to the refrigerator and grabbed a beer. I removed the cap and flung it over to Sam as he raised his hand and caught it. I smiled and sat down on the couch. The girl introduced herself as Monica. I didn't care what her name was and wanted to be left alone. Lucky got up from the table and turned on some music. Sam yelled at him to turn it down. I shot Sam a look because he never told anyone to turn down the music. He liked it loud. He tilted his head to the side, indicating it would be too loud for Lily. I rolled my eyes and went back to watching TV.

It wasn't long before Monica scooted closer to me and started running her finger up and down my arm. I looked at her. She was attractive, but she wasn't my type. She leaned in closer and whispered in my ear.

"I give great blow jobs if you're interested." She smiled as she slowly licked her lips.

I was drunk, and I wasn't going to have sex with her, so I took her up on her offer. It had been a while since I'd had one, and I was more than ready. I got up from the couch and motioned for her to follow me into the bedroom. As I shut the door, Monica knelt and unbuttoned my jeans. She slid them down to my ankles along with my boxers. She wrapped her mouth around my hard cock as I fisted her hair and moved her head up and down. I was just about to come when the door opened. I looked up and saw Lily standing there.

Chapter Four

LILY

    I rummaged through my closet, trying to find the black skirt I wanted to wear tomorrow. I couldn't believe I would be teaching fourth grade for an entire year. The teacher that I replaced took a year off to take care of her terminally ill husband. I unpacked the last of the boxes and found my black skirt. Looking at the clock, it was midnight.

    I needed to take a shower because I felt dirty from unpacking. Walking to the bathroom, I undressed and turned the shower on. As I reached up to adjust the shower head, the pipe broke, and water started pouring everywhere. I screamed, then quickly reached down and turned the water off. I stood there in a fit of rage. It was late. I was dirty, and now, what the hell was I going to do? I had no choice. I had to ask Sam if I could use his shower. I knew he was up because I could hear the loud music through the paper-thin walls. I threw on a tank top and a pair of yoga pants and went next door. After several knocks, Sam finally opened the door.

    "Lily, what's up? Is everything ok?"

    "No, the shower head pipe in my shower just broke, and I start my new job in about seven hours. Can I use your shower really quick?" I asked.

"Sure, come in. The bathroom's right down the hall." He smiled.

I walked into his apartment and quickly scanned for Luke. He was the last person I wanted to see right now. All I saw was some other guy and two half-naked girls. I looked at Sam and raised one eyebrow.

"Sorry, but we're playing strip poker," he said.

"None of my business, Sam," I said as I held up my hand.

Suddenly, standing before me was the guy sitting at the table.

"Sammy, who's your friend?" Lucky asked.

"This is Lily. She just moved in next door."

"Hello, beautiful." He smiled as he softly kissed my hand. "I'm Lucky, and it's my pleasure to meet such a gorgeous woman."

"It's nice to meet you, Lucky," I said with a fake smile. I knew his kind and wasn't about to fall for it.

I excused myself and headed down the hall. I opened the door —to which I thought was the bathroom—and gasped when I saw Luke standing there, getting a blow job. I instantly shut the door and left the apartment. Sam came after me and asked what was wrong. I told him I changed my mind, returned to my apartment, shut the door, and slid down until I was on the ground. I cupped my face in my hands and sat there. I was startled when there was a knock at the door. Getting up and looking out the peephole, I saw it was Luke. I opened the door, and he stood in jeans and a t-shirt, holding a toolbox. I couldn't even look at him after what I saw. I was so embarrassed.

"Sam said the pipe in your shower broke."

"Yeah, it did. What are you, the handyman?" I asked.

"As a matter of fact, I am. I'm the maintenance guy, and I need to take a look so that I can get whatever parts I need and come back tomorrow to fix it."

"Fine. Come in," I snarled as I stepped aside.

I couldn't stop staring at his ass as he walked down the hall. What the hell was the matter with me? I didn't want to look at him or any part of his body. I followed him into the bathroom as he set his toolbox on the toilet.

"So, what the hell did you do to this?" he asked.

"I didn't do anything. I just went to adjust it, and it broke off."

"These things just don't break off that easily. You must've really grabbed it and yanked it hard."

He was making me angry with his attitude, and I thought about something on him that I was going to grab and yank really hard. I rolled my eyes as I stood there, leaning up against the sink.

"You know what, Mr. Handyman? You're right. It must be my superhuman strength that broke it."

He turned his head and looked at me. The corners of his mouth turned into a small smile that grabbed my attention. I couldn't look at him anymore. I was getting turned on, and that was something that hadn't happened to me in a very long time. I was starting to get annoyed with how my body reacted just at the sight of him, and the worst part was I couldn't get what I just saw out of my head.

"I'll be in the kitchen if you need me." I walked out of the bathroom.

I looked at the clock on the stove, and it was two a.m. I was practically in tears because I had to be in my classroom at seven a.m., but I still needed to clean myself up. Luke came walking out of the bathroom with his toolbox.

"I'll get the parts I need tomorrow and come back to fix it. Will you be home?" he asked as he looked at me, and I didn't answer. "Lily, what's wrong?"

I turned towards the refrigerator and acted like I was getting a bottle of water so that he couldn't see the tears that were about to fall.

"Nothing's wrong. I'm just exhausted. I start my new job in a few hours and feel disgusting from unpacking boxes all day. And to answer your question, no. I won't be home tomorrow, at least not until after three o'clock."

I heard him take a few steps closer from behind.

"Hey, grab your things and shower quickly at my place. By the way, I'm sorry for what you saw earlier."

I put my hand up to stop him. "Please, don't apologize. You did nothing wrong. It was my fault for walking in on you and your girlfriend."

"She's not my girlfriend," he said. "Come on. Time's ticking away, and you need a shower."

I turned around and looked at him. "Thank you, Luke. Let me grab my things."

He waited for me, and we walked to his apartment. He opened the door, and as I stepped inside, the only thing I saw were two completely naked girls sitting at the table while Sam and Lucky were fully dressed. Luke sighed, walked over to the table, gathered the girl's clothing, and threw them at them.

"Girls, it's been fun, but it's time to leave now."

"Hey, man, what the hell are you doing?" Lucky said as he stood up.

"Lily, the bathroom's on the left."

I started walking to the bathroom, and I heard Luke tell Lucky the party was over and he needed to leave. Lucky wasn't happy about it, but he did what Luke said. I shut and locked the door. I stepped into the shower, stood under the hot water, and relaxed. As I was shampooing my hair, I heard the door open.

"It's just me. Don't freak out," Luke said.

I froze. "What the hell, Luke? Get out!" I yelled.

"You're not the only one who has to get up early. I need to brush my teeth quickly."

"You can't wait until I'm out of the shower and back in my apartment?"

"No. I'm tired, and I want to go to bed. Besides, you women take long showers."

I heard him start brushing his teeth. I couldn't believe the nerve of him.

"The door was locked. How did you get in?" I asked.

"The lock's broke, so it wasn't locked."

I heard him turn the water off. "I'm going to bed. After you get home, I'll be by your place to fix your shower tomorrow. Night," he said.

The door shut, and he was gone. I stepped out of the shower, dried off, threw my clothes on, grabbed my things, and headed towards the door. Sam was cleaning up the mess that was left in the kitchen.

"Lily, before you go," he said as he walked towards me. "I'm sorry for tonight and for the things you saw."

"Don't be sorry, Sam. What you and Luke do is your business, not mine. You have nothing to apologize for." I smiled.

He leaned over and kissed the top of my head. "Sleep tight. I'm going to give Gretchen a call tomorrow. Could you please not mention what you saw here tonight?" he asked with a twisted face.

"Don't worry. I won't tell her a thing." I smiled and walked out the door.

~

I JOLTED out of bed at the sound of my alarm buzzing. I quickly turned off the irritating sound and looked at the time. It was five-thirty. I didn't fall asleep until three thirty, and I was exhausted. I went to the bathroom and splashed cold water on my face to try to wake myself up. I stumbled into the kitchen and made a pot of coffee. As the coffee brewed, I put on my makeup, straightened my blonde hair, and put on my clothes. After pouring some coffee into my travel mug, I grabbed my purse and school bag and opened the door to leave. As I was locking up, Luke's door opened, and he came walking out. Our eyes met.

"Morning," he said.

"Good morning," I replied. "You're up early."

"I told you last night that you weren't the only one who had to be up," he said as he locked his door.

"Have a good day." I smiled.

"Yeah, you too," Luke said as he walked up the stairs.

On the way to the school, I couldn't help but wonder why he was up so early and why he went upstairs. He said he didn't have a girlfriend. Well, he said she wasn't his girlfriend. I shook my head. He was no different than every other guy, except he was the hottest-looking man I'd ever seen. I couldn't stop thinking about the scar I saw on him and wondered where it came from. Why was I thinking about Luke so much? I couldn't do this. I was starting over, and I couldn't have any distractions. I pulled into the school parking lot and headed to my classroom. I walked through the door and stared around the room. This was going to be my second home for the next ten months. I smiled at that thought and set my things on my desk. My main focus had to be my students, not Luke.

I heard a soft knock on the door. As I turned to look, Chris Channing, Gretchen, Giselle's aunt, and the school's principal stepped in.

"Lily, it's been way too long. How are you?" she asked as she hugged me.

"I'm good, Chris. Thank you again for hiring me."

"You're welcome. You were the perfect candidate. Not only have I known you for the past twenty years, but I know how much you love children. Gretchen told me about your situation, and I want to tell you I'm sorry."

I looked away and started rearranging things on my desk. "Don't be sorry, Chris. I'm moving on and starting over. Things worked out for the best."

"They sure did," she said as she hugged me again. "Your students will be here any minute. If you need anything at all, call me."

"I will," I smiled as the bell rang, and a flock of children entered the classroom.

∼

I SPENT most of the day getting to know the children and having them get to know me. We all had lunch together in the classroom, which they thought was cool. I wanted them not only to like me but to trust me as well. I wanted them to feel safe every time they walked into the classroom. The end of the day approached, and the bell rang. In a matter of minutes, the classroom was empty. I walked around the room and straightened the desks. Grabbing my things, I turned off the light and headed home. When I arrived at my apartment, I unlocked the door, threw my bags onto the chair, and kicked off my heels. I sat on the couch for a minute to relax when I heard a knock. I got up, looked through the peephole, and saw Luke standing there. I opened it and motioned for him to come in.

"Hi," I said.

"Hey," he said without looking at me as he walked down the hall.

I rolled my eyes. I was exhausted and in no mood for his attitude.

I put the kettle on the stove for some tea. All I wanted right now was the comfort of my plush bed. While waiting for the water to heat up, I heard Luke yell from the bathroom.

"Shit!"

It sounded like a yell of pain, so I walked to the bathroom to see what happened. He stood there holding his hand.

"Are you okay? What happened?" I asked.

"Nothing. Just go!" he spat.

"Excuse me, mister, but this is my fucking bathroom, and I'll be in here if I want to be."

He looked up at me. "Do you always use that kind of language?"

"Yes, I do. Now let me look at your hand," I said as I lightly touched it.

He pulled away. "No, it's fine. I don't need your help."

"Maybe you do, or maybe you don't. You're hurt, and I need to see how bad it is. Now sit your goddamn ass on that toilet so I can take a look."

He looked at me with anger in his eyes. "You can come off as being really mean."

"Good, I'm glad you noticed. Now, give me your hand."

He held out his hand, and I removed the blood-soaked tissue. I grabbed a washcloth from under the sink and wrapped it around his wound.

"Put pressure on that while I get the antiseptic and a Band-Aid. It doesn't look like it needs stitches."

I reached into the cabinet and took out the antiseptic and some cotton balls. I could see him staring at me from the corner of my eye. I soaked the cotton ball with antiseptic and set it on the counter's edge. I turned to him and took his hand. I didn't want to look at him because he had the most amazing brown eyes.

"Where are you from?" he asked out of nowhere.

"Why do you care?" I replied.

"I don't. I'm just trying to make small talk."

"Seattle."

"Is your family still there?"

"I don't have any family. They're dead."

I removed the washcloth and grabbed the cotton ball.

"This will sting, but I know you're a big boy who can handle it." I dabbed the cut on the side of his hand.

"Fuck!" he screamed and tried to pull his hand away.

"Do you always use that kind of language?" I asked.

"Only when someone's hurting me!" he exclaimed.

"Stop being a baby and man up."

"Don't tell me to man up!"

"Fine. Be a baby."

I put the Band-Aid on his hand. "There, all better. Now get back to fixing my shower."

He looked at me and got up from the toilet. "Thank you."

"You're welcome," I said as I walked out of the bathroom.

I took a teabag from the cabinet and made some tea. About thirty minutes later, Luke emerged from the bathroom.

"You're all set."

"Great. Thank you. Can I offer you a beer?" I asked, not sure why those words escaped my lips.

"No, I need to go. Enjoy the rest of your evening," he said as he left my apartment.

Chapter Five

LUKE

I opened the door to my apartment and set my toolbox by the closet. I looked at my watch. It was almost time for Mrs. Clements to bring Charley home. I walked outside to wait for her. Charley took a dance class after school with her best friend, Allie. Allie's mom picked the girls up from school, took them to dance class, and then dropped Charley off at my place. When Maddie worked the day shift at the bar, she usually didn't get off work until six. She didn't work many nights, but when she did, Charley spent the night at my place.

"Hey, peanut, how was your first day of school?" I asked her as I carried her backpack inside.

"It was great. I'm hungry," she pouted.

"What do you want to eat?" I asked.

"Grilled cheese." She smiled.

"One grilled cheese sandwich coming right up," I said as I took out the pan. "Tell me about your day."

"I love my new teacher. She's so nice and super pretty."

"Is that so?" I asked. "What's her name?"

"Miss Gilmore."

I made Charley her grilled cheese sandwich and listened to her as she told me all about her day.

"Uncle Luke, what happened to your hand?" she asked as she looked at the Band-Aid.

"Yeah, Uncle Luke, what happened to your hand?" Sam asked as he walked through the door, smiling.

"It's just a cut from fixing the shower next door. It's nothing to worry about. Do you have homework, Charley?" I asked.

"Nope. Miss Gilmore said we would all be too tired from our first day to concentrate on homework, so she didn't give us any."

"She sounds like a cool teacher," I smiled.

"She's really cool. You would like her."

I left the kitchen as she said that and sat on the couch. Sam opened a beer, handed it to me, and sat in the chair across from me.

"How did it go at Lily's?"

"It went fine, except I cut myself," I said.

"I invited Gretchen to the beach this weekend, and I think you should invite Lily."

I looked at Sam and sighed. "Your hang up with Lily and me is getting old. I'm not interested. Ask her yourself if you want her to join us at the beach this weekend."

"Fine, I will," he said as he pulled out his phone.

Charley came over and sat next to me. "Can I watch SpongeBob SquarePants?"

I put my arm around her, and she snuggled against me. I turned on her show and looked at Sam as he laughed.

"What is so funny?" I asked.

"Lily asked if you were going to the beach, and when I told her yes, she said no. You two are going to kill me."

I rolled my eyes. I couldn't stop thinking about how Lily told me that her family was dead. I couldn't imagine not having my family. I hadn't seen any guys coming around, so I was pretty sure she didn't have a boyfriend. Not that it mattered. I was just surprised that someone as beautiful as her didn't have one.

The door opened, and Maddie walked in.

"Mommy!" Charley exclaimed as she jumped up from the couch.

"Baby, how was school?" she asked as Charley jumped in her arms.

"Hey, Maddie," I said as I kissed her cheek. "How was work?"

"It was the same as every other day. I got hit on a few times. A couple of drunken guys grabbed my ass. You know, the usual."

"Yeah, well, I better never see them grabbing your ass. Otherwise, I'll kick theirs," I said.

"Say goodbye to Uncle Luke and Uncle Sammy, Charley."

"Bye, Charley," Sam smiled from the couch.

"Bye, peanut," I said as I held out my fist to her.

"Later, gator," we both said at the same time.

I walked over and sat back down on the couch. "Do you know anything about Lily's past?"

Sam shot me a look. "No. Why are you asking?"

"I don't know. It's just something she said earlier."

"What did she say?"

"I asked her where she was from, and she said Seattle. I asked if her family lived there, but she said that she didn't have any family and that they were dead."

Sam looked at me, and his mouth dropped. "Seriously?"

"Yeah, seriously, dude."

"Wow, poor Lily, to be all alone with no family. That's awful."

Sam got up from the chair to shower because he was taking Gretchen out on a date.

I grabbed an ice-cold beer from the fridge and sat on the couch. My phone beeped, and there was a text message from Lucky.

"Dude, come to the bar tonight. There are some really hot chicks here, and I scored us a gig for Saturday night."

I wasn't in the mood for the bar tonight.

"Sorry, Lucky, not tonight, and thanks for the gig on Saturday."

I got up from the couch and grabbed my guitar. I sat back down, and as I began to play, I heard music coming from the other side of the wall. Lily was playing her guitar. The song she was playing sounded familiar. As I strummed a few chords, the music from the other side of the wall stopped. I played a short tune and waited. Lily played it right back. I strummed another tune, something a little more complicated, and then I waited. A few seconds later, she played it back. I couldn't help but smile.

"Is that a smile I just saw on your face, Luke?" Sam said as he walked by.

"No, and where are you taking Gretchen?" I asked to change the subject.

"I'm taking her to a new restaurant for dinner and maybe a movie afterward."

"Have a good time," I said as Sam headed out the door.

I strummed a few more chords and waited for Lily to strum back, but she never did. I decided to try to write a new song. It had been a year since I'd written anything. Ever since…

Chapter Six

LILY

"Hello," I said as I answered Gretchen's call.

"Guess what I'm doing tonight?"

"I don't know. Taking a bubble bath and shaving your legs?"

"No, Lily, stop it! I'm going on a date with Sam!"

"Ah, so he finally called you. That's great, Gretchen. I'm happy for you."

"Try it sometime, Lily. You might surprise yourself and like it."

"No thanks. I'm happy with my life as it is. I don't need a man to complicate things. Have fun on your date with Sam. You better call me tomorrow and let me know how things went."

"I will. Try not to have too much fun in that apartment alone."

"Goodbye, Gretchen."

"Goodbye, Lils."

I smiled as I hung up the phone and picked up my guitar. I could hear Luke trying to play something. He kept strumming and stopping. The little game we played just before Gretchen called was fun. He would play a tune and stop, and I would play it back. I couldn't help but wonder how his hand was doing. Something about him bothered me. On one hand, I couldn't stop thinking about him.

On the other, I couldn't stand him. I got up and put my guitar back. I had an empty corner in my living room, so I moved my guitar there. That guitar held many memories for me—some bad, some good.

∽

THE FOLLOWING DAY, I stumbled out of bed, tired as hell, and went to the kitchen for coffee. You'd think I'd be used to only getting a couple of hours of sleep a night since it's been over a year. I poured a cup and then headed to the bathroom for a shower. I stepped out of the shower and heard my phone beep. Grabbing it from my dresser, I noticed a text message from Sam.

"*Good morning. I need to see you before I leave for work. Can I stop by?*"

I smiled because he probably wanted to talk to me about his date with Gretchen.

"*Sure. The door's unlocked. Grab a cup of coffee, and I'll be right out. I'm getting dressed.*"

I quickly ran to the door, unlocked it, and returned to my bedroom. As I put on my black pants, I heard Sam come in.

"Hey, Lily, it's just me."

"Hey, Sam, I'll be right out!" I yelled.

I put on my shirt and walked to the living room, rubbing my hair with a towel.

"You look very professional today." I smiled.

He wore a three-piece black suit with a light green shirt and matching tie. Needless to say, he looked hot.

"I have a meeting today with a big client, and he's uptight. He's the 'everything needs to be professional' type of person."

"So, what brings you here for a visit this early morning?" I asked.

"Being a teacher, I knew you'd be up getting ready for work."

"Follow me to the bathroom. I need to start getting ready," I said.

Sam got up from the table and stood in the bathroom doorway while I put on my makeup.

"I had a great time with Gretchen last night. She's an amazing person." He smiled. "I think the four of us should go out."

"The four of us?" I asked as I put on my mascara.

"Gretchen, me, you, and Luke."

"I don't date," I said as I looked at my eyes in the mirror.

"I know you don't, and I'm sorry to hear that."

I instantly looked at him. "Gretchen told you, didn't she?"

"Yes. She told me about your ex and what happened at the church."

"Damn her. Just wait until I talk to her," I said in anger.

"Don't, Lily. She's worried about you. She told me she's happy you moved to Santa Monica because now she can keep a closer eye on you. She doesn't want you to be lonely."

"I like being lonely. Did she say anything else?" I asked as I ran a brush through my damp hair.

"She told me that your family isn't dead and that they're still living in Seattle."

"My family's dead to me, Sam. What my sister and mother did is unforgivable. I want you to forget about that conversation and don't ever mention it to anyone. Do you understand me? I'm starting my life over, and that's my story. I never plan on seeing either of them again."

"Okay. I'll forget about it, but I want you to know that Luke isn't a bad guy like you think he is. He's hiding himself, just like you are."

"I don't care about Luke, Sam. I'm not interested in men, period. I don't care who they are. They're all lying, cheating bastards who break my heart over and over. I refuse ever to let it happen again."

He put his arm around me and held me tight. "I understand, and don't worry. Your secret's safe with me."

"Thank you, Sam."

"I have to go, or I'll be late. Have a good day with your students." He smiled as he turned and left the apartment.

"Have a good professional meeting!" I yelled from the bathroom.

As I blow-dried my hair, I couldn't stop thinking about what

Sam said about Luke hiding himself. I didn't care about Luke or his life. I threw my hair up in a ponytail and headed out the door.

∼

THE STUDENTS WERE WOUND UP, but we had a productive day. I was sitting at my desk as the students were doing a writing assignment when Charley approached me.

"Miss Gilmore," she said.

"Hi, Charley, what's up?" I asked.

"My uncle's taking me to the carnival Friday night," she said with a huge smile plastered on her face.

"Wow, what a nice uncle you have." I smiled back.

"He's the best! He takes care of me a lot while my mom's working. He helps me and my mom out since my daddy isn't around."

Hearing Charley say those words broke my heart. I knew what it was like not having your dad around.

"Your uncle sounds like he's an amazing person."

"He is, and I love him very much. I think you would like him. He doesn't have a girlfriend. She died."

"Oh, Charley, I'm sorry to hear that. I'm sure that I'd like him."

The bell rang, and the end of the school day had arrived.

"Bye, Miss Gilmore." Charley smiled and waved.

"Bye, Charley. See you tomorrow."

The classroom emptied, so I walked around putting things away and straightening the desks. I grabbed my bags, climbed into my Explorer, and started driving. The car began to shake as I was driving and listening to my favorite tunes. I quickly pulled over onto the side of the road, and it stalled. I turned the key to try and start it, but it was dead. I sighed and pulled out my phone. I attempted to call Gretchen and Giselle, but there was no answer.

"Shit—shit—shit!" I said as I climbed out and leaned up against the side of the Explorer. I tried to call Sam, but he didn't answer either, so I left a message and told him where I was.

Thirty minutes had passed, and I was getting ready to start walking when a motorcycle pulled up behind me. I was a little nervous. He pulled off his helmet and looked at me. I couldn't help but smile as Luke climbed off his bike and walked towards me.

"So, you're my knight in shining armor?" I asked.

"Something like that," he said. "Pop the hood so that I can take a look."

I popped the hood and stood beside Luke as he examined the engine. "Try and start it."

I climbed inside and turned the key—nothing. "Sorry, but it still doesn't want to start!" I yelled from the driver's seat.

Luke shut the hood and walked over to the driver's side window. "It's probably the alternator. You're going to have to get this towed."

"Great," I said as I laid my forehead on the steering wheel.

"My buddy owns a garage not too far from here. I'll call him and have him come tow it."

"Thank you, Luke."

"No problem," he said as he walked away and made the phone call.

He walked over to me as I climbed out of the truck and handed me his helmet. "Here, put this on."

I looked at him in confusion. "Why?"

"Because I don't want you on the back of my bike without one on."

I stared at him like he was crazy. "I'm not getting on the back of that thing. I hate motorcycles."

"Suit yourself. The guys won't be here for another two hours if you want to sit in the hot sun or a car. I really don't care either way," he said as he walked away.

I sighed as I sat on the ground, leaning against my broken-down Explorer. This was going to be the longest two hours of my life. Luke got on his bike and started it. He pulled up next to me and yelled over the roaring engine.

"Are you sure? This is your last chance!"

"I'm sure," I said.

He sped away and left me sitting there on the side of the road in the hot sun. I pulled my phone from my pocket, and it was dead. Of course, it was. Could this day get any worse? A few minutes later, I heard the roaring engine of a motorcycle. I looked up and saw Luke getting off his bike. He walked over to me and grabbed my arm.

"What the fuck do you think you're doing?!" I yelled as he pulled me off the ground.

"Taking you home. And watch your mouth," he said.

"I'm not getting on that thing, and you can't make me!" I said as he was dragging me to his bike.

He stopped dead in his tracks, turned around, and looked at me. "What is it that you're scared of, Lily?"

"Nothing," I said as I walked back to the Explorer. "Just leave me alone and go home, Luke."

I sat inside to try and escape him. He opened the passenger door and climbed in. I stared straight ahead and wouldn't look at him.

"Something about motorcycles has you freaked out. Tell me what it is, and maybe I can help you."

"You can't help," I said as my eyes started to tear. He wouldn't stop staring at me, and once again, he made me uncomfortable.

"Please, just tell me, Lily," he spoke softly.

I sighed and took in a deep breath. "I was in a motorcycle accident with my dad when I was a child. I can still remember the pain as if it happened yesterday. I haven't been on a bike since and don't plan on starting now."

"I can understand that, but you'll be safe with me. I promise."

I glanced at him. There was something in his eyes that drew me in. It was hot, and the thought of sitting here for the next two hours wasn't pleasant.

"Fine. I'll go," I said hesitantly. "But just to let you know, I may have an anxiety attack."

He reached over and touched my hand. I should've pulled back, but I couldn't. He cocked his head and smiled. "You'll be fine."

We both climbed out of the Explorer and walked over to his motorcycle. The memories of the accident started to flood my mind. He handed me the helmet and saw I was shaking. He clasped my shoulders.

"Take a deep breath. You'll be safe."

I took the helmet and put it on. Something was soothing about his voice. I trusted him, and I started to calm down. He straddled his bike and started it. Patting the seat behind him, he told me to get on. I climbed on and leaned forward, wrapping my arms around him as tightly as possible. I closed my eyes as he took off down the road, and the only thing I felt was the wind against us and Luke's muscular form. He looked back for a second and asked me if I was okay. I told him I was. The sick feeling I had a few minutes ago had passed, and riding with him wasn't so bad. He made me feel safe.

We reached our apartment building, and I sighed in relief. A car pulled up next to us when he pulled into a parking space. I glanced over and saw my student, Charley, getting out of the vehicle. Luke climbed off his bike as Charley ran up and hugged him. I took off my helmet.

"Miss Gilmore!" Charley's eyes lit up.

Luke looked at her. "This is Miss Gilmore. Your teacher?" he asked in shock.

"Yes, Uncle Luke, that's her." She smiled.

I looked at Charley with widened eyes. "This is your uncle that you've been telling me about?"

"Yes! It sure is!" Her smile widened.

A woman walked over to us with a couple of bags. Luke immediately took them from her. She looked at me and held out her hand.

"Hi, Miss Gilmore. I'm Maddie, Charley's mom."

I smiled as I shook her hand. "It's nice to meet you. Please call me Lily."

"Miss Gilmore, why are you riding my Uncle Luke's motorcycle?" Charley asked.

"Your teacher lives in the apartment next door to me. Her car broke down, so I gave her a ride home," Luke said.

"I had no idea you lived here, Lily," Maddie said. "Charley and I live in the apartments upstairs. My parents own the building."

"Uncle Luke, can Miss Gilmore come with us to the carnival on Friday?" Charley asked.

Luke looked at me, and our eyes locked. I could tell he was uncomfortable.

"Thank you for inviting me, Charley, but I won't be able to make it," I said.

"Uncle Luke, tell her she can come," Charley whined.

"Yeah, you can join us. Maddie has to work at the bar Friday night, so Charley's staying with me."

"Please, Miss Gilmore. Please," Charley begged.

How could I resist her? "Okay, Charley. I'll go." I smiled as I placed my hand on her head.

We walked inside the building, and I said goodbye as they headed upstairs to Maddie's apartment.

I opened the door and threw my things on the chair. I grabbed a bottle of wine and poured some into a glass. Standing against the kitchen counter, I remembered something Charley said about her uncle. She said he didn't have a girlfriend because she died. I was in deep thought when startled by a knock at the door. I looked out the peephole, and Luke was standing there.

"Hi." I smiled. "Come on in."

"I just wanted to tell you I called my buddy's garage. They towed your Explorer, and it'll be ready tomorrow afternoon."

"Thank you, Luke. I appreciate it. Do you want a glass of wine or a beer?" I asked.

Placing both his hands in his pockets, he spoke, "Nah, I need to get going," He opened the door and turned around. "I'm driving Charley to school in the morning. I can give you a ride if you don't already have one."

My heart rate started to pick up the pace. "Thank you, but I don't think we will fit on your bike."

Luke chuckled. "We wouldn't take my bike. I have a vehicle."

"You do?"

"Yes. My sister wouldn't let me take Charley on the bike anyway. She hates motorcycles."

"Thank you for your offer. My students would appreciate you ensuring their teacher made it to work." I smiled.

"Okay then. I'll meet you here in the hall at six forty-five." He smiled back.

I took in a deep breath as he shut the door. Something was

happening to me. That feeling was beginning to come back, and it scared the shit out of me. I couldn't and wouldn't let myself go down that road again. I was happier alone. I needed to be alone for my own sanity because I couldn't take more heartbreak. Just as I was getting caught up in my emotions, there was a knock at the door. I looked out the peephole and saw Luke standing on the other side. I opened the door and stared at him.

"By the way, I'm Luke Matthews," he said as he extended his hand.

"It's nice to meet you, Luke Matthews. I'm Lily Gilmore," I replied as I shook his hand.

He turned and went back to his apartment. I shut the door, smiled, and headed for the shower.

Chapter Seven

LUKE

I couldn't believe that Lily was Charley's teacher. I walked into the apartment, and Sam was cooking dinner.

"What are you making, dude?" I asked him.

"I'm making chicken parmesan. Gretchen's coming over for dinner."

"Thanks for the notice, bro."

"Sorry. I was in meetings all day; it was a last-minute thing. Did you go and pick up Lily?" he asked.

"Yeah. I had her car towed to Huey's Garage. It'll be ready tomorrow. Hey, did you know that she's Charley's school teacher?"

"I knew she was a teacher, but I had no idea she was Charley's. That's pretty cool. Don't you think?" he asked.

"I guess. I'm driving her and Charley to school in the morning. Maddie has to be at the bar early for a meeting. Lily's going with Charley and me to the carnival tomorrow. Why don't you and Gretchen come with us?"

Sam's brow raised. "You asked her to go with you to the carnival?"

"No. Charley asked her to go."

"And she said yes?" he asked in a surprised tone.

"Yes, she did. She wasn't going to turn down Charley."

"That's great, Luke. Gretchen and I already have plans for tomorrow night, though, sorry."

"Wow, you're really serious about this girl."

"I really like her, man. She's all I ever think about."

I walked over and placed my hand on Sam's shoulder. "That's great. I'm happy you found someone. I'm going to Maddie's to give you and Gretchen some privacy."

"Thanks, man." He smiled.

I walked out the door and up to Maddie's apartment. Charley was playing video games, and Maddie was cooking dinner. I could tell something was wrong with Maddie, and it looked like she'd been crying.

"What's wrong, Maddie?" I asked.

"Nothing's wrong. It's the onions," she said.

"Daddy called," Charley spoke from the couch.

"Is that true?" I asked Maddie.

She nodded without saying a word. "What did the bastard want?!" I spat.

Maddie turned and looked at me. "Not in front of Charley, Luke."

I looked over at Charley, who was lost in video games.

"Then let's go into the other room. I want to know what that bastard wanted," I whispered.

We walked into Maddie's room. "All he said was that he's coming to town in a couple of weeks and wants to see Charley. I told him that he couldn't see her until he paid his child support, but he said I better watch it, or he'll take me to court and sue me for full custody of her."

"Over my dead body," I spoke in anger.

"Calm down, Luke. I have a couple of weeks to think of a plan. Technically, I can't keep him from her. He's her father."

I shook my head as I walked out of the bedroom. Walking over to the couch, I took a seat next to Charley.

"Are you and Mom okay?" she asked.

"Yeah. We're okay." I smiled as I kissed the top of her head.

After dinner, I went back to my apartment. Opening the door, I stepped inside and didn't see Sam or Gretchen. I didn't have to see them. I could hear them before I reached the hallway. I rolled my eyes and walked out of the apartment. I didn't need to sit and listen to them having sex. I stood in the hallway and thought about going to Bernie's, but I decided I wasn't up for it, especially since I was driving Lily and Charley to school tomorrow morning. I stood and stared at Lily's door. I couldn't stop thinking about her and how she held onto me while on the motorcycle. She held on as if her life depended on it. She trusted me even though she was scared to get on that bike. I smiled for a moment and thought about knocking on her door. Then, I decided it wasn't a good idea, so I returned to my apartment, took my guitar from the stand, and sat on the couch, playing a few chords as loud as possible to let Sam know I was home.

~

I SLAMMED my hand down on the beeping alarm clock. I was so damn tired from being kept awake all night while Sam and Gretchen acted like they'd never had sex before. I stumbled out of bed and threw on a pair of jeans and my black T-shirt. I ran the brush through my hair and went to the bathroom to brush my teeth. Gretchen was in the kitchen, pouring coffee.

"Good morning. You must be Luke," Gretchen said as she extended her hand.

"Yeah, and you must be Gretchen." I shook her hand.

I looked around and didn't see Sam. "Where's Sam?" I asked as I poured my coffee into my to-go cup.

"He ran to get some bagels. He'll be back soon."

I looked at the clock. It was six forty.

"I have to go. It was nice meeting you, Gretchen," I said as I walked out the door and up the stairs to get Charley. Just as I reached the top step, she was coming out of her apartment.

"Morning, Uncle Luke." She smiled.

"Morning, peanut." I patted the top of her head. "Do you have everything you need?"

"Yes, Uncle Luke." She sighed.

We walked down the stairs as Lily was coming out of her apartment.

"Perfect timing!" She smiled as she held up her coffee cup.

"This is so cool that I get to drive my teacher to school!" Charley shrieked.

Lily looked nice. Oh hell, she looked beautiful. Every time I glanced at her, I felt like I'd met her before. Her long, blonde hair was straight, and she wore a long cream-colored skirt with a light pink top and high heels. Damn. I wish my teachers looked like that when I was growing up. She was going to give those boys their first hard-ons. When she smiled, her bluish-gray eyes lit up.

"Good morning, you two," Lily said.

"Morning," I spoke back.

"Good morning, Miss Gilmore," Charley said as she took Lily's hand and led her to the Jeep.

Charley climbed into the back as Lily sat on the passenger side.

"A Jeep Wrangler fits you. I like it better than that motorcycle you ride."

"Thanks, but I like my bike, so you'll get used to it." I winked.

"Keep dreaming." She smiled.

When I pulled into the school parking lot, Charley climbed out and leaned over to kiss me. "Bye, Uncle Luke." She waved.

"Bye, peanut. Have a good day."

Lily climbed out of the car and slung her bag over her shoulder. "Thanks for the ride, Luke. Have a good day," she said as she started to walk away.

"Hey, Lily!" I yelled out.

She stopped, turned around, and looked at me.

"I can pick you up at the end of the day and take you to the garage to get your car."

"Sounds good. I'll see you later." She smiled.

I caught myself staring at her as she walked into the school. For the first time in over a year, a woman made me smile. Sam was right. Lily was a nice girl—a very nice girl—and I couldn't stop thinking about her. I found myself thinking of her in ways I hadn't thought about since…

Chapter Eight

LILY

    I sat quietly at my desk while the students had their daily reading time. I was trying to concentrate on grading papers, but the only thing on my mind was Luke Matthews. Why did he have to be so damn sexy? Why did the universe have to light up every time he smiled? Why did he have to have such a great body? Why did he have to live next door?

    I found myself thinking about him more and more, which was something I didn't bargain for when I moved to Santa Monica. I was distracted by the chiming of my cell phone. I looked over and saw a message from Giselle.

    "Gretchen had a date last night with Sam, but she never came home. I guess she got a piece of that hot man!"

    "Lucky girl," I replied.

    "Do you want to meet up for dinner and drinks tonight?" Giselle asked.

    "I can't. I'm going with Luke and Charley to the carnival."

    "Who's Charley?"

    "She's Luke's niece, who also happens to be one of my students."

    "We have some catching up to do. Call me later, and let's set up dinner."

    "I will. Bye."

I immediately sent Gretchen a text message.

"Did you have sex with Sam?"

A few minutes later, she replied.

"Yes, I did. It was wonderful, Lily. He's a GOD in bed."

I smiled.

"I'm glad you had fun. Are you still at his place?"

"Yeah, I'm getting ready to leave. I have a photo shoot across town in an hour."

"Is Luke there?"

"No. He's not. Why are you asking?"

"I was just wondering. I have to go. Reading time is over."

I wondered why Luke didn't tell me that Gretchen stayed the night. After all, she was my best friend. The rest of the day went quickly, and before I knew it, the bell rang, and the children hurried out of the classroom. Maddie walked in as I stood by the door, saying goodbye to the students.

"Hi, Maddie." I smiled.

"Mommy!" Charley exclaimed as she came running from the other side of the room.

"I saw Luke outside. He's taking you to pick up your car?" she asked.

"Yes." I nodded.

"That's great. It's good to see that Luke's helping you."

I thought that was odd to say and wondered what she meant by it. My mind went back to what Charley had said about Luke's girlfriend dying.

"Bye, Miss Gilmore. I'll see you later!" Charley smiled.

"Bye, Charley. I'm looking forward to it."

"Have a good time tonight, Lily," Maddie said as she took Charley by the hand and left the classroom.

I grabbed my bags and headed to the parking lot. I smiled when I saw Luke's Jeep in front and Luke sitting in it with his Ray Bans on. I felt a rush of sensation down below. I hated myself for that. He turned to me and smiled as I climbed inside.

"Did you have a good day?" he asked.

"I did. Thank you for asking. How about you?"

"I fixed a couple of toilets, a leaky sink, and changed a light bulb for the woman in 4B."

"I didn't know you changed light bulbs," I smirked.

"I can do just about anything."

"So, if I needed my light bulb changed, you'd change it for me?" I couldn't believe what I just said. What the hell was the matter with me?

Luke looked over at me as the corners of his mouth turned upwards. "Just call me, and I'll be over in a flash. I can change anything you want."

"How can I call you if I don't have your number?" Oh my god, I had no control over my mouth. Why was this happening? This wasn't me.

We were stopped at a light. "Give me your phone," he said as he held out his hand.

I looked at him strangely, then placed my phone in his hand. He typed in his number and handed it back to me.

"There, now you have my number. If you need anything fixed, call me," he said as he took off from the light.

As we drove to the garage to pick up my Explorer, a song that was all too familiar to me came on the radio. Luke reached over and turned it up. I looked the other way. It was one of my dad's songs.

"I love this song," Luke said. "Do you know it?"

"I've heard it a few times," I said as I looked down at my phone.

When we finally reached the garage, Luke parked the Jeep, and we both got out.

"Hey, Huey," he said as they fist-bumped each other.

"Hey, Luke. We need to hit the bar sometime, man."

"I know. It's been a while. This is Lily. Lily, this is Huey."

"It's nice to meet you, Huey," I spoke as I held out my hand.

"It's nice to meet you too, Lily. Your truck's all fixed and ready to go."

I paid Huey what I owed and thanked him as he led me to where the Explorer was parked. Luke followed close behind.

I climbed inside and turned the key. Luke walked over, and I rolled down the window.

"I'll follow you home in case it breaks down again."

"Thank you. I appreciate it." I smiled.

He turned away, and I couldn't help but stare at his fine ass as he walked back to his Jeep. It didn't matter what side of him you saw, front or back. He was still sexy as hell.

I drove home, and Luke followed behind me. We pulled into the parking spaces next to each other and walked inside the building.

"What time should I be ready tonight?" I asked.

"Charley will be at my place around seven. So, we'll pick you up then."

"Sounds great, and thanks again for your help," I said as I slid my key into the lock.

"No problem. I'll see you in a couple of hours." He entered his apartment and shut the door.

I threw my bags on the kitchen counter and walked to the bathroom for a quick shower. I had no idea what I was going to wear. I was standing in my room, in a towel, when I heard a knock on the door.

Shit, I thought. I looked out the peephole and saw Giselle standing there. I unlocked it and opened the door, standing behind it. Giselle walked in and looked at me.

"I bet you were wishing I was Luke right now." She smiled.

"Very funny," I said. "What brings you over?"

Giselle followed me to the bedroom. "I had an appointment not too far from here, and I just thought I'd stop by. What's going on with you and Luke anyway?"

"Nothing. We're just friends. Why do you think something's going on?"

"I don't know. Wishful thinking, I guess." She smiled. "Do you even find him attractive?"

I pulled out my jean shorts from the drawer and put them on. "Of course, I find him attractive. Have you seen his ass? You'd have to be blind not to see that."

"Well, at least you find him hot. That's a start," she said as she sat on the bed.

"You know my past, and I won't go down that road again. I'm happy the way I am."

"Lily, stop trying to convince yourself. You're twenty-six years old and vowed to stay single and not date guys for the rest of your life. Sorry, honey, but it won't happen unless you join the convent."

"Hilarious, Giselle," I said as I put on my black tank top. I picked up my brush from the dresser and ran it through my hair. "Should I wear my hair up?" I asked as I looked in the mirror.

"Why does it matter? It's not like you're trying to impress anyone."

I shot her a look and walked into the bathroom to brush my teeth. Giselle followed behind.

"You know I love you, right?" she asked. "I just want you to be happy and not become some old cat lady who keeps herself locked up with her twelve cats."

I laughed as I rinsed my mouth and spat in the sink. "I don't even have a cat."

"Not yet, you don't. But you've been talking about maybe getting one."

I smiled and smacked her arm as I left the bathroom. I grabbed my black cowboy boots from the closet and put them on. I twirled around the living room.

"What do you think?" I asked.

"I think you look hot, and Luke isn't going to know what hit him when he sees you." She smiled. "There's nothing sexier to a man than short jean shorts, tank tops, and cowboy boots."

I cocked my head. "How do you know that?" I asked.

"I dated a cowboy once."

"Oh yeah. That creepy guy from Montana that wouldn't let you take your boots off during sex and wanted you to ride him on a bull."

"Yep, that's the one." She laughed.

Suddenly, there was a knock at the door. Luke's eyes raked over me when I opened it.

"What did I tell you?" Giselle whispered in my ear as she walked by me. "Have fun, everyone. Lily, make sure you call me tomorrow."

"Hi, Charley," I said as I patted her head. "Hi, Luke." I smiled.

"Are you ready to go?" he asked.

"I am. Just let me grab my purse and camera."

I turned around and headed towards the bedroom. I could feel his eyes staring at me as I walked away. I grabbed my purse, put my camera around my neck, and returned to the living room.

"You look really pretty, Miss Gilmore," Charley said. "Uncle Luke, doesn't she look pretty?" Charley asked as she tugged on his pant leg.

"Yes, Charley. Miss Gilmore does look pretty," Luke spoke in embarrassment.

Charley looked at me and winked. I needed to watch out for this little girl. We climbed into Luke's Jeep and headed for the carnival.

"Nice camera. I take it you like to take pictures," he said.

"Yeah, I love taking pictures. Photography has always been a passion of mine. Someday, I'd love to work for a big magazine."

"You mean like National Geographic or something like that?" He smiled as he looked over at me.

"Yeah, something like that." I smiled back.

∽

Charley's eyes lit up the moment she saw the lights.

"I can't wait to get inside!" she said excitedly as she grabbed our hands and dragged us through the parking lot.

Luke looked over at me and smiled. We got to the gate, and I pulled out my wallet to pay for my ticket.

"I got your ticket," he said.

"I can buy my own ticket, Luke."

"Charley invited you, so I'm buying your ticket."

We stepped up to the window, and he purchased three wristbands. I tried to give him my money, but he refused.

"If I let you buy my ticket, this becomes a date. I don't do dates," I said to him.

He stared at me for a minute. "I can assure you that this isn't a date. I don't do dates either."

"Will you two stop it and hurry up," Charley said with an attitude.

"I'll make you a deal," Luke said. "You can buy the food."

"Deal," I spoke as I held out my hand to him, and we shook on it.

We both held one of Charley's hands as we walked around the carnival. The lights were bright, and the music coming from the games loudly blared through the speakers. Charley saw a ride she wanted to go on, so we waited in line.

"Do you watch Charley a lot?" I asked.

"Yeah. I try to help Maddie out as much as I can. It's hard being a single parent."

"I'm sure it is."

"What about your parents?"

"They help out a lot. Right now, they're on a month-long cruise."

"They own the apartments?" I asked.

"Yes. They've owned those apartments for over twenty years. I remember them buying the building when I was seven years old. It's where Maddie and I spent most of our childhood. What about you?" he asked.

I didn't want to talk about my childhood or my family. It wasn't a topic that I was comfortable with. The only thing I ever wanted was a normal, happy childhood. I can thank Mommy and Daddy for not giving me that. I felt horrible for having to lie to Luke about my family, but I didn't want him to know about how awful they were. I didn't like to be judged for their actions. And as far as I was concerned, my family was dead.

"I grew up in Seattle with my parents and my sister. They died a couple of years ago in an accident."

Luke looked at me, and I could see the empathy in his eyes. "I'm sorry."

"Thank you. I don't like to talk about it," I said so he wouldn't ask me any other questions.

Luke nodded. We finally arrived at the front of the line, and

Charley got on the ride. We stood there, waving to her as the car she was sitting in sped by us.

"She's a great little girl." I smiled.

"She's the best," Luke said. "She's a huge part of my life, and I would do anything to protect her."

The ride ended, and Charley climbed off. She grabbed onto our hands and led us over to the games.

"Miss Gilmore, do you like to play games?" she asked as she looked up at me.

"I love to play games, Charley."

"So does my Uncle Luke." She winked.

I couldn't help but laugh. "Charley, when we're not in school, you can call me Lily."

"Really?!" she asked in excitement.

Luke looked over at me and laughed. "Just remember, though, she's Miss Gilmore during school hours," he said.

"Okay, I'll remember," she said as she led us to the game with the huge, stuffed purple cat hanging from the tent. "I want that cat, Uncle Luke," she begged.

I laughed as we approached the milk bottle toss. There was no question Luke was going to win that cat for Charley. He paid the guy behind the booth, and he handed him three baseballs. He told Luke to stand behind the line. I looked at him and frowned.

"That seems pretty far back," I said.

"Nah, it's fine. I used to play some baseball in high school. I can do this." He smiled.

Luke threw the first ball and knocked down the milk bottles. There was something about watching him throw those balls that made my heart beat faster. I was scared because I suddenly saw him as almost perfect. As promised, he won Charley her cat.

"Here," he said as he handed me the baseball. "Try it."

I shook my head. "No, I can't throw. I'd just embarrass myself."

"Just try it for fun." He smiled.

I sighed as I stepped behind the line and threw the ball. I almost hit the man behind the counter. Good thing he ducked when he did.

Luke and Charley started laughing. Suddenly, Luke was behind me, and he grabbed my hand.

"Here, let me help you," he said as he continued laughing.

He brought my hand up over my head and counted to three. His touch was amazing, and my impulses were starting to go crazy. My heart was rapidly beating, and the sensation deep below was back. I closed my eyes for a moment. On the third count, he helped me throw the ball. I knocked down all of the milk bottles. I jumped up and down, clapping my hands as Charley cheered excitedly, and Luke smiled at me. The carnie told me to pick which animal I wanted, so I chose the smaller version of Charley's cat.

"Look, now we match," I said, holding my cat beside Charley's. "Can you do me a favor and hold it while I take some pictures."

"Sure I can!" she excitedly spoke.

I brought my camera up and started taking pictures of Charley walking in front of us. I would call her name, and she would turn her head right before I pushed the button.

"Why photography?" Luke curiously asked.

"I love to capture people in a way you normally wouldn't see them when they're standing in front of you. Pictures capture true emotions. You know how people say that a person's eyes are the window into their soul?"

"Yeah."

"That's how I feel about pictures. I feel photographs capture the true nature of a person at that moment. The people don't just become images. They become stories. If you know what I mean."

"Yeah, I think I do." Luke smiled.

"I see the world differently through the lens of a camera." I shyly smiled.

I felt comfortable talking to Luke—too comfortable, in fact, and it scared the shit out of me.

Chapter Nine

LILY

Charley wanted to go on the Ferris wheel. She wanted all of us to go together. I hated Ferris wheels because I was afraid of heights, and the thought of being stuck at the top scared the shit out of me.

"Come on, Uncle Luke and Lily. Let's go on the Ferris wheel!" Charley squealed in excitement.

"Okay, Charley. We're coming." Luke smiled as he tried to catch up with her.

"You two go ahead. I'll watch from the sidelines."

"You don't like Ferris wheels, do you?" Luke asked with a slight grin.

"No, I don't. I'm scared of heights."

We walked up to the gate, and Luke grabbed my hand. I looked at him as he smiled at me.

"Luke, what are you doing?" I asked in a panicked tone as he pulled me through the gate.

"Face your fears, Lily. It's the only way you'll get over them."

"Luke Matthews, I'm not getting on that Ferris wheel," I said as I tried to loosen his tight grip on my hand.

"Just like you weren't getting on my bike?" he asked.

He stopped pulling me, turned around, and our eyes met. "You'll be safe. I promise."

Just like with the motorcycle, I trusted him. I took a deep breath as the three of us climbed into the seat of the Ferris wheel.

"Lily, since you're scared, you can sit next to Uncle Luke," Charley said.

I sat in between Luke and Charley. The ride started to move, and I gripped the bar so tight that my knuckles turned white. My heartbeat quickened as my panic grew. I closed my eyes, wishing that the ride would end before it even began. I felt Luke take my hand.

"Take slow, deep breaths, Lily," he whispered as he gently squeezed my hand.

The touch of his warm hand soothed me as my racing heart began to slow down, and a sense of calm slowly washed over me.

"Now open your eyes. You can get some great pictures," he said.

I slowly opened my eyes to see Charley staring at me.

"Are you okay, Lily?" she asked.

"I'm fine, sweetie." I lied.

The time had come for the ride to end, and of course, we stopped at the top. I gasped. Luke looked over and smiled.

"Look at the world through your camera lens. It'll calm you down."

I brought my camera up to my face and began taking pictures of the bright lights and the people below. Luke was right. For a minute, I forgot we were stopped at the top because I was focused on getting the best pictures. Before I knew it, we were back on the bottom, and it was time to get off the ride. Luke took my hand and helped me out of the seat.

"I'm hungry," Charley announced.

"Me too, peanut," Luke said as he picked her up to give her a piggyback ride.

Charley giggled. I wanted to capture the sweetness and innocence of this moment, so I began snapping pictures of the two of them. We stopped at a stand where they sold burgers, hot dogs, and fries. Charley ate a hot dog while Luke and I ate hamburgers. We sat at the wooden table eating when Luke and Charley started throwing French fries and laughing at each other.

"You both need to stop." I laughed at them.

Luke picked up a fry, threw it at me, and smiled. I looked at him and smirked as I threw one back. After our food fight ended, I glanced at my watch and saw it was late. Charley looked exhausted. Luke picked her up and carried her to the Jeep while I carried her oversized cat. He set her down and buckled her in. Being with him tonight and seeing him with Charley told me he would be an amazing father. It was just one more thing about him that seemed to be making him perfect. We arrived back at the apartment building, and I held the door while Luke carried Charley into his bedroom and laid her in his bed. Luke walked out, and I whispered good night to Charley. She opened her eyes and gently took my hand.

"I haven't seen Uncle Luke so happy in a long time," she whispered.

I smiled and kissed her forehead. "I had a great time too."

I walked back into the living room, where Sam and Gretchen sat on the couch, watching a movie.

"Hey, you guys. Did you have fun?" Sam whispered so as not to disturb Charley.

"Yeah. We had a great time," Luke said as he walked into the kitchen.

"It was a lot of fun." I smiled.

Gretchen looked at me and winked. I rolled my eyes.

"Call me tomorrow," she whispered.

As I headed towards the door, I heard Luke ask Sam to keep an eye on Charley while he walked me home.

"One foot out the door, and I'm already home." I laughed.

"You can never be too careful in these parts." He smiled.

I inserted the key into the lock. "Would you like to come in for some adult drinks?" I asked.

"You mean I can have something alcoholic?" he asked jokingly.

I laughed and nodded. "Come on in and have a beer with me. I think after tonight, we deserve one."

Luke followed me in as I walked to the refrigerator and grabbed two beers. After handing Luke his and opening mine, I held my bottle up.

"Here's to a wonderful evening spent in good company and facing my fears of the Ferris wheel."

Luke threw his head back and laughed. "I'll drink to that," he said as our beer bottles came together.

I leaned against the refrigerator while he leaned against the counter. It was one of those awkward moments when neither person was sure what to say next, so I just went for it.

"Let's sit on the couch while we finish our beer."

"Um, okay," Luke said as he followed behind me.

I sat with my back against the arm of the couch so I was facing him. I brought my leg up and tucked it underneath me. Suddenly, I felt the urge to pee.

"I'll be right back." I smiled.

Luke smiled back and took another drink of his beer. A few moments later, when I walked back into the living room, I saw him standing in front of my guitar.

"Hey," I said, placing my hands in my pockets. I knew he would figure it out soon— if he hadn't already.

"This guitar of yours. Only one was made in the whole world, and it belonged to Johnny Gil—" He stopped before he could get my last name out. After pausing for a moment, he continued. "The guitar was handmade by an old man living in a small Southeast Asian village. It was most known for the initials L.G. engraved into the frets. No one could figure out what it stood for." He stared into my eyes. "The initials stand for Lily Gilmore. Don't they?" he asked.

I took in a deep breath. "Yes, the initials are mine. He had that guitar made one week after I was born," I said as tears started to fill my eyes. I quickly looked up at the ceiling. There was no way I was going to let Luke see me cry.

"Wow, I had no idea you're Johnny Gilmore's daughter. He's a legend." He smiled. "How he merged the sounds of the late 70s and early 80s was amazing. He's a musical genius. He created a sound that no one could duplicate, and everyone said it was because of this guitar."

I was getting pissed off with the way he idolized my father. He may have been a musical genius, but nobody knew how he lived his life like I did. Luke's phone went off, so he pulled it from his pocket.

"I have to go. Sam and Gretchen are leaving, and I need to get back to Charley. Thanks for the beer," he said as he headed towards the door. He stopped as he put his hand on the knob and looked at me. "Come to the beach with us tomorrow."

I didn't know what to say at that moment. Did I want to go? Was he only asking me because now he knew who my father was? Were we really friends? I started questioning everything about our time spent together, and he put me on the spot.

"Sure, I'll go. It sounds like fun."

"Great. I'll see you tomorrow then." He smiled.

After locking the door behind him, I pressed my forehead against it, immediately regretting my decision. I couldn't let this happen again.

Chapter Ten

LUKE

 Charley was sleeping peacefully as I carefully opened the door and peeked into the room. Closing the door as silently as possible, I grabbed a pillow and a blanket from the hall closet, set them on the couch, sat down, and ran my hands through my hair. I couldn't believe that Lily was Johnny Gilmore's daughter. I remembered her father having passed away about two years ago, but I didn't recall hearing anything about her mother or sister, so I decided to grab my laptop. I did some online searching, and because her parents had been divorced for the past ten years, I couldn't find anything on them until an article popped up that caught my attention. The headline read: '80s Musical Legend's Daughter Calls Off Wedding.' I clicked on the headline to bring up the article.

 "Lily Gilmore, daughter of 80's musical legend Johnny Gilmore, calls off the wedding after she caught her fiancé having relations with her sister in the church on their wedding day. Sources say Miss Gilmore caused quite a scene outside the church, climbed into a limousine, and hasn't been seen since."

 I looked at the article's date, which was dated a little over a year ago. At that moment, it occurred to me that she lied to me about her family. The only person in her family who passed away was her father, whereas her mother and sister were still alive. I set my laptop on the coffee table and laid on the couch with my hands behind my head. Why would she lie to me? I couldn't understand her motive, and I was pissed. There was one thing in my life that I hated most and would not tolerate—people who lie.

I awoke to the feeling of tapping on my shoulder. I opened one eye and saw Charley standing over me, smiling.

"Wake up. I'm hungry," she said.

"Okay. Okay. I'm getting up."

I sat up on the couch and rubbed my eyes. "What time is it, Charley?"

She looked at the clock in the kitchen. "It's seven o'clock."

"May I ask why you're up so early?"

"Uncle Luke, it's not early for a kid my age."

I couldn't help but smile as I kissed her on the top of her head. "What do you want for breakfast?"

"I want your smiley pancakes." She smiled.

I walked into the kitchen and took out everything I needed to make pancakes. Charley loved the way I made them. Her favorite part was when I used chocolate chips for the eyes and whipped cream for the smile.

"Don't forget the eyes, Uncle Luke!" she shouted from the couch.

"Don't worry, Charley, I won't."

The pancakes were cooking on the griddle when Sam walked through the door.

"Damn, Luke, those smell good."

"Want some?"

"Yeah, I'm starving. Gretchen had a photo shoot this morning, so we didn't get to eat."

I poured more batter onto the hot griddle.

"Hey, don't forget to make them smiley," Sam said as he turned and looked at Charley.

Charley looked at him and giggled. I rolled my eyes. He walked into the kitchen and started a pot of coffee.

"I pulled up an article last night about Lily."

"Are you stalking her or something?" he asked.

"No. Do you know who her father was?"

I could tell by how Sam looked at me that he already knew.

"You asshole. You knew and didn't tell me?"

"Uncle Luke, language!" Charley yelled from the couch.

"Sorry, peanut. Please, don't tell your mom."

"The article said that she caught her fiancé with her sister on their wedding day."

"Yeah, I only found that out from Gretchen," Sam said as he poured some coffee into his cup and sat on the bar stool. "I asked Lily about it, but she got really pissed and told me to forget that I even knew."

"You asked her about it?" I said as I took the pancakes off the griddle. "Why would you do that?"

"Because I think you two would make a great couple, and I wanted to get her feel about dating."

"Bro, leave it alone. Jesus Christ, I already told you I'm not interested in dating anyone."

"Uncle Luke, I'm pretty sure J.C. is a bad word when used that way," Charley said as she sat at the table.

"I'm sorry, Charley." I sighed as I set down the plate of pancakes in front of her.

Sam got up from the bar stool and sat at the table across from Charley. "Dude, what the hel—heck did you do my pancakes? They're frowning cakes," he said with a pout.

I rolled my eyes and poured myself a cup of coffee. Just as I was about to sit down, Maddie entered the apartment.

"Good morning, baby," she said as she walked over and kissed Charley on the head. "Good morning, guys."

"Hey, Charley, would you mind if Sam took you home while I talked to your mom for a few minutes?"

Charley looked at Sam and cocked her head. "Will you give me a piggyback ride upstairs?"

"You bet I will. Hop on, little girl, and we'll giddy up out of here."

Charley climbed on Sam's back and giggled. As soon as the door shut, Maddie asked me what was going on.

"Lily is the daughter of Johnny Gilmore," I said.

"What? As in Johnny Gilmore, the musician?"

"Yeah, and she lied to me about something."

"What did she lie about?" Maddie asked as she poured more coffee into our cups.

"She told me that her family was killed a couple of years ago in an accident, but I did some research. The only person who died in her family was her father, and I remember that day. The reports said he had a massive heart attack. Her mom and sister are still alive and living in Seattle." I grabbed my laptop, set it on the table, and brought up the article I saw last night. "Here, read this," I said, turning my laptop towards Maddie.

"Wow, poor girl." She looked up at me. "She obviously had her reasons for telling you her family's dead. I know that if I had a sister and caught her having sex with my fiancé, I would never talk to her again. But to find them on her wedding day, in the church! Cut her some slack, Luke. You don't know the whole story."

I stood there for a few moments, pondering what Maddie said. "You're right, sis. Thanks."

"You're falling for her, aren't you?" She asked as she put her hand on my shoulder.

"No. We're just friends," I replied.

"It's okay, Luke. Don't fight what's natural," she said as she walked out the door.

I sighed and started cleaning up the kitchen.

Chapter Eleven

LILY

    I lay in bed, staring at the window as the sunlight filtered through the sides of the blinds. It would be another beautiful day, but I wasn't sure if I wanted to go to the beach. After last night, I wasn't sure of anything anymore. I knew for a fact that I was falling for Luke. His brown eyes stared at me intently when I talked. His sculpted face and chiseled chin were perfection, as were his perfectly shaped lips that I've found myself wanting to touch. It was the way he lit up the room when he smiled. And his perfect body—a strong body that I knew could protect me. I fantasized about running my hands across his chest and down to his manhood.

    Snapping out of my fantasy, I threw back the covers and jumped out of bed. I did a little stomping dance because I was angry with myself for thinking about him that way. I refuse to give my heart away. It's mine, and it's my job to keep it safe. It was tucked deep inside, and I wouldn't let it come out. It wouldn't be able to withstand any more pain. After I threw my hissy fit, I picked up my phone and sent a text message to Luke.

    "Something came up, so I won't be able to go to the beach today. Sorry, maybe next time."

I waited for a response, but I didn't get one. Maybe he was pissed at me for not telling him who my father was, or perhaps he didn't care whether I went or not. Whatever the reason, I didn't care. I couldn't care. I wouldn't care.

Walking into the bathroom, I brushed my teeth and threw my hair into a ponytail. I put on my bikini because I decided that I would lay out by the pool when everyone left for the beach. I grabbed my phone from the nightstand after throwing on my jean shorts and a tank top. When I saw I still hadn't received a message from Luke, I sighed and walked into the living room. The beer bottles from last night were still on the coffee table. As I walked over to pick them up, there was a knock at the door. I looked out the peephole, and Luke stood on the other side. My heart started racing as I turned the lock and opened the door.

"Good morning," I said.

"Morning. Can I come in?"

"Oh, sure," I said as I stepped out of the way. "What's up?" I could feel something was off.

"Grab your things. You're coming to the beach," he said.

"Didn't you get my text? I told you something came up."

"I got it, and I don't believe you. So grab your things, and let's go. The gang is probably already there."

"I don't appreciate you being so bossy," I snapped.

He stared at me with his beautiful brown eyes, making me weak in the knees. I had to turn away because I was starting to melt right in front of him. I walked over and picked up the beer bottles. He reached out as I walked past him and lightly grabbed my arm.

"I know you probably think things are weird because of last night, but they're not. You said that you would come to the beach with us. I don't want you changing your mind over something untrue. Things are fine, Lily."

I stood there for a moment before looking at him. I could hear the sincerity in his voice. He let go of my arm, and I set the bottles on the counter.

"Let me go get my things. I'll be right back," I said as I headed towards my bedroom. I grabbed my bag, packed for the pool, grabbed my camera, and slid into my flip-flops.

"Okay, I'm ready."

Luke looked at me and smiled. When we left the apartment, I walked towards the spot where he parked his Jeep, but his Jeep was gone. I looked behind me, and Luke was sitting on his motorcycle with a big grin.

"Oh no! Once was enough. I'm not getting on that bike again!"

Luke started it up and rode over to me. "Come on, Lily. Hop on," he said as he handed me his helmet.

"Let's take the Explorer!" I yelled.

"Hop on, Lily. Let's not keep everyone waiting."

I rolled my eyes, grabbed the helmet from his hands, and put it on. Climbing behind him, I put my bag across my shoulder and wrapped my arms around him.

Here we go again.

∼

THE BEACH WAS CROWDED. I took off the helmet and handed it to Luke as I climbed off the bike. My heart was still racing from the nerves and excitement.

"Now, that wasn't so bad, was it?" he asked.

I looked at him and smirked as I walked through the parking lot. When I reached the end of the sidewalk, I stopped to take off my flip-flops. The minute my toes hit the warm sand, I felt serene. Luke and I walked across the sand and over to where Sam and a group of people were sitting around. Lucky jumped up when he saw me.

"Hello, beautiful," he said, lightly kissing my hand.

As I smiled at him, I could see Luke giving him a dirty look out of the corner of my eye. I said hi to Sam, and Luke introduced me to the rest of his friends.

"Isn't Gretchen here?" I asked Sam.

"She'll be here in about an hour. She had a photo shoot this morning."

I gave him a small smile. They already sounded like a real

couple, and it made me happy that Gretchen had found someone. I couldn't ask for a better man for her. Lucky put his arm around me and started walking me away from the others.

"Every time I look at you, I feel like I've died and gone to Heaven. You're a real angel in disguise, aren't you? I know that we could make beautiful, angelic music together. How about we give it a try?"

I looked at Luke and winked at him. He could tell I wasn't falling for Lucky's bullshit lines.

"You know Lucky," I said, pausing to turn around and face him. "Every time I look at you, I feel like I've died and gone to hell. So please do me a favor and back the fuck off so that I can go on with my day." I smiled politely.

He looked at me for a moment with furrowed brows. He extended his hand to me.

"You are one awesome chick! Friends?"

I smiled and shook his hand. "Friends," I said.

Sam and Luke both busted out laughing. I looked over at Luke as he was shaking his head at me.

"What do you guys want to do?!" Luke yelled to everyone.

"I think I'm just going to lay in the sun for a while," I said as I took off my top and shorts, revealing my bikini.

"Hot damn!" Sam squealed as he ran towards me, picked me up, and ran to the water.

I yelled at him to put me down. He laughed and said he would, but not until we cooled off. We hit the water, and he carried me out until the water stopped at our chest.

"Sam! You wait!"

He was smiling at me, and suddenly, out of nowhere, someone had a tight grip on my waist and pulled me under the water. My heart started racing, but within moments, I was released and returned to the surface. When I turned around, Luke was inches from my face, smiling.

"You asshole! You scared the shit out of me!" I said as I splashed him.

"Watch your mouth, and I couldn't resist! Please tell me you're not mad."

How the hell could I be mad at that face? He was having fun, and I was all up for crazy, wild fun—at least I used to be.

"I'm not mad."

"Good. Then let's get out of the water," he said as we swam back to shore.

Sam was standing at the shoreline with two towels. "Here, dry off, and let's play some volleyball."

I saw Gretchen waving to me as she sat in the sand, so I ran to her.

"Look at you, miss sexy thing in that teeny weeny bikini! You've gone and given all the boys a boner!" she said in her fake Southern accent.

I threw my towel at her and sat down. Putting my arm around her, I laid my head on her shoulder. "I'm glad you're here."

"Looks like you and Luke were having some fun in the water."

"He found out last night about Johnny." I sighed.

"What did he say?"

"He was shocked, but then he raved about him like he was some sort of God."

"Lily, he was a God to many people, and one of them is Luke. How weird is that? You move here to start a new life and live next door to a twenty-seven-year-old guy who worships your dad."

I lifted my head and gave her a dirty look.

"I'm just saying."

Sam walked over and asked Gretchen if she wanted to play volleyball. She jumped at the chance. Little did the boys know she was the captain of her volleyball team and star player. She grabbed my hand and told me to come, but I wanted to lay back in the sun and relax for a while, so I told her I'd play later. I looked around, and Luke was off to the side, talking to a group of people. I decided to wander the beach and to take pictures. I put on my jean shorts, grabbed my camera from the bag, and headed down the beach. The sun was bright, the sand was warm, and the beach was filled with people enjoying a beautiful Saturday. I heard someone shout my name. When I turned around, Luke was running up behind me.

"Hey, where are you off to?" he asked as he caught up with me.

"I was just wandering around, taking some pictures." I smiled.

"I know this great little area with the best view that's perfect for taking pictures. Come on, follow me."

I followed him about half a mile down the beach. When we reached the area, I looked around. It was a cove with large boulders around one side, forming a small wall. There were a few sailboats in the water, but overall, there wasn't anyone else around.

"If you climb those rocks over there, you'll be able to get some great pictures looking out into the ocean," Luke said.

I smiled as we walked over to the area. Luke climbed up first and then held his hand out to me. "I don't want you to fall. These rocks are tricky, and you could slip."

I took his warm, strong hand, and he helped me onto the rock. We climbed a couple more until we were at the top. Luke was right. This was a beautiful place to take pictures. I lifted my camera and began clicking. Luke was staring out into the water as I turned towards him and took his picture.

"I think I took enough pictures from this spot."

Luke took my hand as we carefully stepped down onto each rock. Only when we reached the sand did he let go.

"This is a quiet spot," I said as I sat down.

"I come here when I need to think."

"Think about what?" I asked.

"Life," he replied as he stared out at the water. "There's something that I want to ask you."

I suddenly became nervous and had a sick feeling in my stomach. "Okay, ask away."

"Why did you lie to me about your mom and sister being deceased?"

I felt a knot in my throat. Did I owe him an explanation? Was I obligated to tell him everything? I stood up and grabbed my camera. "They're dead to me," I said as I walked away from him.

He instantly jumped up and followed me. "Lily, wait!" He caught up with me and lightly grabbed my arm. "Please, don't walk away from me."

I sighed and stood there. Luke let go of my arm, and our eyes locked. I shook my head and pursed my lips. The last thing I wanted to do was dredge up the past, but I didn't think I had much choice.

"My mother and sister did horrible things, and as far as I'm concerned, they're dead to me."

"I read the article about you and your ex-fiancé. I'm sorry that happened."

I took in a deep breath as I looked down. "Hunter's an asshole, and my sister's a whore. My mother knew they were fucking behind my back for a long time, but she didn't say a word to me about it. She was going to let me marry that cheating bastard and ruin my life. Just because she stayed in a marriage where her husband did nothing but cheat doesn't mean everyone else wants that life. I hate them for what they did!"

Tears started to fall down my face. Luke stepped closer, and before I knew it, his arms were around me, embracing me and letting me know everything was all right. My heart started racing. His arms were so strong. I wanted to push him away but couldn't muster the strength to try. My head told me to run, but my heart said it was okay.

"I had no idea that your mom knew. I'm sorry, Lily."

I broke our embrace and looked at him. "Thank you, Luke. I moved here to start a new life and forget about them and everything that happened. I'll tell you more sometime over several drinks." I laughed.

Luke laughed and hooked his arm around me. "Come on, let's head back to the gang. They're probably starting rumors about us."

Chapter Twelve

LUKE

As we returned to the part of the beach where everyone had been playing volleyball, I couldn't stop thinking about holding Lily. It felt right, and it scared me to think of us being more than just friends. My feelings were growing for her, and holding her the way I did to comfort her intensified those feelings. Her warm skin against mine felt incredible and stirred up emotions I hadn't had in a long time. We reached our friends as the volleyball game was ending. I saw Sam walk over to Gretchen and kiss her on the lips.

"Break it up, you two, or get a room." I smiled.

"Well, well, if it isn't Mr. Matthews and Miss Gilmore. Where did the two of you go off to?" Sam asked with a smirk.

"I showed Lily the cove. She wanted to take some pictures."

Sam gave me a strange look, and I knew why. He was surprised because that cove was where I practically lived after the accident. I shrugged my shoulders and walked away. It felt right to take Lily there. I wanted her to get some great pictures.

"Let's cook some lunch!" I yelled to everyone.

I started the grill, and Sam took out the hot dogs and hamburgers. I put them on and stood there, watching them cook.

"I'm proud of you, man," Sam said.

"No big deal, bro. Leave it alone."

He patted me on the back and smiled. Lucky walked over and stood beside me while I grilled the food.

"Dude, don't forget about our gig tonight."

"I haven't forgotten."

"What gig?" Lily asked as she walked up.

Lucky put his arm around her. "Lukey boy, didn't tell you that we have a band and occasionally play at Bernie's?"

"No. He didn't tell me." She shot me a look.

"Honestly, I really didn't think about it," I said in my defense.

"Tell me you'll be joining us tonight and listening to the lovely Luke sing his heart out?" Lucky smirked.

"You sing?" Lily asked.

Shit. I wanted to kill Lucky. "A little." I smiled.

"We'll have to talk about this later. I see Giselle coming," Lily said as she walked away.

"Hot damn! Another hottie coming my way. Later, man," Lucky said as he went to check out Giselle.

I rolled my eyes and continued to grill the food. Moments later, Lily approached me with a plate in her hand. "I thought you might need this."

"Thanks." I took it from her and put the hot dogs and hamburgers on it. We walked over to the picnic table, and as I set the plate down next to the other food, the gang started lining up, so I walked back to grill some more. Lily followed me.

"Go eat," I said.

"I will. I want to wait for you." She smiled. "I want to know more about this band you have."

"It's no big deal. Bernie's is the bar Maddie works at. I play guitar and sing a couple of songs every once in a while. Sam plays on the keyboard, and Lucky's the drummer."

"That's cool. I'm surprised you never mentioned it."

"I guess I didn't think about it," I said.

"What's your band's name?" Lily asked.

I froze because I didn't want to explain it. I wasn't ready to open that door and walk down that road with her.

"Well?"

I took in a deep breath. "The band's called Love In Between."

"Cool name. How did you come up with it?"

"You know what, Lily, you really should go eat. Don't wait for me."

"Oh, okay." She walked away.

I could tell by the look on her face that I'd hurt her feelings, so I turned around and watched her walk back to the table. Now, I felt like shit. Damn it. I didn't want to hurt her feelings, but I couldn't talk about anything to do with Callie. It still hurt too much.

I finished grilling the second round of hamburgers and hot dogs and walked over to the table. I sat down and stared at Lily as she sat in the sand across from my friend, Jasper, who was playing guitar. They were talking, and then he handed her his guitar. I watched as she strummed each chord. She looked amazing with a guitar. As I watched her, Gretchen came over, grabbed a hot dog, and sat beside me.

"She's pretty amazing with the guitar. She gets it from her father," Gretchen said.

"I've only heard her play a couple of times."

"Well, I'll ask her to play later. I know you don't want to hear this, but I'm saying it anyway. Sam told me about the accident and Callie, and I'm really sorry for your loss. I was there with Lily when she found out about Hunter and Brynn. I saw the look of pain and betrayal on her face, and I was there the whole night, holding her and telling her that everything was going to be okay. I've never seen someone so hurt in my life until I met you."

I turned and looked at her. "What the hell is that supposed to mean?" I asked.

"It means that the first time I saw you, I saw the same look on your face that I see on Lily's every day. She puts up a good front, but deep inside, she's dying, not only because of what Hunter did but because of her family, including her father. I see that in you."

I turned away. I didn't want to hear anymore and wasn't in the mood to get lectured. I got enough of that from my mom and Maddie. Gretchen got up and left the table. I looked over to where Lily was sitting, but she was gone, so I got up and walked over to Sam.

"Hey, bro, have you seen Lily?"

"Yeah, she's over there in the water." Sam pointed.

"Thanks, man."

I walked to the shoreline. "Want some company?!" I yelled out to her.

"Sure!" she shouted back.

I stepped into the water and swam over to where she was. "I'm sorry about earlier."

"Don't be."

"No. I was an asshole. It's just that I don't want to talk about certain things."

"I get it, Luke. I'm the queen of not wanting to talk about things. Please don't worry about it."

I smiled at her. Every time I saw her, I found myself smiling.

"I want you to come to the bar tonight," I blurted out.

"I'd love to. Thank you for inviting me."

We swam back to the shore, and Lily looked over at me.

"I think I'm going to ask Giselle to drive me home."

"If you're ready to leave, I'll take you."

"No, you stay and enjoy yourself."

"I'm taking you home, Lily. End of discussion."

She shook her head and grabbed her bag.

Chapter Thirteen

LILY

I climbed onto the back of Luke's bike and wrapped my arms around him, making sure to close my eyes as he took off from the parking lot. It was getting easier to ride with him, and I didn't feel as scared anymore. He told me I'd be safe with him, and that's how he made me feel.

We reached the building, Luke parked his bike, and we climbed off.

"Aren't you going back to the beach?" I asked as I handed him his helmet.

"Nah, I think I'm going to practice some songs for tonight."

As we walked to our apartments and inserted our keys into the lock, we both turned and looked at each other.

"See you later," he said.

"Yeah, see you later." I smiled.

I walked into my apartment and threw my keys onto the counter. I went into the bathroom and started the shower. Looking at myself in the mirror, my hair was a hot mess from the water and Luke's motorcycle helmet. I stepped into the shower and washed the salt and sand off my body. After spending a ridiculous amount of time in there, I turned the shower off and stepped out, only to hear my phone chiming. I grabbed a towel and wrapped it around me as I walked over to my bag to get my phone. There was a text message from Giselle.

"Brace yourself, darling. I just got a call from your mom."

I gasped, and my eyes grew wide.

"What the hell did she say?"

"She said she misses you dearly and wants to speak with you. She's trying to track you down. I told her that I hadn't talked to you in months, and you were in Portland the last time I did."

"Thanks, Giselle."

"You're welcome. I'll see you tonight at the bar."

"You're going?"

"Yep, Lucky invited me. He's so sexy, Lily!"

Oh God. I didn't know how to respond to that. Giselle and Lucky are total opposites.

"Okay, see you later."

I felt sick to my stomach. Why the hell would my mom be trying to track me down? I knew why. Because I'm her daughter, and even though she's dead to me, I'm not dead to her. I needed to lie down, so I climbed into bed. When I settled underneath the covers, I heard Luke playing his guitar from the other side of the wall. Lying on my side and tucking my hands underneath my pillow, I lay there and listened as Luke strummed the chords of his guitar. The sound was soothing, and it reminded me of when my dad would sit at the end of my bed, play his guitar, and sing me to sleep.

~

I WAS STANDING ALONE at the main entrance of the dark church. Looking down at my wedding dress, it suddenly turned black. My heart began pounding in my chest as I started to panic. I slowly made my way down the dark halls. As I approached the central part of the church, the white bows that sat upon the pews had turned black. I looked up at the altar and saw several white calla lilies; their arrangements were also black. What's going on? Where is everybody? I started calling Hunter's name. I needed to find him. As I approached a small room by the kitchen, I heard noises coming from it, so I extended my hand and reached for the doorknob. Suddenly, I heard a voice behind me.

"Don't open that door, pumpkin."

I turned to the familiar voice and saw my father standing there, shaking his head.

"Daddy, someone's in there. They can explain what's happening."

"Don't do it, Lily. Don't open that door!" he screamed.

Suddenly, he disappeared. I slowly turned the knob and opened the door. Hunter was standing there, naked, with a nude woman pinned up against the wall. I couldn't understand what was going on. He turned his head, and the woman looked at me. That woman was my sister, Brynn, and they were smiling. I put my hand over my mouth and looked to the corner of the small room, only to find my mother standing there, pointing and laughing at me. I slammed the door shut and ran down the long hallway that kept getting longer and longer. I couldn't breathe, and I started screaming. Tears were falling from my eyes so fast that everything became blurry, and I could no longer see, so I dropped to my knees…

～

"Wake up, Lily. Wake up. You're having a bad dream."

My eyes flew open, and Luke stood over me, clasping my shoulders. I couldn't catch my breath, and my face was soaked with tears. I stared at him, trying to focus on what happened. He sat down on the edge of the bed.

"Are you okay?" he asked as he wiped the tears from my face.

"I'm fine. How did you get in here?" I asked as I sat up.

"I'm the maintenance man, remember?" He smiled. "I heard you screaming, so I came right over. I thought you were in trouble."

I pushed my hair back with my hands and took a deep breath. "I had a bad dream, that's all."

"Do you want to talk about it?"

"No, I just want to forget it," I said as I looked down.

Luke wrapped his arms around me and pulled me into him. I wrapped my arms around him and buried my face in his neck. His scent was captivating, and his arms were strong as he sheltered me. I wanted to run my lips softly against his skin. I was lost in him and the moment. I pushed back.

"Do you always treat your neighbors like this?" I asked.

"Only the beautiful ones." He smiled.

The butterflies in my stomach awoke and started fluttering around as we stared into each other's eyes. He ran his finger along my jawline, then over my lips. My heart was racing. I knew what was coming, and I braced myself for it. Luke leaned in and tilted his head as he softly brushed his lips against mine. He touched each side of my face as our kiss deepened. I parted my lips, allowing access for his tongue to enter my mouth and meet with mine. He stopped and placed his forehead against mine while still holding my face.

"I'm sorry," he whispered.

"Don't be," I whispered back.

He stood up from the bed. "I'll see you later at the bar."

"Yeah, see you later."

I put my fingers on my lips, recalling that breathtaking moment. There was feeling and magic in how he kissed me, and I'd never felt anything like it before, not even with Hunter. I heard music coming from the other side of the wall, and I could tell Luke regretted kissing me. How was I going to face him tonight at the bar? There was also the issue with my mother. I walked to my closet and pondered about what to wear. I pulled out my black strapless sundress, slipped it on, and looked at myself in the full-length mirror. I couldn't stop thinking about Luke. The moment he kissed me, I wanted more of him. My life was unraveling right before my eyes, but I needed to stay in control. I wouldn't let anyone hold power over my emotions or feelings again.

I ran the flat iron through my hair as I looked in the mirror. All I saw was a broken girl who had trust and daddy issues. Suddenly, my phone rang, and Gretchen was calling me.

"Hello," I answered.

"Hey, Lils. Sam is going with Luke to the bar to set up the equipment. Do you want me to pick you up so we can drive together?"

"What about Giselle?"

"She texted to tell me she's going with Lucky. They left the beach together, and I don't know where they went. That situation is weird."

"Sure, we can drive together."

"Great, I'll be over in two seconds. Bye."

I looked at my phone in confusion. Then it hit me: she must be at Luke's. I put the finishing touches on my hair as Gretchen strutted in the bathroom.

"You look great, Lily." She smiled.

"Thanks, so do you."

"Sam and I just had the most amazing sex!"

I sighed as I walked out of the bathroom and into my bedroom. "TMI, Gretchen."

"Did something happen between you and Luke?" she asked as she sat on the bed.

"No, why do you ask?"

"I don't know. When Sam and I got back to the apartment, he looked more depressed than usual."

"I don't know what his problem is, but I don't need it," I said as I slid on my silver bracelet.

Gretchen jumped up from the bed. "Something did happen! You better tell me right now, Lily Gilmore!"

"We shared a small kiss, but he regretted it and left. There's nothing more to tell, and I don't want to talk about it again."

Gretchen came up behind me and put her arms around my neck. "He's badly wounded, Lily, and he doesn't know how to heal. Sam said Luke's pretty much isolated himself since the accident."

"I'm sorry about that and feel really bad for him, but I'm not the person to put him back together again. I'm broken, too, and I have my own issues. I don't need to take on someone else's."

"Wow, Lils. That's deep. But tell me this: what's more perfect than two broken people trying to heal each other?"

"Let it go, Gretchen. I'm done with guys and don't want to discuss it anymore. Let's go now because I need a drink."

"I know you when you get like this, and you better stay away from the vodka," she warned as she grabbed her keys.

Chapter Fourteen

LUKE

"Dude, come on, get out of the shower already," I said as I pounded on the bathroom door. "You're worse than a girl!"

"I'll be out in a minute!" Sam yelled.

I couldn't get my mind off Lily and couldn't believe I kissed her. Her soft lips against mine were intoxicating, and it left me wanting to explore more of her. She probably thought I was a jerk, which would ruin our friendship. How could I be so stupid? I haven't kissed a girl since Callie.

"Bro, what's up?" Sam said as he stood in the doorway of my bedroom.

"Nothing. I'm just thinking about some things."

"I could tell you were in deep thought the way you were standing there. Are you okay?"

"Yeah, I'm fine. I kissed Lily," I blurted out.

"What! Seriously, man?"

"Don't make it a bigger deal than it already is. I'm sure she hates me now, and I'm positive I ruined our friendship," I said as I walked out of the bedroom.

"You didn't ruin anything, Luke. I can tell Lily likes you, and maybe kissing her was what you needed to do to let her know you're interested in her. And don't say you're not because I know you," he said as he pointed at me.

"I can't stop my feelings, but I can stop my actions. I find that when I'm with Lily, I think less and less about Callie, and that's not right, man."

Sam walked over and put his hand on my shoulder. "Luke, you loved Callie, and what you had was great, but she's gone, and you have to start accepting that. Would Callie want you to live in misery and not move on? Wouldn't you want Callie to find someone to make her happy and care for her like you did? Dude, come on, you need to let go."

"You think it's so easy," I said as I wiped away a tear that fell down my face. I grabbed my keys from the counter. "Let's go," I said as I walked out the door and climbed into the Jeep.

∼

Walking into Bernie's, I saw Lily sitting at the bar. Gretchen jumped up and ran over to hug Sam. I didn't know what to say to Lily. I already apologized for kissing her. She turned around and looked at me as I gave her a small smile before walking over to the stage to get things set up. Shortly after, Lucky came strolling in with his arm around Giselle.

"Feeling good tonight, boys." Lucky strutted over with a big smile across his face.

I looked at him and rolled my eyes. "Let me guess, you got laid."

"That's right, Lukey boy," he said as he slapped me on the back. "You should try it sometime."

I ignored him because he was Lucky, and that was how he was. When we set the stage up, the bar had already filled up since Bernie had advertised that we'd be playing tonight. I kept looking at Lily, but she wouldn't look at me. She kept her back turned and drank her beer. I took a deep breath, walked over, and sat on the stool next to her.

"Hey," I said.

She picked up her beer, took a sip, and looked at me. "Hey."

Candi, the bartender, walked over to where we were sitting. "The usual, Luke?"

"The usual." I smiled.

Lily sat and stared at her beer bottle.

"I'm sorry about earlier," I said.

"Sorry about what?" She smiled as she looked at me.

"Um, when I crossed the line and kissed you."

She cocked her head and slowly shook it. "I'm sorry, Luke, but I don't recall you kissing me."

I grinned because that was her way of telling me that everything was cool between us. I held up my beer bottle as she held up hers, and we lightly tapped them together.

"I have to get on stage now."

"Good luck." She smiled.

Chapter Fifteen

LILY

    I sat there while Luke walked to the stage. He was still apologizing for our kiss. I could tell he felt awkward about it, so I had to turn it into nothing, even though it was something to me. It was something real that stirred up desire and passion from within. Something I wouldn't so easily be able to forget. Holding the beer bottle between my hands, I was in deep thought when I heard his voice. I closed my eyes for a moment because it was breathtaking. I saw him standing in his stonewashed jeans and brown boots as I turned to face the stage. His navy blue shirt was tight and emphasized his muscular, ripped body. He was sexy as hell, and I couldn't stop thinking about how much I wanted him to kiss me again. I needed another drink, so I motioned for Candi and ordered a vodka shot. The beer wasn't doing it, and I needed to forget about Luke, the kiss, and my mother. I threw back the shot that Candi set down before me and ordered another. I listened intently as he sang his song. The words haunted me.

    I grabbed another shot glass from Candi's hand before she could set it down. After Luke finished his song and sang a few more, I started to feel the effects of the alcohol. Giselle and Gretchen walked over and sat at the bar beside me.

"Why didn't you sit with us at the table?" Giselle asked.

"I was already sitting here and didn't feel like getting up."

"Are you okay, Lily?" Gretchen asked.

"Sure. Everything's just awesome. My mom, who's dead to me, is trying to track me down. The boy next door kissed me, then apologized, and left me sitting on the bed, looking like an idiot. I found my fiancé and my sister fucking in a closet on my wedding day, and best of all, my mother knew they were seeing each other for a long time. Cheers to my awesome fucking life," I said as I held up my beer bottle.

"What's going on?" Luke said as he walked up behind me.

"Hey, Luke. Great show," Giselle and Gretchen said at the same time.

Sam and Lucky walked over, grabbed their girls, and kissed them. I rolled my eyes.

"Let's dance," Giselle said as she grabbed Lucky's hand.

"Awesome idea! Come on, Lily," Gretchen said.

"You go ahead. I'll join you in a while."

"Come on. Let's sit at a table and talk," Luke said as he lightly touched my arm.

I got up from the stool, grabbed my beer bottle, and walked over to a table with Luke.

"You were really amazing. I want you to know that." I smiled.

"Thanks." He smiled as he looked down in embarrassment.

A waitress named Deb walked over to the table and set down two napkins. "Great performance as always, Luke. You want the usual?"

"Thanks, Deb. Get me a beer and whatever Lily wants."

"What can I get you, sweetie?" Deb asked.

"Two shots of vodka and make them doubles, please."

"Two shots of vodka and a beer coming right up." She smiled.

"Switching over to the hard liquor?" Luke asked.

"I need it tonight," I said.

"Why's that?"

"I really don't want to get into it."

Suddenly, two girls approached the table. I recognized one of them. She was the one giving Luke a blow job that night I walked in on them.

"Hi, Luke." She smiled. "You were so awesome tonight."

"Thanks." He smiled.

"Would you like to get together later and maybe talk or something?" she asked.

"No, not tonight."

Deb walked over with our drinks and just in time. She set the vodka down in front of me and handed Luke his beer. I slammed the first shot and then the second.

"Aw, come on. I promise you'll have a really good time," she whined.

"Back off. He said no! Now, take your little slutty asses and get away from my table!" I yelled.

Luke looked at me in surprise as he drank his beer.

"Who the hell are you?" she asked.

I stood up from my seat. "I'm trying to have a conversation here, but instead, I'm being bothered by some little groupie who thinks she's going to get laid."

Luke stood up and lightly grabbed my arm. "Lily, sit down."

I jerked my arm away. "Don't touch me!" I snapped.

Giselle and Gretchen came running over to the table, with Sam and Lucky following.

"Go down the street. I'm sure there's a very profitable corner with your name on it. If you blow random strangers, you might as well get paid for it."

"Bitch!" she snapped as she turned on her heels and walked away.

Giselle clasped my shoulders, and Gretchen picked up the shot glass and smelled it.

"Shit, she's drinking vodka."

Luke looked at me and then at Gretchen. "Is that bad or something?" he asked.

"Yeah, it is," Giselle answered.

"Lily tends to get mean and violent when she drinks vodka. It's the only alcohol that affects her that way. She can drink anything else, get drunk, and have fun, but vodka turns her into a different person," Gretchen answered.

"Oh, fuck off! I can drink whatever the hell I want. Who are you? My mother?"

Luke leaned over the table. "Watch your mouth."

I leaned over until my face was mere inches from his. "Fuck you too! I want everyone to leave me the hell alone!" I exclaimed as I got up from my seat.

Anger washed over his face. He got up from his seat and followed me to the bar. "You aren't drinking anymore tonight."

"I'm going to the restroom. I'll be right back," I said.

I just wanted to go home. At this point, I was drunk, and I didn't feel good, so I left the bar and started walking down the street. It wasn't too long after when I heard Luke calling my name.

"Are you crazy? You told me you were going to the bathroom. Why did you leave, Lily?"

I stopped, and as I turned around, I started to stumble, but he caught me.

"I just want to be left alone. I want you to leave me alone, Luke."

We were by a dark alley with only a dimmed light post to provide some lighting. Luke pushed me up against the brick and pinned my hands with his to the wall. "I don't want to leave you alone, Lily."

We stared into each other's eyes before he leaned forward and forcefully pushed his lips against mine, forcing my lips to part. He kissed me as if he wanted to devour me. Our tongues were tangled as the alluring scent of him engulfed my senses. I felt helpless, and I couldn't move because he was too strong. My heart was racing. Moments later, he broke our kiss and stared at me.

"I hope you don't remember this tomorrow," he whispered.

Luke let go of my hands and picked me up. He carried me to his Jeep, set me in the passenger seat, pulled the seatbelt over me, and buckled it. I closed my eyes and fell asleep.

My eyes flew open, and I looked around my bedroom. Looking down, I noticed I was still in my dress from last night. Over to the right, the clock read eight a.m. I placed my hand on my head as it felt like there was someone inside pounding it with a sledgehammer. I felt sick, and I was still a little dizzy. I couldn't remember how I got home or in my bed.

Stumbling out of bed, I walked into the bathroom and looked at myself in the mirror at the mascara that was smeared underneath my red eyes. I started the bath and poured some bubbles under the stream of running water. After climbing into the tub, I laid myself back. The last thing I remembered about last night was Luke's band performing. I ran my fingers across my lips, remembering my dream about him kissing me and how real it felt. I closed my eyes to try and soothe my pounding head, but it didn't help. After thirty minutes, I climbed out of the bathtub and threw on a fuchsia cotton sundress. I ran a brush through my hair and piled it in a messy bun on my head. I opened the medicine cabinet for some Motrin. Pulling out the bottle, it was empty. I sighed. As I made my way to the kitchen, I was startled by a knock on the door. I walked over, looked out the peephole, and saw Luke standing there with coffee.

"Good morning. I've come with coffee, which I'm sure you need." He smiled as he held up two cups.

"You don't have some Motrin, do you?" I asked.

He handed me a coffee cup, reached inside the pocket of his shorts, and pulled out a bottle, shaking it in front of me.

"You may come in," I said as I stepped out of the way.

I took the bottle from him and set it on the counter. I caught him staring at me as I grabbed a bottle of water from the fridge.

"What? I know I look like a hot mess, but you don't have to make it so obvious."

He laughed. "You do look like a hot mess, but I like it. It's very becoming on you."

I sighed as I took three pills out of the bottle and shoved them in my mouth, chasing them down with water.

"I bet you say that to all the girls."

"Only the ones I like." He smiled.

"So, how did you know I was up?" I asked.

"I heard you run the bath water."

"Oh, that's nice. Do you also hear when I'm getting myself off?" With a shocked expression, he didn't know what to say.

"I'm joking, Luke."

He shook his head and grinned at me.

"I apologize for anything I may have done or said last night. The last thing I remember is watching you perform," I said as I motioned for us to sit on the couch.

"That's the last thing you remember?"

"Yes. So please enlighten me on my activities so I can decide whether or not to show my face at Bernie's again."

"Well, you told some girl to find a street corner and get paid for giving blow jobs. You told Gretchen and Giselle to fuck off, and then you told me to do the same. After that, you said you were going to the bathroom, but instead, you went out the front door, and I had to chase after you."

"Oh," I gulped. "I'm sorry. It was the vodka. I'm sure Giselle and Gretchen told you how I get when I drink it."

"Yes, they did. If you know how you get, why drink it?"

"It soothes me, and I needed it after yesterday's news."

"What news? Did it have anything to do with that nightmare you had?"

I took in a deep breath before I answered him. "I think it did. After you dropped me off yesterday, Giselle told me that my mother had contacted her and she was looking for me. It upset me, and when I went to lay down for a while, it must have manifested into that nightmare."

"Tell me about your nightmare. I know you'd rather not, but I want to hear about it."

Taking in a deep breath, I told him. Luke reached out, took my hand, and interlaced our fingers.

"That's horrible, Lily." He pulled me into him. "You shouldn't be having nightmares like that. I'm sorry."

He leaned back against the arm of the couch, almost in a laying position, and I was snuggled against his chest. His arms were wrapped around me as if he was keeping me safe. I could feel his heart's rapid beating—a similar beat that matched mine. As he began stroking my hair, I looked up to see him smiling down at me, and the words suddenly flew out of my mouth before I could stop them.

"Kiss me."

Luke hesitated. "Are you sure?"

"I'm positive. Unless you don't want to."

"Believe me, I want to."

"Then shut up and do it."

He slowly brought his lips down to mine and kissed me softly. After a short moment, he stopped and looked at me while gently running the back of his hand across my cheek. I smiled. That was all he needed to be convinced I wanted him as much as he wanted me.

Chapter Sixteen

LUKE

Her lips were soft, and her tongue was smooth. I softly kissed her, nipping at her bottom lip and watching her smile as I did it. Our tongues gave way and accepted each other instantly. I was hard, and I knew she could feel it pressing against her as she moved up and positioned herself perfectly on top of me. I fisted her hair as she held my face in between her hands. Our breathing was rapid, and our hearts pounded at the same pace. I wanted to be inside her and feel her skin against mine. I removed the clip that held up her hair and let it fall over her shoulders. She was a sexy, beautiful person, and I needed and wanted more of her. My hands traveled down the back of her dress and over her ass. I caressed every bare spot until I reached her thong. I ran my hands up and down her back as we kissed deeply and passionately. It felt incredible to be underneath her, but I wasn't sure if this was the right time. I wanted us to make love for the right reasons. I didn't want to be a one-night stand with her, and I was sure she didn't want to be one with me, so I broke our kiss and looked into her eyes. She had awakened something in me that'd been dead for a year.

"What have you done to me, Lily?" I asked her as I ran my fingers through her hair.

"The same thing you've done to me," she responded.

"As much as I want you, we should wait."

She looked at me and nodded. Pulling her into me, I held her tight.

"I'm scared. I don't know where this is going. There's so much I don't know about you and so much you don't know about me. I don't want us to have sex on a whim and end up regretting it later. That's not who I am, Lily, and I need you to trust me."

She whispered in my ear, "I do trust you, and I agree with you."

I tightened my arms around her, knowing this woman before me was perfect. She slowly climbed off me and sat up on the couch. Sitting beside her, I ran my finger along her shoulder, making small circles.

"Will you go on a date with me tonight?"

"I don't do dates." She smiled.

"I don't either, but I thought we could make an exception tonight." I smiled back.

She took my finger from her shoulder and tenderly kissed it.

"I think maybe I could make an exception this one time."

"Me too." I grinned.

I stood up from the couch. "I'm going to go now before it gets any hotter in here," I said as I pointed to the door.

Lily got up and followed me. "Maybe I should call my maintenance guy over so he can cool me off."

"Somehow, I think your maintenance guy will make you sweat." I smiled as I leaned into her and kissed her lips. "I'll pick you up at six o'clock. We'll go to dinner and then figure it out from there."

"That sounds great. I'll be ready." She smiled as she closed the door.

∽

"Dude, where the hell were you?" Sam asked as I walked through the door.

"I was over at Lily's," I replied, heading towards my bedroom.

Sam followed behind me. "Bro, your hair's all messed up. Did you have sex with her?!"

"No, we didn't have sex. We almost did, but I stopped it."

"Dude, are you crazy? Why did you stop it?"

"Maybe I am, but I'm not thinking with my dick. I'm thinking with my head and heart, and I want to—no, I need to know her better. I have too much hurt going on, and so does she. Neither of us needs to have a sympathy fuck just for the sake of it."

"I get it, and I'm proud of you," Sam said.

"I asked her out on a date tonight. I'm going to take her to dinner, and then I think I'll take her to the cove so we can really talk to each other without anyone else around."

I heard the door open and little footsteps running around the apartment. I walked out of my bedroom and saw Charley in the kitchen. "How's my favorite niece?"

"Uncle Luke!" she exclaimed, running to me and hugging my legs. "I'm your only niece, silly."

I kissed her on the head as Maddie walked over to me. "Hey, can you watch Charley for a few hours while I go out with some friends?"

I looked at her, and she could tell something was up. Immediately, Sam spoke up. "Your brother isn't available tonight, but I am, and I would be more than happy to look after Charley for you."

"Not available?" Maddie asked as she looked at me in surprise.

Sam walked over to her and whispered in her ear, "Luke has a date with Lily tonight."

Maddie put her hand over her mouth. "Oh my God, yay!" she exclaimed.

Charley walked up to Sam. "What are your plans for tonight, Uncle Sammy?"

He bent down and looked at Charley square in the eye. "Well, little one, if you must know, Gretchen's coming over, and we're going to grab some chicken fingers and fries for dinner. Then we'll go for ice cream and maybe play a little miniature golf."

Charley's eyes widened. "Can I come?"

"You sure can!"

"Thanks, man. I owe you," I said to him.

Maddie motioned for me to follow her into my room. "I'm so happy for you. I can't believe you actually asked her out."

"Me neither, but both of us still have a lot of personal issues that we need to work out."

Maddie hugged me. "It'll be okay, Luke. You're a great guy, and from what I can tell, Lily's a great girl. Charley loves her."

We walked back to the living room, and Maddie kissed Charley goodbye.

"Thank you, Sam. It's a school night, so I'll be back by nine o'clock."

"We'll be here waiting." He smiled.

"Uncle Luke, where are you going that you can't watch me?" Charley asked.

"I'm going on a date with Lily."

A beautiful smile graced her face. "I hope you have fun."

"We will, peanut. Make sure you give Uncle Sammy a hard time."

"Stop being silly, Uncle Luke." She giggled.

Chapter Seventeen

LILY

I was on cloud nine. Luke left me breathless with that kiss, and I was happy for the first time in a very long time. Nothing was on my mind except Luke and our upcoming date. I stood in my closet and stared at the clothes on the rack. Picking up my phone, I sent Luke a text message.

"Hi. Casual or dressy?"
"Hi. Which do you prefer?"
"Casual?"
"Casual it is then. Actually, it was always casual."
I smiled as I replied. *"Good. See you soon!"*
I heard a soft knock on the wall.
"Did you just knock on the wall?"
"Yes."
"LOL, why?"
"I just wanted you to know I'm right on the other side if you need anything."
"Thank you, but I need to go, or I won't be ready when you come to pick me up."
"Pick you up? Why don't you pick me up?"

"You asked me out, remember?"

"Of course I do, but that doesn't mean you can't pick me up."

I laughed.

"Fine, I'll pick you up."

"Good. I'll be waiting."

I smiled and shook my head as I pulled out a pair of black Capri pants. The floral print maxi dress I bought hung there, with the tag still attached. I hadn't had the chance to wear it yet, so I put the pants back and pulled out the dress—it was casual enough. I picked up my phone and sent another text message to Luke.

"Are we taking your motorcycle?"

"Do you want to?"

"Not really. I needed to make sure because I wanted to wear this dress I bought."

"I thought this was casual."

"It is causal. It's a casual dress."

"Then maybe we'll take my bike. I'd like to see you get on it in that dress."

I smiled as I bit my bottom lip.

"Bye, Luke."

"Bye, Lily."

I took the tag off and slipped it on—it was perfect. Walking into the bathroom, I decided to wear my hair wavy. By the time I was done putting the last wave in, it was already time to leave. I slipped on my sandals, grabbed my purse, and walked next door to Luke's. I knocked on the door and gasped when he opened it. He wore dark jeans with a white button-down cotton shirt that he left untucked. Once again, he took my breath away. He smiled at me, grabbed my hand, and spun me around.

"You look amazing," he said.

I smiled as he pulled me into him, and we shared a small kiss.

"You're looking pretty sexy yourself, Mr. Matthews."

"I try." He winked as he shut and locked the door. "Do you like Mexican food?" he asked.

"I love Mexican food." I smiled.

"Good."

I found myself no longer being nervous around him. He was

such an easy-going guy, and he made me feel safe, unlike the first time I met him when I thought he was an ass. We pulled into the restaurant and climbed out of the Jeep. Luke grabbed my hand, and I looked at him and smiled as we made our way to the entrance. We decided to sit outside on the patio for dinner, and I ordered a margarita while Luke ordered a beer. We talked briefly about Charley, and he asked me how I got into teaching. Just as we finished our drinks, he touched on a taboo subject—my family.

"What was it like growing up with Johnny Gilmore?"

"You want to know the truth?"

"Of course I do," he said, giving me a weird look.

"It was like living in a whore house."

He didn't have a chance to respond because the waitress brought over our food. I took a bite of my taco as he stared at me.

"I'm sorry, Lily."

"Don't be. You didn't know. We can talk more about it later."

∼

We walked hand in hand back to his Jeep, and Luke opened the door for me. Before I climbed in, he cupped my chin in his hand and softly kissed my lips.

"I've wanted to do that since we got here." He smiled.

"I've been waiting for you to do it," I said as I bit my bottom lip.

We climbed into the Jeep, and he drove us to the cove.

"I thought this would be the perfect place to be alone and talk."

"It's the perfect place," I said as he led me to the secluded area.

I sat in the sand as he built a small bonfire. The atmosphere was beautiful, and there was no other place I wanted to be but here with him.

"So, you wanted to know about life with Johnny Gilmore, right?" I asked.

He stopped what he was doing and looked at me. "If you don't want to talk about it, I'll understand."

"My father was a manwhore that slept with any woman who glanced his way. My mother knew about it and threatened to divorce him if he didn't stop. He promised her that he would. So, to try and keep her from finding out, he would use my sister and me as an excuse. He called it 'daddy-daughter day'. Once a week, he'd take us somewhere fun. Then we'd end up at one of his whores' houses, and he'd make us sit on the couch while he went and fucked her in the bedroom. He would tell us that she was a friend who needed something fixed. This went on for years. Sometimes, at night, he'd ask me if I wanted to go for ice cream, and he'd make me sit in the car, alone and in the dark, and wait for him while he went inside someone's house. I'll never forget the feeling of being so scared."

Luke finished building the bonfire and walked over to me. He sat behind me, put his arms around my waist, and pulled me into him.

"Wow, I really had no idea. What an asshole. Didn't you ever tell your mom what he was doing?"

"Johnny said that Mom wouldn't understand and that she'd leave us, and he didn't want me to be responsible for breaking up the family. He said it was our little secret, and I'd be rewarded in the end."

"What the hell did he mean by that?" Luke asked.

"When he died a couple of years ago, I found out there was a bank account in my name that he started when I was a kid. I guess that's what he meant. He did have his good moments. He taught me to play the guitar, sang special songs, and left me a lot of money. But I would've rather had a father who was home and faithful to his wife instead of all that money. I remember many Christmases when he'd be there in the mornings, and then he'd have to leave. He would tell my mom that he and the boys had to practice, but we knew he was going to see one of his whores. I don't know what I would have done if it hadn't been for Giselle and Gretchen. I practically lived at their house to experience some normalcy."

Luke tightened his arms around me as I rested my head on his chest.

"So it's hard for me to hear people idolizing him because he was a shitty father who could have been so much better."

"I'm sure he loved you."

"I know he loved me. He told me every chance he could. But those were just words."

Luke rested his chin on my shoulder. "Why didn't your mom leave him?"

"She was afraid of being alone. She convinced herself that he loved her more than all the other women. They were just distractions, and at the end of the day, he always came home to her."

"That's crazy," he said as he lightly squeezed me.

"She's crazy. Look at how she was going to let me marry Hunter so that I'd live the life she did."

Luke pushed my hair to the side and began kissing my neck. I smiled as I tilted my head.

"Keep that up, and you'll be sorry."

"Somehow, I don't think I'll be sorry," he whispered.

I closed my eyes, and I could feel his erection pressing against the small of my back. I wanted him, but I was scared. It had been over a year since I last had sex, and I was afraid I wouldn't be any good for him. As I brought my hands up to his head and ran my fingers through his hair, he let out a light groan and turned me so that I was lying on my back on the soft sand. He lowered himself on top of me as his lips found their way to mine. His kiss was soft and alluring, and his actions were gentle and slow. His hands traveled to my breasts as he gently squeezed them through the fabric of my dress. Our breathing was rapid, and our hearts were beating fast. He reached his hand under my dress, cupping my ass as he let out a moan of excitement. Pushing the edge of my panties to the side, he dipped a finger inside me. I let out a light moan and arched my back as a feeling of pleasure took over me.

"Do you want me to stop?" he whispered as he kissed my lips.

"No. I don't ever want you to stop."

He groaned as he inserted another finger. I was already wet and getting ready to come.

He softly rubbed my clit in small circles as his fingers moved in and out of me fluently.

"Luke, I'm going to come. Don't stop, please."

"I won't stop. I want to feel you come with my fingers inside you."

This man knew what he was doing, and I wanted more of him. I wanted to feel every inch of him inside me. My body shook as I climaxed, and every tingling nerve in my body heightened. The flickering light of the fire showed off his beautiful smile as he brought me to orgasm. I moaned quietly even though I wanted to scream from the pleasure, but I was afraid someone would hear me.

Luke didn't say a word. He just stared at me and smiled as he gently removed his fingers.

"I want to have sex with you," I whispered.

He took the back of his hand and gently stroked my cheek.

"We aren't going to have sex, Lily. We're going to make love, and it will be beautiful, but not tonight and not here."

I couldn't speak. I was lost in his stare and his words.

"We should get going. You have school tomorrow, and I have a broken garbage disposal that needs to be fixed."

I let out a light laugh. I didn't want our night to end. Luke stood up and put the bonfire out. Moments later, he took my hand and helped me up from the sand, then pulled me into him and kissed me. I smiled as we held each other and danced for a few moments.

We climbed into the Jeep, and I sat there, thinking about how he never told me a thing about his ex-fiancée or the accident. I wanted to know everything about him. I sighed, and he reached over and took hold of my hand.

"Is everything alright?" he asked.

I glanced at him and smiled. "Everything's perfectly fine."

Chapter Eighteen

LUKE

When we arrived home, I walked around and helped Lily out of the Jeep. I couldn't stop thinking about what happened and how much she enjoyed it. Feeling the inside of her was incredible, and hearing her moan as I gave her pleasure was heart-stopping. My feelings for her were strong—stronger than I'd ever imagined. I needed her in ways I didn't understand. I grew weaker every time she smiled at me.

"Please come in and have a beer," she said.

I couldn't resist her. "That'd be great." I smiled.

She threw her keys on the counter, and I pulled out my phone to see if I had any messages. The only one was from Sam's phone.

"Have fun with Lily, Uncle Luke."

I laughed and looked at Lily as she grabbed two beers from the fridge. She handed me one, then we both sat down on the couch.

"You haven't told me anything about you. All I know is that you're the maintenance man, love my father, and are in a band."

Eventually, I needed to tell her about Callie and the accident. It wasn't fair to her that I hadn't spoken about it yet. I looked at her and took in a deep breath.

"I was the high school football team quarterback, and Callie was the lead cheerleader. We met senior year when her dad was transferred here from Ohio. We both felt an instant attraction and dated until the accident."

Lily reached over and grabbed my hand. She could see the tears beginning to fill my eyes. It was still too hard to talk about.

"You don't have to talk about it anymore. I understand how hard it is."

I leaned forward and grabbed her, pulling her into a warm embrace. I needed to feel the comfort of her being in my arms. I drank most of my beer and looked at the clock. It was midnight.

"You need to get some sleep. You have to be up early for work, and I don't want you to be tired," I said as I got up from the couch.

"I don't sleep anyway," she said.

I set the beer bottle on the counter and looked at her. "What do you mean you don't sleep?"

"I can't sleep more than a couple of hours a night."

I walked over and pushed her hair behind her ear. "Have you talked to someone about this?"

She took my hand and kissed my palm. "No, not yet."

"How long has this been going on?"

"Since the whole church ordeal."

"That was over a year ago, Lily!" I exclaimed. "How the hell do you function on only a couple hours of sleep?"

"I don't know. I'm used to it, I guess."

Kissing her head, I wrapped my arms around her. She held me as tightly as I held her.

"I'm staying here tonight to make sure you sleep."

"If you're staying here, then you're going to have to make love to me," she said as she stared into my eyes.

"Lily," I whispered and gently kissed her lips.

I couldn't refuse her. She wanted me to make love to her just as badly as I wanted to. I slowly took down the straps of her dress, letting it fall to the ground, revealing her lace bra and thong. Her body was amazing, and I instantly became hard. I took her face in my hands.

"I don't have a condom. I'll have to go get one."

"You don't need one. I'm on the pill, and I'm clean. I haven't had sex in over a year," she whispered as she stroked my cheek.

"I haven't had sex since the accident, and I'm also clean." I smiled.

"I trust you." She lifted my shirt over my head.

As I picked her up and kissed her passionately, I set her up against the wall. She tightly wrapped her legs around my waist. I was holding her by her perfectly tight ass as my lips traveled down to her neck. I'd never wanted anything so bad in my life, but I had to slow down. I wanted this moment to be as perfect as she was. I stared into her beautiful eyes as she stared into mine.

"I'm nervous," she whispered.

"So am I." I smiled as I carried her to the bedroom and sat her on the bed.

I kicked off my shoes, unbuttoned my jeans, and took them off. I unhooked her bra, exposing her beautifully shaped breasts and hardened nipples. She laid herself back on the bed as I took off my boxers. Hovering over her perfect body, I kissed her tenderly on her breasts. She let out a soft moan when I took her hard nipple in my mouth and lightly tugged on it. Her back arched in excitement, wanting more. I moved my hand down her torso until I reached the edge of her thong, then I grabbed it and slid it off her body. I could feel how wet she was when I touched her, so I slid my finger in and out of her, feeling her warmth. She was ready for me, and she had me throbbing.

Chapter Nineteen

LILY

I gasped when Luke took off his boxers. He was huge and very well-endowed. I silently thanked God but didn't expect anything less, considering his perfect body. As he erotically sucked my nipples, I reached my hand down and took hold of his hard cock. Running my hand down the entire length of him gave me chills. As I stroked him up and down, a moan escaped the back of his throat.

"God, Lily, you're amazing," he moaned as he continued to explore each breast.

My skin was on fire, and I needed him more than air. He brought his mouth up to mine, kissed me passionately, and then whispered in my ear.

"I want to make you come with my mouth before I make passionate love to you."

I gasped as his tongue traveled down to my body. His breath was hot as he began licking the inner edges of my thigh before moving to my swollen lips. I was already on the verge of an orgasm. He reached his hands up and cupped my breasts. He aroused me more than I'd ever been aroused before. His mouth moved swiftly over my swollen, wet area that so desperately throbbed for him, and he moved his tongue in small circles around my clit. Placing my hands on each side of his head, I breathlessly called out his name as my body released itself to him. He softly kissed the sensitive area and smiled before his lips returned to mine.

"You're so beautiful, Lily," he said as he took his cock and placed it between my legs.

"You're amazing, and I want you inside me," I whispered.

He slowly pushed himself into me, inch by inch. He was so hard, and he felt incredible.

"God, Lily, you're so tight. Are you okay?" he asked.

"Yes, Luke. Please don't stop!" I exclaimed as I dug my nails into his back.

He smiled and pushed himself deeper inside me. I wrapped my legs around him as he cupped my ass with both hands and gently squeezed. He slowly moved in and out of me as we stared into each other's eyes. This was the most beautiful moment I'd ever experienced. His thrusting became rapid and brought my body to the heightened state of another orgasm.

"Lily, come with me," he moaned as he pushed himself into me one last time before filling my insides with his come.

Watching the look on his face as he came was the sexiest thing I'd ever seen. He collapsed on me and held me tight, our bodies melting and our hearts racing at the speed of light. I'd just had the best sex of my life, and I wasn't sure if my body would recover. He lifted himself on his elbows and pushed my hair back with one hand.

"Are you okay?" He chuckled.

"I'm fantastic. How about you?"

"I'm great. No, better than great."

I giggled as I ran my hands through his hair. He glanced over at the clock. It was three a.m.

"You need to get up in a couple of hours."

"I know. Don't worry about it, I'll be fine. Will you stay here with me?" I asked as he climbed off the bed and me.

"Of course, I'll stay here. There's no place else that I'd rather be. I want to wake up with you in my arms."

We climbed under the covers, and Luke wrapped his strong arms around me, pulling me in as close as he could.

"You feel good naked," he said as he softly kissed my back.

"So do you." I quivered.

"Good night, Lily."

"Good night, Luke."

∼

I opened my eyes as the buzzing sound of the alarm began, increasing in sound with each buzz. I reached over and turned it off while still wrapped up in Luke's arms. I tried getting up slowly because I didn't want to wake him. As soon as I moved, his arms tightened their grip around me.

"Don't leave this bed. Call in and tell them you're sick. I'm not letting you go."

I laughed as I turned and looked at him. "I have to go. I have a class to teach. Remember, your niece is part of that class."

He sighed as he kissed me. "Fine, but I'm joining you in the shower."

"I was hoping you would." I winked.

He grabbed me, turned me on my back, and started tickling me. I laughed and screamed at the same time. Suddenly, there was a knock on the wall. Luke stopped, looked at me, and we both started laughing. Luke didn't knock back. He banged on the wall.

"Dude, it's called payback!"

Luke got up and took my hand as we stepped into the shower, having sex before starting our day.

I looked at the clock on my phone as I threw my hair up. Luke walked up behind me as I stood there in my bra and panties.

"I made you some coffee," he said as his hands traveled up my sides and his lips met my neck.

"Thank you, and you need to stop, or I'm going to be late." I turned around, kissed him, and then went to the bedroom to get dressed.

Luke followed and stood in my bedroom doorway, leaning against it with one arm while holding his coffee cup.

"I want to see you tonight."

"I want to see you too," I said as I put on my heels and stopped in front of him.

"Kiss me, and I'll let you through." He smiled.

I smiled as my lips met his. I wanted to leave him with more than just a kiss, so I stuck my hand down the front of his jeans and grabbed his semi-hard cock. He moaned. "Lily, how could you?"

"How can't I? You're too damn irresistible," I said as I lifted his arm and walked through.

I heard him chuckle as he followed behind me. I grabbed my bag, keys, and coffee cup from the counter. Luke opened the door, and we both walked out.

"Have a good day," he said as he kissed me.

"Uncle Luke!" Charley exclaimed.

He broke our kiss and looked at her as she ran down the rest of the stairs to him. "Hey, peanut."

"I saw you two kissing." She smiled. "Did you spend the night?" she asked.

Luke looked panicked as we both looked at each other. "No, of course not. Lily had something that needed to be fixed."

Maddie stood behind Charley and smiled at me.

"Let me drive Charley to school for you," I spoke.

"That's okay, Lily. You don't have to do that."

"I want to. I'm going there anyway, and I'm already running late," I said as I looked at Luke.

"Mommy, please!" Charley squealed.

"Okay," she said as she kissed Charley goodbye. "Thank you, Lily."

"No problem." I smiled as I took Charley's hand.

"Bye, Mommy. Bye, Uncle Luke." She waved as we walked out of the building.

Chapter Twenty

LUKE

"Would you like to join me for some coffee? I know you're dying to talk to me."

"Yes, I want coffee, and I'm dying to talk to you." Maddie smiled as she followed me into my apartment.

I entered the kitchen and poured the last of the coffee into a cup. Just as I handed the cup to Maddie, Sam walked out of his bedroom, straightening his tie. He walked over and fist-bumped me.

"Thanks for keeping me awake all night," he said as he picked up the empty coffee pot and looked at it.

"No problem, man."

"As happy as I am that you finally gave in and had sex with the hot girl next door, I have to go to a meeting. We'll talk about it later, dude. Love you, Maddie," Sam said as he walked out the door.

"Love you back, Sammy." She smiled and then turned to me. "I only want to know if you're okay."

"I'm fine, Maddie," I said as I started another pot of coffee.

"You've been depressed for over a year, Luke. You haven't attempted to meet or date anyone, and now, suddenly, you're spending the night with the girl next door."

"That's because the right girl never crossed my path. I didn't think I'd ever fall for anyone after Callie. She was my life, my whole world, and you know that. But since Lily moved in, I started seeing things differently. She makes me smile, Maddie. No one has been able to do that in a very long time."

"I know, and I'm happy for you. I just don't want you or her to get hurt. You both have endured enough pain. Mom and Dad are going to love her. You know they'll want a family dinner when they return from their cruise, right?"

"I know, and I want Lily to meet them." I kissed Maddie on the top of her head and went into the bedroom to change. I had work that needed to be done.

~

I COULDN'T STOP THINKING about Lily and our night together. I didn't plan on making love to her quite yet, but she wanted me to, and who was I to deny her? I needed to tell her about Callie and the accident. I was surprised she didn't ask about my scar last night. My phone beeped with a reminder about the job I needed to do. I snapped out of my thoughts and back into reality. I grabbed my toolbox and headed upstairs to Mrs. Lopez's apartment to fix her garbage disposal.

"You have that look, Luke," Mrs. Lopez said.

"What look would that be, Mrs. Lopez?" I asked as I tightened the pipe under her kitchen sink.

"The look of love."

I chuckled. "Is that so? How can you tell?"

"I can see it in your eyes. They have a new life about them. Who is she?"

I crawled from under the sink and threw my wrench in the toolbox. "I'm not in love, but I have met someone I really like." I smiled.

"Ah ha! I knew it!" she exclaimed. I sure hope it's that cute little blonde who moved in next door to you."

"It is, and her name is Lily," I said as I took the bottle of water she held out to me.

"I'm happy for you, Luke. I know you've had a rough year. You deserve true happiness."

I closed my toolbox and picked it up from the floor. "Thanks for the water, Mrs. Lopez. Everything's working perfectly now. Just call me if you need me," I said as I walked out the door.

I walked back into my apartment, set my toolbox down, then sat on the couch. I missed Lily already. She was always on my mind, and it was driving me crazy, so I decided to send her a text message.

"How about dinner tonight at your place? We can cook together."

"That sounds great! I don't cook, though."

"I'll teach you. We can go to the store together when you get home."

"Sounds fun. I can't wait."

"Me either."

As I was watching TV and thinking about how slow the day was going, there was a knock on the door. Lily threw her arms around me when I opened it, and our lips met. I pulled her into the apartment, kicked the door closed with my foot, and pinned her up against the closet door as I kissed her passionately. After a moment, she broke our kiss and smiled at me.

"I missed you," she said out of breath.

"I missed you too, and I couldn't wait for you to get home," I responded as my lips made their way behind her ear.

The door opened, and Sam walked in. "Really? You do know there's a bedroom down the hall over there, right?" he said.

Lily and I laughed as I shook my head at Sam.

"Seriously, dude. I don't want to come home and find the two of you having sex on the couch. Because I may have to join in."

I smacked him on the back of the head as I walked by. "That's not even funny, bro." I pointed at him.

"Lily thinks it's funny. Look at her. She's laughing."

"Babe, don't humor him, please."

Sam laughed as he walked to his room.

"Are you ready to leave?" I asked as I walked over to her and softly ran my hand across her cheek. She nodded, so we headed out of the apartment and climbed into my jeep.

"What are we making?" Lily asked as I pushed the cart through the grocery store.

"I thought maybe we could cook some spaghetti with a homemade sauce, salad, and bread."

"You make homemade sauce?"

"I sure do, and Charley loves it. My mom never cooked alone. She always made us cook as a family from the time we were six years old."

Lily hooked her arm around mine and laid her head on my shoulder. "Your mom sounds amazing. My mom never cooked. She had her chef do all the cooking, and we rarely ate as a family."

My heart ached for her when she told me that. I leaned over and kissed her head. "Come on. Let's get what we need and get out of here."

While we were walking through the store, I saw Bernie.

"Hey, Luke," he said as he looked at Lily.

"Hey, Bernie. How was Florida?" I asked him.

"Florida was great, and I'm getting closer to retirement. Who's this beautiful woman on your arm?"

"This is Lily Gilmore. Lily, meet Bernie, the owner of Bernie's Bar."

Lily shook Bernie's hand, and he smiled at her.

"I'm going to take a stab in the dark here. You wouldn't happen to be Johnny Gilmore's daughter, would you?"

"Yes, I am. Johnny was my father." She smiled.

"I knew it!" Bernie exclaimed. "Look at you, all grown up. Your dad used to play in my bar when he was in Santa Monica, and he used to show me pictures of you. He was a brilliant musician. I'm sorry to hear about his death."

"Thank you," Lily said. "He was a great musician."

"Hey, Luke. We need to sit down and discuss what you want to do with the bar. This last trip to Florida pushed me closer to selling, and the next time I go, I'm not coming back."

"I know, and I have to give it some more thought. I'll call you."

"Don't take too long, son. I have others who are interested. It was nice to meet you, Lily. Luke, I'll talk to you soon," he said as he walked away.

Lily looked at me as I sighed.

"What was all that about?" she asked.

"We'll talk about it over dinner."

Chapter Twenty-One

LILY

Luke opened the bottle of wine as I took two glasses from the cabinet. He started making the sauce, and I started on something a little simpler—the salad.

"How was your day at work?" he asked.

"It was good. My students were very well-behaved today." I grinned.

"Did Charley say anything to you about us?" he asked as he began to chop the onions.

"No. Though she did smile at me a lot." I laughed.

"She's a great little girl. I hope to have a daughter like her someday."

I stopped my knife halfway through the tomato when Luke said that. A sick feeling in my stomach instantly developed because the talk of family terrified me, but I talked about it anyway.

"How many kids would you like to have?" I asked like an idiot.

"I don't know. Four kids would be nice, I guess."

"Four!" I gasped.

Luke chuckled as he put the onions in the sauce. "What's wrong with four kids?"

"Nothing's wrong with four kids. I'm just surprised you want so many."

"Cal—forget it. I'm sorry I brought it up," he said.

I could see the sadness on his face as he turned to the stove and stirred the sauce. I put down the knife and wrapped my arms around his waist.

"Don't ever be sorry. You need to talk about her, Luke. I never want you to feel like you can't or shouldn't."

He put down the spoon and turned to face me.

"It just doesn't feel right to talk about her like that, and I don't want to hurt you."

"You wouldn't hurt me. She was a huge part of your life for many years, and I want to know about her."

Luke softly brushed his lips against mine. "You're amazing. Did you know that?"

"I've been told a few times." I smiled.

He hugged me and returned to making the sauce as I finished slicing the tomatoes for the salad.

"On the night of the accident, we were on our way home from a trip. We were stopped at a red light a few streets away from here. When the light turned green, and I began to go through the intersection, another car ran the red light and crashed into us, hitting Callie's side. Our car spun out of control, and another car hit my side." He paused for a moment. "I'll never forget the sound of both crashes, the sounds of the squealing tires, the brightness of the headlights as both cars headed towards us, and Callie screaming my name before I blacked out. I'd woken up in the hospital three days later without any recollection of the accident at that moment. My parents told me that Callie had died, and that's when everything came rushing back to me."

I gulped as I heard him tell the story, and my eyes couldn't help but fill with tears. He wouldn't look at me, and I knew if I tried to comfort him in any way, he would lose it, so I quickly changed the subject.

"Have I told you how much of an asshole Hunter is?"

Luke looked over at me and started to laugh. "What?"

"He's an asshole, plain and simple. He's an uptight, cock sucking piece of shit, and I truly despise him. Did I ever tell you that he coordinated his underwear with his clothes?"

"Seriously?" Luke asked.

"I'm dead serious, and not only did he do that, but he also kept a divider in his drawer for his socks. What guy does that? Oh, and the best part, he has pants that he'll only wear on certain days of the week."

Luke was laughing and shaking his head. "What the hell did you ever see in that guy?"

I had to stop and think about that for a moment because I honestly didn't know.

"He wasn't hot, that's for sure. He was cute in a boyish way. I think it was because he's a charmer, and he charmed his way into my life, like the lying piece of shit he is."

Luke walked over to me, put his hands on my hips, and kissed my forehead. "Watch your mouth." He smiled.

"Sorry," I said as I looked up at him.

I grabbed two plates from the cabinet and some silverware out of the drawer and set the table for dinner. I heard the beep on my phone.

"Your phone went off, babe," he said.

I walked over to the counter and picked it up. The message was from Giselle.

"I'm off to Seattle for a modeling job, and Lucky's coming with me. I just thought you and Luke would want to know."

I knitted my brows and quickly replied.

"What the hell's going on with the two of you? Are you a couple or something?"

"We're two adults having fun—without a commitment."

"All right, if you say so," I replied.

Luke set the spaghetti on the table. "What's wrong? You look confused."

"I am confused. I'm confused about this whole Lucky and Giselle thing. She's going to Seattle on a modeling job, and he's going with her. Don't you think that's weird?"

"Lily, Lucky's weird. You should know that by now." He chuckled.

I sat at the table as Luke put some spaghetti on my plate. "Eat up."

I took a bite as he watched me. "Luke, this is the best spaghetti I've ever had."

"You're not just saying that to spare my feelings, are you?"

"Of course not! The sauce is truly amazing."

I left a long piece of spaghetti hanging from my mouth as I motioned with my finger for him to come closer. He smiled and leaned across the table, taking the other end of the spaghetti in his mouth and following it until his lips reached mine. He licked my lips with his tongue and then inserted it in my mouth. We got up from our seats and continued to share a kiss. He slowly put his hands up my shirt, pulling the cups to my bra down and feeling my hardened nipples. I reached my hand down to his stiff cock and stroked it through the fabric of his jeans. Getting lost in the hotness of the moment, our kiss became more passionate with a bit of roughness until we were interrupted by a knock on the door.

"Uncle Luke, are you in there making your famous spaghetti?"

We broke our kiss and looked at each other. Luke's eyes widened.

"What the hell?" he whispered. "Um, yes, Charley, I am!" he yelled.

I started laughing as Luke had to sit back in his chair to hide his erection until it went down. I walked over to the door and opened it.

"Hey, sweetie!" I smiled. "Would you like to come in and have some of Uncle Luke's famous spaghetti?"

"I sure would!" she exclaimed.

Charley walked in and sat down next to Luke at the table. "Hi, Uncle Luke," she said as she kissed his cheek.

"Hi, peanut. How did you know I was making spaghetti?"

"Mommy and I just came back from the store, and I could smell it in the hallway. But the smell was stronger coming from Lily's door."

Luke and I both laughed as I set a plate in front of Charley. I put some spaghetti on it with some bread, and she sat there and ate it. Luke looked at me and smirked.

"So, are you two dating or what?" Charley blurted out with a mouthful of spaghetti.

Luke and I shared a glance at each other. "Yeah, you could say that we're dating." He winked at me.

"I knew it!" Charley giggled. "I can't wait to tell my friends that my teacher and uncle are dating."

Luke pulled his ringing phone from his pocket. It was Maddie calling to ask him to send Charley home.

"Your mom wants you home as soon as you're finished eating, peanut."

"Why?" she whined.

"I think it's because you have homework to do." I smiled at her.

"Oh yeah, I forgot." She giggled.

Luke looked at her and whispered, "Your teacher is mean."

"I am not!" I exclaimed as I picked up some plain noodles and threw them at him across the table.

"Oh, you want a food fight, do you?" He laughed as he reached into the spaghetti bowl, grabbed a handful, and threw them at me.

"Charley, get under the table!" I spoke.

She started laughing and ducked under the table. I reached into the salad bowl and threw what I'd grabbed at Luke. He looked at me and sighed as he brushed the lettuce from his hair. I started laughing uncontrollably until he put some butter on a knife, flung it at me, and it stuck to my forehead. He couldn't help but laugh as he took out his phone and started taking pictures. I took my finger and wiped the butter off as I seductively brought my finger to my mouth and began sucking it. Luke put his phone down and looked at me.

"Come on, Charley. It's time to go home and do your homework."

"Okay," she said with an exaggerated sigh.

Luke looked at me and whispered, "Stay right where you are."

He took Charley by the hand and walked her back to her apartment. I already knew what was going to happen the minute he returned.

Chapter Twenty-Two

LUKE

I ran Charley up to her apartment so that I could get back to Lily. The way she sucked her finger made me hot for her, and there was no time to waste. We were already interrupted by Charley earlier, and I wanted to avoid any further interruptions. I walked into Lily's apartment, but she wasn't sitting at the table, so I followed her clothes trail to the bathroom. She was lying in a bubble-filled tub, waiting for me. I leaned against the door with my arms folded, smiling at her.

"What are you waiting for?" she asked seductively.

"I'm waiting for an invitation to join you. I thought I told you not to move."

"Get your hot, naked ass in this tub right now!" she demanded.

I kicked off my shoes and removed my shirt, jeans, and boxers. Lily moved forward as I stepped into the tub behind her, pulling her naked, wet body into me.

"I thought this would be better. We do need to wash off from our little food fight."

I began kissing her neck as she tilted her head to the side. "This was an excellent idea."

Lily took the soap and washed my arms, holding her against me. I took it from her hands and began to soap her breast. She moved her body against mine as my erection pressed against the small of her back.

"You feel so good like this," I whispered as the water sloshed back and forth. She let out a moan as I inserted my finger inside her. "I don't think we'll last too long in this tub. I want to be inside of you right now."

She moved up as I climbed out of the bathtub and grabbed an extra-large towel she had sitting on the toilet. I held out my hand, helped her out from the tub, and wrapped us both in the towel, holding her closely as she buried her face into my chest. I picked her up and set her on the bathroom counter. Her smile grew as my tongue traveled down her damp body and below where she ached for me. As my mouth sucked and my tongue licked every inch of her, Lily ran her fingers through my hair, pulling and tugging as she enjoyed my movements. Standing up, I thrust myself inside her. I reached under her and grabbed hold of her ass as I moved in and out of her. Her legs wrapped around me. She was so warm inside, making me want to come fast.

"Faster, Luke, faster!" she yelled as her nails dug into my back.

"Ah, baby, you're going to make me come already," I said as I pushed deeper inside her.

I felt her swell around my cock, and I was going to explode any second. Suddenly, she let out a loud moan as we both came at the same time. I held her face, kissed her softly, and stared into her eyes.

"Can we consider us a couple?"

"I don't do boyfriends," she said.

"I don't do girlfriends, but I thought maybe we could make another exception."

"I guess I can make another exception for you." She smiled.

I picked her up from the counter and carried her to the bedroom.

I woke up as Lily got in the shower, and I made a pot of coffee. Grabbing my phone off the counter, I saw several missed calls from my mom and one voicemail.

"Hi, Luke. It's Mom. Your father and I are back from our cruise, and we're having a family dinner this Friday night at six o'clock. Your sister told me you've met someone very special, but she won't tell me anything else, so bring her with you. I'm dying to meet her. I love you, Luke. Bye."

I poured some coffee into a cup, took it in the bathroom, and handed it to Lily as she was getting ready for work.

"My mom called last night and left a message. She's having a family dinner this Friday night and is dying to meet you. Maddie told her about us."

"That sounds great. I'd love to meet your family." She smiled.

"Would you like to go to Bernie's tonight?" I asked her.

"Sure, that sounds fun. We never did talk about that last night."

I moved my hands under the towel she had wrapped around her and placed them on her hips.

"That's because we were too busy making love all night," I whispered as I nibbled on her ear.

She smiled, turned her head, and her lips met mine. I could kiss her all day. She placed her hands on my chest and broke our kiss.

"I'm going to be late if we don't stop."

"I know, and I'm sorry. Finish getting dressed. You have approximately fifteen minutes before you have to leave."

"Thanks for the warning," she said as she brushed her teeth.

I heard a knock on the door and wondered who would be here so early in the morning. I opened it and saw Sam standing there, holding a brown bag in my face.

"Bagels for the two lovebirds."

"Come on in, man. Thank you."

Sam stepped inside the apartment as I took the bag from him.

"Lily and I are going to Bernie's tonight. Do you and Gretchen want to join us?" I asked.

"That sounds good. I'll ask her."

"Want some coffee?" I asked Sam as I walked over and poured some in a cup for myself.

"Nah, I have to get going soon. Are you free to grab a burger at the bar this afternoon?"

"Sure. I'll meet you there around one."

Lily came out of the bedroom, looking smoking hot. We were going to have to role-play in bed. The thought started getting me hard.

"Good morning, Lily. You're looking as beautiful as always." Sam smiled.

"Good morning, Sam, and thank you," she replied as she kissed his cheek.

"Hot damn! I've been kissed by two beautiful women already this morning," he said as he spun around and placed his hand on the doorknob.

"Later, bro. I'll see you later for that burger."

"Later, dude. Bye, Lily," Sam said as he waved and left the apartment.

I poured the rest of the coffee in her to-go cup and handed it to her as I walked her to her Explorer. I opened the door and wrapped my arms around her.

"Have a good day, babe," I spoke as I kissed her lips.

"You too." She smiled.

∽

"Two burgers, medium, with everything, and a side of fries," the waitress said as she set our food in front of us.

"I'm taking Lily to family dinner Friday night."

"Wow! That's a big step in taking a girl home to meet the family. I haven't done that with Gretchen yet. I love how I was right that you and Lily would make a great couple. You are a couple, right?"

I nodded as I took a bite of my burger. "Yep, we made it official last night."

"Dude, that's awesome." Sam smiled as he fist-bumped me.

When we finished lunch, Sam returned to work, and I headed to

Bernie's to talk to Maddie. I walked into the bar and took my usual seat.

"Hey, Luke. What brings you in here today?" Maddie asked.

"I know you talked to Mom last night. I listened to her message this morning, and she knew about Lily."

"I may have mentioned that you've met someone, and she's really special. I hope you're not mad."

"No, I'm not mad at all. It bought me some time before the million questions Mom will ask me about her."

Maddie set a beer down in front of me.

"Luke, my boy. Tell me you're here to give me your decision?" Bernie said as he came from the storage room with a box in his hands.

"Not yet, Bernie. But I promise you'll have my answer by the end of the week," I replied.

"You're actually thinking about buying the bar again?" Maddie leaned over the counter and asked.

"Yeah, but I want to talk to Lily about it first. We were supposed to talk about it last night, but we got distracted by a bathtub, a countertop, and a bed."

"Whoa, stop right there!" Maddie said as she put her hand up.

I finished my beer and got up from the stool.

"Later, Bernie. Lily and I will be in tonight. See ya, sis," I said as I kissed her cheek.

Chapter Twenty-Three

LILY

I grabbed my bags and headed to the Explorer. When I climbed inside, I inserted the key—nothing. The fucking thing wouldn't start. I took in a deep breath and calmly turned the key—nothing. "Damn—damn—damn it!" I yelled as I slammed my hands against the steering wheel. I pulled out my phone and dialed Luke. Please answer, please answer, I thought to myself.

"Hey, babe, are you on your way home?"

"I never made it out of the parking lot. My truck won't start!"

"Sit tight. I'll be there shortly."

"Thank you, I—I'll be here!"

I couldn't believe what almost came out of my mouth. A text message came through from Gretchen.

"Sam and I will be joining you at Bernie's tonight. Make sure you have your dancing shoes on because we're going to get down and dirty!"

I laughed. "Alright, but we must get the guys to dance with us. If Luke dances, he's perfect. I love a man who can dance!"

I looked up and saw Luke pulling into the parking lot. I sighed in relief when he was in his Jeep and not on his bike. Pulling up next to me, he smiled, and I gave him a small wave and a smile in return. I was so happy to see him. I climbed out of the Explorer as he climbed out of his Jeep and hugged him tight.

"I missed you," I said.

"I missed you too. Now, let's see if we can get your truck running."

I popped the hood and stood next to him as he fumbled with some wires. I was turned on by how sexy he looked, trying to fix my truck.

"Go try to start it."

I sat in the truck and turned the key—nothing. I got out and walked over to Luke as he was on the phone with the mechanic. After he hung up, he shut the hood of my truck and put his hands on my hips.

"They're going to tow your truck back to the garage."

I sighed. "I need a new car."

"The good news is that I get to drive you to and from work tomorrow." He smiled.

"There's no school tomorrow. The district's closed."

"That's great! So I guess you don't have to be home early tonight."

"Nope. I can stay out late because it's not a school night." I smiled.

We walked over to Luke's Jeep, and he opened the door for me. I climbed in, and we drove back to the apartment building. We pulled up as Maddie and Charley were getting out of the car.

"Uncle Luke, Lily, guess what? My daddy's coming to visit in a few days!"

I could see the tears in Maddie's eyes as Luke looked at her. She looked away.

"Lily, take Charley to your apartment. I want to talk to my sister for a minute."

I took Charley's hand and led her inside the building. I began to worry about the conversation Luke would have with Maddie. Obviously, no one liked Charley's father. After a few minutes, they walked into my apartment, and Maddie took Charley home. Luke opened my refrigerator and grabbed a bottle of beer. He opened it and flung the cap across the counter.

"Do you want to talk about it?" I asked as I stood there with my arms folded.

"He hasn't seen Charley in three years. He hasn't paid child support, and he hasn't sent her any gifts, nothing. The only thing the bastard's done is make a few phone calls, talk to her for a couple of minutes, and makes up excuses as to why he can't visit her. Now, he's coming here after three years and expects to take her for a weekend."

I walked over to where Luke was standing. "He's her father."

"Don't give me that bullshit, Lily! The only thing that attaches that title to him is his DNA. He's no father to that little girl!"

I could see the pain in his eyes, and I knew he was more of a father to Charley than anyone. I watched him as he threw back his beer. Wrapping my arms around him, I held him tight.

"He's a drunk and a drug addict, Lily. There's no way I'm letting him take her. He can visit her at Maddie's with me sitting there."

"I'm sorry, but Charley seems really excited to see him."

"I know, and that's the sad part. She doesn't even know what he's like. She hasn't seen him since she was six years old."

"Come on. Let's not worry about this now. Let's go to Bernie's and have a good time. Speaking of Bernie, we never discussed what you two were talking about yesterday," I said as I looked up at him.

He took his thumb and softly stroked my cheek. "You're so beautiful," he whispered.

I smiled as I placed my hand on his face. "You're beautiful too, Luke, inside and out. The way you take care of Charley is amazing. You treat her like she's your own daughter, and that's what I love about you."

He took my hand from his face and pressed his lips against my palm while staring into my eyes. "I'm falling in love with you, Lily."

My pulse started racing. Chills ran up and down my spine as he spoke those words. There was no denying that I was falling in love with him. He consumed my every thought, and I always craved his touch. I brought my face closer as I kissed his lips.

"I'm falling in love with you too, Luke."

Picking me up, he buried his face into my neck as I wrapped my legs tightly around him. He didn't say anything. He didn't need to. We both knew as we were holding each other that our love was growing, and whether we wanted it or not, there was no stopping what was happening between us. After carrying me to the bedroom, he stood me up in front of the bed. His fingers deftly unbuttoned my shirt as he slid it off my shoulders, letting it fall to the ground. He unhooked my bra, letting it fall from my breasts as he ran his fingers over my puckered nipples. I was mesmerized by him as he stared into my eyes while he undressed me. He took down my skirt, exposing my thong, and then he cupped my ass in his hands and squeezed it while taking in a sharp breath.

"I can never get enough of you. I can feel your body begging for me," he said as he placed his hand between my legs. He inserted his finger and kissed me gently. Everything he did was gentle and slow. I wanted to reach out and grab him, but he wouldn't let me. He took my hand and placed it on my clit, making me rub it in circles as he bent down and erotically kissed every inch of my throbbing sheath while my body trembled, and I had one of the best orgasms of my life. Moments later, he brought his mouth up to mine.

"I want you to taste what I taste every time we make love," he whispered.

His hand reached around to the back of my neck, and he held me steady while he kissed me passionately, sucking my tongue and nipping my bottom lip. "I need you, babe. I need you so bad it hurts."

As he broke our kiss, he turned me around and laid me on the bed, hovering over me and softly kissing my back. I could feel his hard cock rubbing against my ass and up the small of my back. A low groan turned louder as he pushed himself inside me. He moved in and out of me, making me come with him as he reached under me and rubbed my swollen clit. After lowering himself on top of me, he brought his mouth to my ear and whispered, "Don't ever leave me."

I felt a knot in my throat, finding it hard to catch my breath. He just asked me never to leave him, which meant things were moving faster than the speed of light. I turned my head to the side and kissed his lips as I smiled. He got up and went into the bathroom, and I lay there, pondering his words. A few minutes later, he emerged and walked over to where his boxers and jeans lay on the floor.

"I've been thinking about buying Bernie's bar," he said as he put his boxers on and sat on the edge of the bed.

I sat up and wrapped one arm around his neck.

"That's wonderful, Luke. How long have you been thinking about doing that?"

He took my hand and interlaced our fingers. "It's something I've dreamed of doing since I was a kid. Callie and I talked about it all the time. She encouraged me to go for it, and when I finally decided to take that leap, the accident happened and changed everything."

"Luke, you should still buy it."

"It's not that simple, Lily."

I heard my cell phone ringing, so Luke told me to answer it. I got up from the bed, walked over to the dresser, and saw Gretchen was calling.

"Hey, Gretch. What's up?"

"Are the two of you going to have sex the rest of the night, or are you coming to the bar?"

"Are you already there?" I asked.

"No. We're waiting for you outside your apartment."

"Oh. Give us a minute. The door's unlocked. Come in and make yourselves comfortable."

"Okay," she said as she ended the call.

Luke looked at me, and I could see that the tears and sadness that filled his eyes were gone.

"I didn't realize what time it was."

"They can wait," I said, pulling my black dress from the closet.

"If you wear that, you're going to have me fucking you in the bathroom at the bar."

I giggled as I slipped it on. "I dare you." I smiled.

"Dude and dudette, let's go!" Sam yelled from across the room.

"Shut it, man! We're coming!" Luke yelled back.

"I bet you are!" he exclaimed.

We looked at each other and started laughing. Luke got dressed, and we walked into the living room. Gretchen looked at me, got up from the couch, grabbed my arm, and led me into the bathroom.

"You have sex hair. You can't go to the bar with sex hair."

I sighed as I took the brush, ran it through my hair, and touched up my makeup. "How's that?" I asked her as I turned around.

"Much better." She smiled.

We walked into the living room, grabbed our guys, and headed to Bernie's.

Chapter Twenty-Four

LILY

"Four beers, Candi," Luke said as he walked past the bar, and the four of us sat at a table.

"What's going on with your sister and Lucky?" I asked Gretchen as I grabbed her hand.

"I don't know. She said it's weird because he's not her type at all, yet she can't stop fucking him."

I twisted my face at her as Candi brought the beers to the table.

"It looks like it's a full house tonight, Luke. Maybe you should be up on that stage, playing your guitar and singing us a song." Candi smiled.

"I'd love to, Candi, but I didn't bring my guitar."

"Maybe you didn't bring it, but I did." Sam chuckled.

Luke shot him a look. "You brought my guitar, man?"

"Yeah, it's in the back of the Jeep. I put it in there in case you needed it." Sam replied.

"Great!" Candi grinned. "Thirty minutes, Luke. Get ready to knock the socks off this crowd."

Luke looked over at me as he took a swig of his beer. "How

about you get up on that stage and play what your daddy taught you?"

"No way!" I exclaimed as I took a sip of my beer.

I didn't know if he was joking or not. But there was no way in hell I was getting up on that stage and playing the guitar.

"Come on, Lily. You have a beautiful voice." Luke smiled.

"Since when have you heard me sing?"

"Through the wall. You sing almost every night before you go to bed—at least you did before I started sleeping over."

"Damn it. I have to move. Those walls are too thin."

Luke laughed, pulled me from my chair, and hugged me. "You aren't going anywhere," he said.

Sam went out to the Jeep, grabbed Luke's guitar, and handed it to him as Candi announced Luke's performance from the stage. I smiled at him and kissed him for good luck. He winked at me, walked to the stage, and sat on the bar stool Candi provided for him. Luke adjusted the microphone and said hello as everyone in the bar clapped. His smile captivated me like it always did, and the way he held his guitar and strummed a few chords for a sound check pulled me in. Candi set another beer down in front of me, leaned over, and whispered in my ear as she looked at the stage.

"Luke's a great guy. It's good to see him smile again."

My eyes wouldn't leave him as he sat up on the stage, and I stared straight ahead as I replied, "He is a wonderful guy. Sometimes, I think he's too good to be true."

Candi patted my shoulder and walked away. I sipped my fresh, cold beer and listened as Luke sang a song.

The moment he finished his song, Luke spoke to the crowd. "I've met a very special lady. She's very talented, and I think you'd all like her. Ladies and gentlemen, I'd like to introduce Lily Gilmore."

My stomach dropped, and my heart started racing. There was no doubt in my mind that I was going to kill him, but that would have to wait because people were cheering and clapping for me. Gretchen pushed me up on the stage. I stood there and faced the cheering crowd.

Luke stood up, handed me his guitar, and whispered in my ear, "You can punish me later."

I shot him a look and sat down on the stool with his guitar in hand. Luke made his way off the stage and back to the table. I stared into the crowd, remembering the night my father did the same thing to me. Closing my eyes, I took in a deep breath and started playing a song that I wrote shortly after my father's death.

While the people in the bar clapped and whistled, I strummed the last chord. Standing up, I smiled and thanked them as Sam walked up on stage and took Luke's guitar. He kissed me on the cheek and smiled. Luke got up from the table and stood in the middle of the bar, waiting for me to walk off the stage and into his arms. When I climbed down to meet him, his arms tightly wrapped around me.

"Babe, that was beautiful. Are you okay?"

"I'm fine, Luke," I said, looking at him.

"I didn't know you wrote songs. I thought you just sang and played random ones or the ones your father taught you."

"I write a song here and there." I smiled.

He cupped my face in his hands and kissed my lips.

"I've never heard that song before, Lily. What the fuck, girl? Why didn't you ever sing it to me?" Gretchen started to tear up.

"It's just a song that I kept to myself."

"Just a song you kept to yourself? You just sang it in front of a shitload of people!" she exclaimed.

"Consider it my debut."

Suddenly, our favorite song, Blurred Lines by Robin Thicke, started playing, and Gretchen grabbed my hand, pulling me to the dance floor. We started moving our hips back and forth. Moments later, I felt two hands clasp my waist. As I turned around, Luke smiled, moving his hands up and down my body while dancing to the music. Our bodies kept the same rhythm as we swayed our hips back and forth. As we stared into each other's eyes while we danced, Luke never stopped smiling, and neither did I. When the song ended, Luke put his arm around me, kissed me, and then led us back to the table. Sam held his hand up for a high five.

"You rocked that song, girl. I'm so proud of you. I didn't know you could sing," he said.

"Thank you, Sam." I smiled.

Luke sat in his chair and placed his arm around me. Scanning the crowd, I saw the two girls at Luke's apartment standing in the corner, staring at us. They left the corner and walked over to our table a few moments later. I looked at the girl who so graciously gave Luke a blow job and said, "Keep walking." Then I smiled and threw back my beer. Gretchen spit out her beer, unable to contain her laughter as Luke shook his head.

~

Barely making it through my apartment door, Luke already had my dress pulled up as he worked on tearing off my panties. Our passionate kiss couldn't be broken as we were both engrossed in the moment. This time, I pinned Luke up against the door as I unbuttoned his jeans and took them down, along with his boxers. He threw his head back and moaned as I took his hard cock in my mouth. No longer able to control his movements, his hands fisted my hair as my tongue ran around the tip and my hands moved in sync up and down his shaft. His moan grew louder as I started sucking, and he moved his hips back and forth.

"Oh God, Lily. I'm going to come!" he exclaimed.

Suddenly, a warm, salty liquid filled my mouth. I'd never swallowed before. In fact, I never sucked a guy off until they came before. Usually, I stop and finish them with my hand, but I didn't want to stop with Luke. I didn't know what to do, and I didn't want to seem rude and ruin the moment by running to the kitchen sink and spitting it out, so I just swallowed it. Luke pulled me up and pushed back my hair.

"You're unbelievable." He smiled.

"Correction. You're unbelievable," I replied.

He carried me to the bedroom, wrapped me tightly in his arms, and made love to me. For the first time in over a year, I slept soundly through the night.

Chapter Twenty-Five

LUKE

I spent more time at Lily's place than I did my own. Sam and I worked out a system that if I stayed at Lily's for the night, Gretchen would stay at our place. Another morning had come, and Lily was getting ready for work. As I made the coffee, I texted Sam to ask if he could bring some eggs. I was in my boxers, so I went into the bedroom and threw on my jeans. Hearing a knock on the door, I left the button and zipper of my jeans undone. I walked over, opened it, and froze when I saw Charley standing there. She was looking me up and down, noticing I was half-naked. It's not the first time she's seen me like this, but it's the first time this happened at Lily's.

"Charley, what are you doing here?" I tried to smile casually.

"Why aren't you dressed? Did you spend the night?"

I took in a deep breath. "Peanut, what can I do for you?"

Lily emerged from the hallway, saw Charley, and looked at me.

"Hey, Charley. Come on in," she said.

She ducked under my arm and walked into the apartment. "Are you coming to my grandma's family dinner tonight?" she asked Lily.

"I sure am."

Charley glanced at me as I came from the bedroom with my jeans buttoned and a t-shirt on.

"You didn't have to get dressed on my account," she said.

Lily busted out laughing, and I shot her a look. "Peanut, don't you have to go to school?"

"Yeah, but I was just—"

"You were just leaving." I laughed as I picked her up, threw her over my shoulder, and took her back up to her apartment. When I dropped Charlie off with Maddie, I walked back to Lily's apartment, and Sam walked over and handed me a carton of eggs.

"Dude, I sent you a text like twenty minutes ago."

"Sorry, but Gretchen had me tied up." He winked.

"Thanks, man," I said as I grabbed the eggs and walked inside Lily's apartment.

Lily was sitting at the table, eating cereal and drinking her coffee.

"Babe, I was going to make you some eggs."

"Thank you, but I'm fine eating my cereal. Besides, I don't have time for eggs," she said as she looked at her watch.

I poured a cup of coffee and leaned against the counter as I stared at her. I couldn't believe this loving, beautiful girl was mine. I never thought I would say those words again after Callie, but with Lily, it was so easy.

She looked over at me and smiled. "Do you know how sexy you look leaning against that counter?"

"Why don't you show me?" I smirked.

"Don't tempt me, Luke. As it is, I'm running late again," she said, putting her bowl in the sink.

She turned to me and placed her hands on my chest. "I have to go. Charley will start spreading horrible rumors about us if I'm late."

I chuckled, kissed her lips, and hugged her goodbye. "Have a good day, babe. I'll miss you."

"I'll miss you too," she said as she kissed me one last time.

I walked into my apartment to find Gretchen cleaning up the kitchen.

"Morning, Luke."

"Morning, Gretchen," I responded as I headed towards my bedroom.

As I was gathering my laundry, Gretchen stood in the doorway.

"I need to talk to you about something."

"Shoot."

"Giselle called me. She and Lucky ran into Lily's mother in Seattle. That being said, Lucky accidentally told her that Lily lives here."

"Shit. That's not good, right?"

"No, it's not. Because if she or Brynn come here, there's no telling what might happen."

"Maybe Lily and her mom should talk. Family is really important, and I would hate for Lily to completely lose hers over what her mother didn't tell her. It was for the best that things worked out the way they did, or else I never would have met her."

"You don't understand, Luke. Lily's life has never been normal. She's told you about her father's affairs and his alcohol and drug use, right?"

I turned around and looked at her as I carried the basket of dirty clothes to the living room.

"I knew he had multiple affairs, and he drank, but she never mentioned anything about drugs."

"He did every drug out there and then some. I remember going over to Lily's house one day, and her dad was snorting coke right off the kitchen table."

"Shit, that's terrible," I shook my head as I poured two cups of coffee.

"It really is, Luke. She's made up her mind to remove herself from her family, and I think we need to do whatever we can to protect her. I don't want her to get hurt again. I love her too much to see her go through that pain. She's a good person and doesn't deserve it."

"I love her too, and I will protect her in every possible way. I don't want you to worry." I smiled.

Gretchen grabbed her things and left the apartment. I was bothered that Lucky said something to Lily's mother, but he didn't know what was happening, so I couldn't blame him. I decided not to tell Lily what Gretchen said because I didn't want her worrying about it, especially tonight at my family's dinner. I was excited to bring Lily home to meet my parents, so I sent flowers to my two favorite women. I grabbed my phone and called the local florist. I had a nice arrangement sent to my mother for the dinner table, and I sent Lily a dozen red roses with a card that read:

Beautiful flowers for a beautiful woman.
I'm missing you already.
Love always, Luke.

It was a beautiful day, so I decided to sit outside and write some songs. I took my laundry to the laundry room, threw it in the washer, grabbed a notepad, pen, and guitar, and headed to the pool. As I sat in the chair and set my phone down on the table beside me, I looked up at the sky as the sun went behind a cloud, one of the very few clouds that filtered the sky. I thought about the conversation Gretchen and I had about Lily's family as I grabbed my pen and started writing down the words that came to my mind:

Even the clouds will say
There's nowhere we can get away from everything
There's nowhere we can practice positivity

I strummed the C and F chords to find the perfect tune, and then my mind returned to the first time Lily and I met. She didn't put up with my bullshit when I was an ass to her because I could only focus on myself and my problems.

When all I see is me
So let's drop, let's stop this teenage rivalry

I strummed the C, F, and G chords to produce a tune that fit the words of the song I was writing. Lily's heart had been broken, not only by her father and her mother but also by her ex-fiancé and her sister, and it killed me to see her cry.

And every heart will break
There's just no way to keep it safe from anything
If the only thing that makes it break is somebody
Please don't give it to me
'Cause seeing you cry makes me want to leave
But losing you scares the shit out of me

My phone rang, and Lily's beautiful picture lit up my screen. I smiled,

"Hey, beautiful."

"I just received some beautiful red roses from a really sexy guy named Luke. You don't know him by any chance, do you?"

"Can't say I do. But when I find him, I'm going to kick his ass for sending my girl flowers."

"They're beautiful, Luke. Thank you. My students are very excited and keep making kissy noises at me. Charley came up to my desk and said they better be from you." She laughed.

I chuckled. "I'm glad you like them, babe."

"As you can hear, my class is out of control. I miss you, and I'll see you later."

"Bye, Lily."

"Bye, Luke."

I smiled as I set my phone down. Were things moving too fast? I wasn't sure, but the only thing I knew for certain was that she was the first woman to catch my attention and make me feel something since the accident. I played the chords again and added a couple more lines before Mrs. Kramer called me to come and fix her leaky toilet.

I'd sail the ocean blue
Or I'd fly a rocket to the moon
But I'm good for nothing without you

I got up, headed back to the apartment, grabbed my toolbox, and fixed Mrs. Kramer's toilet.

Chapter Twenty-Six

LILY

I set the vase of roses Luke sent me on the counter as I thought about what I would wear to his family's house. I was getting nervous because I hadn't met anyone's family in a long time. I always worried they wouldn't like me or find something wrong with me. I wondered where Luke was. Usually, he was waiting for me when I got home. Looking out my window, I noticed his motorcycle wasn't there, so I grabbed my phone and texted him.

"Where's my knight in shining armor?"

A few moments later, a message came through.

"I'm at the store, babe. I had something that I needed to pick up. I'll be over shortly."

"See you soon," I replied.

I walked into the bedroom and opened the closet door. I wanted to look perfect for his family, and I didn't want them to see the destruction that had been left inside me, thanks to my family. I took off my work clothes and stood in front of the open closet in my bra and panties. Suddenly, a voice came from behind, startling me from my thoughts.

"Well, isn't this a sight for sore eyes," Luke said as he leaned against the doorway with his hands behind his back.

"Shit, Luke, you scared me," I said as I turned around and looked at him.

"Sorry, babe, but what do you expect when you're standing there in nothing but your bra and that delicious lace thong."

I smiled as I walked over to him.

"What are you hiding behind your back?" I asked as I ran my finger down the front of his shirt. His top lip curled as he looked at me and brought his hands forward, revealing a helmet.

"Surprise!" he said.

I put my hands over my mouth in shock. "Luke!"

"I know. You probably hate me right now for this, but you should have your own helmet if you're going to be riding on my bike."

"I don't hate you at all. I love it!" I exclaimed as I took it from his hands.

The black helmet had white lilies, and my name was engraved on the side. I reached up and kissed Luke's smiling lips. "Thank you, baby. I love it."

He took the helmet from my hands, put it on my head, and then placed his hands on my hips. "God, you're so sexy."

I walked over to my full-length mirror in the corner of my bedroom. I couldn't help but burst out laughing as I stood there and examined myself in nothing but my bra, panties, and a motorcycle helmet.

"Why are you laughing?" Luke asked as he walked over to me.

"I look ridiculous like this."

He cupped my ass and grinned. "I seriously want to fuck you with that helmet on."

I instantly removed the helmet, turned around, and smacked Luke on the chest.

"You're crazy! I'm not having sex with that on!" I exclaimed.

Luke sighed. "Fine. Leave it off then," he said as he pushed me down on the bed and smiled.

I LOOKED out the window of Luke's Jeep as we drove down the street to his parents' house. The streets were lined with trees and huge houses with well-manicured lawns. Luke reached over and took my hand.

"Please tell me you're not nervous."

"Why would I be nervous? I'm only meeting my boyfriend's parents for the first time," I said as I looked at him.

"You're a smart-ass." Luke laughed as he brought my hand to his lips and gently kissed it.

As he pulled into the driveway, I admired the vast number of palm trees in front of the beige-colored, two-story home. I took a deep breath before Luke climbed out and walked around to open the door.

"Close your eyes and breathe, Lily," he said as he helped me from the Jeep. "There's nothing to be nervous about. My family is as easygoing as they come and will love you."

I nodded and smiled as we walked up the driveway to the front door. As Luke put his hand on the handle and pushed the door open, Charley ran over to us.

"Uncle Luke. Lily!" she exclaimed as he scooped her up.

"Long time no see, peanut," he said as he tapped her on the nose.

"Grandma, Grandpa, and Mommy are in the kitchen," she said.

"Well, let's go see them and introduce Lily." Luke smiled.

We walked down the hallway, and I could hear the rapid beating of my heart. Luke put Charley down as we approached the kitchen and walked over to his mom.

"Luke, you're here!" she exclaimed as she hugged him tight. "Thank you for the beautiful flower arrangement."

Maddie walked over and hugged me. "Don't be nervous," she whispered.

Luke broke his hug from his mom and turned to his dad, who patted him on the back as the two of them hugged each other.

"Mom and Dad, I'd like you to meet Lily Gilmore." Luke smiled as he held out his hand for mine.

"Oh, Lily. It's wonderful to meet you! You can call me Annie," she said as she hugged me tight.

"It's nice to meet you as well. I've heard so much about you."

"It better be all good, or Luke will be in trouble," Annie said as she shot Luke a look.

"Of course, it's all good." I smiled.

Luke's father held his arms out. "It's nice to meet you, Lily. You can call me Tom."

"It's nice to meet you, Tom." I smiled.

Luke smiled and put his arm around me. "They love you already," he whispered.

I stood before the island and admired the granite counter amongst the cherry cabinets, which matched the cherry wood floors. I couldn't help but be reminded of the kitchen in my childhood home. The resemblance was incredible.

"Come on, everyone. Let's start cooking dinner!" Annie exclaimed.

"What are we having, Mom?" Luke asked.

"We're making Chicken Marsala tonight, and I have everyone's job assigned," she said as she pulled a white piece of paper from her apron pocket. "Tom, you're in charge of pounding out the chicken breasts. Luke, you're in charge of making the coating for the chicken, and Lily, you're in charge of slicing the mushrooms. Maddie, you're in charge of making the salad, and I will make the potatoes."

"Grandma, what about me?" Charley frowned.

"You, my dear grandbaby, are in charge of helping me with the potatoes. Once I slice them, I need you to place them in the dish."

Luke and I took our place at the counter where all the ingredients were laid out. I grabbed the mushrooms and started slicing them while Luke prepared the coating for the chicken. Being a part of this gave me an incredible feeling.

Annie was a breath of fresh air. She stood about five foot two with a petite stature. Her chestnut-colored, mid-length hair softly framed her face. Her eyes were a deep brown, and her smile reminded me of Luke's. From what I could tell, her personality was bubbly and full of life. She was a natural family person, and I took comfort in the fact that, for this night, I could be a part of it.

"I really like how your mom does this with dinner," I told Luke.

"It's okay now, but it was annoying growing up. Imagine your friends calling you to hang out, and you tell them you can't because you have to cook dinner with your mom. I was teased a lot."

"Aw, poor baby," I said as I put a mushroom in his mouth.

Annie put the potatoes in the oven as Luke handed Tom the coated chicken and put it in the skillet. Tom was a handsome man who stood about six feet tall and was muscular. His short, sandy brown hair and brown eyes reminded me greatly of Luke.

"Okay, everyone, the potatoes are in the oven, the chicken is in the skillet, the salad is made, and now you can rest until it's ready!" Annie exclaimed.

Luke went to the refrigerator, grabbed two bottles of beer, twisted the caps off, and handed one to me. "Come on, babe. Let me show you the house."

He took me on a tour and up to his old bedroom. The blue walls were lined at the top with a football border. In fact, everything in his room was football-themed, right down to the lamp that sat on the dresser. A twin bed sat in the corner of the room with a blue comforter and matching pillow. There were pictures on the wall of Luke and his family. I scanned the room to see if there were any pictures of Callie, but there weren't. My eyes traveled to the closet door where a poster of my father hung. He was sitting on a stool with his guitar. I walked over to where it hung and stared into his eyes. Tears started to fill my eyes as Luke came up from behind and wrapped his arms around me.

"I'm sorry, Lily. I forgot it was still hanging up," he said as he kissed my head.

"It's fine," I said as I wiped my eyes. The anger I thought I'd buried when my father died began to emerge.

"Wait until I show you the backyard," Luke said as he walked me out of the bedroom.

Just as we were going to look at the backyard, Annie announced that dinner was ready. Everyone sat in the dining room, but before Luke sat down, he poured some wine into everyone's glass. He walked over to where Charley was sitting and pretended like he was going to fill her glass.

"Uncle Luke, I can't drink wine. I'm not old enough." She giggled.

"I'm so sorry, Madame. I thought you were at least twenty-five."

I smiled as Charley laughed at him. To see him with her tugged at my heartstrings. You could see and feel the love when he was around her. Luke looked at me and winked.

"Lily, tell us about your family. What do your mom and dad do? Do you have any siblings?" Annie asked innocently.

"Mom, not now," Luke interrupted.

"Luke, don't be silly. I want to know all about Lily."

At that moment, Charley decided to chime in. "Uncle Luke spent the night at Lily's. He answered her door this morning, only wearing a pair of jeans, and his hair was messy like he just got out of bed."

"Charley!" Maddie exclaimed.

Luke shot her a look across the table.

"Well, I'm sure Lily had him over for coffee," Annie said.

"I saw them kissing in the hallway the other day, and he sent her pretty red roses today." She smiled.

"Peanut, you need to be quiet and eat your dinner, or I'm eating your dessert."

"No, you're not!" she whined.

"Watch me!"

"Mom, tell him to stop it!" she whined.

"For goodness sake, the two of you need to stop and eat your dinner," Annie said.

I leaned over to Annie and whispered to her.

"I'll tell you about my family after dinner. I really don't want to do it in front of Charley."

She patted my hand and smiled. "I understand."

Dinner turned out great. The atmosphere was something I'd

always dreamed of. The Matthews were a tight-knit family who would do anything for each other. This was the kind of family I'd craved my whole life. I helped clean up the table as Charley, Luke, and Tom went outside in the backyard per Annie's orders. Charley came running into the kitchen, asking if she could change into her bathing suit and go swimming. Luke walked over to me and placed his hands on my hips.

"Do you want to go swimming with us?" he asked, placing his forehead on mine.

"I'm going to hang back with your mom and dad so we can get to know each other better. You go and swim with Charley. I'll be watching." I smiled.

As Luke leaned in to kiss me, there was a knock on the door. Suddenly, we heard a familiar voice.

"Hey, Mrs. Matthews. How was your cruise?" Sam's voice echoed through the hallway.

"Sam's here?" I asked Luke.

"Sam is mom's second son, and she always invites him, but I thought he said he had plans tonight with Gretchen."

Sam walked into the kitchen, gave Luke a high-five, and kissed my cheek.

"I thought you couldn't make it tonight, man," Luke said.

"Gretchen got called to a photo shoot. The model they had got sick at the last minute, so they needed a replacement."

Charley came running down the stairs in her pink, frilly bathing suit and ran straight to Sam.

"Uncle Sammy, are you going to go swimming with us?!" she excitedly asked.

"You bet I am!"

Sam and Luke changed into bathing suits and took Charley into the pool. I sat on the patio with Annie, Tom, and Maddie as we talked and drank margaritas.

Annie and Tom's backyard was simply breathtaking. The beauty of the stone patio and perfectly placed palm trees gave way to the infinity-shaped pool and hot tub next to it—a built-in grill over to the side and a large glass patio set in the middle. Exquisite flowers were planted in stone pots surrounding the space, and the in-ground lights began lighting up the area as the sun set and dusk settled in.

"So, tell me about your family," Annie said.

I smiled lightly because I knew it was inevitable. If Luke and I were to continue our relationship, they would need to know everything about me.

"My father was Johnny Gilmore," I said as I took in a deep breath and let out a long sigh.

Tom looked at me and cocked his head. "The Johnny Gilmore? As in Johnny Gilmore, the musician?"

I nodded as I took a sip of my margarita. "Yep, that's the one."

Annie put her hand on my knee. "I'm so sorry for your loss. I remember reading about your father's massive heart attack in the papers. He was so young. What a shame."

I lowered my head as I moved my straw back and forth, banging the ice cubes against the glass.

"Well, I'm sure all the alcohol he drank and all the drugs he did didn't help."

"He was a brilliant musician, and that's what you should remember him for." Tom winked at me. "Do you play the guitar, Lily?" he asked.

"Yes, I do. Johnny began teaching me when I was four years old."

"You'll have to play for us sometime. We'd love to hear you play." Annie smiled.

I looked straight ahead at the massive in-ground pool where Luke and Sam swam with Charley. There was laughter and a lot of splashing going on.

"Maddie told us that you just moved to Santa Monica. Where were you living before?" Annie asked.

"I grew up in Seattle but spent the last year living in Portland. I needed a fresh start, and leaving Seattle was the only way. I moved here because I was offered a year-long substitute teaching job."

Annie reached over and grabbed my hand. "May I ask why you wanted a fresh start?"

I looked at her and Tom and pursed my lips. I took a sip of my margarita and sighed. They were great people, and I found them very easy to talk to—as if I'd known them my whole life. I felt connected to them and found comfort in them, just like I did in Luke.

"I caught my ex-fiancé cheating on me in the church on our wedding day."

Annie gasped as she squeezed my hand. "Lily, I'm so sorry."

"The worst part is that my mother knew about it, and I guess it had been going on behind my back for a long time, but she was going to let me marry him anyway."

Annie frowned as she listened to my words.

"Lily, you poor girl. I want to reach over and hug you right now, but I don't want Luke to think something's wrong, so I'll hug you later." She smiled.

Tom looked at me and held up his glass. "You got dealt a raw deal in life, Lily, but look at it this way. You never would have met my son, and we wouldn't be in the presence of excellent company right now."

"Now, I'll drink to that," Annie said as she tapped our glasses.

Luke got out of the pool, grabbed a towel, and walked over to where we were sitting. "What are you toasting to without me?" he asked.

"We're just toasting your beautiful girlfriend." Tom winked at me.

Now I know where Luke gets all his winking from. I smiled as Luke leaned over and kissed me with his cold, wet lips. Maddie came out of the house with two more margaritas and handed one to me.

"I'll be right back, babe. I'm going to go change," Luke said.

Sam carried Charley out of the pool and set her on the patio. Maddie told her to go inside the house, change into dry clothes, and watch TV while the grown-ups talked. She whined a bit, but I could see how tired she was.

Chapter Twenty-Seven

LUKE

I changed out of my bathing suit, rushing to return to Lily and the others to announce that I decided to buy Bernie's Bar. I couldn't believe that I was actually going to do it, and I knew it would be a lot of hard work, but with Lily by my side, it would be worth it. Walking down the stairs, I saw Charley curled up on the couch, watching cartoons. I walked over to her and kissed her on the head, and as she looked up and smiled, her eyes ready to close. I grabbed a beer from the kitchen and sat beside Lily, taking her hand in mine.

"I have an announcement that I'd like to make. I've decided to buy Bernie's Bar."

"Dude! That's awesome!" Sam exclaimed.

Lily looked over at me, smiled, and touched my cheek. I knew she was happy.

"Luke, my boy, that's wonderful news. Let me know if you need any help," my dad proudly said.

My mom got up from her chair and hugged me. "I'm so proud of you, son. You're finally going to put that settlement money to good use."

Maddie stood up and high-fived me because she'd manage the

bar once I took over, which meant better hours for her. I leaned over and kissed Lily's lips.

"It makes me happy that you decided to follow your dreams," she said.

"It's because of you, babe." I smiled.

My good news didn't last long as my father decided to say something to Maddie about Charley's dad.

"Charley tells us that her deadbeat dad is visiting in a few days."

Maddie looked at him and said she didn't want to discuss it. Maddie was good at avoiding things, believing that if she didn't think about it, then the issue didn't exist. But Charley's dad did exist, and she needed to learn to deal with it.

"He said he's changed, that he's off the alcohol and the drugs, he wants to form a relationship with his daughter, and he wants a better relationship with me," Maddie said.

I didn't believe it because I knew Adam too well. We used to be friends in high school until he started hanging with the wrong crowd. Maddie was infatuated with him because he was the bad boy with tattoos and piercings all over his body. I warned her to stay away from him and told her he was trouble, but she didn't listen. They went on a few dates, and she ended up pregnant. He was her first, and I'll never forget the night she told our mom she was pregnant. Of course, being the deadbeat that he was, he denied the baby was his, and my mom cried all night while I went out and beat the shit out of him. Lily sat there and didn't say a word while we went back and forth about what a loser he was. I got up and asked Lily if she was ready to leave. It was getting late, and I wanted to spend time alone with her.

∽

THE FOLLOWING DAY, Lily arranged bagels and muffins on the kitchen table.

"Good morning, babe," I said, kissing her.

"Good morning." She smiled.

"What's all this?"

"I went out and grabbed us some breakfast," she said as she held up the plate. "We have blueberry, banana, and chocolate chip muffins on this side. Now, on this side"—turning the plate—"we have plain, salt, and cheese bagels, with your choice of regular, honey-walnut, strawberry, or non-fat cream cheese."

"Who's going to eat the non-fat cream cheese?" I asked.

"Gretchen will because she and Sam are coming over. They should be here in a few minutes."

"Do I have time to jump in the shower?"

"Yes, just make it quick," she said as she kissed me.

"I really wish you would have woken me up earlier and told me."

"Sorry, baby, it was sort of last minute!" she yelled as I walked down the hallway.

After I finished my shower and dressed, the voices I heard grew quiet as I entered the kitchen. Looking at the three of them sitting at the table, Lily stared at me with tears.

"Babe, what's wrong?" I asked her as I walked over to where she was sitting.

"I'm sorry, Luke. I had to tell her about Giselle seeing her mom in Seattle. I got a phone call from her mom saying she's on her way here and wants to talk to Lily," Gretchen confessed.

Lily looked at me with sad and disappointed eyes as she got up from the table and walked into the kitchen area. "I can't believe you knew and didn't tell me."

"I'm sorry. I wanted to tell you, but I didn't want to upset you," I said as I went to hold her.

She moved away from me and looked down. "There's one thing I will not tolerate in a relationship: keeping secrets. I hate secrets. They do nothing but ruin your life."

I moved closer, but she continued to back away. "Lily, please. I think you're overreacting," I said.

Gretchen and Sam got up from their seats. "Hey, bro, I think we should leave. Call me later," Sam said.

Gretchen walked over to Lily and put her hand on her arm. "Don't stress. We're all here for you."

When they left, my attention immediately went back to Lily. I wanted to wrap my arms around her and take away her pain, but she wouldn't let me.

"Lily, tell me what you're feeling," I pleaded.

She walked over to the table and started cleaning up the plates.

"I feel betrayed that you didn't tell me about this. I feel sad because I trusted you to tell me everything, and I feel angry because you knew something about my family that I didn't."

"Babe, seriously. Don't you think you're overreacting just a little bit? Come on, so what if Lucky told her where you are? So what if she comes here and finds you? She's your mom, and you should talk to her. You were with my family last night. That's how a family should be, not full of anger and resentment. I understand what she did was wrong, but you have to find it in your heart to forgive her at some point."

She turned around and looked at me with rage in her eyes. "Don't you dare tell me that I need to forgive her! I told you about my family and what kind of childhood I had. She was going to ruin my life by letting me marry that cheating bastard!" she yelled.

"You need to calm down, Lily," I said as I cautiously approached her.

"Don't you tell me what I need to do! You have no idea what path of destruction my family has left inside me. So you don't get to tell me to calm down."

Her unreasoning made me angry, and I raised my voice to her. "Don't yell at me. I'm not Hunter, your mom, or Brynn!"

"Since you're so big on forgiveness, why don't you take your own advice and forgive Charley's dad?"

"That's different, Lily, and you know it," I said as I shook my head.

"No, it isn't. What you feel for him is what I feel for my mom and sister. Why is it so easy for you to tell me to forgive and forget when you can't do it yourself?!" she spat.

"It's a totally different situation, babe."

"No, it isn't, Luke."

As I walked closer to her to tell her everything would be all right, she folded her arms and turned away.

"Lily, I'm sorry, but you're being childish right now."

"Then leave this child alone," she replied.

"Do you really want me to leave you alone?" I asked.

She spun around and looked at me. "Yes, I do!"

"Fine. Then consider me leaving you alone. You won't hear from me until you decide to talk, but I don't know if I'll be around when that happens!" I yelled as I opened the door.

"You're an asshole!" she spat.

"Watch your mouth!" I yelled as I walked out and slammed the door.

I stood there for a second with my hand on the knob, listening to her yell, "Fuck you—fuck you—and a triple fuck you!"

Chapter Twenty-Eight

LILY

Taking a deep breath, I stood in my living room and pondered our first fight. Hunter and I fought all the time, and it wasn't healthy. I should've known then the relationship was toxic. Our fights always consisted of him having to work late and canceling plans at the last minute because of some business deal that came up. The more I thought about it, the more I knew those were just lies to see my sister or some other woman who may have been in his sights.

As I sat on the couch and brought my knees to my chest, I realized I didn't even know why I got so mad at Luke. I knew he was only trying to help, and yelling at him wasn't right. It was hard for him to understand the dysfunction of a family when his was so perfect. I jumped up off the couch and ran to the door. I needed to apologize. As I pulled open the door, I saw Luke leaning against the wall, staring at me. I threw my arms around him as fast as I could.

"I'm so sorry. I didn't mean anything I said. Please forgive me," I begged, tears forming quickly in my eyes.

"Shh, babe, it's alright," he said as he held me tight. "I'm sorry. I didn't mean to push you."

I looked at him as he brushed my hair out of my face and gently kissed my lips.

"Does this mean that we get to have make-up sex?" he asked.

I lightly laughed as I pulled him into my apartment, and he kicked the door shut with his foot. He broke our kiss long enough to lift my shirt over my head. A low growl came from the back of his throat when he saw I wasn't wearing a bra. As he unbuttoned my shorts and slid them off my hips, he pushed me up against the wall.

"I don't think we're making it to the bedroom," he said breathlessly.

"I don't think we are either." I smiled.

As Luke wrapped his mouth around my breast, I unbuttoned his jeans and slid them off his hips, wrapping my hand around his cock and feeling the extreme hardness against my palm. My body shuddered as he dipped one finger into me and then another. I tilted my head back as his lips traveled up to my collarbone, licking and light sucking my skin, sending intense vibrations throughout my body. As he lifted me, I wrapped my legs around his waist, and he entered me with a long, hard thrust. My body tightened when his thrusts accelerated, and I found myself moving my body with his as his tongue traveled from my neck, down my jawline, to my chin, and finally, to my lips. Our breathing became shallow, and our hearts were racing as we moved in sync, and our taut bodies gave way to the inevitable pleasure of release we both desperately wanted. Luke buried his face into my neck as he tried to catch his breath.

"I love you, Lily," he whispered.

"I love you too, Luke," I replied as tears filled my eyes.

He looked at me and softly kissed each eye. "No tears."

I smiled as I unwrapped my legs from his waist, and he gently lowered me down and pulled up his boxers and jeans. As he handed me my clothes, I heard my phone chiming. I quickly dressed and walked over to where my phone sat, noticing a text message from Sam.

"Is everything good between the two of you? Because the wall was vibrating, and it had to be a minor earthquake if it wasn't from the two of you!"

I couldn't help but laugh out loud as Luke walked over, and I handed him my phone. He shook his head and responded.

"Dude, don't you have anything better to do than listen to us have sex?"

Luke grinned when he read Sam's reply.

"Bro, when a fucking picture falls off the wall, what the hell do you want me to think?"

"I'm going to change," I said as I walked towards the bedroom.

"And I'm coming to watch," Luke smirked as he followed behind.

Suddenly, there was a knock on the door, and he quickly turned around to answer it.

"I'll get it, babe. It's probably Sam."

As I pulled my white sundress from my closet, my body started to tremble at the familiar voice I heard in the next room. My heart beat out of control, and my hands began to shake. I took a deep breath before walking into the living room and facing my mother for the first time in over a year. I stopped dead in my tracks as I saw her staring at me.

"Hello, Lily," she said in a mild-mannered tone.

"What the fuck are you doing here?" I asked. Turning to Luke, I raised my hand and spoke, "If you tell me to watch my mouth, you're out of here."

"I wasn't going to say anything," Luke said as he stood beside me.

She stood there in her beige pantsuit, looking at me. Her long, brown-dyed hair still looked the same, but her face had aged quite a bit.

"I've missed you so much, baby girl."

"Don't you ever call me that!" I said sternly as I put up my finger in disgust.

"Please, Lily. Let's talk. It's been far too long, and I want to talk to my daughter."

"Maybe you should have thought about that before you let me spend a year planning a wedding with a lying, cheating bastard!"

Suddenly, Luke spoke up. "I think both of you need to get everything out in the open, but here's not the place because it's too easy to start screaming and yelling. I'm taking the both of you out to lunch at a restaurant, where you will do nothing but embarrass yourselves if you raise your voice. That way, you can talk calmly."

"Thank you, Luke," my mother said.

"If you think for one second I'm going anywhere with that woman, then you're delusional!" I yelled.

"Come on, babe. We need to talk," he said as he lightly took hold of my arm and led me to the bedroom. "We'll be right back, Mary," he said.

As we walked into the bedroom, Luke pulled me into an embrace.

"Listen to me. If you ever want her to leave you alone, you need to discuss things with her. Just listen to her, ask her questions, get your answers, and then be done with it. If you still want nothing to do with her after you talk, you can walk away with no regrets."

"I can't, Luke. You don't understand," I said as I began to tremble.

Instantly, he broke our embrace and placed his hands on my face. "Close your eyes and take in a deep breath, babe."

I did what he said and slowly opened my eyes. "Feeling better?" he asked.

I nodded, and he kissed my lips.

"I'll be there with you. I'll be there for you, and I'll be there to catch you if you fall. You've suffered enough, and you need to do this. Okay?"

"Fine, I'll go. Just let me get myself together," I said.

"That's my girl." He smiled, kissed me on the head, and left the room.

∽

LUKE PULLED into the parking lot of a restaurant called The Garden Bistro. I was still unsure about this, but I had Luke there to help through it if things got rough. We walked into the restaurant and were promptly seated at a table. I stopped to see which seat my mother was taking because I didn't want to sit next to her. As the waitress greeted us and handed us our menus, she asked us for our drink orders.

"I'll have a melon ball, please." I smiled.

Luke looked at me with furrowed brows and then glanced at the waitress.

"Doesn't that have vodka in it?" he asked her.

"Yes, it does," the waitress replied.

"No melon ball for her. She'll have a glass of red wine."

I looked at him, cocked my head, and then looked up at the waitress. "Just bring the bottle, please." I sighed.

I looked across the table at my mother as our eyes met, and she took that opportunity to begin her sad attempts at changing my mind about her.

"I miss you, Lily. You have no idea how hard this has been for me since you left."

I felt the fire starting to rev up in my body. "This has been hard on you?" I asked as I raised my voice, and Luke grabbed my hand. I took a deep breath because I wouldn't embarrass myself or him. I promised him, and I was going to keep that promise. As I was preparing to speak, the waitress set the glass and bottle of wine on the table. Luke grabbed the bottle and poured some into my glass. I took a sip and asked my mother the question I wanted an answer to.

"Okay, Mother. Why? Why didn't you tell me about Brynn and Hunter?"

She looked down at the glass that held her gin and tonic. "They both promised me they'd end it, and I thought they had. You already had trust issues with men, and I didn't want to hurt you."

"Once a cheater, always a cheater. You, of all people, should know that!" I spat.

I could see the tears beginning to form in her eyes. Luke looked over at me. "Lily," he said.

"What? It's the truth. Dad promised you that he wouldn't see other women, but he did anyway, and he did it until the day he died. I remember walking past your bedroom almost every night and hearing you cry yourself to sleep. How could you live like that? How could you want that life for me, your own daughter?"

She took in a sharp breath. "You put up with certain things when someone is your life and consumes you. I know Hunter loved you, so I didn't tell you. You deserved to have a good man love you after what your father put you through."

I stared blankly at her as I couldn't comprehend where she was coming from.

"I have a question for you, Mother, and I want you to be honest with me. Are you on drugs?"

"Lillian Grace Gilmore! How dare you speak to me like that!" she spat in a loud enough voice that managed to turn a couple of heads.

"Lillian?" Luke smiled.

"I was named after my grandmother. Be warned that you are never to call me that!" I said sternly as I held up a finger to him.

The waitress walked over with our food and set our plates down in front of us as I got ready to spit fire back at my mother.

"Brynn misses you. She's torn up over everything that has happened," she said calmly.

I finished the last of my wine, grabbed the bottle, and poured more into my glass.

"She's broken up? What about me? Don't you even care how this has affected me? Why is everything about you and Brynn? What about my feelings and what happened to me? Jesus Christ, Mother. Sometimes, I think we aren't even cut from the same cloth."

She looked at me, and a single tear fell from her eye as she quietly spoke, "We aren't."

In that instant, every part of me froze. My pulse started racing, and I felt my throat constricting.

"What the hell, Mary!" Luke said as he looked at her.

I got up from my seat. "I need to get out of here," I said as I grabbed my purse and ran out of the restaurant.

I had only reached the parking lot when I needed to stop to try and catch my breath. My legs felt like lead, and they didn't want to move anymore. My stomach was tied in knots, and I wanted to vomit. Luke came up from behind and wrapped his arms around me, but I broke away from him.

"Don't. Because if you do, I'll lose it, Luke, and I can't lose it!" I raised my voice.

Suddenly, I heard my mother's voice in the distance. "She was only seventeen years old and a baby herself."

As I started to take a few steps forward, I stopped and turned around. With sarcasm, I responded, "Let me guess. You swooped in and saved the day!"—raising my voice—"Or better yet, her life!

"The two of you aren't going to do this in the middle of the parking lot," Luke snapped. "Get in the Jeep, and we'll return to the apartment where you two can discuss this."

As much as I hated her at that moment, I needed to hear everything she had to say. I couldn't spend the rest of my life wondering about the truth Mary had kept hidden all these years. As hard and painful as it would be, I needed some answers.

"Luke's right. Let's go back to my apartment. I want to hear about what a lie my life has been."

We climbed into the Jeep, and Luke drove us back to my apartment.

Chapter Twenty-Nine

LILY

We walked into my apartment, and I immediately took out a bottle of wine. My mother looked at me as I took a glass from the cabinet.

"You seem to drink a lot. Do you have a drinking problem?"

I gasped as I set the glass on the counter. "Considering everything I've been through in my life, I should have one."

She shook her head and sat down at the table. Luke sat across from her, and I stayed at the kitchen counter.

"So, go ahead and tell me how my whole life's been a lie," I said.

She cleared her throat as she began to speak. "I had some problems, and the doctors told me that I would never be able to conceive a child. You have no idea how much that devastated me because the only thing I wanted was a child with Johnny. I started drinking a lot, I stayed in bed all day, and I isolated myself from the world. One night, Johnny came home with this seventeen-year-old girl, Allison. He told me she was pregnant with his child and that she agreed to give us the baby. Her mother was a prostitute and a drug addict, and her father had run off after she was born. She could barely take care of herself, let alone a child. So, Johnny paid for her medical care, and after you were born, he gave her money to start a new life." Her eyes filled with tears as she continued. "I know you'll probably ask me why I stayed after that. It was because of you, Lily. I may not have given birth to you, but you were my baby, my daughter, and you were a part of Johnny, which made you even more special."

I gulped before throwing back my glass of wine. I closed my eyes, and Luke got up from the table and walked over to me.

"Lily, are you okay?" he asked as he placed his hand on top of mine.

"I raised you, Lily. You're my daughter, and you cannot say otherwise! I loved you and nurtured you. I took care of you when you were sick, and I was there for you when you cried while your father was out playing his shows and having sex with any woman who looked his way."

Luke tightened the grip on my hand.

"Mary, I think Lily's heard enough."

"It's okay, Luke. Let's go sit down."

I walked over to the table and sat across from my mother, and I had a moment where I felt incredibly sorry for her.

"Mom, please just tell me why you would let me marry Hunter if you knew about him and Brynn. All I want is an honest answer."

She looked at me with pursed lips, and I could see the pain in her eyes.

"You seemed happy with Hunter, and I couldn't ruin that for you. All I wanted was for you to be happy. I know I was wrong, and I should have told you when I first found out," she said as she shook her head.

"When did you find out?" I asked.

"Does it really matter at this point, Lily?"

"Yes, Mother, it does. It matters to me."

She took a deep breath before spilling the words I didn't want to hear. "I found out the day we went shopping for your wedding dress."

My stomach instantly felt sick as I placed my shaking hand over my mouth, and my eyes swelled with tears.

"But Brynn was with us that day, trying on maid of honor dresses. How did you find out?"

"I received a text message from Mrs. Kendall with a picture of Hunter and Brynn going into a hotel room together. She said she saw them, and she thought I should know. Why do you think I broke down and cried when you came out in your dress? Part of it was because you were so beautiful, and I couldn't believe you were getting married, and the other part was because I knew it would destroy you, and I couldn't let that happen. So, one day, not too long after that, I confronted the two of them and warned them that they were to end it immediately."

Luke leaned over and clasped my shoulders, rubbing them gently. I took a deep breath and buried my face in my hands. As I thought of something, I lifted my head and looked at my mother.

"If you couldn't get pregnant, how did you with Brynn?"

She looked at me as a light smile crossed her lips. "Brynn was a complete surprise. The doctors couldn't explain it either. They just said she was a gift from God."

"Yeah, a real gift," I mumbled.

Mary reached over and put her hand on mine, and I instantly froze. "Lily, what your sister did was wrong, and please don't think I'm defending her, but you also need to remember that you're supposed to love your children unconditionally."

As I slid my hand out from under hers, I got up from the chair and walked over to the window. A part of me understood where she was coming from and why she didn't tell me. As I turned around and looked at my mother, I saw a weak woman who was scared and alone. I saw a forgiving woman who took in someone else's child as her own because she desperately wanted a baby with the man she loved. I walked over, sat in the chair, and grabbed her hand.

"Our relationship is going to need a lot of work. It will take time to get back to where we were before all of this happened. I can't instantly forgive you and pretend it never happened. I need time to process everything you've told me."

She gave me a small smile. "At least it's a start. I want our relationship back, Lily."

"We'll get there eventually, but you must give me space. As for Brynn, don't expect miracles because I don't think I'll ever be able to forgive her."

My mother stood up and hugged me.

"I'll give you the space you want now, but please keep in touch. You're a very lucky woman to have such a wonderful man in your life. Even though I don't know him very well, I can tell he's a great man and very sexy, too." She winked.

When I walked her to the door, she turned to Luke.

"I'm counting on you to take care of my daughter."

"Don't worry, Mary. I'll take excellent care of your daughter." Luke grinned as he winked at me.

Shutting the door behind her, Luke walked over and pulled me against him.

"I'm so proud of you. Trying to mend things with her took a lot of strength." He kissed the top of my head. "That's one of the qualities I love about you, Lily."

"Oh yeah?" I smiled as I looked up at him. "Tell me what other qualities you love about me."

His hands began to travel up and down my sides as he softly kissed my lips.

"I love how soft your skin is," he whispered as his lips touched my neck. "I love how perfect your ass is," he said as he squeezed it with both hands. "I love how beautiful and firm your tits are." He smiled as he pulled the strap to my sundress down and exposed one breast, taking it in his mouth and lightly sucking my nipple. "But most of all, I love how wet you get when I touch you," he whispered as his finger dipped into me.

I moaned as I ran my fingers through his hair, threw my head back, and brought one leg up to his waist so his finger would deepen inside me. My body instantly knew pleasure when he touched me. Hell, it knew pleasure just by the way he looked at me. As he removed his finger, he looked at me and smiled.

"Come on, babe. Let's take it to the bedroom this time." He picked me up, carried me, and gently laid me on the bed.

Chapter Thirty

LUKE

As Lily and I were snuggled against each other in bed, I heard my phone beep. I reached over, grabbed it, and read a text message from Maddie.

"Adam just called and talked to Charley. He said that he was sorry and something came up, so he won't be able to visit her. She's devastated and won't stop crying."

I sighed, and Lily asked what was wrong. I showed her the message from Maddie. I was relieved because I didn't want him near her, but I felt sorry for Charley. I kissed Lily on the forehead and sent a message back to Maddie.

"Typical douchebag, Adam. I'll be up there in a second."

As we climbed out of bed, Lily and I got dressed and headed upstairs to Maddie's apartment. Opening the door, Maddie walked over and told us Charley was in her room. I could hear Charley crying down the hallway. As Lily and I entered her room, we saw Charley lying face down and crying into her pillow.

"Hey, peanut," I softly spoke as I rubbed her back.

"Go away, Uncle Luke. I don't want to talk to anyone," she sobbed.

"Your mom told me about your dad, and I think it's pretty crappy what he did, but he'll come see you soon."

"You don't know anything!" Charley snapped at me.

Lily walked over to the bed and motioned for me to move down. "Let me try," she whispered.

Sitting next to Charley, she began to tell Charley about her father.

"I know what it's like to be disappointed by your dad, Charley. My dad disappointed me almost my whole life."

Charley turned her head, looked at her, and sniffled. "Really?"

"Yeah, really," Lily answered in a soft, sweet voice.

"But he promised, Lily. He promised me that he would come see me."

Lily took her hand and started stroking Charley's hair. "I know he did, sweetie, but sometimes when you're grown up, things come up, and it can hurt the ones you love. My dad made me a lot of promises that he didn't keep. Sometimes, he wouldn't be home for my birthday, even though he said he'd be."

"What did you do?" Charley asked as she sat up, and Lily handed her a tissue.

"I cried, just like you are right now, and then I got over it because I had plenty of people at home who loved me, just like you do."

"But I wanted to see him," she whined.

Lily embraced Charley and kissed her on the top of her head.

"I know you do, sweetie, but sometimes certain things can't be helped. You have to be a big girl and try to understand."

As Lily looked at me, I smiled. Seeing her with Charley was incredible. All I saw when I watched her was the mother of my children.

"Thank you, Lily," Charley spoke as she hugged her.

"You're welcome, baby."

"Hey, what about me?" I asked as I leaned over and began tickling her.

Charley giggled and tried to push my hands away. "Thank you, Uncle Luke."

"How would you like to spend the night at my apartment tonight? We can dance, eat junk food, sleep on the floor, and, best of all, watch scary movies!" Lily said with excitement.

"Really?!" That would be so fun! Can Uncle Luke spend the night with us?" Charley asked.

Lily looked at me and then twisted her face as she looked at Charley. "Are you sure you want boys at our sleepover?"

"Only Uncle Luke." Charley giggled.

Lily leaned over and kissed me. "I guess he can come, but he has to behave himself."

"Is that so?" I growled at her.

As Lily and I left the room, I told Charley to pack her bag. We walked into the living room, where Maddie sat on the couch.

"Charley is going to have a sleepover at Lily's tonight. If that's okay," I said.

She looked up at me and smiled. "That's great, Luke. Thank you, Lily. I'm sure that made Charley very happy."

Charley came running down the hall with her bag. "I'm ready!" she squealed as she kissed Maddie goodbye.

The next morning, I rolled over and looked at Lily as she slept beside Charley on the floor. We had a great night, and Charley was happy. Before getting up, I softly kissed Lily on the head and returned to my apartment to shower. While standing under the warm water, I kept thinking about Callie and how she'd be happy I'd moved on. I grinned as I thought about Lily and how all I saw was my future with her. As I turned off the water and wrapped a towel around my waist, there was a knock on the bathroom door.

"Bro, I have to take a piss! Can you hurry it up?"

"I'm done, man. Relax," I said as I opened the door and walked to my bedroom. After getting dressed, I saw Sam sitting on the couch alone.

"Where's Gretchen?"

"She had a photo shoot."

I walked into the kitchen and grabbed what I needed to make pancakes because I wasn't sure if Lily had everything.

"Dude, come over to Lily's for pancakes. Charley's there."

Sam turned his head. "Why is Charley there?"

"Adam called her yesterday, said something came up, and that he couldn't visit her. She was upset and crying, so Lily asked if she wanted to sleep over at her place."

"I bet she loved that." He smiled.

"We had a lot of fun."

"Hold on a second, and let me throw on some clothes." He got up from the couch and headed to his room.

We returned to Lily's apartment, and I put the stuff on the counter. Lily wasn't on the floor anymore, and Charley was up watching cartoons.

"Hi, Uncle Sammy." She smiled.

"Good morning, darling."

"Charley, where's Lily?" I asked as I plugged in the griddle.

"She's in the shower. Are you making pancakes?"

"I sure am." I smiled.

Sam cracked the eggs and put them into the bowl as I measured the pancake mix. Lily emerged from the bedroom with a smile on her face.

"If I didn't know any better, I'd think you two were gay."

I smiled at her as she walked over and kissed me.

"Maybe I am, and you just don't know it yet."

She hit me on the arm with the back of her hand as she walked over and kissed Sam on the cheek. "Where's Gretchen?"

"She's at a photo shoot. We're leaving tomorrow afternoon for San Francisco. I'm taking her home to meet my parents."

"That's great, Sam." I smiled.

As Lily reached into the cabinet, Sam grabbed and hugged her.

"Dude, what the hell are you doing?" I said as I looked over at them.

"I'm just thanking her for moving in next door because if she didn't, I never would have met the love of my life."

"Uncle Sammy! Lily is Uncle Luke's girlfriend. You shouldn't be hugging her like that."

"Yeah, Sammy. Hands off." I chuckled.

"It's okay, Charley. It's just a friendly hug," Lily said as she set the plates on the counter.

I made the pancakes exactly how Charley loved them, and the four of us had an excellent breakfast. As we were cleaning up, and Charley was gathering her things, my phone rang, and my mom appeared on the screen.

"Hey, Mom," I answered.

"Good morning, Luke. Your father and I were wondering if you and Lily would like to go to Bernie's bar tonight for some drinks."

I told her to hold on as I looked at Lily and asked her if she wanted to go. She smiled and nodded as she took a sip of her coffee.

"Sounds good, Mom. How about we meet around seven?"

"Excellent! We'll see the two of you tonight. I love you, Luke."

"I love you too, Mom."

Chapter Thirty-One

LILY

After spending the day with Charley, Luke took her back to her apartment as I got ready to meet his parents at the bar. I couldn't stop thinking about how devastated Charley was when her father told her he couldn't visit. It was a feeling that I knew too well, and I wish I didn't.

As I stood in front of my full-length mirror and stared at the girl looking back at me, I thought she looked happy and fulfilled. Had fate finally led me to where I was supposed to be? I'd never been this happy, and now that I'd settled things with my mother, an overwhelming sense of peace had landed in my life. It was a feeling I never wanted to lose.

"What are you thinking about?" Luke asked as he came up from behind and wrapped his arm around me, burying his nose into my neck.

"I was just thinking about how my life has worked out and how happy I am because of you." I smiled.

A low growl came from his throat as he took in my scent. "Do you have any idea how good you smell?"

"Judging that you have one hand squeezing my boob and the other up my dress, I think I have a pretty good idea." I laughed.

"Can you feel that?" Luke whispered as he pushed his body against me, looking at me through the mirror.

"Yes, I can feel how hard you are, baby, but we don't have time." I smiled as I turned around and kissed him on the cheek. "Look at the clock. It's six forty-five, and we have to meet your parents in fifteen minutes." I walked over to the closet and grabbed my shoes.

"Damn, Lily. You sure know how to give a guy blue-balls!" he exclaimed as he adjusted himself.

"Sorry, baby. I don't want to be late for your parents. I promise I'll make it up to you when we get home." I winked.

"I just want you to know that you're mean, babe!" he yelled as he stood in the bedroom.

"Yep, and I will show you how mean I am later!" I yelled back, walking towards the living room.

Suddenly, Luke came up from behind, grabbed me, and spun me around.

"You better keep that promise because that's all I'll be thinking about all night," he said as he kissed my neck.

"Do you ever think about anything else besides sex?" I laughed.

"Not when I'm around you. You're all I want 24/7, babe." He put me down and kissed me.

I grabbed my purse as Luke grabbed his keys off the counter, and we headed out the door.

∽

Walking hand in hand and Luke carrying his guitar, we strolled into the bar and over to the table where his parents were sitting. Before sitting down, I hugged them each while Luke went to the bar and grabbed us a couple of beers.

"It's so good to see you again." I smiled at Annie.

We sat at the table and talked as Luke showed his father around the bar. I could tell how excited Annie was that Luke would finally buy it. She reached over and placed her hand on top of mine.

"You have no idea how happy I am that you're in Luke's life. The past year has been so difficult for him and us all."

I smiled at her. "I'm sure it's been very difficult. It seems the past year wasn't good for any one of us."

"No, it wasn't. But the only thing that matters is that you and my son found each other and are both happy. I'm thrilled he's decided to buy this bar. It's all he ever talked about for years. Now, he'll finally put that settlement money to good use."

"He never mentioned the settlement money to me."

"He doesn't like to talk about it. I think it's a reminder of the accident. The man who ran the red light was drunk and driving on a suspended license. He was a partner at a prestigious law firm in Los Angeles. He'll never be practicing law again. Luke settled for five hundred thousand dollars. His attorney said he could probably get more, but Luke just wanted to be done with it. It was settled out of court to avoid publicity."

As I sat there, pondering that my boyfriend had five hundred thousand dollars he didn't tell me about, Luke and his dad sat at the table.

"What have the two of you been talking about?" Luke asked.

"Just girl talk." I smiled. "You haven't told Bernie yet that you're buying the bar, have you?"

"No, I just sent him a text message telling him I need to meet with him tomorrow and that I've decided."

I reached over and kissed him on the cheek, leaving a lipstick mark on his face. I laughed as I grabbed a napkin and wiped it off. We ordered some chicken wings, had a couple of beers, and enjoyed his parents' company. Luke leaned over and told me he'd be right back as he got up from his seat. As I continued conversing with Tom and Annie, the lights on the stage caught my eye. I looked up, and Luke sat on the stool before the microphone.

"Good evening, everyone." He smiled and waved to the patrons in the bar.

Everyone cheered and said hello as Luke strummed his guitar. "This song I'm going to sing for you tonight is one I wrote for an extraordinary woman in my life."

Annie looked over at me and smiled as she placed her hand on mine and gently squeezed it. My eyes started to swell with tears before he even started singing. He strummed the chords as our eyes met and began to sing the words he wrote.

Even the Clouds will say
There's nowhere we can get away from everything
There's nowhere we can practice positivity
When all I see is me
So let's drop let's stop this teenage rivalry
And every heart will break
There's just no way to keep it safe from anything
If the only thing that makes it break is somebody
Please don't give it to me
'Cause seeing you cry makes me want to leave
But losing you scares the shit out of me.

Or maybe, I'll sail the ocean blue
Or I'd fly a rocket to the moon
But I'm good for nothing without you
It doesn't matter what you say
I think about you every day, girl, I
Am good for nothing without you

Even the clouds will say
That Saturdays and rainy days were meant to be
If you're indoors and in the arms of somebody
Under the blankets and sheets
Well the sky is clear; it's the middle of the week
So come my dear, let's make believe.

Love In Between

Or maybe, I'll sail the ocean blue
Or I'd fly a rocket to the moon
But I'm good for nothing without you
It doesn't matter what you say
I think about you every day, girl, I
Am good for nothing without you

Cause I want you
I want you
I want you
To want me to
I want you
I want you
I want you
I do
But I won't fool this heart anymore
Or maybe, I'll sail the ocean blue
Or I'd fly a rocket to the moon
But I'm good for nothing without you
It doesn't matter what you say
I think about you every day, girl, I
Am good for nothing without you

Even the clouds will say
There's nowhere we can get away from everything
And if the only thing that breaks your heart is somebody
Please don't give it to me
'Cause seeing you cry makes me want to leave
But losing you scares the shit out of me.

Annie and Tom looked over at me as the tears that swelled in my eyes slowly fell down my face. The crowd cheered as Luke strummed the last chord and exited the stage. I stood up from my chair and wrapped my arms around him when he approached me.

"I love you," I whispered, tightening my grip around him.

"I love you too, babe. I'm glad you liked it."

"I loved it, Luke. It was perfect. You're perfect."

Sitting down, he brought me onto his lap and kissed me.

"That was a beautiful song, honey," Annie said.

"Great tune, son." Tom smiled as he held up his glass.

We talked for a while longer and then called it a night. I had work in the morning, and Luke had to meet with his lawyer to discuss the purchase of the bar. As we said goodbye to Annie and Tom, we climbed into the Jeep and returned to my apartment. I made sure Luke received his punishment for calling me mean.

Chapter Thirty-Two

ONE MONTH LATER

LILY

My life was perfect. Luke and I were perfect. I'd never been more in love with anyone than with him. He consumed me, and he owned me. He held my heart and soul, and I thanked God for him daily. He had completely changed my life. When I didn't think it was possible to trust someone again, he walked into my life and showed me it was.

As Luke was still sleeping, I slipped out of bed and headed to the kitchen to make a pot of coffee. When the coffee began to brew, I walked over and opened the blinds. It was cloudy outside, and I could smell a hint of rain as I opened the window. It was the perfect day to stay in bed and watch movies. Walking back into the bedroom, I took off my nightshirt and climbed into bed, wrapping my arms around Luke and softly kissing his back. He rolled over and smiled.

"Good morning, beautiful."

"Good morning," I whispered as my lips traveled across his chest.

Reaching down, I stroked his erection through the soft fabric of the sheet.

"Someone's horny." He smiled as he ran his fingers through my hair.

"I'm always horny when you're around."

"I know you are, and I love it." He flipped me on my back and climbed on top of me.

As Luke ran his tongue behind my ear and softly nipped my neck, I could feel the warmth deep in my belly. His hard cock pushed against my thighs as his lips made their way down to my breasts. His hand cupped me down below before his fingers found their way inside of me.

"Someone is more than ready." He smiled.

My hips moved in sync as his fingers moved in and out of me slowly. He was teasing me. I could tell by the smirk on his face.

"How bad do you want me inside you?"

"Very bad. Can't you tell by how wet I am?" I spoke breathlessly.

"Yes, but I want you to tell me how bad you want me inside of you."

"If you don't put that hard cock inside me now, you're not going to have one anymore."

The look on his face was priceless. "Well, that wasn't the answer I wanted to hear, but it'll do."

He asked me to put my arms above my head. Then he locked my wrists tight with his hand as he pushed himself into me. I threw my head back as he did it with such force that it made me gasp. His eyes gazed into mine while he pounded into me and gave me exactly what I wanted. I needed to run my hands through his hair, but his grip was too tight, and I couldn't free my hands.

"You want to touch me, don't you?" He smiled.

"You know I do."

"Should I let your hands go?"

"Yes. Please," I spoke breathlessly as my heart raced at full speed.

The grin on his face grew wide. "I'll let go if you come first."

I wrapped my legs around his waist as he took in a sharp breath. He took his free hand and placed it flat on my breast, with his palm face down and pressed hard against my nipple. He rubbed it in slow circles as he moved fluently in and out of me. My body was ready to release, and he knew it.

"That's right, baby. Let go and come all over me."

His words were all I needed to hear as a moan escaped my lips, and my body shook, releasing my pleasure all over him.

"That's it, Lily. I can't hold back anymore, baby," he grunted as his grip tightened around my wrists, and I felt the warmth of him spill into me as he pushed himself one last time deep inside me.

Letting go of my wrists, he touched each one and softly kissed them.

"I hope I didn't hurt you."

I gently rubbed the side of his face with the back of my hand. "You could never hurt me."

As he leaned down and kissed me, I heard my phone chime. He broke our kiss and looked at me.

"Why are we always getting interrupted by someone?"

"It's probably Sam telling us to shut the hell up." I laughed.

Luke climbed off of me, and we got out of bed and headed to the kitchen for coffee. As he poured some into our cups, I checked my phone and saw a text message from Giselle.

"Lunch, 1:00 p.m. at The Southside Grill. You have no choice, and don't be late. It's important."

I read her text with a twisted face, wondering what the hell was going on and what could be so important.

"I'll be there at 1:00 p.m. sharp!" I replied.

"What's wrong?"

"I just got this weird text from Giselle," I said as I handed him my phone.

"Hmm. I'm sure it's nothing serious. She's probably having a bad hair day."

I rolled my eyes as Luke looked over at his beeping phone.

"It looks like I'll be fixing Mrs. Blake's toilet again while you're at lunch with the girls."

"That's the third time this month. I swear she does it intentionally to get you to her apartment."

Luke held up his coffee and smiled. "Maybe she does. The women in this building can't seem to resist me."

"Very funny." I shot him a dirty look and got up from my chair.

He extended his arm, grabbed my waist, and pulled me onto his lap. He made me straddle him on the chair so we were face to face. Pushing the strands of my hair behind my ears, he kissed my lips.

"You know how much I love you, babe. It's only you. It will always be you, and you better never forget that," he spoke as his deep brown eyes stared into mine.

"I know, and I love you too. I love you so much that sometimes it hurts, and I get scared."

"There's nothing to be scared of, Lily. You know my feelings for you, and I know your feelings for me." He lifted my nightshirt over my head.

I bit my bottom lip and smiled as I felt his erection underneath me. He leaned his head slightly forward and took my nipple between his teeth while he looked up at me. He wrapped his lips around my breast, tenderly sucking and circling his tongue around my nipple, making it harder than it already was.

"I only want these beautiful breasts in my face." He smiled as he reached down and dipped one finger inside of me, lifting me. "And I only want my fingers inside you."

I let out a hiss and tilted my head back as he found my G-spot and started moving his finger back and forth. I moaned with desire as a warm, flushing sensation resonated throughout my body, and I released myself on him.

"And I only want your come all over me." He smiled.

He had me so hot that I could barely stand it. After removing his finger, he scooted me back a bit and pulled his hard cock from his boxers. Grabbing my hips, he pulled me forward and gently set me on him. I slowly pushed myself down as I cupped his face, and we stared into each other's eyes.

"And last, I only want to be inside of you."

Once he was entirely inside me, he lifted my hips slightly as I moved back and forth. He made sure to keep a tight grip on my hips as he started to swell inside me. As I felt the warmth of him shoot through me, he wrapped his arms around me and held me tightly on him as he finished himself off, pouring every last drop of pleasure inside of me.

Gazing into my eyes, he placed his hands on my face. "Do you understand?

I nodded and spoke softly. "Yes."

Luke embraced me as he whispered, "You better."

∽

WALKING INTO THE RESTAURANT, I saw Gretchen and Giselle sitting at a table in the corner. I made my way through the restaurant and joined them.

"You're exactly five minutes late," Giselle said as she looked at her watch.

"Sorry, but I couldn't find a place to park. This joint is busy."

A waitress with long black hair walked over to the table and set a glass of red wine in front of me.

"I took the liberty of ordering your drink," Gretchen said.

"Thank you. Do you want to tell me what's going on? You have me freaked out."

"I'm pregnant," Giselle yelled out as I was taking a sip of wine.

I spat my wine all over the table and started choking. "What?! Did you say you were pregnant?"

I must have said it too loudly because a few heads turned and looked in our direction. Gretchen took her napkin and started wiping the spilled wine from the table.

"Yes, Lily. You heard right. She's pregnant."

"Who's the baby daddy?" I asked.

Giselle looked at me. "You don't have to say it like that. The father is Lucky."

"WHAT?!" I exclaimed as a few heads turned once more.

"Will you please keep it down," Giselle whispered.

"How far along are you?" I asked quietly.

"About six weeks."

"How do you feel about this?"

"I'm not sure."

I looked at Gretchen, who was sitting there in silence.

"Have you told Lucky yet?"

"No, not yet, and I don't know how to."

"How did this happen? I thought you were on birth control?"

"I am, but sometimes I forget to take it. You know I have a hectic schedule."

"Yeah, and it's about to get busier," I said.

Giselle reached across the table and took my hand. "Listen, Lily. I'm thinking about getting an abortion, and I need your support."

"You know how I feel about that, Giselle."

"I know, and that's why I'm begging you."

"There's always adoption. Do you know how many couples can't have children?"

Suddenly, this conversation hit home, and tears started to form in my eyes.

"Listen, I'm not getting into this discussion with you both right now. I'm about to say something, and I don't want you to ask any questions. We'll discuss it further at my apartment, over dinner, one night. Mary isn't my biological mother."

Giselle and Gretchen looked at me as shock took over their faces. I held up my finger.

"If my biological mother decided to have an abortion, I wouldn't be sitting here with the both of you."

Gretchen picked up her phone off the table. "Everyone look at their schedules right now because we're setting up a dinner night over at Lily's."

I laughed lightly while Giselle took a sip of her water and looked at me. "Lily, I promise I will tell Lucky tonight, and we will decide together."

"I'm here for you, Giselle. Don't get me wrong. I will always be here for you, no matter your decision."

"We're here for you, Lily, and you can't keep something like that from us," Gretchen said.

"I know, and I'll tell you everything. Let's have dinner at my place next Tuesday, and we'll do Chinese take-out. No guys. Just us girls."

∽

As I OPENED the door to Luke's apartment, I saw him lying on the couch watching TV. I threw my purse on the table, walked over to where he was, and lay beside him, snuggling into his chest.

"How was lunch, babe?"

"A clusterfuck," I mumbled.

"Watch your mouth," he said as he kissed my head.

"Sorry. But wait until I tell you something."

"Did something happen?"

I propped myself up and kissed him. He smiled as he nipped at my bottom lip.

"Giselle is pregnant, and Lucky's the baby daddy."

Luke's eyes widened, and his jaw dropped. "Are you serious?"

"Yes. I wouldn't make something like that up."

Luke pushed himself into a sitting position as I laid my head across his lap.

"Does Lucky know?"

"She's telling him tonight, and she wants to have an abortion. I told both of them about Mary not being my biological mother, and we're having dinner at my place Tuesday night so I can tell them the whole story. I couldn't stop thinking about it because what if my birth mother had an abortion?"

Luke ran his fingers through my hair. "I don't want to think about that. I'm sorry lunch was such—"

"A clusterfuck?" I said, knowing he'd tell me to watch my mouth.

He tapped me on the mouth with his fingers as he looked down at me. "Watch your mouth, babe."

Sam and Gretchen walked through the door as I grabbed Luke's fingers and stuck them in my mouth. I sat up and looked over at her.

"Long time no see, Gretch."

"Ugh, what a clusterfuck of a day!" she exclaimed as she fell into the recliner.

I stared at Luke. "Aren't you going to tell her to watch her mouth?"

"No. Why would I tell her that?"

"You tell me that all the time!"

"That's because you're my girl, and I don't want you talking like that." He smiled as he kissed me on the nose.

"Wait a minute!" I exclaimed. "I wasn't your girl when you told me that in my bathroom while fixing my shower."

"Well, I sort of liked you."

"Sort of?" I asked.

"Babe, drop it."

I rolled my eyes and sighed as I got up, and Luke slapped my ass. Sam laughed, and Gretchen followed me to the kitchen to grab a beer.

"What do you think Giselle's going to do?" I asked her.

"I honestly don't know. You know Lucky is totally not her type, and our parents will die when they find out."

"Well, let's hope they make the right decision." I walked over to Luke and handed him a beer.

Chapter Thirty-Three

LUKE

"Congratulations, Luke. You are now the owner of this bar!" Bernie smiled as he handed me the keys.

"Thanks, Bernie," I said as I shook his hand.

"This was my legacy and passion for many years, son, and now it's your turn. Do whatever you need to and make this bar your legacy."

"I will, Bernie. Enjoy the retired life," I spoke as I hugged him.

"I will, Luke. You two take care." Bernie smiled as he tipped his hat and walked out the door.

As I picked up Lily and swung her around, I kissed her. "I can't believe it, babe. I can't believe this is all mine!"

"I'm so happy for you."

The door to the bar opened, and my mom, dad, Maddie, and Charley walked in.

"Uncle Luke!" Charley exclaimed as she ran over to me.

I picked her up and kissed her on the cheek. "Welcome to Luke's Bar and Grille, peanut."

"Yay!" she exclaimed.

I put her down as my mom and dad walked over and hugged me.

"We're so proud of you, Luke."

"Damn proud, son," my dad said.

"Congratulations, manager." I smiled as I threw the extra set of keys at Maddie.

I stood there and looked around the bar. My life was exactly where I always wanted it to be. I owned a bar and had a woman I was madly in love with standing by my side. Lily looped her arm around my neck as I was in deep thought.

"What are you thinking about?" she asked.

"Just how lucky I am to share my dream and this moment with you."

She leaned in and softly kissed my lips. "I'm the lucky one." She smiled.

Candi burst through the bar's doors as we were having our little moment.

"Hey, boss." She smiled as she hugged me. "You have no idea how happy I am that you bought this joint."

Candi was one of the best bartenders I knew. She was forty-two years old, and she had never been married. Maddie had always been jealous of her long, curly black hair, and they worked together for years. Both being single, they were constantly getting hit on by the customers. Candi used to be a prostitute. She stumbled into the bar one night after being beaten up by her pimp. She was only twenty-two years old at the time. When Bernie saw her, he took her to the hospital. After she was released, they had a long talk, and Bernie brought her back to the bar, taught her how to make drinks, and gave her a job. That was twenty years ago, and she told us every day how Bernie saved her life and offered her a second chance.

I decided to have a celebration party with family and friends tonight. I put a sign on the door saying the bar was closed for tonight only and would re-open tomorrow. Lily walked over to me and kissed me goodbye. Chris, the school's principal, had called her for a meeting. Looking at the stage, I chuckled when I saw Charley up there, pretending she was holding a microphone and singing her little heart out. My mom and dad left just as Sam came walking in.

"Dude, congratulations!" he said as we fist-bumped. "I never thought I'd see this day."

"Me either, Sam. You and Gretchen are coming tonight, right?"

"Of course we are, and depending on how Giselle is feeling, she and Lucky will be here."

"Oh yeah, that's right. Today is the day of her appointment at the clinic. Lily wanted to be there with her, but Giselle told her that Lucky was taking her."

"It sucks that they got themselves into this situation in the first place," Sam said as I handed him a beer.

"Uncle Sammy!" Charley shrieked. "Did you hear me singing?"

"I sure did, and I think you're going to be the next Taylor Swift."

Charley's eyes widened as she smiled. "Do you really think so?"

"Yes, I do. I'm calling American Idol and telling them I have a nine-year-old celebrity sitting beside me."

I chuckled as I poured Charley a Coke. "Here, peanut. Take this and go sit over at the table."

"Thanks for the beer, man. I'm going to head home, get changed, and then wait for Gretchen to finish her photo shoot. I'll see you later," Sam said as we did our handshake.

As I was sitting in my office, reviewing some paperwork, Lily walked in, and I immediately knew something was wrong.

"Hey, babe. What's wrong?" I got up from my chair and wrapped my arms around her.

"The teacher I'm subbing for is returning to work on Monday. Her husband passed away sooner than they thought, and she said she needs to come back to teaching to take her mind off of it."

"Aw, babe, I'm sorry," I said as I held her tight.

"I mean, I can understand her needing to return, and I'm sorry her husband passed away, but I'm going to miss my students." She started to cry.

"I know you will. I know how much they mean to you." I kissed her head.

My heart broke for her. She loved her job and her students. I wanted to take away her sadness, but I didn't know what to do for her.

"You can work here at the bar."

She broke our embrace and looked at me.

"Thank you, but no. As much as I love you, I don't want to work for you. Anyway, Chris said that one of the teachers will be retiring at the end of the year, and when they move some other teachers around, there will be a position available, and she said it's mine. I'll focus on photography for a while."

"That's my girl." I smiled, brought her face closer to mine, and softly kissed her lips.

"You know, to make this place perfect, we have to have sex here."

"Is that so?" She smiled as she bit her bottom lip.

"My office is the perfect place to start, Miss Gilmore." I grinned as I slowly undid the buttons on her shirt, then pushed it off her shoulders.

"I agree, Mr. Matthews." Her smile grew wide as her fingers grabbed the bottom of my t-shirt and lifted it over my head.

Chapter Thirty-Four

LILY

Luke and I left the bar and returned to my apartment to change and prepare for the party. The whole staff was going to be there, along with all of Luke's family and friends. It would be a great night, and I wouldn't ruin it for Luke or me.

As much as I loved my students, maybe it was best that I focused on what I'd always wanted to do—photography. Walking into my apartment, with Luke following behind, I set my purse on the counter and grabbed a bottle of water from the refrigerator. Turning around, Luke put his hands on my hips and looked at me.

"Are you sure you're okay?"

"I'm fine, Luke." I smiled.

"I'm going to run next door and grab some fresh clothes. I'll be right back," he said, kissing me on the forehead and walking out the door.

I couldn't stop thinking about Giselle and what she must be going through right now. She told Gretchen and me that she didn't want us to go with her to the clinic because she and Lucky needed to do it alone. She told me that she'd call me when she had the chance. As I headed to my bedroom to change clothes, Luke opened the door and walked in.

"That was quick," I said as he followed me into the bedroom.

"I'm a guy. Give me a pair of jeans and a T-shirt, and I'll be happy. We're not like you women who spend hours deciding what you'll wear, how you'll do your makeup, and how you'll style your hair."

"I don't do that!" I exclaimed as I took a dress from my closet, looked at it, and then put it back. "Okay, guilty as charged." I smiled.

Walking over to my dresser, I looked at Luke as he dressed.

"I'm worried about Giselle. Have you heard from Lucky?"

"No, not yet," he replied, slipping his dark gray t-shirt over his head.

"What are your feelings about all this?"

Luke sat on the edge of the bed and watched me as I ran a brush through my hair. "I don't know what to think. I'm not happy about their decision, but it's their life, and they have to live with it. Who knows? Maybe fatherhood would have changed Lucky."

"Their relationship is weird. They're more friends with benefits than anything else," I said as I twisted my hair in a clip.

"Some people prefer their relationships that way. It's way less complicated."

"Are you saying our relationship is complicated?"

"Yes, our relationship is very complicated because I can't just have sex with you and leave. You plague my thoughts and my dreams when you're not around. So, that complicates things because when you're not with me, I feel like life has stopped until you're by my side again."

His words were like poetry to me, and they reached deep down to the very core of my soul. What he had just said made tears spring into my eyes. I couldn't speak a word because if I opened my mouth, I would lose it and cry like a blubbering idiot.

As Luke stood up from the edge of the bed and wrapped his arms around me, I took a deep breath and tried not to let the tears fall.

"I'm sorry, babe. I said too much, and if you respond, you'll cry, right?"

Once again, I nodded and closed my eyes.

"I love you, Lily."

"I love you, Luke."

"I hate seeing you sad. Don't worry about this teaching thing. Everything will work out, and I'll be by your side every step of the way."

The one thing I could always count on Luke for was that he always made me feel better, and suddenly, losing my job as Charley's teacher didn't seem so bad anymore.

∼

LUKE AND MADDIE were behind the bar, setting up the glasses, while Candi and I ensured the tables were set up.

"How many people are you expecting, Luke?" Candi shouted across the bar.

"About fifty or so."

"Who's watching Charley tonight?" I asked Maddie.

"She's spending the night at her girlfriend's house."

Maddie walked over and hugged me. "I'm really sorry to hear that Charley will have a new teacher on Monday. I haven't told her yet. She's going to be devastated."

"Thanks," I said as I looked down. "I'm going to miss those kids, but I'll still see Charley every day, and she's more than welcome to come over whenever she wants. Just send her down."

Maddie laughed as she placed her hand on my shoulder. "That's sweet of you, Lily, but I'll give you a call first in case you and my brother are busy."

"Ah, that's a good idea." I winked.

Looking over Maddie's shoulder, I saw Tom and Annie walk into the bar.

"Your mom and dad are here," I said to her.

"Great, keep them occupied for me." She smiled as she walked the opposite way.

Following behind them was another couple who walked over to Luke and hugged him. Luke looked over to where I stood and motioned for me to come over.

"Lily, I want you to meet my Aunt Rose and Uncle Matt."

"My, aren't you a sight for sore eyes," Aunt Rose said as she hugged me. "We've heard so much about you from Annie and Tom that we feel like we already know you."

"It's great to meet both of you." I smiled.

Rose was Annie's younger sister, and Matt was her husband. She was a cake decorator and owned a bakery in San Francisco, and he was a retired accountant who did the books for Rose's bakery. As we were talking, Gretchen and Sam walked in.

"Hey, bro." He smiled as he and Luke shook hands.

"Hi, Sam," I said as he hugged me.

"Have you heard from Giselle yet?" I asked Gretchen with concern.

"I texted her, and she said she's fine—she's…"

Before Gretchen could finish her sentence, Giselle and Lucky walked through the door. I put my hand on Luke's shoulder, and he turned around. The four of us stood there and stared at them.

"We're having a baby!" She smiled as she threw her hands in the air.

We stood there, unable to say anything. Luke spoke the first words.

"Awesome." He smiled as he hugged Giselle and high-fived Lucky.

Sam followed behind Luke and did the same as I smiled. Gretchen, Giselle, and I walked over and sat down at a table.

"I couldn't do it. I was lying down on the table with my feet in the stirrups. Lucky held my hand, and the doctor asked if I was ready. I told him I was, and then he went to check me, and I yelled, 'Stop.' I looked at Lucky and told him I couldn't do it, and he said, 'Please don't.' So, I sat up, got dressed, and we went out to lunch and talked about what we would do."

"And what are you going to do?" Gretchen asked as she grabbed Giselle's hand.

"Lucky and I are going to raise the baby together as friends, with some occasional sex thrown in." She smiled.

"Is he moving in?"

"No, we're not moving in together. We will keep our separate places fully furnished with everything the baby needs."

I leaned over and looped my arm around her neck. "If that's what the two of you want, I'm happy for you. I can't tell you how glad I am that you didn't do it."

"I know you are, Lily, and I gave a lot of thought to what you said about your birth mother. By the way, nobody better cancel on Tuesday because I want to hear all about it," she said as she pointed her finger at Gretchen and me.

I felt two strong hands clasp my shoulders. As I looked up, Luke bent down and kissed me. "Come on, babe. There are a few people I want you to meet."

After meeting all of Luke's family and friends, Luke walked over and got up on the stage. As he positioned himself in front of the microphone, he held up his beer and yelled, "Welcome to Luke's Bar and Grille!"

Everyone in the bar whistled and cheered as I stared at Luke's smiling face. As he looked at me and winked, I held up my beer and blew him a kiss. His happiness was the only thing that mattered to me, and I would do everything I could to make sure he stayed that way.

∼

THE NEXT COUPLE OF WEEKS, I barely saw Luke at all. He was at the bar from morning until night. I would have to go to the bar to visit him. When he came home, he would quietly slip into bed and wrap his arms around me. We'd have dinner at the bar every night, and he still tried convincing me to work there. He even went as far as to ask me if I would play the guitar and sing a few nights a week. I didn't have to say a word. He could tell my thoughts on it just by the look on my face.

As planned, I had Giselle and Gretchen over for dinner, and I told them everything about Mary. Charley cried almost every day at school because I was no longer her teacher. It had been a clusterfuck of a week, and certain emotions from my past were being stirred up. As I was sitting on the couch, feeling sorry for myself, a text message from Luke came through.

"Hey, babe. Why aren't you here yet?"

"I'm not coming to the bar tonight."

"Why not? What's wrong?"

"Nothing's wrong, Luke. I want to stay home."

"But I miss you, Lily."

"Yeah, I miss you too, but you don't seem to care about that."

As I sat there and stared at my message to him, I couldn't believe I had just said that. I didn't know what was happening to me, and I just wanted to be left alone. When he didn't respond, I threw my phone across the table. About twenty minutes later, the door opened. I turned around as Luke walked in, threw his keys on the counter, and stood before me.

"What the hell was that last text supposed to mean?"

I suppose I was looking for a fight because I jumped up without hesitation and got in his face.

"It means exactly what I said."

"What's the matter with you?" he asked as he softly grabbed my arm when I started to walk away. "Don't you dare walk away from me!"

I jerked my arm out of his grip. "Don't you dare tell me what to do!"

"Babe, please tell me what's going on with you because you're not acting like yourself right now."

"You want to know what's wrong? Fine. I'll tell you what's wrong. I never see much of you anymore, and when I do, it's always at the bar with everyone else. We barely eat together anymore, and we don't go out. You spend every damn fucking minute at that bar."

"Watch your mouth, Lily."

"Oh, and that's another thing. You don't get to tell me to watch my mouth because I can talk however I want. I'm an adult, and if I want to scream FUCK to the world, then I fucking will!"

"We talked about this before I bought the bar. That's why I discussed it with you first, and now you're behaving like this. Why, Lily? Are you trying to hurt me? You knew the first few months were going to be difficult."

"Yeah, but then the first few months turn into another few months, and then they turn into years. It's your passion, and that's all you'll ever do, and that's all you'll ever think about, Johnny!" I screamed.

The expression on his face nearly killed me. It was filled with pain, disgust, and anguish. As he walked to the door and placed his hand on the knob, he turned around and looked at me.

"I'm not your father, Lily."

He slammed the door behind him, and I stood there with my hand over my mouth as I dropped to my knees. I couldn't believe I called him "Johnny." As I closed my eyes, the memories of my mother and father fighting became more vivid. Brynn and I would sit on the stairs and hear them scream back and forth at each other. I remember my mother yelling at him about never being around and how he promised things would be better. I began to sob as I buried my face in my hands. I felt two arms wrap around me, and I heard Sam's voice telling me it would be okay. He helped me up from the floor and led me to the couch.

"Lily, please calm down."

"Sam, I said horrible things to him. I called him 'Johnny.' I'm more fucked up than I thought I was."

Chapter Thirty-Five

LUKE

As I hopped on my bike and sped out of the parking lot, I couldn't stop thinking about Lily's behavior and attitude towards me. She was irrational, and I was disturbed by her calling me her father. We'd had a long discussion about how many hours I'd be working at the bar the first few months, and she told me that she understood and that she'd be with me and support me through it all. As I pulled into the parking lot at the bar, I parked my bike on the side of the building and walked through the doors. I sighed as I stepped behind the bar and poured myself a cold beer.

"Where'd you run off to?" Maddie asked as she was making drinks.

"Lily's apartment."

"You didn't bring her back with you?"

"No. We got into a fight."

Maddie stopped what she was doing and looked at me. "About what?"

"The bar and how she's sick of not seeing me and spending time with her," I said as I slammed the glass down on the counter and looked at her. "See, this is what I don't get. We spend time together, and we see each other every day. She comes here, and when I leave, I go home to her place and spend every night with her."

"You have to realize that things for Lily have significantly changed over the past couple of weeks. She lost her teaching job, and her boyfriend, who spent every waking minute with her, became a bar owner. She barely sees you anymore. That's a lot to take in at the same time."

"She called me 'Johnny,'" I said.

"What? Why did she do that?" Maddie asked in confusion.

"I don't know. She said this will consume me because it's my passion and dream."

As I looked down, Maddie placed her hand on mine.

"It sounds like she's having flashbacks of her father and how he was never around. Didn't she say that her ex-fiancé was never around and started spending less time with her?"

I nodded and clenched my jaw. "You're right. Now things are starting to make sense."

"You need to talk to her, Luke. I love you both and don't want to see your relationship go in the toilet because of a misunderstanding."

"I'm going to talk to her, don't worry. I'll be leaving after I finish the budget. I want to give her time to cool down."

Pulling my phone from my pocket, I swiped the screen and saw I had a text message from Sam.

"I just left Lily's, and she's a mess, man. I know it's none of my business, but I'm not sure if I've ever seen a girl like that. She's pretty messed up, and if you love her, you'll get your ass back there."

"Thanks for being there for her. I'm heading over there now."

I looked at my watch and walked to my office. I shut down the computer and stacked the paperwork into a neat pile for tomorrow. I wandered over to Maddie before leaving the bar.

"Starting tomorrow, I want you out of here by five p.m. You've been here late, and I appreciate it, but it's not fair to Charley. I know it's only temporary, but things are returning to normal. We need to sit down tomorrow and have a meeting, so head here right after dropping Charley off at school," I said as I kissed her cheek.

I didn't see her when I opened the door to Lily's apartment and stepped inside. I walked down the hall, stopped in her bedroom doorway, and stared at her lying on the bed curled up. My heart broke seeing her like that. She must have heard me because she rolled over and tried to open her swollen eyes. As I walked over and sat on the edge of the bed, I pushed her hair behind her ear and leaned over, kissing her teary eye and moist cheek. She raised her arm and looped it around my neck, bringing me closer as I buried my face deep into her.

"I'm so sorry for everything I said." She began to cry.

"I'm sorry for not being here when you needed me, Lily."

We lay there briefly in silence before I pulled back and looked at her. Her eyes were swollen and red. She grabbed my hand as I got up from the bed, and I told her I'd be right back. I walked to the bathroom and grabbed a washcloth from under the sink. I ran the cloth under warm water and folded it as I walked back to the bedroom. Gently wiping her face, the corners of her mouth curved up, forming a small smile.

"That's what I like to see." I smiled back.

She sat up with her back against the headboard. I put the washcloth on the nightstand and took both of her hands in mine, interlacing our fingers.

"We need to talk, babe. You need to tell me your feelings, where that last argument came from, and why you called me your father's name. Because if we don't, it'll happen again, and that's not good for our relationship."

"I know," she replied.

"Are you hungry?" I asked her as I was starving.

"Yeah. I haven't eaten all day."

"How about Chinese food? I'll call and have it delivered, and we can sit on the couch, eat it, and talk."

"I love that idea." She smiled as she placed her soft hand on my cheek.

I brought her hand to my mouth and kissed her palm before picking up my phone and calling in our dinner order. Lily got up from the bed and grabbed a pair of yoga pants and a tank top from her drawer. She changed her clothes and put her hair up in a ponytail.

"Ugh, look at my face!" she exclaimed as she wiped her eyes.

Wrapping my arms around her, I spoke, "You have a beautiful face, tear-stained and all."

She smiled and wrinkled her nose as she turned around and kissed me. While I grabbed the bottle of wine and a couple of glasses, Lily took down two plates from the cabinet and got out the silverware. Not too long after calling in the order, there was a knock at the door. As the delivery boy handed me the brown bag, I reached into my pocket and took out some cash. Lily walked over, took the bag from my hands, and sat on the couch.

"I'm going to call a therapist tomorrow morning and schedule an appointment," Lily said as she took the Chinese food cartons out of the bag.

"Do you really think you need to?"

"Yeah. It's something I should've done a long time ago. When I yelled at you earlier, I felt like I was reliving my childhood and watching my mom and dad having the same argument. Mary would scream at him because he was never around, and he kept telling her that it was part of the business and that things would get better. But instead of getting better, they got worse. He would be gone for months on tour, which was understandable, but when he'd get back to Seattle, he wouldn't come home for a few days."

I set my plate down on the table, reached over, and hugged her. "I'm sorry you had to grow up like that."

"I felt abandoned, Luke, and then I felt it again after the church incident with Brynn and Hunter. All those emotions and feelings were coming back to me these past two weeks when you were so busy at the bar, and we weren't spending as much time together. That's an issue that needs to be addressed, and I think a therapist can help me."

"I love you, Lily. I don't know how to make that any clearer to you."

"I know you do, baby. Believe me. It's not you. I'm the one who has these issues, compliments of Johnny and Mary Gilmore, and

I'm the one who needs to take care of them. I know you love me; I really do. It's just that this change over the past couple of weeks has really messed with my head."

"Then you do what you must to free yourself of your past. I'll be here for you every step of the way." I smiled as I brushed my hand over her cheek and kissed her.

Chapter Thirty-Six

LILY

After having the best sex of my life last night, I rolled over and ran my tongue along Luke's shoulder. I was extremely sore, but it was worth it.

"Good morning, babe. What time is it?"

"It's seven o'clock. Don't you have to meet Maddie at the bar?"

"Yeah, but I can be late. Just let me send her a text."

After texting Maddie, he set his phone on the nightstand and pulled me into him.

"Ouch," I said as I scooted closer.

"What's wrong?" he asked.

"I'm just a little sore down there, that's all."

"God, after what we did last night, I believe you are. I'm sorry, babe. What can I do to make it feel better?"

I smiled as I lifted my head and kissed his lips. "There's nothing you can do. It'll feel better in a few days."

"Umm, I don't think I can go a few days without having sex with you."

I rolled my eyes as I struggled to get out of bed. "You're such a guy." I smiled.

Luke chuckled as he followed me into the bathroom. I started the shower, turned around, and noticed as he removed his boxers.

"What are you doing?" I asked.

"Taking a shower with you like I always do," he replied with a confused look.

"That could pose a problem since we can't have sex."

"Don't worry, babe. I can control myself. Let's get in, wash up, and get out."

"All right, but you better behave yourself."

Luke smirked as we stepped into the shower. I closed my eyes and let the stream of hot water run down my hair and body. When I opened my eyes, I saw Luke staring at me. My eyes glanced down and noticed his hard cock. I looked at him and cocked my head.

"I can't help it, Lily. This is what you do to me. I tried to stop it, but you're standing there, naked, with the water running down that hot body of yours. What do you expect?"

I couldn't help but burst into laughter as he stood there, naked and hard, trying to defend himself. I reached my hand over and took hold of him, stroking his entire length as his erection pressed against my palm. Taking my thumb, I skillfully circled his smooth head as I reached under and deftly stroked his balls with my other hand. A loud groan escaped the back of his throat as he threw his head back.

"Just stand there and enjoy it. This is about you, Luke."

"Babe, I need to touch you," he moaned as he grabbed both of my breasts and began rubbing them.

"You can have my tits, but nothing else." I smiled as I got down on my knees and took his length in my mouth while the hot water beat down on us.

As I sucked up and down his shaft, his moans became louder. Keeping my fingers wrapped around his base, my tongue licked its way up to his head, circling the wet, smooth area before my lips wrapped themselves around the tip, sending him into a near convulsion.

"I'm going to come any second, babe," he moaned as he thrust his hips back and forth.

I continued to fist his base as I gave his cock one hard suck, feeling and tasting his salty liquid exploding in my mouth. He pressed both hands against the shower wall as he let out one last moan and gave me every last drop he had. I looked up at him and smiled as he took my hand and helped me up. He pulled me against him as his mouth smashed with mine. His kiss was strong and forceful, letting me know he was grateful.

"God, babe, you're amazing."

"I know." I smiled.

He chuckled, and we finished our shower. He dressed, kissed me goodbye, and flew out the door. As I put on my make-up in the bathroom, my phone rang. I grabbed it off the shelf, only to see that my mother was calling.

"Hi, Mom," I answered.

"Hi, Lily. I'm sure you know that tomorrow is your sister's birthday, and I was hoping you could call her."

I sighed, as we'd been over this a thousand times. "Mom, I don't know if I'll ever be able to forgive Brynn for what she did. Listen, I don't have time to discuss this right now. I've got a lot of things to do, and I'm already running late. I'll talk to you later," I said as I ended the call.

I finally finished getting ready, so I decided to call Giselle.

"Hello," she answered sleepily.

"Hey, did I wake you?"

"No, I've just been dozing on and off. I've spent half the morning puking."

"Would you mind some company? I need to talk to you about something."

"Sure, come on over. I don't have anything going on today."

"I'm on my way," I said as I hung up.

∽

"Come on in, girl." Giselle smiled as she opened the door.

I reached over and hugged her. She stood there in her white

satin robe. Her long brown, ordinarily perfect hair was pulled back into a messy ponytail.

"You look like you're not doing too well."

"I'm not. I have severe morning sickness."

"I brought some bagels. I thought the baby might like one."

"Ugh, this kid doesn't like anything," she said as she sat on the couch and hugged the pillow.

"Have you tried crackers?"

"Yes, and they don't work either. I throw up for four hours, and then it stops."

"Your morning sickness will go away soon."

"Not soon enough." She pouted. "Anyway, what did you want to talk about?"

"Do you know the name of a good therapist around here?"

Giselle cocked her head and pushed out her bottom lip as she looked at me. "You're seeking therapy, sweetie?"

"Luke and I got into a huge fight yesterday over him not being around as much since he took ownership of the bar. It was my entire fault, and I called him 'Johnny.'"

Her eyes widened as she reached over and grabbed my hand. "Why on earth would you call him 'Johnny'?"

"Because at that moment, I was having flashbacks of my parents and the things my dad used to say. Music was his life and his world. It was his passion, and he put every waking moment into it. Suddenly, I saw that in Luke with the bar, and I freaked out, especially since Hunter never had time for me."

She sighed. "You need therapy!"

"I know I do. Now give me a name because I know in your industry, ninety percent of the models are in therapy."

Giselle laughed as she got up from the couch and grabbed her cell phone. As she scrolled through it, she asked me if I wanted a male or female therapist. I looked at her with a twisted face because it didn't matter. I wanted the therapist who was the best.

"I would call Dr. Evelyn Blakely," she said. "Marissa sees her, and she said she's a godsend, so I'm taking that to mean she's good."

As I took my phone from my purse, I noticed a text message from Luke.

"I just wanted you to know that I can't stop thinking about your beautiful, talented mouth, and it's distracting me from my work."

I smiled as I quickly responded.

"Good, that was the plan, baby."

"Are you going to be coming to the bar?"

"Yeah, I'll be there later. I have a few things that I need to do first."

"See you later, Lily. I love you."

"I love you too."

I tapped the contact button and asked Giselle for the number for Dr. Blakely. She rattled it off, sprang from the couch, and ran to the bathroom.

I dialed the number and waited for someone to answer.

"Dr. Blakely's office, Janelle speaking. How may I assist you?"

"I would like to schedule an appointment to see Dr. Blakely, please."

"Are you a new patient?"

"Yes."

"I know this is short notice, but can you be here in thirty minutes? I just had someone cancel about an hour ago."

"Wow. Yeah, I can be there in thirty minutes," I said.

"Your name, please."

"Lily Gilmore," I replied.

Giselle emerged from the bathroom and sat down next to me. "I swear this kid is going to kill me."

"Aw, don't say things like that." I smiled as I placed my hand on her flat stomach. "Anyway, I have to go. Dr. Blakely's office told me to be there in thirty minutes."

"Wow! Who gets into therapy that fast?"

"They just had a cancellation."

"See, it was meant to be." Giselle smiled as she got up and walked me to the door.

I parked the Explorer in the Santa Monica Sunset Medical Center parking garage. Upon entering the building, I took notice of the large saltwater fish tank in the middle of the lobby. I looked to my right at the directory and found Dr. Blakely's suite number. I suddenly became nervous when I entered the elevator and took it up to the fourth floor because I had to relive my past for Dr. Blakely to try and help me. I took the long hallway to Suite 413 as the elevator doors opened.

As I walked through the door, I was greeted by a petite brunette who handed me a clipboard with paperwork and asked me to complete it. Sitting down, I filled out the papers and returned them to the desk. Shortly after that, the petite brunette called my name and walked me into Dr. Blakely's office.

Dr. Blakely emerged from behind her desk, walked over to me, and extended her hand.

"You must be Lily Gilmore. It's a pleasure to meet you." She smiled.

I politely shook her hand and told her it was lovely to meet her. She asked me to sit on the beige leather couch as she offered me coffee or water. I opted for coffee as she walked over to where her coffee pot sat and poured me a cup. Looking around her meticulous office, I couldn't help but notice the burning of incense. I asked Dr. Blakely what the scent was. She told me it was sandalwood and burned it to help her patients relax. She sat in the oversized beige chair next to the couch as she handed me my cup of coffee.

"Why don't we start by you telling me why you feel like you need therapy?"

I looked down as I traced the rim of the coffee cup with my finger.

"For the first time in my life, I've met someone I truly love, and I can't let the effects of my past ruin it. I realized that last night when we argued, and I called him by my father's name."

Dr. Blakeley listened intently as she nodded and wrote things down on her notepad. I went on to tell her about Johnny and my childhood. Before I knew it, our time was up.

"I would like to see you at least two times a week to start if that's alright with you," she said.

"Yes, that would be fine."

"Take care, and I'll see you in a couple of days," she said, putting her hand on my shoulder.

Walking out of her office and heading towards the parking garage, I pulled out my phone and saw that I had a missed call from Luke. I quickly dialed him.

"Hey, babe."

"Sorry, I missed your call. I was in an appointment with Dr. Blakely."

"Who's Dr. Blakely?"

"A therapist."

"You got in that fast?"

"Yeah, they had a cancellation. I'll tell you about it later."

"Are you coming to the bar now? There's something I want to show you."

"Yep, I'm on my way now," I said as I climbed into the Explorer and shut the door.

"Good. I'll be waiting, babe. Park around the back. I love you."

"I love you more." I smiled as I quickly ended the call before he could say anything.

~

I PULLED into the back lot of the bar like Luke had asked, and he was standing there waiting for me. As I parked the Explorer, he walked over and opened my door. Leaning in with a smile, he brushed his lips against mine.

"I've been waiting to do that since this morning," he said.

Climbing out of the truck, Luke bent down and picked me up.

"What are you doing?" I laughed.

"Close your eyes. Make sure they're closed tight because I don't want you peeking."

"Luke, what's going on?"

"I want to show you something. Just do as I say and keep your eyes closed."

He carried me through the parking lot while I closed my eyes. He stopped, put me down, and told me to open my eyes. When I opened them, they darted to the new bar sign, 'Luke's Bar & Grille.' I covered my mouth in excitement as I stared at the artistry that officially made this Luke's bar.

"It's perfect, Luke!" I squealed as I threw my arms around him.

"They put it up this morning. Do you know how awesome it is to see my name on that sign? I've dreamt of this for so long, Lily, and it finally happened."

"I know, baby, and I'm so happy for you," I said as a damn tear rolled down my cheek.

"Babe, don't." He wiped it away with his thumb.

"It's a tear of happiness. I love you so much," I whispered as I hugged him tight.

"I love you more." He smiled. "Come on. Let's have some lunch. Are you hungry?"

"I'm starving."

As Luke walked to the back, I sat at the bar where Maddie was putting glasses away.

"Hi, Lily."

"Hi, Maddie. How are you?"

"I'm good. I'm glad to see you here today."

I gave her a strange look, and then it dawned on me that Luke must have told her about last night.

"I'm assuming Luke told you about our argument."

"Yeah. He was so upset last night when he walked in here."

"I know, and I feel awful about that, but we're good, and I'm seeking help to deal with my past."

"You have no idea how proud of you I am. You're an amazing person, and Luke deeply loves you."

I smiled at her as Luke came up behind me. "What do you want to eat, babe?" he asked.

"I'll just have a burger. You know how I like it."

"Yes. I do," he growled, leaning in and kissing my neck.

"Okay, that's enough!" Maddie smirked.

I got up from the bar and sat down at a table. I pulled my phone from my purse, and there was a text message from Brynn. My heart started racing, and a sick feeling emerged in the pit of my stomach.

"Lily, please don't be mad. I went through Mom's phone and got your number. I really need to see you or, at the very least, talk to you."

As I threw my phone on the table and sighed, Luke walked over with our burgers. He set the plate down and took the seat across from me.

"What's wrong, Lily? You have that look."

I picked up my phone and handed it to him. He looked at me as he set my phone down on the table.

"Don't let that upset you," he said.

"How can I not?!"

"I hate to say this, Lily, and I know your therapist will tell you the same thing, but you need to talk to Brynn to let go and get closure. I told you the same thing about your mom, and look how that turned out. The two of you are speaking again and trying to put the past behind you."

I took a bite of my burger. "OMG, this burger is amazing! Why is this burger so amazing?!"

Luke threw his head back and laughed. "I hired a new chef yesterday, and he uses some secret ingredient. It's so secret that he won't even tell me what it is. I'll be sure to tell him that you love his burgers."

Once I got over how amazing the burger was, I went back to the subject of Brynn.

"I can't believe you would suggest I talk to her after what she did. Have you forgotten that she carried on a relationship with my fiancé and then fucked him in the church on my wedding day?!"

"No, babe. I haven't forgotten that. But maybe you need to hear why she did it. You're carrying an awful lot of anger around with you about Brynn and Hunter, and maybe it's time you hear her out and let it all go. Besides, look at where you are right now. Just think. If you hadn't found them in the church, you'd be living your dream life with a big real estate agent in a big house with a white picket fence, pretending that everything was great, and I'd be sitting in my apartment, all alone and feeling sorry for myself. It's called fate, Lily. You were meant to find out about them that day."

A part of me knew he was right. Luke was always right, and it drove me up the wall. I got up from my chair and sat on his lap. He wrapped his arms around me and buried his face into my neck.

"You're right, Luke. It's time to let go," I said as I kissed him.

"Do you think you two could either get a room somewhere or lock yourselves in the office?" Maddie said as she walked over to us.

"Go away, or you're fired," Luke mumbled.

Suddenly, we heard a crash. Luke looked up as Maddie dropped a glass on the floor and stared straight ahead towards the door. I got up from Luke's lap and looked over to where she was looking at someone standing in the doorway.

"Who's that?"

"It's Adam, that motherfucker!" Luke said as he quickly got up and started walking over to him.

Chapter Thirty-Seven

LUKE

Lily grabbed my arm to prevent me from kicking Adam's ass out of my bar.

"Don't, Luke. Please. Think of Charley," she said as she tried to pull me back.

As I approached Adam, he put his hands up.

"Hey, Luke. I'm not here to cause any trouble. I just want to talk to Maddie."

"Well, she doesn't want to talk to you!" I spat.

"Why don't you let her decide that for herself," he said as Maddie walked over.

"Luke, pull back," Maddie said as she looked at me.

"Maddie, you can't be serious!"

As Lily pulled me over to the side, Maddie and Adam sat at a table.

"Luke, take your own advice!" Lily said between gritted teeth.

"What are you talking about, Lily?"

"We just had a conversation about letting things go and moving forward. You told me that I need to talk to Brynn. Well, maybe it's time you talk to Adam."

"It's different. There's a little girl involved here."

"I understand that, but he's her father, and you at least owe it to Charley to listen to what he has to say."

I rolled my eyes and turned away from her. She was throwing my advice back in my face. She wrapped her arms around my waist and asked me to please stay calm for her. I sighed, turned around, and kissed her forehead. I grabbed her hand and led her to Maddie and Adam's table.

"Hi, Adam. I'm Lily Gilmore, Luke's girlfriend. It's nice to meet you," she said as she extended her hand to him.

"Hi, Lily. It's nice to meet you." He smiled as he shook her hand.

Seeing him touch Lily made me sick, and I wanted to fucking punch him right then and there. But I promised I would stay calm for Lily's sake.

"Would you explain why you just showed up here without calling?" I asked as I folded my arms and leaned back in the chair.

"Before I answer that, I want to congratulate you on the bar. I was shocked when I walked up and saw the sign."

I didn't say a word to him. I just sat there and stared him down as he continued to speak.

"I'm a changed man—"

"The fuck you are!" I exclaimed.

Lily looked over at me and gave me a dirty look. "Watch your mouth," she said with a severe tone.

"I'm clean and have been for over a year. I don't drink, I don't do drugs, and I've quit smoking cigarettes. If you don't believe me, then I can do a drug test for you."

"Why this sudden change of character?" I asked.

"Because I hit rock bottom and almost died. I guess you could say I had an epiphany because when I woke up in that hospital bed, alone and scared, I knew I couldn't live my life like that anymore. So, I checked myself into one of the best rehab programs in the country, and they helped me."

"Then why the hell didn't you come to see your daughter as you promised her you would? Do you know how you broke that little girl's heart?"

Adam sighed and looked at Maddie. "The reason I couldn't visit was that I'm a sponsor, and the person I'm sponsoring, who had been clean for six months, decided to shoot himself up with heroin the night before I was supposed to leave. I had an obligation to be there for him and help him."

I got out of my seat and slammed my fists on the table. "You have an obligation to your daughter!" I yelled.

Lily grabbed my arm. "Luke, that's enough!"

As I took in a deep breath, I sat down. I was angry that he would put a drug addict before his daughter, and I wanted to kill him.

"I understand you being angry, Luke. Trust me, I do. After waking up in that hospital and realizing that I had almost died, the only two people I could think about were Maddie and Charley, and how I was given a second chance."

"Wow," Lily said.

I looked at her and rolled my eyes as she smacked me on the arm. "Stop it!" she spat.

"You're full of shit, Adam, and I don't believe one word of what you're saying. You've done way too much damage, and you left a trail of tears and scars with Maddie and Charley, and I will not let you walk back into their normal lives and fuck everything up!"

Suddenly, I heard a small voice from across the bar. "Daddy?" Charley said as she stood a few feet away from Adam.

"There's my baby girl." He smiled as he stood up and held his arms out to her.

Charley ran to him and threw her arms around him as he picked her up and swung her around.

"Let me look at you," he said as he put her down. "You're beautiful, and you're so grown up," he said as he hugged her.

"Daddy, what are you doing here?" she asked.

"I came to see you and Mommy."

I looked at Maddie as she took in the moment between her daughter and her father. I shook my head because I knew by the look on her face that she believed him and she was going to let him back into their lives.

"Can I talk to you for a minute, Maddie?" I asked as I took hold of her arm and led her to the back room.

"I know what you're going to say, Luke, but a part of me believes him."

"Damn it, Maddie! I knew this was going to happen."

Maddie pointed her finger in my face. "Listen to me. I owe it to Charley to give her father a chance."

"You can't relate, Luke, because you grew up with a mother and father who loved each other and were there for you and Maddie," Lily said as she walked up behind me. "Let's go out to dinner tonight and have some general conversation. Maybe you'll be able to see things differently."

"That's a great idea, Lily." Maddie smiled.

"What do you say, Luke?" Lily asked me as she wrapped her arms around my waist.

"Whatever. I have to go. I have work to do," I said as I stormed off and went to my office.

Chapter Thirty-Eight

LILY

I could see the anger in his eyes as he stormed off into his office. Maddie looked over at me with tears in her eyes.

"He's so angry and has so much hatred for Adam that I don't think he'll ever accept him."

As I hugged her, I told her I would talk to him. We walked back to the table where Adam was talking to Charley. Maddie excused herself as she pulled out her phone to make a call. When she returned to the table, she told Charley to get her things ready because Mrs. Clements was coming to pick her up, take her to dance class, and then go home with her so she could play with Allie for a while. Charley whined, and she said that she didn't want to go.

"You have to go to dance class if you're going to dance for me," Adam told her.

"But I want to stay with you," she whined.

"I want you to stay too, but dance class is more important. So, I'll tell you what. You go to dance class, and tomorrow, when you get home from school, I'll take you and your mom out somewhere really fun."

Charley's eyes lit up as she looked over at Maddie. "Can we, Mom?"

Maddie smiled and patted her head. "Yeah, that sounds great," she said as she looked at Adam.

Charley hugged and kissed Adam goodbye as Maddie took her outside to wait for Mrs. Clements. I looked Adam over as he watched Maddie and Charley leave the bar. As much as I hated to admit it, he was hot. He stood over six feet tall with a nice build, and he wore his light brown hair short. I saw a lot of him in Charley, especially in their bluish-green eyes.

Adam turned and looked at me. "Regardless of what everyone tells you, I love that little girl more than anything in this world, and I came back here to make things right with her."

"Listen, Adam. I don't know you, and I'm not judging you. But you have a track record and a history. I came from a father that was somewhat like you, and he fucked me up, and now I'm in therapy because of him. So, I want to let you know that I love that little girl too, and I won't stand by and let you ruin her if you decide to return to your old life."

Luke came walking up behind me just as I finished my sentence. "Are you ready to go?" he asked me.

"Yes. Adam, we'll see you later for dinner. Maddie will fill you in on the details."

He looked down and nodded his head. "Thanks, Lily. Luke. I'll see you both later."

Luke shot him a look and put his arm around me as we walked out of the bar.

"I heard what you said to him."

"Okay. And?"

"Nothing. I just thought you were pretty badass." He smiled as he brushed his lips against mine.

As I climbed into the Explorer, Luke got on his bike, and we headed home.

"You better be nice at dinner," I said to Luke as he was in the shower and I was touching up my makeup.

"I can't make any promises when it comes to that douchebag."

"Luke, I swear, I'll be so mad at you if you don't let him talk and explain everything."

"What's to explain, Lily? He's a drunk, a drug addict, and a thief. He'll always be those things to me."

"Wow, I never took you for the grudge type."

"Only with him, babe."

I took the towel Luke had waiting for him off the counter and hid the one on the towel rack. As he turned off the shower, I stepped out of the bathroom. "What the hell," I heard him say as he opened the shower curtain.

"Lily, where's the towel I had sitting on the counter?"

As Luke stood there dripping wet, I stopped in the bathroom doorway and held up the towel.

"Do you mean this one?"

He cocked his head and furrowed his brows. "Yes. That one," he said as he held out his hand.

"Sorry, but you're not getting this towel until you promise me that you'll give Adam a chance."

"Damn it, Lily. Give me the towel," he said with irritation.

"No. Not until you promise me."

"Come on. It's cold standing here."

My eyes wandered down to his flaccid cock. "Yeah, I can tell." I smiled.

"That's it!" he exclaimed as he stepped out of the tub and started coming towards me.

"Oh shit!" I ran down the hall and out the apartment door, knowing he wouldn't open it.

Sam was coming out of his apartment. "What's going on, Lily?" he asked as he stopped.

"Oh, nothing. How are you?"

Sam gave me a strange look, and he said he was good. Just as he was about to ask me why I was standing in the hallway with a towel in my hand, my apartment door opened, and Luke grabbed me from behind, pulling me into the apartment and shutting the door.

"Now you're in trouble, babe," he said, taking me to the bedroom and throwing me on the bed.

He was in a pair of sweatshorts and no shirt. His hair was dripping wet, and he looked as sexy as hell. He pinned me on the bed, climbed on top, and sat on my legs so I couldn't move. He took both my hands and brought them over my head as he tightly held my wrists.

"Tell me how much you love me." He smiled.

"No," I said as I tried to wiggle myself free.

"What do you mean, no?" he asked as he leaned down and smashed his lips against mine.

His kiss was rough as I parted my lips, and his tongue slipped into my mouth. He stopped and looked at me.

"Tell me how much you love me."

"Let go of my wrists, and I will." I smiled.

As he let go of my wrists, I brought my hand to his face and stared into his beautiful brown eyes.

"I love more than anything and anyone in this entire world."

"I promise you, Lily. I'll be nice tonight and won't get out of line." He smiled.

I wrapped my arms around him, pulled his body on mine, and whispered in his ear, "Thank you, baby."

∽

We met Maddie and Adam at a restaurant called The Falcon's Landing. As the hostess led us to the table where they sat, Luke tightened his grip on my hand when he saw Maddie laughing.

"You promised," I whispered.

"I didn't do anything," he said as he looked at me.

We arrived at the table and took our seats. I was amazed that Luke shook Adam's hand. Maddie glanced at me and smiled.

"Adam is moving to Los Angeles and attending UCLA," she announced.

I looked over at Luke and saw his jaw tightened. I squeezed his thigh under the table, and he loosened it.

"That's great, Adam. What are you studying?" I asked.

"Drug abuse and alcohol counseling."

"You want to counsel drug addicts?" Luke asked.

"Yes, I do. I already have a year of classes under my belt, and they've all transferred to UCLA. I'm starting over, man. I'm walking away from my past, and I'm stepping into a brand new life— a life that includes my daughter and Maddie."

"Where are you living?" Luke asked him calmly.

"I've rented an apartment by UCLA. That way, I can be close to Charley and the campus."

"I'm sorry, man, but I have to ask this. How the hell are you affording all this?" Luke asked.

"I've been working as a computer tech the past year, and the owner was paying me under the table. He warned me that if he caught me using drugs, he would report me to the state. He did a drug test on me once a week. I saved every dime I made to go to school and make something of my life."

"You always were a genius with computers." Luke laughed.

At that moment, Luke realized maybe Adam was telling the truth, and we had a great dinner and a good conversation.

As we left the restaurant, Adam touched Maddie's back. Luke glanced at me, and I squeezed his hand. We hugged and said our goodbyes, and Luke and I climbed into his Jeep.

"They have a chance at being a real family," I said.

"I guess." Luke sighed as he pulled out of the parking lot.

As we were on our way home, my phone rang. I pulled it from my purse and saw it was Giselle calling.

"Hey, girl. What's up?" I answered and put her on speaker.

She was sobbing so hard that I could barely understand her. She said something about an accident. Suddenly, Lucky's voice came through the speaker.

"Lily, it's Lucky. Are you with Luke? I tried calling him, but it went straight to voicemail."

"I'm right here, Lucky. What's going on?" Luke asked.

"Gretchen and Sam were in a car accident. They were rushed to Cedars."

I started shaking, and instantly, I felt sick.

"Lucky, how bad is it?" Luke asked as he quickly turned the Jeep around and headed toward the hospital.

"I don't know, man. The hospital called Giselle and said there had been an accident and to get there immediately. I'm freaking out, Luke. What if—"

"Stop it, Lucky. They'll be fine. We're on our way."

With shaking hands, I ended the call. Luke reached over, grabbed my hand, and brought it to his lips.

"They're fine, babe. I know they are."

Chapter Thirty-Nine

LILY

Luke pulled into the medical center parking garage and quickly found a parking spot. As we climbed out of the Jeep, he grabbed my hand, and we ran to the emergency room entrance. When we approached the reception desk, Giselle ran up to me, crying.

"Lily, they won't tell me anything," she sobbed.

"Giselle, you have to calm down. Think of the baby," I said as I tried to console her.

Suddenly, Sam came walking through the automatic double doors. He had a white bandage on his forehead, cuts on his face, and his hand was wrapped.

"Sam, are you okay?" I asked.

"How's Gretchen?" Giselle cried.

"I don't know. She's still in surgery."

Luke hugged him, and Lucky grabbed hold of Giselle and made her sit in the chair.

I looked at Sam because I needed to be strong, not only for Gretchen but also for him.

"Sam, what happened?" I asked.

"I'll tell you as soon as we get upstairs to the surgical waiting room."

"Did anyone call Gretchen's parents?" I asked.

"I did," Lucky said. "They're on their way."

Lucky helped Giselle up, and we all rode the elevator to the third floor, where the surgical waiting room was. It was quiet, and we were the only people in there. I sat down next to Giselle and offered her some water. She wouldn't take it as she continued crying on Lucky's shoulder. I walked over to the coffee machine and put in some change. I pressed the button, and nothing. The damn thing was broken. I pounded on the machine as I pressed my forehead against it and started crying. Suddenly, I felt Luke's arms from behind.

"Babe," he whispered, laying his head on my back.

"All I wanted was a cup of coffee," I sobbed.

Luke turned me around and took my face in his hands. "I can get you a cup of coffee." He smiled as he wiped away my tears.

I was scared that Gretchen wouldn't make it, and I felt like I was on the verge of a breakdown. When Luke went to get me a cup of coffee, I walked over and sat next to Sam. He looked at me with tears in his eyes.

"She's going to be okay," I said, grabbing his hand.

"She has to be okay, Lily. If she dies, I don't know—"

"Don't talk like that. Nobody is dying here. She's a strong person, and she'll pull through."

Just as Luke returned and handed me a cup of coffee, a doctor in blue scrubs followed behind him.

"Are you all here for Gretchen Williams?" he asked.

Giselle jumped up from her chair. "Yes. I'm her twin sister."

"Gretchen is going to be fine."

We all sighed in relief as he continued telling us about Gretchen's condition.

"She had some internal bleeding we had to repair, and we also had to remove her spleen. Her right leg is broken in four places, and we had to put in some pins and screws. She'll be in a cast for several weeks while the bones heal, and when the cast comes off, she'll have to go through physical therapy."

"When can we see her?" I asked.

"I can take you to her now, but I want you to be prepared. She's very swollen, and she's hooked up to some machines. We're keeping her comfortable on pain medication, and she hasn't woken up from the surgery yet."

Luke put his arm around me, and we followed the doctor to Gretchen's room. Giselle ran to her and started sobbing. Lucky walked over and tried to calm her down. I instantly felt sick to my stomach when I saw her lying there. I barely recognized her since her face was so swollen.

"Are you okay, Lily?" Luke asked me.

"I'm fine. Are you?"

"Yeah. I'm just glad they're here with us."

"I know this must be bringing back a lot of memories for you," I said, bringing his hand up to my lips.

"It is. But it's cool. I'm just thankful Gretchen's okay."

We walked over and stood at the end of the bed. Sam pulled up a chair, grabbed her hand, and brought it to his lips.

"Please, sweetheart. Please wake up," he pleaded.

It broke my heart to see Sam like that. A few moments later, Gretchen squeezed Sam's hand, and she slowly opened her eyes. Lucky had to hold Giselle back from throwing herself on top of her.

"Let her wake up and focus, Giselle," he said.

Gretchen tried to talk but could only mumble a few words.

"Don't try and talk, sweetheart. You're going to be fine. Just get some rest," Sam said.

She took her other hand and laid it on Giselle's arm as she mumbled, "Stop crying. I have a headache."

As we all laughed, Sam leaned over, gently kissed her lips, and told her how much he loved her. I took a few steps back and looked around the room at the people I called my family. Looking at Sam, I remembered the first time I met him and how he held the door open as I brought in my boxes. Then I glanced at the twins, remembering the day they moved next door and how we instantly became best friends. As I looked at Lucky, I was remembering the night we met. I couldn't help but smile at how he tried to flirt with me, thinking he would get lucky.

"You okay, babe? You look like you're in deep thought." A slight grin graced Luke's face.

As my eyes stared into his, I remembered the first time he told me to watch my mouth, and I knew at that moment he was the one I needed to complete my life.

"I'm wonderful." I smiled as I reached up and softly brushed his lips against mine.

Thank you for reading Love In Between. I hope you enjoyed it!

Luke's and Lily's story continues in book two, The Upside of Love.

DOWNLOAD HERE

I invite you to join my Sandi's Romance Readers Facebook Group, where we talk about books, romance, and more! Join the fun!

Newsletter
Website
Facebook
Instagram
TikTok
Bookbub
FOLLOW ME ON AMAZON

The Upside of Love

LOVE SERIES, BOOK TWO

The Upside of Love

(Love Series, Book Two)

New York Times, USA Today & Wall Street Journal Bestselling Author
SANDI LYNN

Mission Statement

Sandi Lynn Romance

Providing readers with romance novels that will whisk them away to another world and from the daily grind of life – one book at a time.

Chapter One

LILY

"Have I told you how much I love you, Luke Matthews?" I asked as I ran my hand across his chest.

"You have, babe, and I don't ever want you to stop telling me."

I lifted my head from his chest and kissed his lips – the lips that devoured every inch of my skin last night from head to toe. The lips that made me warm when I was cold and the lips that gave me the security I desperately needed.

It had been two months since Sam's and Gretchen's accident. Gretchen's leg was healing nicely, and Sam waited on her hand and foot, practically never leaving her side. Luke moved into my apartment since Sam moved Gretchen into his. Lucky was staying with Giselle at her place because his apartment building had a flood and was being renovated. Their relationship was still weird. Even though Giselle was pregnant with Lucky's kid, it didn't stop them from seeing other people. It was awkward when one of them would bring the other out with us.

"I guess I should get up and head to the bar," Luke sighed.

I tightened my arm around him because I didn't want to move. "No," I said.

"What do you mean?" Luke laughed.

"I think we should stay in bed all day and do nothing but have wild sex." I smiled as my hand traveled down to his hard cock.

"You sure know how to turn me on, babe," he said as he rolled me over and hovered over me. "I have to go to the bar. You have to edit those photos for Mrs. Braxton, and we have a lunch date with Charley today." He smiled as he took down my panties.

"You're right. But promise me we'll schedule a day to stay in bed and not worry about the outside world."

"You got it." He smiled as he plunged his finger inside me. "Now, give me your lips and shush. I'm going to make sweet love to you."

After a sweet round of lovemaking, Luke took a shower, and I made a pot of coffee. As I waited for it to finish brewing, I stared out my window at the perfectly blue sky and the sun shining brightly into my living room. Settling in Santa Monica was the best decision I ever made.

Lost in my thoughts, I felt strong arms wrap around me. I tilted my head back and looked up at Luke's smiling face.

"What are you doing?" he asked.

"Just admiring the beauty of the day."

He was wearing only jeans, and his hair was still soaking wet. He was the sexiest man alive, as far as I was concerned, and I couldn't seem to get enough of him.

"Well, I'm admiring the beauty in front of me." He softly kissed my neck.

I giggled. "You sure have a way with words, Mr. Matthews."

"And you have a way with those lips." He smiled as he kissed me again.

Luke walked to the coffee pot, poured some coffee, and sat at the table.

"Do you want me to make you breakfast?" I asked.

"Nah, I'm good, babe. I'll grab something at the bar."

There was a knock at the door, and Sam's boisterous voice came through loud and clear.

"Dude, are you up? Are you decent?"

Luke sighed as he got up from his chair and opened the door.

"Morning, Sam. Morning, Gretchen."

I smiled as my best friends walked into the apartment. I immediately grabbed two cups and poured coffee into them.

"Sit down," I said to Gretchen, lightly taking hold of her arm and leading her to the table.

"Thanks, Lily." She smiled.

"Have you talked to Giselle?" I asked.

"Yeah. She said that she and Lucky were shopping for furniture for the baby's room."

"For both places?" Luke asked.

"I'm not sure. She didn't say anything, and I know his apartment still isn't ready. I think she likes having him around."

"They're weird." I laughed.

Luke got up from the table. "Okay, friends. It's been fun seeing you, but I have to finish getting dressed and head to the bar. Maddie and I have some liquor orders to go over."

"We playing tonight?" Sam asked.

"Yeah. I already talked to Lucky, and he said he and Giselle will be there. I'm also interviewing new bands to play on the weekends after we play our gig. I want Lily to play, and she won't," he pouted.

"Get over it, Matthews." I winked.

Luke headed to the bedroom to get ready, and Sam and Gretchen got up to leave. "I can't wait to get this cast off today. So, when you see me tonight, I'll be strutting in."

I laughed as I hugged her.

"I can't wait to finally make love to her without that cast getting in the way." Sam smiled.

"Just keep it down," Luke yelled from the bedroom.

"Paybacks, bro. Paybacks." He laughed.

~

Since I couldn't get another teaching job immediately, I decided to make photography my full-time work. I mostly just worked out of my apartment but wanted to rent a small space and turn it into a studio. It was something that I'd thought about over the past couple of months, and Luke was supportive. He told me I needed to follow my dreams and go for it like he did with the bar.

I did a photoshoot with Rory Braxton and her twin girls. It was a surprise gift for her husband's birthday. I photographed them at the beach, and then Rory wanted some sexy pictures for Ian. I brought her back to the apartment once I set it up with the backdrop. I'd never photographed sexy images like the ones I did for her, and I was nervous at first. But after seeing the photographs, I knew she'd be more than pleased. I met Rory through Giselle. Rory's husband's best friend, Adalynn, owned Prim magazine, for which Giselle did a lot of modeling. She instantly thought of me when she overheard Rory and Adalynn talking about finding a female photographer. Since the pictures that Rory wanted for Ian were of her practically naked and very seductive, she thought it would be best to have a female photograph her so as not to upset her husband.

While I was sitting at my computer, editing the photos, Luke walked up and kissed me.

"Bye, babe. Have fun today, and I'll see you later at the bar for lunch with Charley."

"Bye, baby." I smiled.

I looked at the photos of Ashley and Ariel Braxton and smiled as I envisioned a family like Rory's and Ian's one day. I picked up my phone from the desk and called Rory.

"Hello," she answered.

"Hi, Rory. It's Lily. Your pictures will be ready by tonight, so I was hoping we could meet for lunch tomorrow, and I can show you the final shots."

"Excellent, Lily. Tomorrow will be perfect. If you're in the mood for Mexican food, we can meet at the Border Grill around noon?"

"Sounds great, Rory. I'll see you tomorrow."

As I was editing the photos, one popped up of Luke. I smiled as I ran my fingers across his perfect six-pack on the screen. It was one of him lying on the bed in only a pair of unbuttoned jeans. His arm was behind his head, and he was looking out the window.

I was the luckiest girl alive to be loved by him, and my life was perfect. It was more perfect than I had ever dreamed it would be.

Chapter Two

LUKE

I walked into the bar and saw Adam talking to Maddie. So far, he had kept his word and was turning his life around. He attended UCLA like he said he would, and he also worked full-time in the IT department at Rocket Corp. He saw Charley and Maddie as much as he could, and I could tell that Maddie was falling in love with him again. She had always loved him. I thought he should make computers his career, but he wanted to be a counselor for drug and alcohol abuse. I was cool with him as long as he kept true to his word about changing. Charley loved having him around and so close. And if she was happy, that was all that mattered.

"Hey, you two," I said as I approached the bar.

"Hey, man," Adam replied.

Maddie looked at me and smiled. "Charley is really looking forward to having lunch with you and Lily today."

"Yeah, we are, too. We better go over the liquor order before she gets here."

Adam kissed Maddie goodbye and told me he'd see me later. I took out the invoice with the liquor order on it, and Maddie and I started to check the boxes.

"Can I ask what the two of you were talking about?"

"Not really, but I'll tell you anyway," she smirked. "He wants to take Charley and me to Disneyland this weekend. Just the three of us, like a family."

"How do you feel about that?" I asked.

"I love him, Luke. I always have. I want us to be a family."

"Please tell me he's not spending the night at your place. I don't want Charley to get her hopes up."

"He's not," she said as she looked at the invoice.

"Go to Disneyland and be a family." I smiled as I kissed her cheek. "Charley will love it."

As I was pulling the liquor bottles out of the boxes, my phone buzzed in my pocket. I pulled it out, and there was a text message from a number I didn't recognize.

"Hi, Uncle Luke. It's me, Charley. Hehe."

I looked at my sister and showed her my phone. "What the hell is this?"

"We bought Charley a cell phone last night, and before you say anything, she's only allowed to text Adam, you, Lily, Mom, Dad, Sam, and me. It's for emergency purposes only."

"Really, Maddie? You don't think she's a little young to be responsible for a cell phone?"

She rolled her eyes. "All the kids her age have them, and I like knowing I can get a hold of her any time I want."

"So if all the kids her age had horses, you'd buy her a horse?"

She twisted her face and looked up at the ceiling. "Yeah, I would. I love horses." She smiled. "Relax, Uncle Luke. It'll be fine."

"Don't come crying to me if she goes over her minutes, and you're paying a small fortune for your bill."

"She won't. Now text her back." She winked.

"Awesome, peanut. I'll see you for lunch, and you can show me your new phone."

"Okay."

Maddie and I finished putting the liquor away, and I went to my office. I had so much paperwork to catch up on. I was finding it difficult to do everything on my own. Sure, Maddie helped, but she tended the bar with Candi. Neither one of them was suited for secretarial work. I was beginning to think I needed to hire someone to come into the bar three days a week and do the paperwork and help with the books. I got up from my chair, and just as I opened the door, my two beautiful girls stood there.

"Why, hello there, beautiful ladies." I smiled.

"Uncle Luke!" Charley exclaimed as she threw her arms around my waist.

"Hi, Charley. Hey, babe." I smiled as I leaned over and kissed Lily. "Did you get those photos done?"

"I did, and I'm meeting Rory tomorrow for lunch to show her."

"Great. Now, let's eat. I'm starving," I said.

"You should have let me make you breakfast." Lily smiled.

"If I recall, I had a great breakfast this morning." I winked.

We left the bar, and Lily gave me her Explorer's keys.

"Where do you want to go eat?"

"At the beach." Charley smiled.

"The beach? We can't have lunch at the beach."

"Sure we can, Uncle Luke. We can get some sandwiches and then take them to the beach. Lily has a blanket back here."

"Smart little girl." Lily smiled as she looked at me.

"Okay, then. The beach it is."

We spread out the blanket and took our sandwiches out of the bag. "One ham and cheese on white for you," I said as I handed Charley her sandwich. "And one tuna on whole wheat for you, babe."

"Thank you."

It was a beautiful day to spend at the beach. I just wished we could have spent the entire day there. But there was way too much to get done at the bar. As soon as we finished our lunch, Charley played by the shoreline. She loved the way the waves crashed into her feet. I leaned over and pushed Lily's hair behind her ear. She placed her hand on mine and interlaced our fingers.

"What's wrong? I can tell something's bothering you," she said.

I sighed. "I think I need to hire a secretary or an assistant to handle all the paperwork at the bar. It's becoming too much to do on my own."

She softly smiled as she brought my hand up to her lips. "Then hire someone. If you need the help, then do it. I don't want to see you so stressed out."

"Maybe I will." I smiled as I leaned in and kissed her seductively on her lips.

"Hey, no kissing in public." Charley smiled.

"Is that so, little girl?" I laughed as I grabbed her and tickled her in the sand.

We picked up the blanket, shook it out, and Lily dropped me off at the bar. "Bye, babe. I'll see you later. Ask Sam to give you a ride to the bar tonight, and we can ride home on my bike."

"Aren't you coming home to change?" she asked with disappointment.

"I have so much paperwork to catch up on and want to jump on it. Does that make you mad?"

"No. I'll call Sam and ask him." She smiled.

I leaned over and kissed her and then kissed Charley on the cheek. I went straight to my office and shut the door. I didn't want to be disturbed until the gang arrived later.

∽

"Is it safe to come in?" Lily asked as she poked her head through the door.

I looked up from what I was doing and smiled. "Of course it is, babe. Get in here."

She walked in and sat down on my lap, wrapping her arms around my neck and kissing my lips.

"I missed you," she said.

"I missed you too."

"Have you even made a dent in any of this?"

"Some. Not much. I did place an ad for help. It runs tomorrow, so keep your fingers crossed that people respond. Is everyone here?"

"Everyone except Giselle and Lucky. I called them, and they're on their way."

She climbed off my lap, and I got up from my chair. We walked into the bar together, and I saw Gretchen and Sam standing and talking to Candi.

"Look at you." I smiled as I kissed Gretchen. "No more cast. How does it feel?"

"I'm still trying to get used to it." She laughed.

"You look great, Gretchen," I told her.

"Thanks, Luke."

"Sammy, let's get the equipment set up. Why isn't Lucky here yet?"

"Keep your panties on, dude. I'm here." Lucky smiled as he held out his arms.

The three of us went and set up the stage. I looked across the bar at Lily as she stood there, talking to our friends. I never thought I could love again since Callie. But Lily changed all that for me. She breathed life into me again. Now, every breath I took was for her.

Chapter Three

LILY

I was nervous to show Rory the pictures. I knew I shouldn't have been because they turned out great, but I was always anxious about showing my work. I put the photos in the Explorer and drove to the Border Grill. When I arrived, Rory was already sitting in a booth, waiting for me.

"Hi, Lily." She smiled as she got up and hugged me.

"Hi, Rory."

"I took the liberty of ordering you a margarita. I hope that's okay."

"Of course. I love margaritas." I smiled.

I sat down and set the box of photos on the table.

"So, I'm dying to see my pictures," she said.

I took the lid off the box and first pulled out the pictures of her and the girls. I displayed them nicely on the table in front of her. She looked at them and then at me.

"These are absolutely gorgeous! Oh, Lily, these will look wonderful in my house."

"I'm glad you like them."

"I don't like them. I love them!" she exclaimed. "And?" she said with a smile.

I took out the photos that she had made for Ian. "You might want to keep these in your seat while looking at them." I laughed.

"Right." She laughed with me.

She didn't say anything at first. She just kept staring at the half-naked pictures of herself. Finally, she looked at me with a tear in her eye.

"These pictures are amazing. You have captured my heart and soul, and Ian will love them. In fact, he may have a heart attack." She smiled.

"Let's hope that doesn't happen." I laughed.

"Can you put all of the photos of me in a hard-bound photo album? And, if possible, I would like Ian's name engraved on it. No, I want it to say: To the love of my life, my husband, best friend, and lover."

"Of course I can. Don't worry, Rory. I'll take care of it."

She reached over and grabbed my hand. You are an amazing photographer, and I'm so happy Giselle introduced me to you."

"Thank you. I'm thrilled that you had the confidence in me to hire me to photograph you and your beautiful girls."

We placed our order with the waitress and continued talking while sipping on margaritas.

"Have you thought about opening up a studio?" she asked.

"I have. I've been thinking about it for the past couple of months, but I wouldn't know where to start looking."

She picked up her glass and took a sip of her drink. "My husband, Ian, is in real estate development and owns a small strip mall right down the road from here. I know there's a shop for rent because it's next door to the hair salon where I get my hair done. It's the perfect location, and it gets a lot of traffic. I think it would make a great photography studio. I can call Ian and tell him to meet us there after lunch."

I sat there, blown away at this fantastic opportunity that Rory was giving me. "That would be great, Rory. Thank you." I smiled.

She reached into her purse and pulled out her phone. She called her husband, who said he could meet us there in about a half hour.

"If he asks how we met, we'll just tell him we met through Giselle at Prim, and we got to talking. I don't want him to know you photographed me and the girls."

"No worries. Your secret is safe with me."

Rory took care of the bill, even though I tried to fight her on it, and I followed her to the strip mall. Ian was waiting for us inside the shop. As we walked in, he turned around, and I couldn't help but notice how incredibly handsome he was.

"Ian, this is my new friend, Lily Gilmore. She's the one who is looking to open up a photography studio."

"It's very nice to meet you, Lily. I'm Ian Braxton." He smiled as he held out his hand.

"Thank you for coming out here on such short notice, Mr. Braxton."

"Please, call me Ian, and it's no problem."

I smiled as he showed me around the shop. Instantly, I could envision myself opening up a studio here. It was the perfect size and perfect location. "I love it, Ian. I can totally see me working out of this space."

"Great. Why don't you have dinner with Rory and me at our house tonight? I'll draw up the contract and go over the specifics with you. Bring your husband along."

"I'm not married, but I have a boyfriend," I said.

"Perfect. Bring him along, and we can have a nice dinner and talk. I better get going. Bye, sweetheart," he said as he kissed his wife. "I'll call Charles and tell him about dinner. It was great to meet you, Lily, and I look forward to seeing you and—"

"Luke."

"You and Luke tonight." He smiled as he shook my hand.

We left the store, and he climbed into his limo and pulled away. I looked over at Rory, who was smiling from ear to ear.

"I told you this would be perfect," she said.

"Thank you, Rory. You have no idea how much this means to me," I said as I hugged her.

"No problem. You're an incredible photographer, and you should have your own studio. I'll see you tonight. Around seven?"

"Seven is great. Bye, Rory."

I climbed into my Explorer and called Luke.

"Hey, babe. What's up?" he answered.

"Please tell me you can get off early tonight."

"Why? What's going on?"

I was so excited to tell him the news. "We are having dinner tonight with the Braxton's at their home."

"Okay. Why?"

"Because I found the perfect place to open up a studio, and it just so happens that Mr. Ian Braxton owns it."

"Ah, perfect. Okay. Are you at the place now?"

"Yeah. I was just leaving."

"Give me the address, stay put, and I'll be there quick. I want to see it."

"Okay, baby. I'll wait for you."

I texted him the address, sat in the vehicle, and waited for him. About ten minutes later, he rode up on his motorcycle. I climbed out of my truck and wrapped my arms around him.

"Thank you for coming."

"Anything for you, babe. Show me the shop."

"It's this one right here," I said as I pointed to the empty shop in the middle of the strip mall.

He looked through the window and then looked around at the area. "I think this would be a great place for you to start. It has great space, a great location, and great shops around. "Good choice, babe." He smiled as he kissed me. He looked at his watch and then at me. "I think I'll come home for the day. I need to make sweet love to you and then shower." He smiled.

"Really?" I asked with excitement.

"Yep. I've been thinking about you all day and how badly I want to take you to bed."

"We just did it this morning." I giggled.

"Exactly, and it was so magical that I wanted more. You know I can never get enough of you, babe."

"I can never get enough of you either. Let's go."

Luke hopped on his bike and took off, and I followed behind. As soon as we pulled into the parking lot of the apartments, He climbed off his bike and opened my driver's side door. He reached in and smashed his mouth against mine. I turned my body around and wrapped my legs tightly around his waist as he picked me up and carried me to the building. His kiss was forceful and loving. I ran my fingers through his hair as he put me up against the wall outside the building. As he was devouring my mouth and then my neck, I reached into his pants pocket and took out his keys. He held me up against the wall with one hand as the other inserted the key to the building, and he unlocked the door. I started to giggle because he couldn't open it.

"For God's sake. Can't the two of you wait until you get inside your apartment?" Sam said as he opened the door and held it for us.

"No time, bro. I've been thinking about this all day," Luke said as he kissed me.

"Here, let me open your door for you," Sam said as he rolled his eyes.

He took the keys and opened my apartment door. "There you go. Have fun, you two."

Luke carried me to the bedroom, and we both fell on the bed. He broke our kiss, stood up, and lifted his shirt over his head. While he unbuttoned his jeans and took them down, I sat up and got undressed, throwing my clothes on the floor.

"Don't take your bra off yet, babe. I want to do it." He smiled.

I sat there as he stood in front of me, naked, looking like a god. He leaned over and unhooked my bra from the back while slowly taking down each strap.

"God, I'll never get tired of looking at you. You are more and more beautiful every day," he said as his lips hovered over mine.

He lifted my hips and took down my thong. His mouth consumed every inch of my body before he plunged two fingers inside me, making sure I was ready for him.

"Babe, you're so wet. God, I need you now."

I spread my legs wide open for him as he hovered over me and began to thrust in and out of me. I was so aroused by him that it felt like I was already going to come. His moans were deep and sensual as he moved fluidly inside me. I wrapped my legs around his waist as he kneaded my breast. My moans were growing louder by the minute as I felt him swell inside me. His finger reached my clit and began making small circles around it, sending me over the edge.

"That's it, babe. I know you're about to come. Fucking come for me because I can't hold back anymore."

My legs tightened as the orgasm overtook my body. Luke moaned as he pushed himself deeper inside me, filling me with every last drop of pleasure he had inside him. As he collapsed on top of me, we tried to catch our breath.

"I love you, Lily."

I smiled as I pressed my lips against his neck. "I love you too."

Once our breathing returned to normal, Luke sat up and smiled at me. "Are you ready for round two in the shower?"

"I am if you are."

He looked down between his legs. "What do you think that means?" He winked.

∼

"Come in. It's good to see you again, Lily." Ian smiled as he kissed my cheek.

"Ian, this is my boyfriend, Luke Matthews," I said as they shook hands.

"Rory will be down in a minute. Please, come sit down. Luke, you look like a beer kind of guy."

Luke chuckled. "I am."

"I have some imported beer I'd like you to try."

"I would love to," he said.

Ian looked at me and smiled. "Lily, you're a red wine type of girl."

"That's right, Ian. I am."

Rory walked into the room, and we lightly hugged. I introduced her to Luke, and the four of us went and sat down on the patio for dinner. We talked, laughed, and ate the excellent food Charles had prepared. Ian kept staring at me from across the table. It was making me really uncomfortable, and I thought he could tell.

"I apologize for staring at you, Lily. But you seem very familiar to me, and I can't put my finger on it."

Luke looked at me and smiled. Then he turned his attention to Ian. "You probably know her as the daughter of Johnny Gilmore."

Ian immediately snapped his fingers. "That's it! I knew your name was familiar. Your father was a brilliant musician. I'm so sorry about his death."

"Thank you, Ian."

"You know, his picture is on the wall at the Piano Bar. Rory's father is the owner."

"Wait," Luke interrupted. "Jimmy O'Rourke, is your dad?" he asked as he looked at Rory.

"Yes, he is." Rory smiled. "Do you know him?"

"Yeah. I've known him for years. He and Bernie go way back. He used to come into Bernie's bar all the time. I didn't know he had a daughter."

My head was going back and forth, listening to their conversation.

"It's a long story," Ian said.

"Wow, what a small world."

After we finished our dinner, Ian and I got up and went into his office to go over and sign the rental contract. As he reviewed the contract, Ariel and Ashley came running in. They stopped when they saw me.

"That's the lady who took our picture," Ashley said.

Ariel walked up to me and placed her hand on my cheek. "Hi again." She smiled.

Ian looked at me strangely. "Girls, it's way past your bedtime. Now give Daddy kisses and head to your rooms. I'll be up in a few minutes to tuck you in."

"Okay, Daddy." They giggled as they kissed his cheeks.

Ariel turned to me. "Will you take our picture again?"

"I'd be happy to." I smiled.

They ran out the door, shutting it behind them, and Ian cocked his head. Before he could say anything, I spoke first.

"Listen, Ian. Rory wanted this to be a huge surprise for you, so please don't let her know that you know. It will really upset her."

"It's for my birthday, isn't it?" he asked.

I nodded my head.

"I won't say a word about it. I promise."

"Your girls are beautiful." I smiled.

"They are the loves of my life. All three of them."

I sat there thinking what an incredible man Ian Braxton was and how much he loved Rory. I could see it in his eyes whenever she walked into the room. I signed the last piece of paper, and Ian smiled at me as he held out his hand.

"Congratulations, Lily."

"Thanks, Ian. Thank you for everything."

"You're quite welcome. Once you get your studio set up, I'd love to come see it."

I smiled, and we returned to the patio where Luke and Rory were. We drank a couple more glasses of wine and then headed home.

Chapter Four

LUKE

I threw my keys on the counter as soon as we walked into the apartment. Lily headed straight for the bathroom, and I went into the bedroom. As soon as I climbed into bed, I checked my email and was surprised when I saw I had over twenty responses to my help wanted ad.

"Lily, hurry up, babe."

She walked into the bedroom in nothing but her bra and panties, with her hair piled on top of her head.

"Damn, woman. You're killing me." I smiled as I watched her take off her bra and slip on the nightshirt she pulled from the drawer.

"Behave yourself, Mr. Matthews," she said as she climbed beside me.

"Look, babe. Look at all these responses to my ad."

"That's great. Are you going to start interviewing soon?"

"Yep. I'll start setting them up tomorrow morning."

I set down my phone and wrapped my arms around her, pulling her close and inhaling her scent as she snuggled against my chest.

"I loved you taking half of the day off from the bar and

spending it with me. When I open the studio, I'm afraid things will get so busy that we won't have time for each other anymore."

"Aw, babe. Don't say that. We will always have time for each other. We'll make time. Don't worry about that. Remember, no matter how crazy life gets, there's always time for Love In Between."

She smiled as she looked up at me. "That's how you came up with the name for your band."

"Yeah. That's right," I said as I kissed her head.

"I love you, Luke. Good night."

"I love you more, Lily. Good night, babe."

∼

I AWOKE to the aroma of coffee going up my nose. I opened one eye and saw Lily sitting over me, holding a cup of coffee in my face.

"Morning," I said as I rubbed my eyes.

"Good morning. It's time to get up, sleepy head. You have interviews to schedule, and I have a shop to put together."

I took the mug from her and sat up. "Okay. Okay. I'm up. But I refuse to get out of this bed until my beautiful girlfriend kisses me."

"I think that can be arranged." She smiled as she leaned in and kissed me.

She jumped up from the bed and pulled a sundress out of the closet. "I'm so excited. I texted Gretchen and Giselle and told them I was taking them somewhere today. I'm going to surprise them and take them to the shop. They're going to flip!" she squealed.

Seeing the excitement pour out from Lily was amazing. I was so happy that she would finally live as a photographer with her own studio. I wanted nothing more than for her to be happy. My phone buzzed, and there was a text message from Lucky.

"Dude, fuck me, man. Giselle is so hormonal she's driving me up the wall. We're laughing together one minute, and she's screaming at me the next."

I chuckled.

"Pamper her and just take it. She's the mother of your child. Remember that."

"Somehow, I knew you'd say something like that."

"It seems Giselle is being overly hormonal with Lucky." I laughed.

"She's overly hormonal when she's not pregnant." Lily smiled.

I got out of bed and jumped into the shower. When I finished, Lily stood in the bathroom doorway, staring at me.

"You want some of this?" I smiled.

"Yes, but later. I need to lay down some rules for you when interviewing these women who applied to be your assistant."

"Oh? And what rules would that be?" I asked with a smirk as I dried off.

"They must not be attractive. They must be fully clothed and have the personality of a doormat. Actually, a lesbian would be perfect."

I walked over to her and placed my hands on her hips. "Are you really worried, babe?"

"I'm a woman, and sometimes a woman can be insecure when it comes to other women working with the man she loves."

"Please, Lily, you know me better than that," I said as I kissed her forehead.

"It's not you I don't trust. It's the other women. I mean, look at you. You are an incredibly sexy man, and any woman would be stupid not to try and get her hooks into you. I deal with it every time we go out."

"I love you and only you, babe. You know that. Now stop with the nonsense. But I will keep your rules in mind." I winked.

"Thank you, baby. Okay, I'm off to the studio! I love you." She smiled as she kissed me goodbye.

"I love you too, Lil. Have fun, and I'll see you later."

∼

When I arrived at the bar, Lucky was doing some wiring on the stage.

"Dude, when are the chicks coming? I need to sit in on the interviews with you so you can make the right choice."

"You are not sitting in on the interviews, and you're going to be a father."

"So. What's your point?"

"Focus on your kid."

"Man, Giselle is busting my balls. You know, I love her, but then I hate her. Do you know what I mean?"

"Actually, I don't," I said as I walked to my office.

"What's going on with you?" Lucky asked.

"Nothing. Lily is worried about who I'll hire for my assistant."

"Why would she be worried? You're…you." He laughed.

"Exactly, and I told her that."

"Chicks are weird. It's probably just a hormone thing like Giselle."

"Lily's not pregnant."

"No, not yet anyway!" He winked.

As I was about to kick him out of my office, a brunette stood in the doorway.

"Well, hello, Angel. How may I help you?" Lucky smiled as he took her hand and lightly kissed it.

"I have an interview with the owner, Luke."

"Well, that would be—"

"Me," I said as I stepped from behind my desk. "I'm Luke Matthews."

"Hi, Mr. Matthews. My name is Cody Chase."

"Cody, I love that name, and it's so you." Lucky smiled.

"Lucky, get the hell out of here."

"I'm going. I'm going," he said. "Maybe Cody and I can chat later." He smiled.

I shut the door and shook my head. "Ignore my friend. He has way too much testosterone."

She giggled and sat down in the chair across from me.

The interview went well, and she was very qualified for the job, but I had others I had to interview today and tomorrow, so I told her I'd get back to her either way. After I walked Cody to the door, I sat at the bar.

"How was she?" Maddie asked.

"She was good. Very qualified. I liked her. She's a good candidate."

"She's very pretty," Maddie said as she wiped a glass.

"I didn't notice."

"Good answer." She smiled.

"The next girl should be here in about five minutes. Just send her to my office."

"Will do, boss."

Chapter Five

LILY

I couldn't wait to show Giselle and Gretchen the studio. It was something I'd talked about for a long time. They had no clue about any of this. I wanted it to be a total surprise. Gretchen and I watched as Giselle waddled her way to the car. I couldn't help but smile at her because she looked so damn cute, and she was the last person that I thought would have a baby.

"So, where are you taking us?" she asked as she climbed into the car.

"It's a surprise. How are you feeling?"

"Besides fat and bloated, I'm feeling pretty good. Lucky and I have an ultrasound scheduled for tomorrow. We're going to find out the sex of the baby."

"That's awesome! You better call me the second you find out."

"Nope. I'm having all of you over tomorrow night for dinner, and then you'll find out." Giselle smiled.

"Hopefully, Luke can make it. He's been so buried at the bar."

I pulled into the parking lot and the space in front of the studio.

"Follow me, ladies." I smiled as I unlocked the door.

"Lily, what is this?" Gretchen asked.

"Welcome to A Day In The Life Photography Studio."

"What?! Oh my God!" they exclaimed.

"This is amazing, Lily. Congratulations!" Giselle said as she hugged me.

"I can't believe it. You finally have your own studio, and Luke has his bar. You two are so perfect, and you're going to have an incredible future," Gretchen said as she hugged me.

"Life is really good." I smiled. I have to look into hiring a contractor to come in and fix up the inside. I have all kinds of equipment I need to buy. Oh my God, I think I'm freaking out."

Giselle and Gretchen laughed. "Don't stress, and take it one day at a time. We'll help you as much as we can. Plus, you have your handsome boyfriend to help," Giselle replied.

"Luke is so busy with the bar that he needs to hire an assistant. This morning, I laid down the ground rules about who he can and can't hire."

"Well, if he hires some hottie, you'll have to do the same because you'll need help here."

"Very true." I smiled.

"I may have the name of a contractor for you. He's the boyfriend of Sierra Adams over at Adams Advertising, the agency Prim uses to help with the magazine."

"Perfect!" I smiled.

"I'll text you his number later. Now, can we grab some lunch? This little one is starving," Giselle said as she rubbed her tummy.

Giselle craved Mexican food. She ate it every day. We sat down in the booth, and I pulled out my phone and texted Luke.

"Hi, baby. How did your interviews go?"

"Hi, babe. They went really good. What are you doing?"

"I'm having lunch with Giselle and Gretchen. I hope they were ugly?"

"They were smokin hot, babe. I can't help it."

"Very funny. You'll pay for that when you get home."

"I know. That's why I said it."

"Bye."

"Bye."

After we placed our order, I asked Giselle about Lucky.

"So, what's going on with you and Lucky?"

"What do you mean? He's my baby daddy, and that's about it. We've been fighting a lot like an old married couple."

"I walked in on them the other day having sex on the couch," Gretchen said as she bit into a chip.

"When's he moving out?"

"As soon as his place is ready. They said probably about another month."

"Do you want him to leave? I mean, you are going to need help with the baby."

"He's messy, and he doesn't listen. He left the toilet seat up, and I almost fell in the other night when I went to pee because it was dark. He leaves his dishes in the sink and his socks in every room. His shoes are always in the middle of the floor, and he leaves glass rings on my tables."

Gretchen and I sat there laughing. We both silently thanked God that Sam and Luke weren't like that.

"Well, I guess it's time for him to leave." I smiled.

"I love him, but then I hate him. He's very immature. Anyway, dinner is at seven tomorrow night."

"We will be there." I smiled.

~

I picked up Charley from school because Maddie was tied up at the bar, and Adam was in class. As much as I missed teaching, my passion was photography.

"Hey, baby girl." I smiled as Charley climbed into the Explorer.

"Hi, Lily. Guess what?"

"What?"

"I got Student of the Week!" She smiled as she showed me her award.

"Fantastic, Charley! Give me a high five. Wait until your mom and Uncle Luke find out."

"Can we go for ice cream?" she asked.

"We sure can. Let's go."

I drove us to the ice cream parlor, and when I opened the door, Charley walked through, and I stopped. I couldn't shake the feeling that someone was following or watching me. After looking around and seeing nothing and no one, I joined Charley at the counter, and we picked out what kind of ice cream we would have. As we were eating our ice cream, I had an idea.

"Let's FaceTime Uncle Luke and show him what we're doing."

"Yeah! He'll be so jealous."

I pulled out my phone and FaceTimed him.

"Hey, babe. What are you doing?" He laughed.

"Charley and I are sitting in the ice cream parlor having ice cream, and we wanted to show you."

"Hey, peanut!" Luke said as Charley appeared on the screen.

"Hi, Uncle Luke. Look. I got your favorite ice cream." She laughed as she showed him her cone.

"No fair. I want some."

"You can't because you're not here." Charley smiled.

"You two have all the fun."

"I know you're busy. So I'll see you later."

"I love you, babe."

"I love you too." I smiled as I kissed the screen.

"That's gross," Charley said. "My mom and dad are always kissing on the couch. Yuck!"

"Someday, when you're older, you'll want to kiss the boy you're in love with," I said.

"No way. I don't want to get cooties. My mom said that all boys have cooties."

I laughed as I tapped her on the nose. Once we finished, I took Charley back to my apartment, and she did homework while I went into the bedroom. I looked at the guitar sitting in the corner and picked it up. I began strumming the chords.

"Lily," Charley said as she stood in the doorway.

"Yeah, baby."

"Will you teach me how to play?"

"Of course I will. Come here," I said as I held out my hand.

She walked over to me with a smile and sat beside me. I set the guitar in her lap and positioned her fingers on the strings to form a D chord. As she strummed, I adjusted her fingers so she was playing correctly. I had flashbacks of my father sitting on the edge of his bed, teaching me.

"What's going on in here?" Luke smiled as he stood in the doorway.

"I'm teaching Charley a few chords."

"Look, Uncle Luke, I'm playing!" she exclaimed as she strummed the chords.

"I see that, peanut, and I'm jealous. You never asked me to teach you to play."

"You can teach me too." She smiled.

I got up from the bed and kissed Luke.

"How did it go at the studio?" he asked.

"It went well. Giselle and Gretchen loved it, and they're excited for me. Giselle has the name of a contractor she's giving me to get in contact with."

"Good. Maddie should be here shortly. She and Adam are taking Charley out to dinner."

"What are we doing for dinner? Do you want to stay in and cook?" I asked.

Luke softly kissed my head. "That sounds like a plan. Do we have anything here?"

I laughed. "No. We'd have to go to the store and buy something."

"Then I think it sounds like a take-out kind of night." He smiled.

Maddie arrived a few moments later to pick up Charley. She didn't want to leave because she wanted to practice playing the one chord I taught her.

"Have a great dinner, Charley." I smiled as I kissed her on the cheek. "You can come over and practice anytime you want."

"Thanks, Lily. I love you." She smiled as she hugged me.

"I love you too, baby."

She kissed Luke goodbye, and as the door shut, I had a thought.

"We need to buy Charley her own guitar," I said.

"I was thinking that too. I have an older guitar I can give her to practice on, and if she becomes really serious about playing, then we can buy her one."

"That's a good idea." I smiled as I wrapped my arms around him.

Chapter Six

LUKE

Lily and I sat in bed and shared cartons of Chinese food. It had been a while since we just relaxed and did nothing.

"Are you going to tell me about the girls or what?" she asked.

"What girls?" I smiled as I fed her a piece of pork from my chopsticks.

"The girls you interviewed today?"

"Oh, them. What about them?"

"Did you like any of them?"

"There's one girl that I think would be good."

"Is she ugly?"

"Lily!"

"Is she a lesbian?"

"Lily!"

"Come on, Luke, give me something here."

I grabbed the bottle of wine from the nightstand and asked Lily to hand me her glass. As I poured some in, I began to tell her about Cody.

"Her name is Cody Chase, and she's very qualified. She has plenty of secretarial experience and is great with computers."

"What does she look like?" she asked.

"I don't know, Lily. To be honest, I didn't even notice."

"Liar."

I chuckled. "Babe, you're killing me here. There's no reason for you to be acting like this."

She turned away, got up from the bed, and went into the bathroom, shutting the door behind her. She looked upset, but I didn't understand what I said to make her feel that way. I lightly knocked on the door.

"Babe, are you okay?"

"I'm fine. I just had to pee."

She was lying because she never closed the door when she peed. I turned the knob and opened the door to find her leaning up against the counter with tears streaming down her face.

"What's wrong?" I asked as I walked over to her and wrapped my arms around her.

"I'm sorry, Luke."

"Was it something I said?" I asked as I gently wiped the tears from her eyes.

She nodded.

"Babe, talk to me."

"You said there's no reason for me to act like this. I have a reason, which led me to Santa Monica in the first place."

I closed my eyes because I felt like a complete bastard. I completely disregarded her fears and what Hunter did to her. I held her face in my hands.

"Look at me. I love you, Lily Gilmore. You and only you. I don't know how to make that any clearer to you."

"I know you do. This is something I need to work out for myself. It has nothing to do with you, Luke. It's what Brynn and Hunter did to me. I need to get over it."

"Maybe you should call Dr. Blakely and talk to her about it. I don't want you to be upset about this. I need to hire an assistant, babe. I have no choice because I'm drowning."

She buried her face into my neck and softly brushed her lips against my skin.

"I know, and I'm sorry. I love you, Luke, and I promise not to say another word about it. I feel like such an idiot."

I lightly smiled as I kissed the side of her head. "You are not an idiot." I moved my hand up her shirt and began to rub her back. She moaned and tilted her head back. My lips lightly brushed against her skin as I leaned in closer to her, pressing my hard cock up against her. Her hands traveled down to the button on my jeans as she unbuttoned it and took the zipper down. I stared into her beautiful eyes as I lifted her shirt over her head and quickly undid her bra, releasing her breasts and taking each one in my mouth. She released my cock, which was throbbing for her, and stroked it up and down in her soft hand. I lifted up her skirt, took down her panties, and grabbed her hips, setting her up on the bathroom counter.

"I need you inside me now," she whispered as I kissed her lips.

My fingers softly rubbed her clit and then found their way inside her, feeling her excitement. She was more than ready.

"You're ready for me, babe," I said in between kisses as I brought her closer to the edge of the counter and pushed deep inside her with one thrust. We both gasped at the same time. She placed her hands on the counter and arched her back as I held on to her hips and moved in and out of her.

"Luke, oh my God."

"Come for me, babe. You're so wet, and I want more. I want to feel you come all over me."

Her moans heightened, and I felt her tighten around me. She was ready to explode, and so was I.

"Lily, I can't hold back anymore."

She wrapped her arms around me and dug her nails into my back as we came together. I slowly moved in and out of her as I poured every last drop of pleasure inside her. We smiled at each other as I pushed a few strands of her hair behind her ear.

"I'll never be able to get enough of you. We could make love a million times, and it still wouldn't be enough," I said.

She brought her finger up to my mouth and traced the outline of my lips, then softly brushed hers against them. Her legs were still wrapped tightly around me, and I was still inside of her. I picked her up from the counter and carried her into the bedroom, lying on the bed and hovering over her.

"Do you feel that?" I asked as I took her hard nipple in my mouth.

"Yes." She laughed.

"Shall we?"

"Of course." She smiled.

Chapter Seven

LILY

I started the day off by making pancakes for Luke. I knew he had to get to the bar, and I had to get to the studio, so I got up extra early and made sure they were ready when he woke up.

"It smells delicious in here, babe," he said as he poured some coffee.

"Thanks. The pancakes will be done in a second. Go sit down."

He walked up behind me, gripped my hips, and nuzzled his face into my neck.

"I love it when you're bossy."

I heard my phone beep in the bedroom and asked Luke if he could grab it while I put the pancakes on his plate.

"Who's Cameron?" he asked, holding up my phone.

"Oh. What did he say?"

"He said he'll meet you at the studio at ten o'clock."

"Great. I'll trade you." I smiled as I held up his plate.

Luke handed me my phone and stood there, staring at me. "Are you going to tell me who the guy is texting you and meeting you at ten o'clock?"

"You're cute when you're jealous." I smiled. "He's the

contractor that Giselle set me up with. He's coming to see what work needs to be done."

I sat at the table with Luke and replied to Cameron's text message.

"Sounds great. I'll be there."

I couldn't believe this was finally happening. I was going to own my own photography studio. The first pictures I would hang on the wall would be of Rory and the girls. I also thought I could go through the pictures I took on my road trip when I left Seattle. I hadn't looked at those pictures since I developed them in Portland almost two years ago.

"Hello? Babe?" Luke waved.

I snapped out of my daze and looked at him.

"Are you okay?"

"Sorry. I was just in la-la land over my new studio. There's so much to do."

"Don't stress about it. I'll help you any way I can," he said.

"I know you will."

Luke finished his coffee and pancakes and got up from the table to finish getting dressed. As I cleaned up, Luke's phone beeped with a text message that flashed across the screen.

"Bro, are you hiring that hot babe today? If you are, I'll be hanging out at the bar more often."

I felt sick but couldn't let Luke know I read it. I needed to control my insecurities, and maybe talking to Dr. Blakely wasn't such a bad idea.

"Okay, babe. I'm off," Luke said as he kissed me goodbye and grabbed his phone from the counter. "Have a great day at the studio, and I'll see you later."

"Bye, baby. I love you."

"I love you too," he said as he walked out the door.

∼

I STEPPED INTO THE STUDIO, turned on the lights, and deeply

breathed. The door opened, and a hot guy was standing when I turned around.

"Hi, you must be Lily. I'm Cameron Cole." He smiled as he held out his hand.

"Hi, Cameron. It's nice to meet you. Thank you for meeting me here today."

"No problem. Thank you for getting in contact with me. So, this will be a photography studio?" he asked.

"Yes, and if you follow me, I'll explain my vision."

We talked for almost two hours, and then he took measurements. I told him my ideas. He gave me some of his, which were great, and things I didn't think of, and then he told me he could start tomorrow.

"Thank you again, Cameron. I'll see you tomorrow."

"You're welcome, Lily. Enjoy the rest of your day." He smiled.

I had so much to do and many supplies to order. Cameron said it would only take about a week to do what he needed to get done, so I got online and ordered the equipment and supplies I needed for the studio. I looked at the clock, and it was lunchtime. I decided to go by the bar and tell Luke that Cameron would start tomorrow. When I walked in, I saw Luke sitting at a table, eating lunch with a woman across from him. I instantly felt sick.

"Hey, Lily." Maddie smiled.

"Hi, Maddie."

"Luke is right over there."

"Yeah, I saw him."

I walked over to the table, and as soon as Luke saw me, he stood up and kissed me.

"Lily. What are you doing here, babe?"

"I thought maybe we could have lunch together, but I see you're already eating."

"Cody, I want you to meet my girlfriend, Lily. Lily, this is Cody, my new assistant."

She was pretty. Too pretty. The kind of pretty that would make any woman extremely jealous having her working so closely with their husbands or boyfriend. Her short, brown hair looked perfect, and she had piercing green eyes.

"It's nice to meet you, Lily." She smiled as she held out her hand.

"It's nice to meet you too." I smiled with such a fakeness that I thought my face would fall off. "I don't want to interrupt you. So I'm just going to get going."

"No, babe, stay. Have lunch with us," Luke pleaded.

"No. That's okay. You two have a lot to discuss. I should have called you first," I said as I walked towards the door.

I couldn't get out of there fast enough. It felt like my airway was constricted, and I was unable to breathe. I pushed the door open, and Luke took hold of my arm as soon as I stepped outside.

"Are you okay?"

"I'm fine."

"Please, Lily. Stay and have lunch with us."

"I don't want to. I'm sorry, but I have to go."

"It's because of Cody. Isn't it?"

I touched his chest and stared into his eyes as I softly spoke.

"Listen to me. You go finish your lunch and show Cody the ropes. That way, you'll be able to get back home to me quicker."

"Are you sure?" he asked.

"More than sure." I smiled.

He softly kissed my lips and then walked back inside. I pulled out my phone and dialed Dr. Blakely.

"Dr. Blakely's office. This is Camille. How can I help you?"

"Hi, Camille. It's Lily Gilmore. I need to see Dr. Blakely as soon as possible."

"Okay, Miss Gilmore. Let me see what her schedule looks like. She has an opening at one o'clock."

"I'll take it, and I'll see you then."

I looked at my watch and saw it was twelve-fifteen, so I decided to walk down the street to Starbucks. As I was standing in line, I heard someone call my name.

"Hey, Adam." I waved.

I took my sandwich and coffee over to his table and sat down. "Are you studying?" I asked.

"Yeah. For some weird reason, I study better in a Starbucks setting."

I laughed. "How are you? I haven't seen you in a while."

"I'm good. How are you?"

I shifted in my seat as I bit into my sandwich. "I'm okay." I smiled. "The contractor is starting work on the studio tomorrow morning, so I can't complain."

He sat there and stared at me, knowing I wasn't telling him something.

"Anything else? I can tell something's bothering you."

"It must be your counselor instincts, right?"

He chuckled. "Yeah, I guess so."

"It's just me being stupid about something. Luke hired this beautiful girl as his assistant, and I'm having some issues with it. I just walked in on them having lunch at the bar, nearly had a panic attack, and had to get out of there. I have an appointment with my therapist at one o'clock."

"It's understandable for you to have certain fears about that, considering what you've been through, but Luke is a great guy, and I greatly respect him. He would never cheat on you."

"I know he wouldn't. That's why I don't understand why I feel like I do."

"You'll figure it out, Lily. Just take things one day at a time. You'll be so busy with your new studio that you won't have time to give that girl a second thought."

"You're right." I smiled as I looked at my watch. "I better get going, and you better get back to studying. Thanks for the talk."

"You're welcome, Lily."

I got up from my seat and returned to the bar parking lot to get my car. As I approached, I saw Luke around the front, showing off his motorcycle to Cody. I already hated her. Knots began to form in my stomach. I turned down another street that led to the back of his parking lot because I didn't want him to see me. I hopped in the Explorer and drove to Dr. Blakely's office.

Chapter Eight

LUKE

I could already tell that Cody was going to be a lifesaver. She really seemed to know her stuff. Lily looked very uncomfortable when she walked over to the table, and I thought she was pissed when she saw us eating together.

"How long have you been dating your girlfriend?" Cody asked.

"About seven months." I smiled.

"And how about you?" Lucky said as he strolled in.

Cody smiled and shook her head. "Let's just say that I'm in between boyfriends at the moment."

"Perfect. It just so happens that I'm in between girlfriends."

"Don't listen to him, Cody. He's living with a woman, and she's having his baby."

She looked at him in disgust. "How dare you," she said.

"What? We have an open relationship. She sees other guys all the time. In fact, we're having some people over for dinner tonight. Why don't you join us and you can meet all of our friends."

"Are you going?" she asked me.

"Yeah."

"Okay. Thanks for the invite, Lucky. I look forward to it."

I sent Cody to the office to start some paperwork and grabbed Lucky by the arm.

"What the fuck, dude? How could you invite her? Why would you invite her? I told you that Lily isn't comfortable with this situation."

"Relax, bro. Lily will be fine."

I rolled my eyes and went into my office. I didn't know if I should have told Lily that Cody would be there tonight. Fuck Lucky for putting me in this position. I went about my day and made sure I left the bar early enough to go home, shower, and change before the clusterfuck of the night was going to start.

~

WHEN I WALKED through the door, Lily was sitting at the table on her laptop. I walked up behind her and softly kissed her neck.

"It's so good to be home."

She cupped the back of my neck with her hand and tilted her head to the side so I had better access to her soft skin.

"It's good to have you home."

My hands cupped her breasts and squeezed them tightly. I wanted her, and I wanted her now.

"Stand up, Lily," I said.

She did as I asked, and I lifted her shirt over her head and unclasped her bra, throwing it onto the floor.

"Luke," she moaned as I took her breast in my mouth.

I unbuttoned her shorts and pulled them down, along with her panties, as my tongue slid down her torso and to her clit. Her moans became louder as I pleasured her with my mouth. She was swollen and about to come.

"Don't stop, Luke. I'm going to come!" she yelled.

I flicked my tongue around her clit before softly sucking it and plunging my fingers deep inside her. That was all I needed to do to send her over the edge with an orgasm. Her fingers tightened through my hair as she gasped and moaned with pleasure. I stood up and removed my pants as she lifted my shirt over my head. She wrapped her fingers around my cock and stroked me as I passionately kissed her. There was no more time to waste. I picked her up, and she wrapped her legs around me. I put her up against the wall as I thrust inside of her, never breaking our kiss. I moved in and out of her rapidly until I was about to come. I couldn't hold back anymore. I wanted nothing more than to release myself inside her. Her moans excited me. I loved knowing that I made her feel so fucking good. One last deep thrust, and we both came together. As I buried my face into her neck and tried to catch my breath, she told me how much she loved me.

"I love you, too, babe." I smiled as I stared into her eyes. "Don't you ever forget it."

She released her legs, and I carefully set her down. As we were in the bathroom getting ready to go to Giselle's, Lily told me she went and saw Dr. Blakely.

"How did it go?"

"It went well. She pointed out many things to me that I never thought of."

Do I or don't I tell her about Cody? Damn Lucky.

"Lucky was in the bar today and invited Cody to dinner at Giselle's tonight."

She stopped putting on her mascara and stared at me through the mirror. "What?"

"I tried to stop him, but you know, Lucky. He doesn't care, and he doesn't listen."

"Okay."

"Okay? You're not going to yell at me?"

"Nope. It's not your fault, and she seems like a nice girl. Maybe getting to know her better wouldn't be such a bad idea since she'll be working with you every day."

"You're amazing." I smiled as I kissed the side of her head.

"Yeah. I know." She winked.

~

LILY

An uneasiness settled inside me. Dr. Blakely said that Luke wasn't Hunter, and I needed to remind myself of that. She also told me that if I ever wanted to be at peace with what had happened, it would be a good idea to talk to Brynn and Hunter and get my feelings out. I wasn't so sure about that. I was afraid that I'd murder both of them if I saw them face to face. Brynn still sent me text messages every once in a while, asking for my forgiveness. I never replied. I just hit the delete button. According to my mother, the two of them were still together, and as far as I was concerned, they deserved each other. Luke and I arrived at Giselle's house fifteen minutes late.

"It's about time," she said as she hugged me.

"Sorry. Luke had me pinned to a wall."

"Oh my. I can't wait to get that kind of action on again. It's hard right now with the large baby bump and all." She laughed as she rubbed her tummy.

Luke walked over to where Sam was standing, talking to Cody. Gretchen walked up to me and hooked her arm around mine. Giselle did the same, and they walked me outside on the patio.

"Who the fuck is that Cody chick, and why is she here?" Gretchen asked.

"Luke's new assistant and compliments of a douchebag named Lucky," I said as I looked over at Giselle.

"He's an asshole. You already know that," she said.

"I saw Dr. Blakely today, and she said a few things that helped. So, I'm trying not to think about how gorgeous Cody is and how she'll see my boyfriend more than I do every day." A tear started to form in my eye.

"What are the three of you doing out here?" Luke asked as he and Sam stepped out the door.

"Having girl talk. Would you care to join in on our birthing conversation?" Gretchen asked.

"Um, no. I think we're good. Right, Luke?"

"Yeah. We're totally good. Go back to talking, and we'll see you inside."

The three of us laughed. "So, did you find out the sex of the baby?" I asked.

"The answer is in that big box in the living room. I brought in a bunch of blue and pink balloons to the doctor's office, and I had the nurse find out the sex of the baby and then put the appropriate color balloons in the box. So, when we open the box, we'll all know together."

"What a fabulous idea. I'm so excited. Let's find out now." I grinned.

"After dinner. It's almost ready. We should get back inside."

I noticed that Luke and Cody were talking alone. I walked over to where they were standing and made sure she knew he was mine. I wrapped my arms around him and laid my head on his shoulder. I was staking my claim.

"Hey, babe. Are the three of you done with your conversation?"

"Yes, we are, and it's almost time to eat, so we better sit down."

I was on alert as to where Cody thought she was sitting. The next thing I knew, Lucky had taken hold of her arm and led her to the seat next to his. Luke and I sat down, and he poured me a glass of wine. I smiled and thanked him with a kiss on the lips. Giselle kept looking at me and rolling her eyes as Lucky fed Cody his lines of bullshit. Once dinner was over, we all gathered in the living room and sat down, except for Giselle and Lucky, who stood in the center of the room behind the box.

"Okay. Is everyone ready to find out what gender our kid is?" Giselle asked with a smile.

Lucky carefully ran the box cutter across the top, and many pink balloons emerged. Lucky hugged Giselle, and everyone screeched and clapped, but I thought Luke was the loudest when he stood up and yelled, "YES! THANK YOU, GOD!"

Gretchen and I ran over to Giselle and hugged her tightly.

"Dude, what the hell was that for?" Lucky asked Luke.

"Paybacks. You're having a daughter, and there will be guys exactly like you trying to get into her pants."

"The hell they will. My daughter isn't allowed to date, and I will protect her against guys like me."

I looked at Lucky and smiled as I hugged him.

"Congratulations on your baby girl. May you have many sleepless nights when she's a teenager," Sam said.

"You two are mean people," Lucky pointed out.

Giselle was so excited she was having a girl that she could barely stand it. Luke and I decided it was time for us to leave because he needed to be at the bar early in the morning, and I had to be at the studio.

Chapter Nine

TWO WEEKS LATER

LILY

The studio was finally finished, and everything was set in its place. Cameron did an amazing job, and I couldn't be happier. I hung up Rory's picture of her, the girls, and a few of Charley I'd taken. Giselle and Gretchen stopped by a lot and helped me organize things. The doors would be ready to open in just a few short days.

Later that night, Luke got home from the bar later than usual. When he walked in, I could instantly tell he was in a bad mood.

"What's wrong?" I asked as he walked over and gave me a kiss.

"Just a bad day, babe. The liquor order didn't show up today, the dishwasher broke, and the toilet overflowed."

"I'm sorry."

He walked to the refrigerator and grabbed a beer. He threw the cap on the counter and looked at the box that was sitting on the table.

"What's in the box?"

"Pictures I took when I left Seattle. I just took it down from the closet shelf. I haven't opened it or looked in it since I first arrived in

Portland and had them developed. I was going to see if there were any pictures I could blow up and put in the studio."

"Great idea, babe. Do you mind if I open it?"

"No. Go right ahead. I have to brush my teeth. I'll be back in a second."

I went into the bathroom and brushed my teeth. When I walked back into the living room, the pictures from the box were scattered all over the table and floor, and Luke stood there staring at me with a look I'd never seen on his face before.

"Luke, what is it?"

The anger on his face grew, but he wouldn't say a word.

"Luke! What's going on?"

"It was you," he said in a low voice.

"It was me what? What are you talking about?"

He held out a picture to me. I walked over, took it from him, and gasped when I saw the couple sitting at the table. Tears immediately filled my eyes as I looked at him.

"You were the woman who gave us the tickets to Aruba. It was you. The night Callie was killed was the night we were on our way home from the airport from Aruba. The trip YOU gave to us."

I began to shake, and I felt like I was going to pass out. "Luke. I—"

"You what, Lily? Answer me one question. "Did you remember me when you saw me?"

"NO! Of course not. I would have said something. You didn't remember me?"

"I thought you looked familiar, but I blew it off when I found out you were Johnny's daughter. I can't believe this. I can't believe that I—"

"That you what? What exactly are you saying?" I yelled as tears poured down my face.

"If you had never given us those tickets, we wouldn't have gone, and Callie would still be alive today."

The knife that plunged into my heart at that moment hurt like nothing else. I'd never felt such pain as I did right then, not even when I caught Brynn and Hunter together. This pain was far worse and something I'd never experienced before.

"Are you blaming me for Callie's death?" I screamed.

He turned away. "I guess I am. I have to get out of here," he said as he walked to the bedroom and slammed the door shut.

I was shaking uncontrollably and needed to sit down on the couch before I collapsed. I couldn't believe what just happened, and I couldn't believe Luke blamed me for Callie's death. He left the bedroom with his bag and headed towards the door.

"Where are you going?" I cried as I jumped up from the couch and grabbed his hand.

He jerked away from me. "I can't stay here for a while. I need to think about things."

"Think about what? Please don't leave me, Luke."

"I need space, Lily. This is too much for me to handle right now."

"If you walk out that door, then you're blaming me for Callie's death, and that's not fair."

"I'm leaving before we both say something we'll regret."

"It's too late! You already said it!" I screamed as he walked out the door.

I grabbed my head and paced back and forth. I picked up the box from the table and threw it against the door. I fell to my knees and sobbed like a baby. How could he do this to me? How could he blame me and then walk out and ruin us? I didn't know what to do. I needed him. I needed him to hold me and tell me everything would be all right. I curled into a ball in the middle of the floor and didn't move.

Chapter Ten

LUKE

"What the fuck is going on?" Sam yelled as I slammed the door shut.

"Leave me alone," I said and stormed into the bedroom.

He followed me. "Gretchen and I could hear you and Lily screaming next door. What happened, man?"

I looked at Sam, standing in the doorway with Gretchen behind him.

"You want to know what the fuck happened? I'll tell you. Lily had a box of pictures she took when she left Seattle. There was a picture of Callie and me. She was the girl who gave us the tickets to Aruba!"

"So what? What the fuck are you saying, Luke?"

"If she had never given us those tickets, the accident never would have happened."

Sam closed his eyes and shook his head. "Oh my God, Luke. Please tell me you didn't say that to Lily."

Suddenly, Gretchen flew out the door.

"Get out, Sam. I don't want to be bothered. I need to think. I can't do it with you and Gretchen here. Can the two of you go stay somewhere else?"

"Really, Luke? You can't stay with Lily, but it's okay to stay next door? Fuck you. Gretchen and I aren't going anywhere. You need to grow the fuck up, man. How dare you blame Lily? In fact, I hope she never speaks to you again."

I grabbed my bag. "Fuck this. I'll leave."

I strapped the bag to my bike and drove to my parents' house. They had just left for another cruise and wouldn't return for two weeks. My mind was a total clusterfuck. I didn't know what to think or what to do. I just needed to get drunk and forget about it, at least for tonight.

~

Lily

I heard the door open, and for a second, I thought it was Luke coming back to tell me he was sorry until I heard Gretchen's voice.

"Lily," she whispered as she walked over to me, got down on the floor, and wrapped her arms around me.

"I don't know what happened. We were so happy one second, and he was leaving the next. I had no idea he was the one I gave the tickets to. I never opened that box after I developed the pictures."

"I know, sweetie. Come on. Get up and at least lie down on the couch."

She helped me up and over to the couch. I sat there as the tears poured down my face, and Gretchen tried to console me. At this point, there was nothing anyone could say or do to make me feel better.

"I need a drink," I cried.

"I'll get you a beer."

"No. There's a bottle of wine in the rack."

Gretchen got up, grabbed the wine with two glasses, and sat down. The door opened, and Sam walked in.

"Lily, I'm so sorry," he said as he walked over and put his arm around me.

I buried my face into his chest and cried some more.

"Just give him some time. He's just freaked out right now. He'll come around."

"What if he doesn't? What if he hates me forever? He blamed me, Sam. He pretty much said that I killed Callie. How the fuck am I supposed to go on? He's my life. Finding Hunter and Brynn on my wedding day was nothing compared to this."

"You won't have to. He'll come around. He's Luke, and even though he's a fuckhead right now, we all know what an amazing person he is."

"I need to be alone right now," I said as I looked at Sam and Gretchen.

"Okay. We're right next door if you need us."

As soon as they left, I grabbed the bottle of wine and took it to the bedroom. I wasted no time downing half of it before I laid down and passed out.

Chapter Eleven

LUKE

When I arrived at my parent's house, I threw my bag down in the hallway and headed to the bar area in the living room. I took out the whiskey bottle, grabbed a glass, and went outside to the patio. It wasn't too long before I polished off half the bottle. I was so angry. I was furious that Lily and I had met before, and neither remembered. Angry that she was the one to give us the tickets to Aruba. Angry that the accident happened on the way home from the airport. Angry that I had to find out. There was no reasoning with me at this point. Once the shock settled, I would be able to process things better. But for now, I was ready to pass out.

I awoke the following day to the constant ringing of my phone. I rolled over and grabbed it from the other side of the bed to see that Maddie was calling.

"Hello," I sleepily answered.

"Luke, where are you? Aren't you coming in today? I've been trying to call you and Lily all morning, and there's been no answer. What the hell is going on?"

"I'll be there soon." Click.

I sighed as I rubbed my face and jumped in the shower. As I let the hot water run down me, I felt numb. When I finished, I dressed, grabbed my keys, hopped on my bike, and drove to the bar.

"You look like shit," Maddie said as I walked in. "Cody has been waiting for you. What the hell is going on?"

"I don't want to talk about it right now," I said as I walked past her.

I went into my office, and Cody was sitting behind my desk.

"Good morning, boss. Or should I say 'afternoon.'" She smiled.

"Sorry. I had a rough night."

"Are you okay?"

"Yeah. Record all the receipts from last night. That should be the first thing you do when you come in."

"Already done."

"Oh. Well, then, get my files organized. I'll have a desk moved in here so you don't have to sit at mine."

I walked out and went behind the bar. I grabbed a bottle of beer and opened it. Maddie stood there, staring at me with a disgusted look.

"I found out last night that Lily was the woman who gave me the tickets to Aruba."

"What? How did you find that out?" she asked.

"I found a picture she took of Callie and me in Portland. It was in a box with other pictures she took when she left Seattle."

"Okay. So then what?"

"We argued. We fought. I screamed. Callie would still be alive today if she had never given us those tickets."

Maddie's eyes widened. "Luke, no. Are you blaming Lily for the accident?"

I brought the bottle to my lips and took a long swig before answering her.

"Maybe I am. Maddie, you have to understand where I'm coming from," I pleaded. If anyone would get me, it would be my sister. "If we didn't go to Aruba, we wouldn't have been on our way home that night from the airport, and that accident never would have happened, and Callie would still be alive."

Her eyes filled with tears as she stared at me. "Luke, Lily means the world to you. The two of you are so in love. You can't possibly forget that. Did you tell her that you blamed her?"

I nodded.

"Oh my God, Luke. I can't even imagine someone saying that to me. I love you, but you're wrong."

"Somehow, I knew you'd take her side."

"It's not about sides. What are you going to do?"

"I have no clue. I need some time away to think. I can't do that here, surrounded by everyone. Will you be okay with running the bar while I'm gone?"

"Yeah, but where are you going?"

"I'm going to rent a cabin in the mountains for a few days and go hiking. It's the best way to think."

"Please be careful," she said as she kissed my cheek.

I gave her a small smile and left the bar. I contacted Joe, a friend of my parents who owned a string of mountain cabins. He had one cabin left, and I reserved it. I returned to my parent's house and my apartment to get my hiking boots and jeep. Walking through the door, I saw Gretchen standing in the kitchen. She turned and looked at me and then turned back around without saying a word.

"I know you're pissed off at me, and I'm sorry."

"I'm not the one you should be apologizing to," she snapped.

"I'm going away for a couple of days."

"I don't really care," she snapped again.

"Have you talked to Lily?" I asked with hesitation.

She turned around in anger and pointed her spoon at me. "That, mister, is none of your fucking business. If you care so much, then go and talk to her and find out how she is yourself," she yelled as she stomped away and into the bedroom.

I grabbed my boots and stepped into the hallway, locking the door behind me while I stared at Lily's door. Fuck. I shook my head and headed to the jeep.

∼

LILY

I tried to open my eyes, but they were too puffy and swollen shut. I had nightmares last night—nightmares about the accident. I needed to talk to Luke. I picked up my phone and sent him a text message.

"Please come over and talk to me. I'm begging you, Luke."

I waited a few minutes, and there was no response.

"Please, Luke. We can talk this out. We can work through this."

Still, no response. I didn't have the strength to do anything. All I wanted to do was sleep. Suddenly, there was a knock on the door, and I heard Giselle's voice.

"Lily, are you in there? Open the door before I break it down."

I stumbled out of bed and out of the bedroom to unlock the door. As soon as I opened it, Giselle threw her arms around me.

"I'm so sorry. Gretchen called last night, but she said you kicked her and Sam out and didn't want to be bothered."

"I can't do this, Giselle." I began to cry.

Her hands firmly clasped my shoulders. "Yes, you can! This is a bump in the road where your relationship is concerned. As soon as that bump is smoothed out, everything will be fine and return to normal."

"Not this time. You didn't see the anger on his face. You didn't see the hate in his eyes. You didn't hear the disgust in his voice."

"He'll realize he's being an ass and come begging for your forgiveness," she said.

"I'm such a mess. I can't even believe this happened," I continued to sob.

"Shh, sweetie. Do you want me to talk to him? Because I'll punch him in the balls for you. I've done it before, and I'll do it again." She smiled.

I let out a light laugh in between sobs. Giselle was the one who always had a way of making light of a horrible situation.

"Go shower, and I'll make you some coffee. You're a hot mess right now, and you'll feel better after a hot shower."

I nodded and slowly walked to the bathroom. Once I was in the shower and the hot water was beating down my back, the tears started up again, and I crouched down in the corner and sobbed.

Chapter Twelve

LUKE

I received Lily's text messages on the way up to the cabin. I couldn't bring myself to answer her back. I needed time to sort things out: my feelings and my anger. I finally arrived at the cabin where Joe was waiting for me with the keys.

"Well, if it isn't Luke Matthews. Long time no see, buddy." He smiled as we lightly hugged.

"Pastor Joe, how are you?"

"I'm good. How are you doing?"

"I'm okay."

"What brings you up here?"

"I have a lot on my mind and a lot of thinking to do."

"Your mom and dad told me you finally bought Bernie's Bar."

"Yeah, I did."

"Well, here's your keys. The place has everything you need. It's the same one you used to stay in with your parents as a kid."

"I can see that. Thank you."

"If you need anything, I'll just be down the road."

"Thanks, Joe."

I walked through the door and looked around. Nothing had changed. I set my bags down and walked out to the back, where the lake was. I'd been wanting to bring Lily here for quite a while, but with the bar, I hadn't had the time. I knew she'd like it here. It was peaceful and quiet, and it would have been just the two of us like she was always asking. My phone beeped in my pocket, and when I pulled it out, I had a text message from Lucky.

"Dude, you're fucking crazy. How could you do that to Lily, of all people? You need to talk to her. I know I'm not an authority on relationships, but I admire yours."

"You don't understand, so drop it. I want everyone to leave me alone for a while. Tell Sam that I've gone up to the cabin."

"You're crazy, bro. I hate to say this, but I'm disappointed in you."

I didn't respond. He didn't understand. Nobody understood. I wasn't sure if I even understood. I hopped in my jeep and drove to the liquor store for a case of beer and a pizza.

~

Lily

For the first time in seven months, I was alone. Alone in my apartment like I was when I first arrived here. Being alone before I met Luke was fine. But then he came into my life, swept me off my feet, and loved me like no other person ever had. And now he was gone. I walked to the living room, where Giselle had picked up all the pictures and put them back in the box. I didn't want to see that box ever again. I picked it up off the counter, and as I opened the door to go and throw it in the dumpster, Maddie was standing there.

"Hey, Lily. I didn't know if you were home. I'm not even going to ask you how you're doing because I already know."

"Come on in, Maddie."

I couldn't turn her away, and now I was worried about Charley and how she would react to the news of Luke and I not being together anymore.

"Have you eaten, Lily?" she asked.

I shook my head. Food was the last thing on my mind. The truth was that if I even attempted to put food in my mouth, I'd probably throw it up.

"You need to eat. Let's go out somewhere. I know you probably don't want to, but it'll be good for you to get out, even if it's only for a couple of hours."

"I can't, Maddie."

"Yes, you can. Grab your purse, and let's go. We'll go somewhere small where there's not a lot of people."

She was persistent, and I knew she was trying to help. Maybe I needed to get out of this apartment for a couple of hours.

We hopped into her car, and she drove us to a cute little diner.

"Luke will come around," she said as she grabbed my hand. "He's just upset right now, but once he calms down, he'll be back."

"He never should have left. He should have stayed and talked to me. I know we could have worked this out. I swear to you, Maddie, that I had no idea he was the one I gave the tickets to. I swear."

"Sweetie, stop. I believe you, and so will Luke."

"Luke doesn't care about that. He only cares that I gave him the tickets, which in turn led to the accident that killed Callie."

"He's an ass, and I don't want you to listen to him."

"I sent him some text messages earlier, and he never responded."

"He might not have gotten them. He's up at a cabin in the mountains, and the service is not all that great."

"Why did he go there?"

"He said he needed to think and clear his head."

I sat there in disbelief that Luke would leave town like that. I knew he was pissed and upset, but I never thought he would leave town.

"Once he has time to think things over, he'll be back at your door."

Something inside me started to happen. Something that I'd never expected. A rage grew. Rage that he said what he did and rage that he blamed me for Callie's death. I was returning to the place I was at almost two years ago—the place where anger was comforting and consumed my life.

"Well, I may not be around if he does decide he's wrong."

"You have every right to be upset with him," Maddie said.

She didn't even know the half of it. I ordered a bowl of chicken noodle soup, and Maddie ordered a sandwich. I could barely eat, and with every bite I took, I wanted to vomit.

Chapter Thirteen

LUKE

I spent a few extra days than I originally planned at the cabin. Maddie said everything was fine with the bar and to take as much time as I needed. Pastor Joe stopped by one evening and brought a large pizza with him. He said we had some catching up to do before I went back home. We took the pizza out on the patio and I talked to him all about Lily.

"Listen, Luke. We're all on a timeline. We never know when the big guy upstairs plans to take us back home. As much as I hate to say it, it was Callie's time to go home and that accident would have happened anyway. Maybe you would have gone out to dinner that night. You don't know, and you never will, but blaming Lily for Callie's death was not the right thing to do. You've let your anger for that accident cloud your judgment."

"I know I have," I said as I sipped my beer.

"There's a plan for all of us. People just don't come into our lives by accident. They come with a purpose. You were at the lowest point of your life after Callie died, and then, when you least expected it, Lily walked into your life. Do you think it's a coincidence? Do you believe in fate? When one door closes, no matter how painful it is, another opens for a greater purpose."

I sighed as I sat there and listened to him. "I get what you're saying, Joe. I really do. I just needed these last few days to clear my head and get over the shock. I mean, how the heck is it possible that Lily was the one to give us those tickets and then, a year later, show up in Santa Monica and move in next door?"

"That was the higher power doing his job, my son. Have faith and believe." He smiled as he patted my shoulder. "I best be going now. I have to prepare for a funeral tomorrow."

I got up from my seat and hugged him. "It was good seeing you, Joe. Thanks for the talk and for listening."

"No problem, Luke. It was good to see you again. Tell your parents that I expect to see them up here sometime soon. They keep going on those fancy cruises, and I feel a little unloved."

I chuckled. "I will."

I brought the plates and beer bottles into the kitchen and grabbed my phone. I missed Lily, and I wanted to get home to her. God, I had a lifetime of making up to her and owed her a huge explanation. I loved her and wanted to spend the rest of my life with her. I decided to send her a text message.

"Hi, Lily. I'm heading back to Santa Monica tomorrow, and we need to talk."

I waited for a response. Nothing. I set my phone down and jumped into the shower. When I was finished, I looked at my phone again, and still no response. Shit.

∽

LILY

I spent the last few days locked in my apartment. The only time I left was when I went to dinner with Maddie. Gretchen, Giselle, and Sam kept calling and checking up on me, and even Lucky stopped by for a visit. I hopped into my Explorer and drove to my appointment with Dr. Blakely.

"Come in, Lily. I'm glad you're here. You really had me worried on the phone."

"Thanks, Dr. Blakely," I said as I sat in the oversized leather chair.

"Have you heard from Luke?" she asked.

"No. I sent him a couple of text messages, but he never responded."

"I want you to tell me how you're feeling right now."

"I'm sad and hurt, but I'm mostly angry. I'm really angry!" I spewed.

"That's understandable. Words can hurt louder than actions. I think you and Luke both have issues you need to work on. His issue is with Callie's death. I don't think he ever put closure on that. Then there's your issues with your sister and Hunter."

I sat there, playing with a string hanging from the bottom of my shirt.

"He pretty much called me a murderer. He blames me for Callie's death, and maybe he's right. Why did I have to give those tickets away? I should have just thrown them in the garbage. I don't know if he'll ever forgive me."

"Saying never is pretty harsh."

"Yeah, well, my life has been pretty harsh."

"What if he were to walk through that door right now and beg for your forgiveness? What would you do?"

"I don't know because, right now, I'm so angry."

"Angry at what? Him or the fact you gave him the tickets?"

"Both."

"Are you still angry at Brynn and Hunter?"

"Yes."

"Your mother?"

"We're working on our relationship. Things are going well with her right now."

"Good. Then, it would be best to resolve your anger one step at a time. You can't go through life being angry. You will never be your true self, and it'll always get in the way of your life."

"Maybe you should be telling Luke that," I said.

Her phone chimed, alerting us that my session was over. I got up from my seat, thanked her, and left her office. I climbed in my Explorer and put my head on the steering wheel. I was being forced to return to the place I swore I'd never go back to.

∼

LUKE

Not responding to my message, told me that she didn't want to talk to me. I dialed her number, and it went straight to voicemail. I dialed Sam.

"Hey, Luke. How are you?" he answered.

"Hey, is Lily home?"

"I don't know, bro. Gretchen and I are out to dinner. Why?"

"I texted her earlier, and she never texted me back."

"Do you fucking blame her? I wouldn't text you back either."

"Thanks, bro. I'll be home tomorrow. If you see Lily, tell her that I need to talk to her."

"I will, man. Safe travels."

I sighed as I hung up. I opened another bottle of beer, lay on the bed, and scrolled through the pictures of Lily and me on my phone. I slowly ran my finger across Lily's face, taking in how happy she looked and how I had possibly destroyed her. I had been in shock over my discovery. I said things I didn't mean. Words that I would take back in a heartbeat. She had to forgive me because I didn't know what I'd do if she didn't. I needed to stop thinking and go to sleep for the night. Tomorrow would be a new day and beginning for us. I would make sure of it, get down on my hands and knees, and beg her for forgiveness.

Chapter Fourteen

LILY

I booked a non-stop flight to Seattle. When I walked out the door, Sam came out of his apartment. He looked at me and then at my suitcase.

"Hey, Lily. Where are you going?"

"I'm flying to Seattle for a while. I have some things I need to take care of there."

"Ah. I see. I talked to Luke last night. He said he texted you, but you never responded."

"I didn't get a text message from him," I said as I pulled out my phone and took a second look.

"He's at the cabin, and service isn't the best. Anyway, he's coming home today and wanted me to tell you that he needs to talk to you."

"Well, that's too bad because I'm leaving. He had a chance to talk to me the day he left me sobbing hysterically in the middle of my apartment. Now he thinks it's okay just to come back and want to talk because he's had time. It doesn't work that way, Sam. I'm hurt and distraught, and, to be honest, I feel betrayed. He doesn't just get to talk to me when it suits him. If you excuse me, I have a plane to catch, and do me a favor. Don't tell him where I am. Please."

The sadness in his eyes bothered me, but I had no choice.

"I won't tell him. Have a safe trip, Lily, and I'll see you when you get back," he said as he leaned over, kissed my cheek, and helped me load my suitcase into the back of the Explorer.

～

As I sat on the plane and stared out the window, I couldn't stop thinking about what Sam had said. Maybe Luke wanted to talk to me to put closure on our relationship because he still blamed me for what happened. The only thing I knew at this point was that my stomach was in a permanent knot, and I'd never felt so lonely. When the plane landed, I rented a car and drove to my mom's house. The hardest part was going to have to face Brynn and possibly Hunter. I no longer cared about what he did because I realized he wasn't my true love. But my baby sister, Brynn, was a different story. Blood doesn't do that to each other, and it was mostly my anger with her that I needed to control.

～

LUKE

I pulled up to the apartment building, and Lily's Explorer wasn't there. Instead of going to my and Sam's apartment, I inserted the key into Lily's lock and opened the door. I looked around. Lily had all the blinds shut. A blanket was lying on the couch, and an empty bottle of wine was on the coffee table. I walked straight to the bedroom, and she wasn't there. I opened the closet doors and noticed some of her missing clothes and her suitcase was gone. FUCK! Where the hell did she go? I pulled out my phone and texted Sam.

"Where's Lily?"

"I take it you're back. I don't know, dude. She said she was leaving and wouldn't tell me where she was going."

"What about her studio?"

"Don't know. She'll be back eventually. She didn't move for good."

"How the fuck do you know that?"

"She only had one suitcase. Chill out, Luke. You left, and now so did she. Give her the space she wants."

I threw my bag down on the floor and headed to the bar. When I walked in, I saw Cody talking to Maddie.

"Well, look who's back." Maddie smiled.

"Do you know where Lily went?"

"No. I didn't know she left."

"Her suitcase is gone, and so are some of her clothes. Sam said she wouldn't tell him where she was going."

"I'm not surprised, Luke. She was really broken up."

I shook my head and went to my office. A few moments later, Cody walked in.

"Hey, Luke. Welcome back. I'm really sorry. If there's anything I can do, just let me know."

"Thanks, Cody. Can you please shut the door on your way out?"

She nodded and walked out of the office. Sam was right. Lily didn't take all her things, so she'd be back. I would have to wait until she was to talk to her and apologize.

~

LILY

I pulled up the driveway, and an even worse sickness took over me. I walked up the porch steps and opened the front door with my shaking hand. I heard my mother's voice in the kitchen, and when I stood in the doorway, she turned and looked at me.

"Lily? What—"

The minute she said my name, the tears streamed down my face.

"Oh, baby. Come here," she said as she held out her arms.

I walked over to her as she wrapped her arms around me, and I cried, just like I did when I was a child.

"What happened?" she asked sympathetically as she walked me into the living room.

We sat down on the loveseat, and I told her everything. Right down to the day I left Seattle.

"Lily, the accident was not your fault. How could he blame you like that?"

I told her exactly how I felt and why I returned here.

"Where's Brynn?" I asked as I wiped my eyes.

"She and Hunter went out. They'll be back later."

"So they're still together?" I asked. It was a subject that both of us avoided when we talked over the phone.

"Yes."

I asked my mother for a glass of wine, and when she went to get it, I sat there and thought about Hunter and Brynn. After all that happened, they were still together. Maybe that was why I was a part of Hunter's life. So he could meet Brynn. They must really love each other to be together still. Maybe they had the passion that Luke and I did. I didn't know, and I didn't want to know. I was handed my glass of wine, and my mother asked if she could get me something to eat. Food wasn't really on my agenda. I still became sick with each bite. I got up from the couch and took my suitcase to my old room. It looked the same as it did the day I left.

"I never touched it," my mother said as she stood in the doorway. "The maid dusts it once a week. I wanted it exactly the same in case you came back."

I looked out my window at the gazebo in the middle of the lawn, surrounded by flowers. My dad had it built for me when I was a kid. He told me it was my special place to go when I was having a bad day or just needed to think. I liked to play my guitar there. Everyone, including the staff, knew that I wasn't to be disturbed when I was in my gazebo. It was my sanctuary and my safe haven. A place where all my troubles disappeared the minute I stepped inside.

"Excuse me, Mother," I said as I walked out of my room and to the gazebo.

I took a deep breath before stepping inside because I wanted all my troubles to magically disappear. After a few moments, I heard something. I froze in place, and it seemed like time stood still.

"Hi, Lily," Brynn said with a soft voice.

I had to compose myself before turning around to face her. Once I took in several deep breaths, I slowly turned around and saw my sister standing there before me with tears in her eyes.

"Brynn."

"It's so good to see you," she said nervously.

"We have a lot of talking to do," I said.

"I know. It's been a long time," she replied.

Looking at her didn't make me as sick to my stomach as I thought it would. Maybe it was because I was already sick enough over Luke. I looked across the way and saw our mother walking towards us.

"I think the two of you should go out to dinner. Talk over some greasy food like you used to. I think that maybe a public place would be best for your first time talk."

"I agree. Is Cabala's still around?" I asked Brynn.

"Yeah. It is. I'll drive." She smiled.

I climbed into her car, and we drove to the place that made the world's best lobster macaroni and cheese. I could tell Brynn was uncomfortable and that she was on pins and needles, waiting for me to explode and go off on her. But I didn't. I kept reminding myself of what Dr. Blakely said about letting anger consume me.

"Why, Brynn?" I finally asked.

"Do you want the truth?"

"Of course. That's all I ever wanted," I said.

She pulled into the parking lot of Cabala's and waited to spill the truth until we were seated.

"I fell in love with him, and I don't know how it happened," she said as she looked down.

"Go on."

"I didn't want to hurt you, and neither did he, but the attraction between us was stronger than we were, and we didn't know how to stop it."

I set my menu down and looked at her. "You're my sister. How could you carry on with him the way you were and still have the nerve to look at me every day?"

"It was hard and unbearable. You have to believe me when I tell you that. I swear, Lily, neither one of us wanted it to happen, but it did."

I understood what Brynn was saying because it sounded like the same attraction Luke and I had. When two people are meant to be together, there's nothing anyone can do to stop it.

"Do you know how many times I wanted to tell you? I tried on so many occasions, but I just couldn't."

"So instead, you were going to let me marry him? What were the two of you going to do? Continue to fuck behind my back until I found out?"

"I don't know, Lily." She began to cry. "All I know is that I love him and can't help how I feel. I'm so sorry for everything, and I'm sorry for what I've done."

"But you and Hunter are still together. So how sorry could you be?"

She looked me in the eyes.

"We love each other more than life, Lily," she spoke seriously.

And there it was. They weren't just carrying on like two people who got off because they knew it was wrong. They were supposed to be together, and I was the middleman that helped make that happen. Could I be so reasonable? Would I forgive her? Would I forgive Hunter? I didn't know. I guessed that was something only time would tell.

Chapter Fifteen

LUKE

I left the bar and went for a ride on my motorcycle. I rode along the coast just like I used to do after Callie died. When I returned to the apartment, Gretchen and Sam sat at the table.

"Hey, bro," Sam said as he gave a small wave.

"Gretchen, do you know where Lily went?"

"No, and even if I did, I wouldn't tell you," she snapped.

I grabbed a beer from the fridge and sat at the table beside them. Gretchen went to get up, and I grabbed her hand and asked her to sit down.

"Listen, I know you hate me right now, but I must talk to Lily. I need to apologize to her for everything I've said and done. I can't lose her."

"Oh, so now you want to apologize? She trusted you. She gave herself to you when she swore off everything about love and relationships. She loved you so much that nothing else in this world mattered to her. And now you decide to come back when it's convenient for you and try to fix things?"

"I know, Gretchen. I'm sorry. I will spend the rest of my life making it up to her. Please, do you know where she's at?"

"No, I don't, but she'll be back when she's ready."

"Have you been in contact with her?" I asked.

"No. I haven't. She instructed Giselle and me not to call or text her and that she'd talk to us when she returned. I'm sure she's fine. She's a strong woman."

Suddenly, there was a pounding at the door. Sam jumped up, and as soon as he opened the door, Charley came running in and over to me with tears in her eyes.

"Where's Lily, Uncle Luke?"

"Peanut, what are you doing here?"

"I'm sorry, Luke. She ran out of the apartment before I could stop her," Maddie said.

"Where is she?" Charley cried.

"I don't know, peanut. I'm trying to figure it out."

"I overheard my mom talking to my dad about how you blamed Lily for Callie's death."

I looked over at Maddie and gave her a stern look.

"I'm sorry. I thought she was asleep."

"She didn't cause Callie to die." She continued to cry.

"I know she didn't, peanut. I'm so sorry," I said as I grabbed her and hugged her.

She pushed me away. "I hate you for making Lily go away. I hate you!" she screamed as she ran out of the apartment.

Tears rolled down my face as I looked at Maddie and screamed Charley's name. Maddie left the apartment, and I threw my bottle cap against the wall. "FUCK!" I screamed.

Sam walked over and put his hand on my shoulder. "I'm sorry, Luke. Just give it time. She'll be back, and you'll work things out. You're meant to be together, and you'll find a way."

"I hope so, Sam. I really do."

∼

Lily

I was up in my room when I heard the front door open. My mom and I had plans to go shopping, but first, she had to run an errand, so we'd go when she returned. I grabbed my purse and stopped in the middle of the stairs when I saw Hunter standing in the foyer.

"Lily," he said.

"Brynn isn't home," I said as I continued down the stairs and into the kitchen.

"I know. I'm waiting for her. She told me that you and your mom were out shopping."

"She told you wrong," I said as I grabbed a bottle of water from the fridge.

"I think we need to talk."

"You think?" I snapped.

"I'm sorry, Lily. I really am. I know you hate me, and you probably dream every day of new ways to murder me, and I don't blame you. I would too. But I am truly sorry. Your mom told me you found someone great, and I'm happy for you."

I stood there and listened to his bullshit, taking in the stench behind every last word.

"Are you done?" I asked.

He looked nervous as he placed his hands in his pockets and slowly nodded.

"Cancel your plans with Brynn. You're taking me to the park."

"What? I can't do that."

"You can and you will. I need to put this to rest and behind me once and for all."

He pulled out his phone, called Brynn, and told her what I had demanded. I called my mother and told her there was a change of plans and that I wouldn't be going shopping with her. She wanted to know what was happening, and I told her I'd explain later.

Hunter and I hopped into his BMW and headed to the park. It was the one place he always kept his promise and took me to.

"Why are you doing this, Lily?" he asked. "Why the park?"

"Why not? You said we needed to talk, so that's where we will do it."

"You're not secretly planning to kill me, are you?" he asked with seriousness.

"I can't make any promises."

He looked at me, and I busted out laughing. Oh my God, it was good to laugh again. As much as I hated him, he still could amuse me. As soon as we arrived at the park, we sat under a tree like always.

"After talking with Brynn, I can see that you are really and seriously in love. I wish you had told me before we got into the wedding planning. I don't get it, Hunter. Why? Why didn't you just tell me?"

"Because I didn't want to hurt you. Lily, I loved you. I really did, and every time Brynn and I would say it was over, we couldn't seem to end it. I'm so sorry. You have no idea how many times I wanted to call you, but I couldn't because I truly hated myself for what I did to you. I guess you could say I was a coward."

I could hear the sincerity and remorse in his voice, just like I had heard it in Brynn's. The scar that the two of them left me would forever be there, but maybe with a little more understanding.

"Yes, you and Brynn were both cowards, but the fact that the two of you are still together tells me that you were meant to be with her and not me."

He reached over and lightly placed his hand on mine, and I instantly jerked it away. "This doesn't mean we're going to be besties or anything like that."

"I know. Just the fact that you understand means the world to us. Why don't we all have dinner tonight?" he said.

"Don't push it."

I got up from the ground, wiped the dirt off my ass, and told him to take me home.

~

LUKE

I went to the bar to check on things, and as soon as Candi saw me, she motioned for me to talk to her. I stepped behind the bar and grabbed the bottle of vodka and a glass.

"What's up, Candi?"

"I don't like that Cody girl you hired," she said.

"Why?"

"She's been nosing around, asking a bunch of questions about you and Lily. I think she likes you."

"There's no need to worry about her," I said as I downed my shot.

"I know her type, Luke, and she's looking to get you into bed."

"Like I said, don't worry about her. She's a good employee, and if she crosses the line, I'll take care of it."

"Have you heard from Lily yet?" she asked.

"No. I guess I will when she's ready."

"I'm sorry, boss," she said as she put her hand on my shoulder.

"Yeah, me too." I walked away and headed straight to my office.

It was two a.m., and the last customer finally stumbled out. I helped the crew clean up and walked the girls to their cars. When I got home, I headed straight for bed. I was tired, and thinking about Lily all day wore me out, not to mention that I was lonely without her.

Chapter Sixteen

LILY

    I spent the last two weeks thinking about my life, thinking about the anger I had finally let go about Brynn and Hunter, but the anger I still harbored with Luke and his accusation that I was the one responsible for Callie's death. It had been over three weeks since I'd seen or talked to him, or anyone else, for that matter. My relationship with Brynn over the past couple of weeks was tolerable, but things would never be the same again. I thought about my studio and how I never opened it. I put all the work and long hours into getting it ready, and it just sat there. I had planned on staying in Seattle for a few more days until my phone beeped with a text message from Gretchen.

    "Giselle went into labor, and she's in the hospital. It's way too early, Lily. Things aren't looking good. She's asking for you."

    "I'm on the next flight out. Tell her I'm on my way."

    I couldn't believe Giselle was in labor. She still had eight weeks left, and we hadn't even had her baby shower yet. I called the airlines and booked the next flight out, which would get me into Los Angeles around eight p.m. I quickly threw everything in my suitcase and drove to the airport. My mother and Brynn weren't home, so I texted them, explaining why I suddenly had to leave and return to Santa Monica.

As I sat on the plane, I couldn't stop fidgeting. Not only was I scared for Giselle, I was a nervous wreck to see Luke. When the plane finally landed, I climbed into my car and drove straight to the hospital.

As the elevator doors opened, Lucky was standing there. I stepped off and gave him a tight hug.

"How is she?" I asked.

He looked different. He had a look of worry and despair that I'd never seen before. A seriousness that made me worry even more.

"She's scared, and so am I. Thank you for coming back, Lily. She's been asking for you. I've never seen her like this. She's always so strong and sure of everything. But now, she's terrified and nervous."

"Don't worry. I'm sure everything will be fine. I'll go see her now. Where are you heading?"

"To grab something to eat. Do you want anything?" he asked.

"No. I'm good." I smiled as I patted his shoulder.

I walked down to Giselle's room, and when I opened the door, she looked up at me and started crying. My problems suddenly disappeared, and my main focus was my best friend, who needed me. I walked over to her bed, sat down on the edge, and hugged her with tears in my eyes.

"I'm so happy you're back," she cried. "Lily, I'm so worried. The doctors aren't sure what's going to happen. They're running all kinds of tests and put me on some medication."

"Shh. The doctors know what they're doing, and the baby will be fine." I smiled.

Gretchen reached over and grabbed my hand.

"Welcome home." She smiled.

"Where's Lucky?" Giselle asked.

"He went to get something to eat. He'll be back soon. He better be treating you right," I said.

"He is. He's so worried," she said as she closed her eyes.

Gretchen motioned for me to step to the other side of the room.

"Thank you for coming. I know this has to be hard for you right now, and I'm sorry," she whispered.

"Don't worry about me. I'm fine. The three of us have been through so much together and I would never not be here for either of you," I said as I hugged her.

Lucky returned to the room and went right over to Giselle's bedside. I stood there and watched him as he held her hand and gently rubbed his thumb back and forth across her skin.

"I'm going to get some coffee," I said.

"The coffee bar is closed now, but there's a machine down the hall. Believe it or not, the coffee is pretty good," Gretchen said.

As I exited the room, I looked to my left and saw Luke standing a few feet away. I started to tremble, and my heart began to beat at a rapid pace. All I kept hearing in my head was our conversation and how he said he blamed me for Callie's death. I turned away and walked down the hall towards the coffee machine. I prayed he didn't follow me. The rapid beating of my heart ached so badly that I felt like I was having a heart attack. I turned to the right and into the small waiting room with the coffee machine.

"Lily, please don't turn away from me," he said from behind.

I put my money in the machine and hit the coffee button with a shaking hand.

"I have nothing to say to you, Luke. I'm back for Giselle."

"I know, babe."

I turned around and looked at him as I held up my finger. "Don't. Don't call me that. You lost that right. I'm not doing this with you. I have my best friend lying in a hospital bed, ready to give birth two months early, and that's what I'm focusing on."

I grabbed the cup from the machine and stormed past him. I heard him yell my name, but I didn't care. I couldn't care. Because if I did, I'd fall to pieces yet once again.

∼

Luke

I sat down in the chair and cupped my face in my hands. She hated me. I could see it in her eyes and didn't blame her.

"Bro, are you okay?" Sam said as he sat down next to me.

"No," I replied as I looked up at him. "I saw Lily, and she ran from me."

"What did you expect? The last time the two of you spoke, you said some awful things to her."

"I know that, and I'm trying to apologize to her, but she won't let me."

"She will, in time."

"I don't have time, Sam. I need to make things right, now!"

"Come on," he said as he placed his hand on my shoulder. "Let's go see how Lucky and Giselle are doing."

I didn't know if that was a good idea because Lily was in the room. But Lucky and Giselle were both my good friends and I needed to make sure everything was going to be okay. Sam and I walked into the room, and my eyes went straight to Lily, sitting on the edge of the bed, holding Giselle's hand. She knew we walked in but refused to turn around and look at us.

"Hey, Lily." Sam smiled as he walked over to her and kissed her cheek.

"Hi, Sam," she replied.

"Welcome home."

"Thank you."

Lucky approached Sam and me, asking if we could step outside with him. He took us to a courtyard and pulled a cigarette from his pocket.

"Dude, when did you start smoking again?" Sam asked.

"Since all of this. I'm scared, guys. This is my baby, my daughter we're talking about and not knowing anything is driving me crazy. I'm ready to punch someone."

"You need to stay calm for Giselle's and your daughter's sake," I said.

"I know I do. It's hard, though. Thanks, guys, for coming to the hospital. It means a lot to us."

Lucky wasn't being typical Lucky anymore. He was legitimately scared, and he had every reason to be. He was acting like a responsible adult. As soon as he finished his smoke, we returned to the room, where the nurse told all of us that visiting hours were over for everyone except Lucky. I watched Lily kiss Giselle on the cheek and tell her she'd return in the morning. I also watched her walk out the door without looking at me and possibly right out of my life.

"Luke, she needs time," Gretchen said as she put her hand on my arm.

"Everybody keeps telling me that," I said as I left the room.

Chapter Seventeen

LILY

Just as I parked the Explorer and grabbed my suitcase from the back, Luke's Jeep pulled up. Shit. I pulled up the handle on my suitcase and began rolling it to the door. I heard his car door shut, and suddenly, his hand grabbed my suitcase.

"Let me help you, Lily," he said.

"I can do it myself," I snapped as I jerked the suitcase away from him.

"Hate me! Hate me all you want because I'm sorry for everything!" he yelled. "I'm sorry for what I said to you. I want you, Lily. I want our relationship back. I love you!"

I stopped walking when I heard his words and let the rage build inside me. I turned around in a fit of anger and looked at him underneath the bright street light.

"You think you can just return to town when you're ready and expect things to return to normal? You broke me. You shattered me when you stood there and said you blamed me for Callie's death. You crushed me into even more tiny pieces when you walked out and left me. You, Luke Matthews, did that to me!" I screamed.

By then, I was a sobbing mess, and that was when Gretchen and Sam pulled up.

"We needed each other for support, and you turned your back on me. You wouldn't even listen to me, and for that, I hate you! Do you hear me? There is no 'us.' You broke us way beyond repair!" I screamed.

Gretchen came running over and hugged me as tightly as she could. She grabbed my suitcase and the keys out of my hand and led me into my apartment.

"Who the hell does he think he is?" I cried.

She went into the kitchen and pulled a bottle of wine from the cabinet. She poured some into a glass and handed it to me, then went into the bathroom and grabbed some tissues.

"Here," she said as she handed them to me.

I sat on the couch and brought my knees to my chest.

"Lily, I'm really worried about you."

"Don't be. I just exploded. He had it coming. You better get back to Sam. I'll call you in the morning."

"I don't want to leave you."

"Go. Please. I love you, but I need to be alone."

She leaned over and kissed my forehead. "You better call me first thing in the morning."

"I will. Thank you, Gretchen."

"I'm so happy you're back," she said as she hugged me.

∼

LUKE

She made it very clear that she didn't want anything to do with me. I fucked up in such a way that I didn't know how the hell to fix it. Gretchen walked into the apartment and looked at me. She stood there with an angry look and shook her finger at me, but the words wouldn't come out of her mouth.

"Don't, Gretchen. I already know," I said with a tear as I looked down.

Sam was sitting at the table, not saying a word. Gretchen walked over and wrapped her arms around me.

"I love you, Luke. You're my friend just as much as Lily is. You're both hurting so much that I feel so helpless."

"I need her back. I want her back. She won't listen to me, and I don't know what to do."

"I think the best thing you can do is slowly try to rebuild your friendship. She can't hate you forever. I know she won't. I think it's just the shock of seeing you again after so many weeks. She'll calm down, and when she does, she'll need you. I know Lily, and you're the best thing in her life, and she'll realize that once she calms down."

Sam walked over and wrapped his arms around both of us.

"Yeah, what she said."

I couldn't help but let out a soft laugh. Gretchen was right. It was time to focus on winning Lily back, and that was what I would do, no matter the cost. And now it wasn't only Lily I needed to win back. I also needed to win back Charley.

~

LILY

The next morning, I got up at the crack of dawn and was going to go to the studio before I headed to the hospital to see Giselle. I had just finished getting dressed when my phone rang. I picked it up and saw Lucky was calling.

"Hello," I answered.

"Lily, Giselle is in labor, and the doctors say she has to deliver the baby. She's asking for you. She wants you in the delivery room."

"Tell her I'm on my way."

I put on my shoes and grabbed my keys. As soon as I climbed into the Explorer, I inserted the key and turned it. It wouldn't start. "FUCK! Come on, come on," I said as I tried multiple times. I started pounding the steering wheel with my fists when I saw Luke walk out of the building. I climbed out and had no choice but to ask him if Sam and Gretchen were still home.

"Is Sam or Gretchen still home?" I asked with an attitude.

"No. They went to breakfast."

I was fidgeting again and a nervous wreck, but I had to put Giselle and the baby first.

"Lucky called, and Giselle is in labor."

"I know. He just called me. I'm heading there now. The Explorer won't start, will it?" he asked.

"No."

"Get in my Jeep. I'll drive you there."

I took in a deep breath. This was not supposed to happen. I had no choice but to go with him. I climbed into the Jeep, fastened my seat belt, and looked out the passenger window.

"Lily—"

I put up my hand to stop him. "No words. Just get me to the hospital."

He sighed and sped out of the parking lot. The ride there was silent. I wouldn't look at him. I couldn't look at him because, if I did, I'd break down again. He dropped me off at the door, and I ran up to Giselle's room. When I walked in, she was yelling in pain. Lucky was putting a cool cloth on her head and holding one hand while Gretchen held the other.

"Lily," Giselle cried. "It's too early. I can't have her yet. It's too early."

"Shh. It's going to be all right. I promise," I said as I ran my hand across her hair.

I looked at Gretchen. "Why did you and Sam have to go to breakfast so early? The Explorer wouldn't start, and I had to get a ride in with Luke. Do you know how uncomfortable that was?"

"Sorry, but we were hungry," she said. You really need to get a new car."

Giselle yelled with another contraction. The doctor returned to the room and told her it was time to start pushing. She was crying and telling the doctor that it was too early. Lucky was trying to soothe her and make her comfortable. Finally, she delivered her baby girl.

"We need to take her to the neonatal unit right away," the nurse said with sympathy as she held the baby up to her.

"Can I just touch her?" Giselle asked as she cried.

The nurse brought the baby closer to her and Lucky. He kissed her lightly on the head, and Giselle touched her tiny hand. The nurse took her out of the room immediately, and Giselle began to sob uncontrollably. Lucky did his best to calm her down. We thought it would be best for the two of them, as parents, to be left alone. Gretchen and I walked out of the room and saw Sam and Luke sitting in the waiting room across the hall. Gretchen went over to them, and I walked down to the coffee bar.

I took my coffee outside to the courtyard and sat on a wrought-iron bench. I looked at my phone. I had a text message from my mom.

"Just checking in and making sure you're okay."

"I'm as good as I can be. Giselle had the baby about thirty minutes ago, and we're not sure what will happen."

"I'm sorry, Lily. Girls are strong. That baby of hers is going to be just fine."

"Thanks, Mom. I'll talk to you soon."

I sipped my coffee and then looked down at the ground.

"Hey," Luke said.

I closed my eyes and was ready to lash out at him and tell him to get the fuck away from me, but I didn't have the strength. So I just looked up at him with sad eyes.

"The baby is going to be okay," he said.

"You don't know that for sure. There are so many complications for a baby born prematurely."

"Do you mind if I sit down?"

I put my hand out, signaling that I had no choice because other people were in the courtyard, and I didn't want to cause a scene. He sat there with his elbows on his knees and his face cupped in his hands.

Chapter Eighteen

LILY

"I can look at your car and see what's wrong," Luke said.

"Nah. I'll have it towed again. I don't need your help," I snapped quietly.

"I know you don't, but I want to help."

I turned my head and looked at him. "You really want to help me? You can do that by leaving me alone," I said, shaking my head while tears stung my eyes.

I got up from the bench and walked back into the hospital. I couldn't escape the pain that constantly flowed throughout my body, the gut-wrenching pain that was such a huge part of my life. I walked into Giselle's room, sat beside her, and grabbed her hand.

"The doctor said that her lungs aren't fully mature yet, and they have her on a breathing machine. He said the next twenty-four hours are critical, but he's optimistic she'll pull through."

"Of course, she'll pull through. She's a girl. A strong girl who comes from a line of strong women like her mom." I smiled.

"She is strong, isn't she?"

"She sure is," I said. "Have you picked a name for her yet?"

"Yeah, we did." She smiled as she looked at Lucky.

"Isabella Grace Chambers," Lucky replied.

"That's a beautiful name. You look tired, Giselle. You better get some rest. I'm going to head out unless you want me to stay."

"No. You go do what you have to do. I'll see you later."

I kissed her and Lucky on the cheek and walked to the neonatal unit. Luke was standing there, looking through the window. I took a deep breath as I walked up and stood beside him.

"She's so tiny," he said.

"Yeah, she is. She'll be okay. I know she will."

Luke looked over at me and then back at Isabella.

"Look, I'm sorry for snapping at you today. Last night, no. Today, yes."

"I don't blame you. How are you getting home or wherever you have to go?"

"I was going to catch a ride with Sam or Gretchen, but I can't find them."

"They left already. Sam said he had to go to work, and Gretchen had something to do."

"That's great. I'll call a cab then."

"I can drive you home, Lily," he replied as he stared straight ahead.

"Don't you have to get to the bar?" I asked.

"The bar can wait."

"Thanks," I softly said.

"Are you ready now?" he asked.

"Yeah. I guess I'll go home and call a tow truck."

I followed behind him out of the hospital and into the Jeep. A part of me wanted to reach over and hold his hand, but the bigger part of me wanted to hit him.

~

LUKE

As soon as we pulled into the parking lot of the apartment building, Lily got out and climbed into her Explorer to try to start it one last time before she called the tow truck. She looked at me when it suddenly started.

"What the hell!" she exclaimed.

I shrugged my shoulders. It was weird that it just started after it wouldn't turn over this morning. I climbed back in my Jeep and drove to the bar. I decided that I had no choice but to respect Lily's wishes and leave her alone. I could see the pain that resided in her eyes because it was the same pain as mine.

"Hey," Maddie said as I walked into the bar.

"Hey. Giselle had the baby."

"Is she okay?" she asked.

"The next twenty-four hours are critical, but I think she'll pull through. How's Charley? I sent her some text messages, and she won't respond."

"She really wants nothing to do with you."

I rolled my eyes and sighed. "She's not the only one."

"Have you talked to Lily yet?"

"You mean have I been screamed at and been told that she hates me and that I broke her? Yes."

"Aw, Luke. I'm sorry."

"I don't want to talk about it anymore," I said as I walked to my office.

Cody was sitting at my desk again, and it looked like she was reviewing the books.

"Hey, Luke. I'll be done in a second."

"Hey. I really need to have another office built," I said as I turned and walked out.

I pulled my phone from my pocket and sent Lily a text message.

"Hey, I'm sorry to bother you, but do you still have the phone number of the contractor you used for your studio?"

A few minutes later, her reply came with only his name and phone number. What the hell did I expect? I dialed the number and waited for him to answer.

"Hello, Cameron Cole here."

"Cameron, my name is Luke Matthews. I got your number from Lily Gilmore. You did some work in her photography studio."

"Hi, Luke. What can I do for you?"

"I own a bar and was looking to build a small office for my assistant."

"Sure. I can come by later this afternoon, take a look, and give you an estimate if you'll be around."

"Sounds great, Cameron. I'll be here."

I gave him the address, and he knew exactly where it was. I walked behind the bar and started drying off the rack of glasses.

"Cameron, a contractor, will be stopping by later to look at building an office for Cody," I told Maddie.

"Oh. So you plan on keeping her around?"

"Don't start with me, Maddie. She's a good employee."

"I have a feeling that we're going to see how good she really is," she said as she walked away.

I rolled my eyes as I placed the dry glasses on the shelf. I saw Cody walking across the bar in her short skirt and tight shirt. She perched herself on the barstool and showed me some figures on a report.

"See these numbers? This is your profit, and this is your loss. They almost equal out. So technically, you didn't make any money last month."

"That's nice to know," I sighed.

"Don't sweat it. We'll get you up there so you're rolling in the dough. I remember you mentioned bringing in other bands to play on the weekends. I think you should do Friday, Saturday, and Sunday."

"I know. I've already thought of that, and I'm going to do it. I just haven't had the time to contact any bands or listen to them."

"I have an idea." She smiled as she placed her hand on my arm. "I'm going to place an ad online. I know of a few sites that a lot of bands visit, and the ad will grab their attention."

"Thanks, Cody. I'm sorry that I haven't been here much for you since you started. It's just with Lily and all the shit going on—"

"Luke, I understand. Don't worry about it." She smiled. "Remember, I'm here if you ever want to talk."

I smiled at her and looked up when the bar door opened.

"Luke Matthews?" the guy asked as he walked towards me.

"Yep, that's me," I answered as I held out my hand.

"I'm Cameron Cole."

"Great to meet you, Cameron. Follow me, and I'll show you where I thought about putting the office."

He followed me to the back, and I showed him the space. He looked around, stood back, took out his measuring tape, and nodded.

"Okay. This will work." He smiled.

We stood and talked for quite a while. Lily had told me how nice he was, and she was right. He was a great guy, and he knew his stuff.

"I have a job that'll be finished in a few days. I can start then."

"Sounds good, man," I said as I held out my hand. "Thank you for coming out."

"No problem. Tell Lily I said hi. She's a great photographer."

I gave a small smile. "Yeah, she is."

As he left the bar, Cody walked over to me with a smile on her face.

"What's the verdict?"

"You'll have your own office soon."

She looped her arm around mine and laid her head on my shoulder.

"Thanks, but I really don't mind sharing with you. You can tuck me in a corner, and I'll be just as happy."

I looked up and noticed Sam walking towards me. Cody immediately let go of my arm and walked away.

"What the fuck was that, Luke? Are you already giving up on Lily and moving on?"

"Hell no. She was thanking me for the new office I'm having built so she doesn't have to share mine. Jesus Christ, man. You can fuck off for even thinking that."

"Really, bro? What if Lily walked back here instead of me?"

"Well, I don't have to worry about that, do I? She won't even speak to me, let alone walk into my bar," I said as I walked away and punched the wall.

"Are you going to the hospital later?" he asked.

"Yeah. I want to bring Giselle some flowers."

"Good idea. I'll talk to you later," he said as he started to walk away.

"Sam," I called. "Why did you come by the bar?"

"Oh, I was going to talk to you about something, but it can wait."

"Are you sure? You're already here."

"I'm sure. We'll talk later." He smiled.

Chapter Nineteen

LILY

I stepped inside my apartment and threw my keys on the counter. I'd been at the studio doing the final cleanup because I decided that I was going to open within the next couple of days. Now that I was back, I needed to focus on something other than Luke. I jumped into the shower, cleaned up, and put on fresh clothes before I headed to the hospital. As I locked up my apartment, Luke walked out of his. My heart felt like it was going to jump out of my throat.

"Hey," he said without looking at me.

"Hey," I replied and then walked to the Explorer.

I climbed in and tried not to watch Luke get in his Jeep, but my eyes couldn't help it. I put the key in the ignition, and nothing. Luke drove off, and I was about ready to have a breakdown. I turned the key again. Nothing. My phone rang, and it was Luke.

"Hello," I answered softly.

"The Explorer won't start again, will it?"

"Nope," I said quietly because I would lose it any second.

"I'm back," he said as he hung up and pulled up beside me.

I rolled down my window and looked at him.

"Are you going to the hospital?" he asked.

"Yeah."

"Me too. Hop in," he said with a small smile.

For fuck's sake. You have got to be kidding me. I grabbed my purse and climbed into the Jeep.

"We have to stop at the florist first. I want to pick up some flowers for Giselle," he said.

I nodded. "Okay."

I kept my head turned and looked out the passenger window. Luke pulled into the florist's parking lot, and we went inside. I wanted to get some balloons for Giselle and Lucky. Luke stood in front of the cooler, looking at the pink roses. He told the sales lady he'd take a dozen while I had another sales lady blow up a few balloons. This was awkward, and first thing tomorrow morning, I was having the Explorer towed and looking for a new vehicle. When we returned to the Jeep, Luke asked me if I would mind holding the roses. I took them from him and continued to look out the window.

"I met Cameron Cole today," he said out of the clear blue.

"Really?" I asked.

"Yeah. He's going to build a small office for Cody."

"That's nice."

"He's a really nice guy. I can see why you liked him so much."

"Yep. He's great."

I heard him sigh, and then there was silence until he asked me about Charley.

"Have you seen Charley yet?"

"No. I was planning on seeing her tomorrow."

"She told me she hated me."

"Why would she say that?" I asked as I looked at him.

"Because you left."

"I'm sure she didn't mean it. You know how kids are."

That little girl meant everything to him, and it must have killed him to hear her say that. I didn't stop to think how she would be affected by what happened between Luke and me, and now I felt like total shit, worse than I already did.

He pulled into a parking space at the hospital, and we went up to Giselle's room. Luke walked over, kissed her, and handed her the beautiful pink roses. I looked over at Gretchen and Sam, who stared at each other when Luke and I walked in. I gave Lucky the balloons and sat on the edge of the bed.

"How's she doing?" I asked.

"So far, she's doing well. The doctor is really optimistic. We got to sit with her earlier. It's so hard to see her hooked up to all those monitors and that breathing machine." She began to cry.

I leaned over and hugged her. "I know, but it's helping her. Just remember that. You'll be holding her in your arms soon, and this will all be behind you."

Lucky, Luke, and Sam stepped out of the room, and Gretchen walked over and sat down in the chair by us.

"Did you come here with Luke? What's going on?"

"The damn Explorer was dead again, and Luke was leaving to come here, so he offered me a ride."

"That's the second time today, Lily," Gretchen said.

"No shit, and I can't believe it."

"Have the two of you talked?" Giselle asked.

"You mean besides Lily screaming at him last night in the middle of the parking lot?"

I shot Gretchen a look. "Very little and nothing but small talk. I told him this morning to leave me alone."

Giselle took hold of my hand. "Sweetie, don't you think you should listen to him? Hear what he has to say?"

"He said all I needed to hear that night he accused me of killing Callie and left. Obviously, he isn't over her, and I don't think he'll ever be."

"That's not true," Sam said as he returned to the room.

"Sam, I'm not talking about this anymore."

"Where's Lucky?" Giselle asked.

"He and Luke are looking at Isabella. She's a beauty, Giselle. Thank God she looks like you." He laughed.

We all laughed, and it felt good. It felt good to be in the company of my best friends when I needed them most. When Luke and Lucky returned to the room, I walked out and headed for the coffee machine. I pulled my phone from my pocket and sent Maddie a text message.

"*Hi. Would it be okay if I pick Charley up from school tomorrow and take her to the studio with me for a while?*"

"*Sure. She'll love that. She misses you so much, and so do I.*"

"*I miss you both too. Don't tell her that I'm picking her up. I want it to be a surprise.*"

∼

LUKE

I didn't know if following Lily out of the room was a good idea, but I didn't care. I just wanted to be where she was. I took some change from my pocket and walked into the waiting room with the coffee machine.

"Excuse me," I said as Lily looked at her phone and stood before the machine.

"Sorry," she said as she moved out of the way.

I put the change in the machine and pressed the button for a cup of black coffee.

"Is this stuff any good?" I asked her.

"It's no Starbucks, that's for sure. But it's pretty decent."

She left the waiting room, and I followed behind. We walked back into Giselle's room and noticed Sam and Gretchen were gone.

"Where did they go?" Lily asked Giselle.

"They left. They said they had to do something and be back tomorrow."

"Great. I was going to get a ride home with them."

"Why? Luke's here. He'll drive you home. Right?" Lucky smiled.

"Of course," I said.

"Anyway, I'm exhausted. Thank you for the flowers and the balloons." Giselle smiled.

"You're welcome." I walked over and kissed her goodbye.

Lily and I walked out of the room, and I turned and looked at her.

"Did we just get kicked out?"

"Yeah. I think we did." A small smile framed her lips.

God, it was good to see her smile again. I wanted to run my hand down her cheek and tell her how much I loved her, but at the risk of getting slapped, I kept my hands to myself and my mouth shut.

"I can't believe Gretchen and Sam took off like that," she said.

"I know. They did that this morning, too."

"The least they could've done was tell us," Lily said.

We climbed in my Jeep, and as we pulled out of the parking lot, I had a thought, a thought that would piss Lily off, but at this point, I didn't care.

"I'm sorry, Lily, but I'm starving and need to grab something to eat."

"NOW?!" she exclaimed.

"Yeah. I haven't eaten all day. We can stop at that diner up the street. It's two minutes from here."

"Just drive through a McDonalds or something and eat it in your apartment."

"The closest McDonald's is three miles from here," I said as I pulled into the diner's parking lot. "See? We're already here."

She looked at me and rolled her eyes.

"Listen, I promise I won't talk to you. But I'm driving, starving, and getting something to eat before I drive you home."

"Whatever," she said as she opened and slammed the door shut.

We walked into the diner. She was pissed. I would take advantage of any opportunity to be alone with her.

Chapter Twenty

LILY

The nerve of him. We were seated in a booth, and I looked around to see if another was available—another booth just for me.

"Are you looking to sit somewhere else?" he asked.

Damn him. I hated that he knew me too well in these types of situations.

"Yes. Yes, I am because this is bullshit that you brought me here," I spoke through gritted teeth across the table.

I picked up my menu and held it up to my face so he couldn't see me. This wasn't right and did not help my state of mind.

"I'm sorry, Lily. You're right. Let's go," he said as he got up from the booth.

I took in a deep breath. Every piece of me wanted to get up from my seat and follow him, but I couldn't.

"Sit down and look at the menu," I said.

"No, seriously. Let's go. I can't do this with you either. I thought I could, but I can't."

"You're making a scene, Luke. Sit down, and let's order dinner."

He sighed, sat back down, and opened his menu. The waitress walked over and took our drink order. Since this place didn't have alcohol, I ordered coffee, and Luke stuck with water. I picked up my phone and sent a text message to Gretchen.

"*Thanks a lot for leaving the hospital without giving me a ride home.*"

"*Sorry. We forgot you didn't drive. But Luke was there. He gave you a ride home, right?*"

"*Not yet. He was starving, so he stopped at a diner to get something to eat.*"

"*Oh. Well, use this time to talk to him.*"

"*Goodbye, Gretchen.*"

"Are you bitching to Gretchen about having to stop here?"

DAMN. HIM. "No. I was—It's none of your business."

The waitress came back with our drinks and took our order. I only ordered a side salad because I wasn't hungry, but I didn't want Luke to start in on me. The couple sitting at the table next to us were being overly affectionate. They were holding hands across the table, stealing little kisses, smiling, laughing, and being what Luke and I used to be like. I could feel the tears spring to my eyes. The waitress brought our food just in time.

"I saw you staring at that couple over there," he said as he took a bite of his burger.

"I wasn't staring."

"They remind me of two other people."

"Really? Because nothing's really as it seems. They'll wake up one day."

He took another bite of his burger and stared at me while nodding. That was the end of our conversation for the rest of the night. After we finished eating, Luke drove back to the apartment. I walked in mine, and he walked in his without as much as a goodnight.

∼

LUKE

I walked into my apartment and threw my keys on the table. Sam and Gretchen were snuggled on the couch, watching a movie.

"Hey, what took you so long to get back?" Sam asked.

"Before coming home, I stopped off and got something to eat."

"Wasn't Lily with you?"

"Yeah, she was, and it didn't go so well. It's over between us. I can't do it anymore. She won't even listen to me. She won't talk about that night, and she won't let me explain. It's over, so stop trying to push us together."

"What are you talking about?" Sam asked.

"I suspect the two of you had something to do with Lily's SUV not starting. I started piecing some things together the second time it happened. Thanks, but no thanks," I said as I walked to my room.

"We were only trying to help you two out," Sam yelled.

I heard my phone beep and pulled it out of my pocket. I had a text message from Cody.

"Hi, Luke. I just wanted you to know that I posted the ad for band auditions, and about twenty bands already want to play at the bar."

I smiled.

"Thanks, Cody. I appreciate your hard work. Now stop thinking about business and take the night off."

"I'm just sitting at home with nothing to do. No big deal."

"I appreciate it. Good night."

"Good night, Luke."

I removed my t-shirt and lay on the bed with my hands behind my head. I thought about what Sam and Gretchen had done to try to get Lily and me alone. I needed to tell her because she would have the Explorer towed tomorrow and possibly buy a new one.

"Sorry to bother you, but I thought you should know that Sam and Gretchen were responsible for the Explorer not starting today. They were scheming to try and get us alone. You won't need to have it towed tomorrow."

"Real special friends. Thanks for letting me know."

What I wouldn't have given right then to be in her bed with my arms wrapped tightly around her. I missed her touch, her smell, the softness of her hair, and her beautiful smile. I was desperate to run my hand gently up and down her silky skin, and I was desperate to hear her soft moans when my fingers went deep inside her. Shit. I was getting hard.

Lily

I didn't sleep anymore. I was lucky if I could get in three hours' worth. I was back to where I was two years ago after I left Seattle. My mind wouldn't settle down with thoughts of Luke, and my anger still consumed me. I rolled out of bed and took a hot shower. I couldn't believe Sam and Gretchen would do such a thing, especially knowing how I felt. I got dressed and grabbed my coffee, and when I opened the door, I saw Charley coming down the stairs. She looked at me, threw her backpack down, and ran to me, throwing her arms around my legs.

"Lily!"

"Hi, baby," I said as I hugged her. "How are you?"

"I knew you'd come back."

"Of course. I just went to visit my mom and my sister in Seattle."

Luke walked out of his apartment and looked at us.

"Uncle Luke, did you know that Lily's back?"

He smiled at her as he patted her head. "Yeah, I knew, peanut."

She could tell something was up because neither one of us said a word to each other. She looked at him and then at me as Maddie walked down the stairs.

"What's wrong? Why aren't the two of you talking?" she asked.

"Come on, Charley. You're going to be late for school," Maddie said.

I bent down and placed my hand on her cheek. "Guess what. I'm picking you up today and taking you to my new studio. I need some help, and I couldn't think of a more qualified person to help me."

"Really!"

"Yes." I smiled. "Now go to school. I'll see you later."

She kissed me on the cheek, gave Luke a dirty look, and then walked out the building door. I locked up my apartment, and Luke walked out.

I stopped by the hospital on my way to the studio to see how Giselle and the baby were doing. When I walked in, she was eating breakfast.

"Just in time. Would you like some of this crap they claim is oatmeal?" she asked.

"No thanks. I'm good." I smiled as I sat down in the chair next to her bed. "How is Isabella doing?"

"She's doing great. The doctor said she'll probably be ready to go home in two weeks. Lucky and I held her last night, and we both cried. I can't wait for my parents to meet her; they're flying in today. I told Lucky he better be on his best behavior or else. The last time they were here, after Gretchen's accident, they weren't impressed with him."

"Speaking of Lucky, where is he?"

"Right here." He smiled as he walked into the room, holding a brown bag. "I bring real food."

He walked over to me and kissed me on the head. I got up from the chair and hugged Giselle.

"I'm going to go. I need to head over to the studio."

"Oh, I forgot to tell you. Adalynn over at Prim wants you to give her a call. She wants to talk to you about doing a photo shoot for the magazine. She was impressed by the pictures of Rory and the girls."

"Seriously?"

"Yeah, so call her today. This could be a huge opportunity for you."

I leaned over and kissed her cheek. "Thank you. I'll call her as soon as I get to the studio. Bye, Lucky."

"Bye, babe. Hey, do me a favor."

"What is it?" I asked.

"Talk to Luke. He misses you in a really bad way."

"Then he shouldn't have said what he did. I love you both. I'll see you later," I said as I left the room.

As soon as I got to the studio, I dialed Adalynn over at Prim.

"This is Adalynn," she answered.

"Hi, Adalynn. It's Lily Gilmore. Giselle said that you wanted me to give you a call."

"Oh yes, Lily. How are you?"

"I'm good. How are you?"

"Doing great. I was hoping you'd be available to do a photo shoot for a fall fashion spread I'm doing for next month's issue of Prim."

"I would be honored. Thank you."

"I saw the pictures you took of Rory and my sweet girls, and the way you captured their emotions was really good. I especially loved the sensual pictures you took of Rory."

"She showed you those?"

"Yes, and so did Ian. He was blown away and wouldn't stop raving about you and your work. I want to do the shoot in a couple of days if you're available. I want some shots on the Santa Monica Pier, and then at your studio would be great."

"Sounds good. I'm available whenever you need me."

"Great. Let's meet at the pier at noon. I'll meet with the models and tell them it's a go."

"Thank you, Adalynn. I really appreciate you giving me this opportunity."

"No problem. I'll see you Friday."

I couldn't believe it. Excitement shot throughout my body for the first time in a long time. Shit. I was going to need an assistant. There was no way I could do that shoot on my own with all that equipment. How was I going to find someone on such short notice? I decided to call Sam, hoping that maybe he knew someone who would be interested.

"Hey, Lils," he answered.

"Hey, Sam. Do you know anyone looking for a job as a photographer's assistant?"

"No, I don't. Why?"

"I'm doing my first photo shoot for Prim magazine in a couple of days and need an assistant. I thought maybe you'd know someone around your firm or someone who knows someone."

"Sorry. But why don't you call the art department over at UCLA? I'm sure there are college students in the photography program who would love to do that."

"Great idea. I didn't even think about that. Thanks, Sam. Oh, you and Gretchen aren't off the hook about the little stunt you two pulled with my truck."

"Oh. You know about that? Sorry."

"Yeah, I know, and I'm not happy, but we'll talk about it later."

"Okay. I'll warn Gretchen," he sighed.

I was pleased about Sam's suggestion to call UCLA. I googled the number and dialed their art department. The director, Mr. Smith, seemed friendly and told me to come right over because he had the perfect person for me.

L.A. traffic was the worst. What should have taken me fifteen minutes to get to UCLA took me an hour. I found my way to the art department and met Mr. Smith. When we reached the photography room, he introduced me to a guy named Wyatt. He was a second-year photography student and one of the best in his class.

"Wyatt, I would like you to meet Lily Gilmore. She's the photographer I was telling you about."

"Nice to meet you, Miss Gilmore." He smiled as he held out his hand.

"Please call me Lily. It's nice to meet you, too."

"I'll leave you two alone to get acquainted." Mr. Smith smiled.

Chapter Twenty-One

LUKE

I was sitting at my desk, reviewing some invoices, when Cody walked into the office.

"Hey, Luke."

"Hey," I replied without looking up.

"The first band will be here to audition in a couple of hours."

"Okay."

"Are you okay?" she asked.

Am I okay? No, I wasn't, but I wouldn't let her know that. I wasn't sure I'd ever be okay again unless I got Lily back.

"Yeah, I'm fine. I have a lot on my mind."

She gave me a small smile and walked out of the office. A few moments later, there was a knock on my door. I looked up and saw my mom and dad smiling at me.

"Mom, Dad, you're back. How was your trip?" I asked as I got up and hugged them.

"It was marvelous." My mom smiled.

"How are you, son?" my dad asked as we lightly hugged.

"I'm good."

"I'm having Charley's birthday party this weekend at the house, so you and Lily better not have other plans. I'm excited to see her. How is she?"

Shit. Shit. Shit. How would I tell my parents that we weren't together anymore and that I royally fucked things up?

"Let's go take a seat and have some lunch. I have something to tell you."

"Now you're worrying me, Luke," my mom said.

I told Maddie to join us, but she said I needed to talk to our parents alone. We took a seat at the table and ordered some lunch.

"Something happened while you were gone. Lily and I broke up."

I watched as tears sprang to my mother's eyes. "Why?"

"Son, I'm sorry," my dad said.

"It was all my fault, and now she hates me. I found out something about her. I was in shock. I accused her of something horrible and took off for a while. When I came back, she was gone. Now she's back because our friend had her baby, and Lily won't talk to me or let me explain."

The sad look on my mother's face broke my heart. She reached over and placed her hand on mine.

"What did she do?"

"Remember when Callie and I were in Portland for the weekend, and I told you that a woman came up to us at the restaurant and gave us those tickets to Aruba?"

"Yes."

"That woman was Lily, but neither remembered each other because it had been a little over a year."

She slowly slid her hand off of mine and glared at me.

"What exactly are you saying, Luke?" my dad asked.

My mother spoke before I could get any words out of my mouth. "I think he's trying to tell us that he blamed Lily for the accident."

"That's ridiculous. She didn't cause the accident."

"I know that. But when I first found out, I was in shock, and I told her that if she hadn't given us the tickets, then Callie would still be alive."

"Oh, Luke," my mother said as a tear ran down her cheek.

Maddie walked over and clasped her shoulders. "He's trying to win her back, Mom."

"I rented a cabin from Pastor Joe, and we had a long talk. He made me realize some things. I'm so sorry, Mom and Dad."

My dad reached over and squeezed my arm lightly while my mom got up from her seat and hugged me.

"She'll come around. Lily loves you too much to give up. She just needs time."

"I hope so, Mom, because I can't live without her."

Cody walked over to let me know that the first band was here. I had them set up on the stage, and then I sat back with my parents and watched them perform.

∼

Lily

"I like you, Wyatt, and I think we'll work well together. You're hired." I smiled.

"Thank you, Lily. I'm so excited."

Wyatt's passion for photography was what drew me to him. His feelings about photographs and art reminded me so much of myself. I took a look at some of his photos and was very impressed. He still had much to learn, so working for me would be perfect for him.

"Who is this fine, ripped-looking man?" I asked as I studied the black and white photograph.

"That's my boyfriend, Grant. He's trying to break into the modeling biz."

"Well, it looks like he should have no problem."

"He is a hottie, isn't he?" Wyatt smiled.

I looked at the clock on the wall. It was almost time for Charley to get out of school. If I didn't leave now, I would be late.

"Why don't you stop by my studio after classes tomorrow so we can review a few things before Friday's shoot?"

"I'll be there! Thank you for this amazing opportunity, Lily," Wyatt said as he hugged me goodbye.

I drove to the school to pick up Charley. I made it just in time, seeing her walking out the doors when I pulled up. A huge smile graced her face as she climbed into the Explorer and hugged me.

"How was school?" I asked.

"It was okay. I couldn't wait for it to be over to go with you to your studio. I'm so excited to see it."

As we stepped through the door, Charley looked around at all the pictures on the wall.

"I like your pictures, but you don't have one in this spot, and it looks weird," she said as she pointed to the corner.

"That's because I was saving that spot for someone special."

She looked up at me and smiled. "Who?"

"You." I tapped her on the nose.

"Really!" she exclaimed.

"Yep." I stepped behind the counter, pulled the bag from the shelf, and handed it to Charley. "I bought these outfits for you a while ago. I was saving them for your birthday, but now is as good a time as any to give them to you."

She opened the bag and took out the articles of clothing with a big smile on her face. "Lily, I love them. Thank you," she said as she hugged me.

"Go in that room over there and get changed. I'll do your hair, and then we'll have a photography session. I think it would be a great gift for your mom and dad. Plus, you will look amazing hanging on my wall."

Charley went to change, and I heard my phone ring. Maddie was calling.

"Hi, Maddie."

"Hi, Lily. I just wanted to let you know that my parents are having a birthday party for Charley this weekend at their house, and I'm hoping you'll come. Charley would be devastated if you didn't, and my parents would be upset. Luke told them what happened, but my mom said you're still a part of the family and wants you to come."

"I don't know, Maddie."

"Listen, I totally understand the awkwardness, but if for

anything, do it for Charley. It's just one day. Plus, Adam and I want you there."

She was right. I had to think about Charley and nothing else. It was her birthday, and the last thing I wanted to do was ruin it.

"I'll be there, Maddie."

"Great. Thank you, Lily. The party starts at noon, and it's all day. I'll talk to you later."

Charley walked in with her first outfit on. She looked so cute.

"I love this outfit!" She smiled.

I walked over to her and ran my fingers through her hair. "I'm thinking maybe some curls would complete this adorable outfit."

We walked back to the changing room, where I had the makeup vanity set up. She sat in the black chair, and we talked while I curled her hair.

"Someone has a birthday coming up." I smiled.

"I know. I can't wait." She giggled. "I thought this year's birthday would be the best ever because my dad is back. But now, you and Uncle Luke aren't talking to each other, so I guess it won't be so great after all."

I felt the most significant ache in my heart after hearing Charley say that. She didn't understand, and it killed me to see her hurting so much.

"Charley, things are complicated right now between your Uncle Luke and me. I can't explain it to you because you're too young. But I can promise you that you'll have the best birthday ever! I'm going to make sure of it. I don't want you to worry about Luke and me anymore. In fact, I don't want you to be mad at him. He loves you more than life, and it really hurts him deep down that you won't talk to him. This is a grown-up situation, and there are no sides to take. Make sense?"

She nodded and looked down. I lifted her chin and swept a slight pink blush across her cheeks. I brought her curls over her shoulders, and she smiled as she stared at herself in the mirror.

"Come on, Miss Model. Let's get this photo shoot rolling."

She giggled as she got up from the chair, and we headed to the photography room. After we had some dinner and ice cream, I walked Charley up to her apartment. The door opened as soon as we reached the top step, and Luke walked out.

"Hi, Uncle Luke." Charley smiled.

"Hey, peanut. How was your day?"

"It was great. Lily and I had so much fun!"

"That's great." He smiled as he patted her on the head and looked at me.

Maddie came to the door and thanked me. I said goodbye to Charley and then headed for the stairs.

"Hey, Lily?" Luke said as he followed me down the stairs. "About Charley's birthday. I don't want it to be awkward for either of us or her. I appreciate you putting everything that happened aside to come and be a part of her birthday."

"It's for Charley. I wouldn't hurt that little girl. I want her to have the best birthday ever, so let's make sure that she does."

He gave me a small smile as I went into my apartment, and he went into his.

Chapter Twenty-Two

LILY

"Great studio, Lily," Wyatt said as he walked around.

"Thank you. Let's go over tomorrow's shoot."

We spent the next two hours reviewing the location, equipment, and overall plan. Wyatt was great, and I knew I had made the right decision in hiring him.

"Lily, is that what I think it is?!" he asked excitedly as he stared at one of my cameras on the shelf.

"Yep. It sure is."

"Oh my God. I've always dreamed of shooting with this kind of camera."

"Go ahead and snap some pics. I don't mind." I smiled as I turned around and continued looking at some orders.

He took the camera outside, and when he walked in, he called my name. When I turned around, he snapped a picture of me.

"Are you done playing?" I asked.

"Yeah. Thanks. I need to go now. I have a class I need to get to. I'll meet you at the pier at eleven to set up."

"Sounds great, Wyatt. Enjoy the rest of your day."

Later that evening, as I opened the building door, I saw Luke unlocking his door and Cody standing next to him. My stomach instantly felt sick and twisted, and my heart started beating at a rapid pace. He looked at me.

"Oh, hey. Hi, Lily." Cody smiled.

"Hi," I softly said as I opened my door. Once I stepped inside and closed it, I leaned my back up against it and began to cry.

Did I have the right to cry? My chest felt heavy, and my breathing felt constricted. I had wrapped myself in a cocoon to protect myself from feeling any more hurt. Obviously, my cocoon wasn't tight enough because the pain and hurt were seeping through at a rapid pace.

~

LUKE

I gave Cody the files I left on the counter and escorted her to the door. The look on Lily's face when she saw her standing there was torturous. I could only imagine what she thought. Fuck. Maybe I should have gone over and explained. She would probably have slapped me. I pulled my phone from my pocket and began to send her a text message. I stopped. She was the one who wouldn't give me the time of day, and she probably wouldn't have believed me anyway. I set my phone on the counter and picked up my guitar. There was a knock at the door as I was strumming a tune. I jumped up, hoping it was Lily. It wasn't.

"Lucky. Come on in."

"Hey, man. I need to talk to you for a minute."

"Sure. Beer?" I asked.

"Yeah."

"What's up? Is everything okay with Giselle and the baby?"

"Yeah, they're fine. I love her, bro. I mean, I'm in love with her."

I sat there confused. "Okay. Are we talking about Giselle?"

"Of course, we're talking about Giselle. I want us to be a couple."

"As in marriage?"

"No. I'm not ready for marriage. I want us to be exclusive."

"You do know that means you can't be hitting on other women, right?"

"I know that. I don't want to see other women. I only want Giselle. Despite some of her annoying ways and flaws, I love her."

"That's great, bro. But your emotions are running high right now. I think you should wait."

"That's what Sam said. Oh well. Maybe you're right. When are we going to play at the bar again? I'm missing it."

"Funny you should mention that. I was watching a band audition today and thinking the same thing."

"Then let's do it." He smiled. "I think we all need to get back to some normalcy."

I chuckled. He was right, and music was the perfect place to start.

"I'll look at my schedule and let you and Sam know. You're a daddy now, and you'll be busy."

"Nah, never too busy for the band. I'm off, bro. I need to get back to the hospital. Thanks for the talk."

When he left, I picked up my guitar again and started strumming the song "Don't Fear the Reaper" by Blue Oyster Cult. It was time to escape inside my music.

~

LILY

I opened up my laptop and connected the camera to it. I hadn't had the chance to review all the pictures I took of Charley, and I wanted them done in time for her birthday. When the file opened, I noticed Wyatt's picture of me. I was looking over my shoulder, and the way he captured the look on my face was unnerving. I had a look of sadness, torture, and distress. Was that how people saw me? I shook my head as I poured another glass of wine. I scrolled through the pictures of Charley and was very happy with the results. I picked my favorites, and as I began to edit them, I could hear Luke playing his guitar through the wall. I sipped my wine, edited my pictures, and listened to the melody he played.

The next morning, I called Dr. Blakely to see if she had time to see me after my photo shoot. I packed the Explorer yesterday with everything I needed from the studio, so I had some extra time this morning before leaving. I heard Luke's door shut, and then there was a knock on my door. I opened it, and Luke held something in his hand.

"Sorry to bother you, but I need to change the furnace filter. It's that time of year. I figured I better do it now while you're home and before I head to the bar."

I waved my hand for him to come in but said nothing. Looking at him made me crazy because all I could picture was Cody. I went to the kitchen to pour another cup of coffee and heard Luke's cuss from the hallway. I didn't react.

"Lily, can you grab me a towel? I'm bleeding."

Shit. I walked over and handed him the towel.

"Thanks," he said as he wrapped the side of his hand.

"Are you okay?"

"I'm fine," he said as he shut the door to the furnace.

I could see the blood soaking through the towel. "Luke, what did you do?"

"I cut myself on a piece of metal that I never shaved down like I was supposed to."

"Let me see," I said as I made him sit at the table and slowly removed the towel from his hand. "Oh God, you need stitches."

"I'm fine. I don't need anything. I have to go. If it doesn't stop soon, I'll go to the ER."

"It's not going to stop. It's a deep gash." I looked at the clock. I had three hours before I had to be at the photo shoot. I grabbed another towel from the linen closet and replaced the blood-soaked one.

"Come on. I'm driving. Don't get blood on my seats," I said as I grabbed my keys.

"Lily, I'm fine."

"GET YOUR ASS IN THE TRUCK NOW!"

"Watch your mouth," he said with a slight smile.

We climbed in, and I took off. "Keep it wrapped tight."

"I'm trying."

"They better not be busy because I have a photoshoot in less than three hours."

I pulled up to the doors of the ER and told him to go inside and that I'd meet him as soon as I parked. They had already put him in a room when I found a spot.

"Excuse me, but where is Luke Matthews?" I asked the nurse.

"Right this way," she said as she led me down the hall.

I walked in, and Luke sat up with his hand over a silver tray.

"The doctor will be in shortly. Just hold on," the nurse said.

"You can go. I'll get a ride back," he said as he looked at me.

"Do you want me to call Cody for you?" Shit. The words just slipped out.

He looked down. "No, Lily, and what you saw yesterday was business. I left a folder she needed on the counter, and she followed me back to get it because I wasn't going back to the bar."

"You don't need to explain anything to me. It's none of my business."

"I didn't want you to think anything else," he said as the doctor walked in.

He gave Luke a tetanus shot and then placed five stitches in the side of his hand.

"Okay, you're good to go. Keep that dry for the first twenty-four hours."

"Thanks, Doc."

He got up from the bed and looked at me. "Thank you, Lily. I appreciate it."

"You're welcome," I softly replied.

We climbed back into the Explorer, and Luke asked me a question on the way home.

"Did you say you have a photo shoot today? That's great. I'm happy for you."

"Thanks. It's for Prim Magazine. It's their fall fashion shoot. We're doing it at the Santa Monica Pier."

Why the hell did I tell him all that?

"Congratulations. You'll do great." He smiled.

His smile. It made me weak every time. It always did. He would smile even in the middle of an argument, and I would instantly forget what we were arguing about.

"Thanks."

I dropped Luke off at the door and told him I had to get to the pier. He gave me a small wave before closing the car door.

Chapter Twenty-Three

LUKE

"What happened to you?" Maddie asked as I walked into the bar.

"I cut myself changing the furnace filter. There was a piece of metal I forgot to shave down."

"Ouch. Are you okay?"

"It hurts a little, but I'm fine."

"How did you drive to the hospital?"

"Lily drove me. It actually happened in her apartment while I was changing her filter. Oh, by the way, I'll be changing yours later tonight."

"Oh, okay. How did that go? I mean, with Lily driving you to the hospital."

"It went okay. Is Cody here?"

"Yeah, she's in your office."

"I have a few errands to run. I need to get Charley's birthday present and some flowers for Mom. I'll be back later."

I hopped into the Jeep and drove to the guitar store, where I picked an excellent guitar that Charley could grow with. I then headed to the flower shop down the road, and I bought two dozen roses. One dozen was for my mom, and the other was for Lily. I wanted to thank her for taking me to the hospital, but I was not sure they'd be well received. It was a small gesture. A thank you. How could she deny that? She still cared about me, even though when I looked at her, all I saw was anger in her eyes. Maybe tomorrow, at Charley's party, we could make some progress. I liked to think that what happened today when she drove me to the hospital was progress. One day at a time. I'd get her back, and our love would be stronger than it was before.

~

LILY

It was a perfect day for the photo shoot. It went better than I expected, thanks to Wyatt and his assistance. The day seemed to fly by. Since it was my first magazine shoot, I was in my glory and loved every minute of it.

When we wrapped, Adalynn asked if we could finish the shoot at the studio on Monday morning. She overbooked a couple of the models, and they needed to be somewhere else. I told her that it was fine and I'd be there. As Wyatt and I gathered the equipment, I saw the Ferris wheel that Luke and I went on together when we first brought Charley here. I remembered being so scared because I hated heights, but he made me face my fear, and when I did, I saw things differently. I'll never forget that night.

"Hey, are you okay?" Wyatt asked.

"Yeah. I'm fine," I said as I snapped back into reality.

We loaded the equipment in the back of the Explorer, and I hugged Wyatt goodbye.

"You are an amazing assistant, and I want to keep you working for me. I really don't have much for you to do right now, but I'll be in touch."

"Sounds great, Lily. I had a great time. Let's do coffee, lunch, or dinner."

"Definitely!" I smiled as I climbed into the Explorer and drove to Dr. Blakely's office.

"Come on in, Lily." She smiled as she opened her office door. "Tell me what you've been doing since our last session."

I sat in the oversized leather chair and brought my knees to my chest.

"I went back to Seattle and confronted Brynn and Hunter."

"Oh? How did that go?"

"It went better than I expected. I didn't break down or murder them like I thought I might. They explained that they didn't do it to hurt me and that it was something that just happened. They tried to stop it but couldn't because they loved each other. I finally realized that I was the middleman in bringing them together."

"How do you feel about that?"

"It still hurts, and I don't think our relationship will ever return to what it was. But, I can understand that when two people are supposed to be together in this life, nothing can tear them apart."

"Like you and Luke?" she asked.

I wrapped my arms around my legs and looked at her.

"By the way you're sitting, it seems like you're protecting yourself from something."

"Maybe I am."

"Tell me about Luke."

"He wants to talk and explain himself. He said he was sorry and he didn't mean it. I won't let him in. I don't want to hear what he has to say."

"Why is that?" she asked.

"Because I'm angry. So angry."

"Angry at what? What are you really angry about, Lily? The fact that he accused you of Callie's death or the fact that he left you because of her?"

I looked at her blankly and then lowered my head to my knees.

"Lily? Am I right? Your father left you, so to speak when he cheated on your mother. He left you physically and emotionally. Hunter left you when he cheated on you with Brynn. Now, Luke left you when he found out you were the one who gave him the tickets. His reason was because of Callie. It's always been in your mind that he still cared for her more than you and that his leaving because of something that involved her confirmed it for you that night."

I lifted my head and looked across the room. "Everyone that has been a vital part of my life has left me. My father, my biological mother, my fiancé, Luke. When he walked out that door and left me standing there, I felt like I had been prosecuted, and he was the attorney that closed the case and walked out of the courtroom," I said as the tears began to fall from my eyes. "He said Callie would still be alive today if I hadn't given them the tickets. At first, I was so scared that he would never forgive me and that he'd hate me. But then anger started to settle inside me."

She handed me a tissue. "It sounds like he realized what he did and how badly he hurt you. He wants to apologize, and you won't let him. Why is that? Do you want to hurt him like he hurt you? An eye for an eye? Or are you just protecting yourself from ever being hurt again? Because if you forgive him, then that would mean you run the risk of him hurting you again or you hurting him."

"Luke has already been hurt enough by me. I've caused him so much pain and heartache. If I let him back into my life, he'll hurt more. Every time he looks at me, he'll be reminded of how I was the one, that girl that caused Callie's death. I love him too much to watch him go through that. So it's best that I stay away."

"And there it is." She smiled as she reached over and took hold of my hand. "You aren't angry at Luke. You're angry at yourself."

I nodded. She was right.

"So you're letting him go so you don't cause him any more pain?"

I nodded again.

"Don't you think that you should let Luke decide that? Are you being fair to him by letting him suffer two losses?"

"Two?" I asked.

"Yes. The loss of Callie and now you."

"He'll be fine eventually. He doesn't need to be reminded of what happened when he looks at me."

"Do you honestly think that's how he feels?"

"I think so."

"Well, I think you're mistaken, and you need to talk to him."

I got up from my seat when I noticed we were thirty minutes over our allotted session time.

"Thank you for seeing me, Dr. Blakely. I'll give everything you've said consideration."

∽

Luke

Before returning to the bar, I set the bouquet of roses outside Lily's door. When I walked into my apartment, Gretchen was getting ready to leave.

"Hey, Luke. You shouldn't have." She smiled.

"Sorry, Gretchen. They're for my mom."

"What did you do to your hand?"

"I cut it over at Lily's place while changing the furnace filter. It hurts like a bitch."

"Stiches?"

"Yep, five."

"Ouch. Feel better. I have to run. I have my first photoshoot since the accident." She smiled.

"Congratulations. I'll see you later."

I walked into the kitchen and pulled out a vase from the cabinet. I set the roses for my mom in water to keep them fresh for tomorrow. I heard the door open, and Gretchen walked back in.

"Hey, didn't you leave some roses for Lily?"

"Yeah. Those are from me. She drove me to the hospital, and I wanted to thank her."

"Aw, she'll love them."

"Or hate them and me for giving them to her."

"Stop being negative. She'll come around. Time, Luke. Remember that."

I sighed because that was what everyone kept telling me. I hated time. I hated waiting. I craved her arms wrapped around me. I longed to hold her and to tell her how much I loved her.

Chapter Twenty-Four

LILY

I stopped by the studio to drop off most of the equipment before heading home. When I opened the door to the building, I saw a bouquet of roses sitting outside my door, wrapped in a pretty pink print paper. Attached was a card. As I picked up the roses and unlocked the door, I set my keys down and walked over to the table, where I pulled the card out and opened it.

> *Lily, thank you for taking me to the hospital this morning.*
> *I appreciate it.*
> *Love,*
> *Luke*

I picked up the roses and smelled them. The fragrance was calming as I lightly touched the smooth petals that curled up with my finger, taking in their silky nap. They were beautiful, just like our relationship used to be. I took a vase from the cabinet and filled it with water, arranging the roses inside, one by one. I set the vase in the middle of the kitchen table and softly smiled as they brightened up my apartment, which had been dark and dreary lately. I needed to thank Luke for the flowers because I wasn't the cold, heartless bitch that everyone seemed to think I was. I was protecting the one I loved. If you love someone, you'll set them free. Isn't that how it goes? I picked up my phone and sent him a text message.

"You're welcome, and thank you for the beautiful roses. You shouldn't have done that. It was unnecessary."

"You're welcome, and it was necessary. I hope you'll keep them."

I tapped the camera button on my phone, snapped a picture of the roses in the vase, and then sent it to Luke.

"They look great on the table."

"They certainly do," he replied.

∼

I DIDN'T ROLL out of bed until after nine a.m. when I was awakened by another nightmare, covered in sweat with my heart beating rapidly. Today was Charley's birthday and party, and I needed to get ready to drive out to Luke's parents' house. I didn't know what this day would bring emotion-wise, but I had to keep positive and happy for Charley.

As soon as I stepped out of the shower, I heard my phone ringing. I grabbed it from the nightstand in my bedroom and saw that Luke's mom was calling. My stomach did a sick flip.

"Hello," I answered nervously.

"Hi, sweetheart. It's Annie."

"Hi, Annie. How are you?"

"I'm doing okay. Listen, I'm calling because I want to tell you how happy Tom and I are that you're coming to Charley's party today."

"I wouldn't miss it for the world."

"I wanted to make it very clear that no matter what's going on between you and Luke, it doesn't affect how we feel about you. We don't want you to feel out of place or awkward in our home. You're just as welcome and loved here as anyone else."

Hearing her say those words to me was comforting. I was

nervous about seeing them and not knowing how they felt about the situation.

"Thank you, Annie. That really means a lot."

"You're welcome, sweetheart. We'll see you later. Bye."

"Bye." I hung up and felt a little more at ease.

∼

I PULLED into the driveway of Tom and Annie's house and grabbed the bottle of wine from the front seat. Before climbing out of the Explorer, I took a deep breath and tried calming my knotted, sick-feeling stomach. This wasn't going to be easy. I walked up to the door with perfect composure and lightly knocked. After a few moments, Annie opened the door and hugged me.

"Thank you for coming, Lily."

"This is for you." I smiled as I handed her the wine.

"Oh, you're such a doll. Thank you."

"Hi, Lily." Adam smiled as he walked over and lightly hugged me.

"LILY!" Charley exclaimed as she ran from the kitchen and threw her arms around me.

"Happy birthday, Charley." I smiled as I picked her up and kissed the tip of her nose.

I put her down, and she took my hand and led me to the kitchen decorated with birthday signs and balloons.

"Lily, it's so good to see you." Tom smiled as he hugged me.

"It's good to see you too, Tom."

Luke was bent over in the refrigerator, turned around, and looked at me. He gave me a small smile, twisted the cap off his beer, and went outside to the patio. Not too long after, Gretchen and Sam showed up.

"How did the photo shoot go?" she asked.

"It was amazing. I loved every minute of it."

"Hey, Lily," Sam said as he walked over and kissed my head. "You okay?"

"Yeah." I smiled with uncertainty.

I asked Maddie if she could come into the kitchen, and I handed her the box that contained the photos of Charley.

"Here. These are for you."

She smiled as she carefully took off the lid and gasped when she saw the pictures of Charley.

"Lily, these are beautiful. Oh my God. Look at our little girl, Adam."

"Wow, Lily." He smiled as he looked at them.

Luke walked in from the patio and came over to see what we were all looking at.

"Lily, those are wonderful pictures. Look at how cute Charley is."

"Thanks," I said. "How's your hand?"

"It's so-so. It still hurts a little." He smiled as he placed his hand on the small of my back and walked away. I froze. It was only for a moment, but it felt like his touch was imprinted on my skin. I sat on the patio next to Gretchen while Maddie, Sam, and Luke helped the kids with the party games. I couldn't stop staring at him and how he was with the kids.

"You okay?" Gretchen asked.

"Yeah, why?"

"Because you seem to be in a daze and staring at Luke. I know how much you love him, so why are you fighting it? Just work things out with the man. How long are you going to let this go?"

"It's complicated, Gretchen. You don't understand."

"What's complicated about two people who are deeply and madly in love working things out? Luke wants you back. He told me so."

"He thinks he wants me back," I said with a tear in my eye.

"What do you mean by that, Lily?"

I got up from my chair and looked down at her. "It means exactly how it sounds. Now, if you'll excuse me, I need to get another drink."

I walked into the house. Annie was getting Charley's birthday cake ready.

"Is there anything I can do to help, Annie?"

"No, sweetheart. Just sit back and enjoy yourself." She smiled.

Enjoy myself. How the hell was I supposed to enjoy myself when I was nothing but miserable? It took everything I had to come and be with Luke's family. The party was a huge success, and Charley was happy. That was all that mattered. I took the margarita that Tom had made for me and stepped back out onto the patio. The only seat available was one next to Luke. I took in a deep breath and sat down.

"Hey."

"Hey," I replied.

"The party was a success, and Charley seemed to have a great time," he said.

"It was a great party."

As we sat there in awkward silence, Luke reached over and touched my hair. I looked at him with furrowed brows.

"Sorry. You had a small leaf in your hair."

"Thanks," I said as I ran my hand through my hair.

When I looked at him, the only thing my mind would think was how much he resented me for everything that happened. He only thought he wanted us back together until he realized he couldn't be around me every day and night because it would constantly remind him of Callie and the accident, just like I was the constant reminder to my mother about my father's affair.

Chapter Twenty-Five

LUKE

It had been a week since Charley's party, and I hadn't seen Lily. But then again, I hadn't been coming home from the bar until the middle of the night. Lucky and Giselle were bringing the baby home next week, so Sam and I decided to prepare the nursery. Gretchen wanted to help but had to go out of town for a photo shoot. Lucky wasn't very handy, and we didn't trust him with paint and putting together the furniture.

It was a Saturday afternoon, and we were going to start painting. Giselle had all the colors picked out before she went into labor and had the paint delivered. So, all we needed to do was get it up on the walls. We had just arrived and laid the plastic on the floor when we heard someone walk through the door.

"What are you two doing here?" Lily asked.

"Painting," Sam replied. "What are you doing here?"

"I picked up some things for the baby and thought I'd drop them off. Plus, I was going to clean up around here. I didn't know anyone else would be here."

"Surprise," I said.

She walked away, and Sam's phone beeped.

The Upside of Love

"Ah, shit. I have to go, bro. Work needs me. Apparently, there's a big problem with one of the accounts."

"What?! It's Saturday, man."

"I know. Sorry. I'll try to get it worked out and come back," he said as he walked out the door.

I shook my head as I poured some paint into the tray, and Lily walked in.

"Where did Sam go?"

"Work. Something happened with one of his accounts."

"Oh."

I rolled the paint on the wall, and Lily stood staring at me.

"Is something wrong?" I asked.

"Since Sam had to leave, I can help you paint if you want."

"Nah. I'm fine."

"I can paint, you know."

"I never said you couldn't."

"You refusing my help tells me you think I can't paint a wall."

"Where are you getting that from? That's not what I'm saying."

"Good. Then I can help."

I sighed. "There's an extra roller over there. Be my guest."

I found myself having a bit of an attitude with her because being in the same room with her, especially after not seeing her for a week, killed me. We still never talked about that night. She wouldn't. I didn't know what to do anymore to try and get her to listen to me. Sometimes, I felt I needed to give up, but the thought destroyed me.

∾

Lily

He was Mr. Attitude today. Was I surprised? No. I hadn't seen him for a week, and it was one of the longest weeks of my life. But then again, I wasn't home much. I spent my days and most nights at the studio, editing the pictures from the photo shoot for Prim. I delivered the photos to Adalynn, and she loved them. She immediately booked my services for another shoot next month. Things in my career zone seemed to be moving forward, but my personal life stayed at a miserable standstill. Silence filled the room. The only significant sound heard was the sticky noise of the paint rolling on the walls.

"Are you going to be able to paint with your hand like that?" I asked.

"I'll be fine."

Luke put down his paint roller and turned on the radio. The song that was on was ending, and "Don't Fear the Reaper" began to play. That was the tune I heard Luke playing on his guitar that night.

"This was one of Dad's favorite songs. He used to sing and play it all the time. I always wondered about the meaning behind it."

"It's about eternal love," Luke said.

"Oh. Then, clearly, my father wasn't thinking about my mother when he would sing it."

Luke laughed. "Lily!"

"What?" I smiled as I turned around and looked at him.

He stared at me for a moment, looking for something to say. "I'm hungry. Are you?" he asked.

"A little."

"How about we order some pizza and take a break? The first coat will have to dry before we can put on the second one anyway."

"Pizza sounds good." I smiled.

"The usual?" he asked as he pulled out his phone.

"Yeah. The usual."

For the first time since that life-altering night, my stomach wasn't twisted in a knot. It felt somewhat normal, and I didn't know what to think. As Luke called in our pizza order, my phone beeped with a text message from Sam.

"Is Luke pissed that I'm not there?"

"No. I'm helping him paint the room."

"Oh. Thank you. I appreciate it. Unfortunately, I have to go out of town for a couple of days to smooth things over with this account, so I'll see you when I get back."

"Have fun!"

"You too!"

"The pizza will be here in about twenty minutes," Luke said.

"I just got a text message from Sam, and he said he has to go out of town for a couple of days for work."

"Is that so?" He sighed.

I walked to the kitchen and washed off the paint spots all over my hands. I took two paper plates from the cabinet and set them on the table. Luke walked in and went straight to the refrigerator.

"Beer?" he asked as he held up a bottle.

"Sure," I said as I walked over and took it from him.

Luke sat at the table while I put the bags I'd brought over on the couch.

"What did you buy?"

"Just some baby stuff. Towels, washcloths, burp rags, and bibs. You know, the usual baby things."

"I still can't believe the two of them had a baby," Luke smirked.

I shook my head as I took the seat across from him. "I know. I hope they can stand each other long enough for that little girl."

Luke threw his head back and laughed. "I was thinking the same thing."

I smiled as I arched my eyebrow and held up my beer bottle. A few moments later, there was a knock at the door. I went into my purse, took some cash out, and handed it to Luke.

"No, Lily. It's on me."

"No. Take it."

He opened the door, and it was Gary, our normal pizza delivery guy from the apartment.

"Hey, you two. Did you move?"

"Hey, Gary." Luke smiled. "Nah, this is our friend's house. We're doing some work."

I tried to hand Luke the money, but he kept shooing my hand away. Gary looked at me and smiled.

"Lily, Luke always pays. What are you doing?"

"Exactly!" Luke smirked.

I sighed and took the pizza over to the table. Later, I would shove the money in the pocket of the hoodie he brought. We sat down, and each took a couple of slices. It felt normal, like the way things used to be.

"How's your mom doing?" he asked out of the clear blue.

I took a sip of my beer before answering him. "She's good. Why?"

Luke shrugged his shoulders. "I heard you tell Charley that you went back to Seattle. How did that go? You know, with—"

"Brynn?" I interrupted.

"Yeah."

"We talked, and we cried. Same with Hunter, without the crying part."

"You saw him?"

"Yeah. They're still together and oh so in love. It made me realize a few things and see things differently."

Instantly, I saw a change in his face. "So let me get this straight. You went all the way to Seattle to talk to your sister and ex-fiancé about their relationship and what they did to you, but you refuse to talk to me about us? That's real nice, Lily," he said as he got up from his chair, threw the plate in the garbage, and then walked out of the kitchen.

Great. Just fucking great. I didn't know what to do. I cleaned up the table and put the leftover pizza in the refrigerator. When I walked back into the room, Luke turned around and looked at me.

"You can leave now. I got this."

"Luke, please."

"Lily, I mean it. Get the hell out of here, NOW!" he yelled.

I flinched at the anger in his voice. Reaching into my pocket, I grabbed some cash and threw it on the floor.

"Fuck you, Luke. Just fuck you!" I yelled as I stormed out.

Chapter Twenty-Six

LUKE

I called Maddie and asked if she could swing by Giselle's place. I needed to talk to someone because if I didn't, I would lose it. It didn't take her long to come over because she was shopping in the area. She entered the bedroom and grabbed a paint roller.

"What happened?"

"Lily. That's what happened. I just don't get it, sis. She goes back to Seattle and makes amends with her sister and that scumbag ex-fiancé of hers, and it's okay, but she won't fucking talk to me. She won't talk about our relationship."

"Luke, you need to calm down for a minute."

"I told her to get the hell out of here, Maddie. I was so angry that she wouldn't talk to me."

She walked over to where I was standing and wrapped her arms around me. "There's something else going on."

"What do you mean?" I asked as I pulled back.

"I'm not so sure anymore that it's about what you said to her. Your love for each other is so strong and so pure that it should be able to overcome anything. I don't know, Luke. Maybe I'm crazy, but there's something else going on with Lily."

"Whatever the hell her problem is, I don't have time to waste anymore. I'm done, and I mean it this time. If Lily doesn't want to talk to me or discuss what happened, fine. She can go off and live a happy life by herself because, obviously, it's what she wants."

Maddie and I didn't say another word after that. She stayed, helped me finish the walls, and then we headed home. Lily's truck wasn't in the parking lot, and it was almost midnight. Not that I should have cared, but it wasn't safe. I said goodbye to Maddie, and I stepped inside my apartment. Sam and Gretchen were both gone, and I was all alone. There was no way I would sleep until I knew Lily was home safe. About an hour later, as I was sitting on the couch, I heard her door shut.

I returned to Giselle's the following day and helped Lucky build the crib. When I arrived, he was sitting in the middle of the nursery, swearing up a storm with crib pieces and parts all over the floor.

"Dude, it's about time. Do you have any idea how fucked up this is?"

I chuckled. "They aren't that hard to build. Move over and hand me the directions."

"How's Lily?"

"Why are you asking me?"

"Sam said she was over here yesterday, helping you paint. Oh, by the way, thanks for doing that."

"Things were going good until she told me something, and I told her to get the hell out," I replied.

"Whoa, dude. Come on. What the fuck is going on?"

"She went to Seattle to talk to her sister and ex, and she won't talk to me," I said as I grabbed the screwdriver.

"She talks to you. I've seen her."

"She won't talk about us. She can forgive and talk to the people who cheated on her and made her life a living hell, but she can't talk to me about our relationship."

"Well, you did tell her that she killed Callie."

"Thanks for that, Lucky. I don't want to talk about Lily anymore."

The Upside of Love

Just as I was tightening one of the bolts, my phone rang. It was Cody.

"Hey, Cody. What's up?"

"Hi, Luke. Sorry to bother you on a Sunday, but I think there's a problem with the invoice for the liquor order."

"It's your day off. Why are you at the bar?"

"I had nothing else to do today, so I thought I'd come in. Do you think you can stop by later and have a look?"

"Yeah. I'm in the middle of building the crib for Giselle and Lucky's baby. I'll be there in a while."

"Thanks. I'll be waiting."

I hung up and looked at Lucky, who was staring at me. "Dude, she is so into you. You better be careful."

"She is not," I snapped.

"Yes, she is. I know when women are into guys. I know their tricks. Trust me, she's into you."

An hour later, the crib was built and put in its place, and after I helped Lucky clean up, I took off for the bar.

When I arrived, I walked straight to my office and saw Cody sitting behind my desk. She held the picture of Lily and me I had in my drawer.

"What are you doing?" I asked.

"Oh, Luke. Sorry. I was just looking at your picture."

"Why?"

"I couldn't find a paperclip, so I opened the drawer, and there it was. I'm sorry."

I walked over and took it from her hands.

"It's a nice picture."

"I'm not here to talk about the picture. What's up with the invoice?" I asked.

"I'm sorry. I already figured it out. I forgot to call you. But since you're here, would you like to grab a bite?"

"No. I already ate. Since the invoice is fine, you can go now."

"Okay," she said with a sad look as she grabbed her purse and started to walk out the door. She turned around. "You're a really nice and special guy. You shouldn't be alone. If you would like some company, call me."

I nodded. Maybe Lucky was right. I was going to have to keep a closer eye on her. After talking to Candi for a bit, I decided to go home. I couldn't stop thinking about Lily and how rude I was to her last night. I needed to apologize. When I pulled into the parking lot, her Explorer was in its usual spot. I knocked on her door before going to my apartment.

"Luke," she said as she opened the door.

"I need to talk to you."

"I think you said enough last night," she said.

"Please, Lily. I want to apologize for my behavior last night. I was way out of line, and I'm sorry."

She motioned for me to come inside.

"I just want you to know that I'm not going to try and push you to talk to me anymore. What's done is done. Obviously, I can't change that night. I didn't mean what I said, and you are in no way responsible for what happened. I was a jerk, and I was in shock. That's all. I would give anything to rewind that night and do things right. I'm really happy that you talked to Hunter and Brynn because I know it had been weighing heavy on your mind for a long time."

She stood across the room and listened to every word I said. She never interrupted, and she never moved from her spot.

"I just wanted you to know that. I'll leave you to whatever it was you were doing." As soon as I put my hand on the doorknob, she spoke.

"Thank you, Luke. I appreciate you saying what you did."

I nodded and smiled at her as I walked out the door.

Chapter Twenty-Seven

LILY

He was hurting. I could tell. He was hurting just as bad as I was. This pain he was feeling would pass. The pain of looking at me, talking to me, and making love to me would always be there in the back of his mind if we were together. Maybe he wouldn't realize it at first, but little things would remind him of Callie, and then he'd look at me, wishing I'd never given him those tickets. It wasn't only about how he felt. It was also about the guilt that I would carry for the rest of my life. Maybe I was protecting the both of us.

I spent the next week photographing children and helping Gretchen plan Giselle's baby shower that was going to be held at Luke's bar. He offered, and Gretchen jumped on it without talking to me first. She thought it would be perfect, and so did Giselle.

Since the shower was today and I hadn't seen or talked to Luke since that Sunday he stopped by, it would be awkward. There was a knock at the door as I was putting the shower favors that I was in charge of in the box.

"Come on in. It's open," I yelled.

The door opened, and I heard Luke's voice from behind.

"Hey, Lily."

After I gasped, I turned around. "Hi, Luke."

"I was wondering if you needed any help with the boxes for the shower. Gretchen said that you'd have a few. I could load them in the jeep."

He looked so hot. As I stared at him, I thought about all the times we made love. I missed him so much that I didn't know what to do anymore. Gretchen and Giselle told me daily how stupid I was, but they didn't know why I couldn't let him back into my life.

"I have these right here," I said as I pointed to the boxes on the table.

"Are they ready to go?"

"Yeah."

He walked over to the table, grabbed the first box, then smiled at me.

"You look beautiful."

I could feel myself blushing as I thanked him. He gave me a small smile as he loaded the boxes in his jeep.

"Okay, I guess that's it. I'll see you at the bar."

The bar was decorated throughout with pink balloons and streamers. When I walked in, the first person I saw was Cody. What the hell is she doing here? Sam walked over to me and kissed me on the cheek.

"You look gorgeous, Lily."

"Thanks, Sam."

"I live next door to you and haven't seen you lately."

"I've been busy at the studio, and then, with planning the shower, I really haven't had much time for anything else."

"Well, stop being a stranger. I miss you." He smiled.

"I miss you too," I said, patting his chest.

The shower got underway and was a huge success. A little over a hundred people came and showered Giselle and Lucky with gifts for Isabella. Luke was behind the bar making drinks when I walked up.

"Hi. What can I get you?" he asked.

"A glass of red wine will be fine."

He smiled, and as he poured it into a glass, Adalynn walked up to me.

"Lily, I need to talk to you about something."

"Sure, Adalynn. What's up?"

"How would you like to go to New York for a couple of weeks?"

"That would be great. What's happening in New York?"

"I'm launching a fashion blog, and I would like you to do the fashion shoot for it."

"I would love to."

"Great. I know it's last minute, but I need you to leave the day after tomorrow. It's a two-week shoot, and Prim will pay all your expenses. I knew you'd be game, so I booked a room at The Plaza. It overlooks Central Park, where I want most of the shoot."

I could feel Luke's eyes on me as Adalynn and I were talking. As soon as she walked away, he spoke.

"Wow. New York. That's exciting," he said.

Suddenly, Cody stepped behind the bar and put her arm around his waist. "When you get a chance, I need to talk to you privately."

"Excuse me, Lily," he said as he walked away with her.

My stomach started to flip out, and I became overly hot. Was he seeing her? Was that why he came over and told me that he wouldn't pressure me into talking to him anymore? Thoughts of the two of them together consumed me, and I felt like I couldn't breathe. I walked towards the back to see if I could hear their conversation, and when I approached Luke's office, I saw him kiss her on her forehead as he clasped her shoulders. I put my hand over my mouth and quietly walked away so he didn't hear me. I went into the main area of the bar and found Adalynn.

"If it's okay with you, I will leave for New York tonight. I haven't been there since I was a kid, and I think I should scout locations in Central Park first."

"Great idea! I didn't think of that. I'll call the hotel and tell them you'll arrive tonight and you can fly on the company jet. Give me a second, and let me check the flight schedules."

As she pulled out her phone, I saw Luke and Cody. He had his hand on the small of her back as they walked into the main area.

"Great news. Your flight leaves at seven o'clock." She smiled.

I looked at my watch and saw it was four. I guessed I had better get home and pack.

"You're leaving tonight?" Luke said.

He must have overheard our conversation.

"Yeah," I replied as I turned around and began to walk away.

"I thought you weren't leaving for a couple of days."

"Change in plans. I need to get the fuck away from here." I didn't mean for those last few words to spew out of my mouth, but they did.

"Why the sudden change, Lily?"

"It's none of your business, Luke. Why don't you focus on your little girlfriend over there and leave me the hell alone."

By this time, all the guests had pretty much left. I told Giselle and Gretchen what was happening and that I had to leave and go pack. I hugged them goodbye, and when I walked out of the bar, Luke was standing up against the Explorer.

"Get out of my way, Luke," I said.

"I'm not moving until you tell me what the hell that remark was about Cody."

"I saw you kiss her, Luke. Okay. There. You wanted to know, so I told you."

"When?" he asked in confusion.

"In your office. Just a little while ago."

He threw his head back and laughed. "Lily, she quit. I was wishing her good luck."

"Luke, I have to go. I have a lot of packing to do and a plane to catch, so if you'll excuse me and please move away from my vehicle, I'd appreciate it."

"Whatever, Lily. I'm over you." He hit the hood of the Explorer and walked away.

His words hurt, but what did I expect? Tears filled my eyes, as I would never get over him.

Luke

This was tearing me apart. I told her that I was over her and I wasn't. I'd never be. I was so in love with her that I had to put an end to all of this once and for all. We needed to talk, and if I had to lock her in a room until I got some answers, I would. I called Candi to join me behind the bar so I could talk to her and Maddie.

"What's up, boss?" she asked.

"I need the two of you to do me a favor. I need you to run the bar while I'm gone."

"Where are you going?" Maddie asked.

"I'm going to New York to get my girlfriend back. I'm done with this game, and she will listen to me."

"Good for you, Luke." Candi smiled as she patted me on the back.

"What if she won't?" Maddie said.

"It's not even an option for her anymore. I'm going to ask Mom and Dad to help out here, too. As you know, Cody quit."

"It's about time," Candi said.

"I had to talk with her, and she didn't like what I had to say, so she thought it would be best to move on."

"Smart girl." Maddie smiled. "When are you leaving?"

"I'm going to try and get a flight out of here first thing tomorrow morning."

Maddie and Candi both hugged me. "Good luck. You do whatever you have to and get her back."

"Trust me. I will."

I left the bar and called my parents. They said they would be more than happy to help at the bar while I was gone, and my dad said not to worry about the paperwork or the books. As I was unlocking the door to my apartment, Lily walked out with two suitcases. She looked startled when she saw me.

"Let me help you with those," I said.

"No need. I've got this."

"Too fucking bad, Lily. I'm helping you," I said as I grabbed one of her suitcases from her hand.

"Watch your mouth, Matthews."

I silently smiled. I loaded her suitcase in the limo that Adalynn had sent to pick her up. She climbed in, and I stopped her from shutting the door. I poked my head inside.

"Have a good time in New York."

"Thank you," she said quietly.

Little did she know that she'd be seeing me tomorrow.

Chapter Twenty-Eight

LILY

I lay down on the plush king-size bed in the hotel room and noted the bottle of champagne and plate of chocolate-covered strawberries sitting on the table in front of the window. I got up and walked over to find a card with my name on it.

> *"Enjoy your stay, and have a great photo shoot.*
> *Best, Ian and Adalynn, Prim Magazine."*

I smiled as I set the card down and bit into a large, juicy strawberry. I had wished that Wyatt could have made the trip with me. But with his classes, he couldn't. I didn't know what to do because I needed an assistant. I'd have to contact Adalynn and see if anyone here would be willing to help. I walked into the bathroom, looked at the amazing sunken jet tub, and decided it was time for a glass of champagne and a relaxing bubble bath. I started the water and got undressed. It was one morning here, and I was still in California time.

As I poured myself a glass of champagne, I sank into the bubbly tub until the water reached my neck. I took a sip of my champagne and closed my eyes. I couldn't stop thinking about Luke and his attitude before I left for New York. The way he grabbed my suitcase from me was a bit rough. Then, how he told me to have a good time in New York was weird. It sounded like he was happy that I was leaving. I didn't know. I couldn't put my finger on it, but he sounded different. Somewhere in the back of my mind, I had wished he was here with me. Exploring New York with him would have been fun under different circumstances. Once I was finished with my bath, I changed into my pajamas and climbed into bed. I was surprised at how quickly I fell asleep.

～

LUKE

I checked into The Plaza at 10 a.m. Thank God my room was ready.

"Here you go, Mr. Matthews. You will be staying in room 2212. I'll have the bellman bring up your luggage."

"Nah, that's okay. I can take it up myself. Thank you."

I boarded the elevator and rode it up to the twenty-second floor. This had to be the most beautiful place I'd ever stayed at. I was on the lookout for Lily, but I hadn't planned what I would say to her when I saw her. I had a feeling once she saw me, she'd be pissed. I sent a text message to Gretchen, asking her if she knew which room Lily was in.

"Do you know what room number Lily is in?"

"No. Hold on a sec, and I'll see if Giselle knows."

I waited, and a text message came through after a few moments.

"She doesn't know either. Sorry, Luke."

"It's okay. I'll think of something."

I left the hotel and walked a couple of blocks. It was going to be tough trying to find Lily here. It would be like trying to find a needle in a haystack. After a couple of hours and a Starbucks later, I pulled out my phone to see if I had any messages. As I was walking, I accidentally ran into someone, which wasn't hard to do in this city.

"I'm sor—" We both started to say at the same time as I looked up.

"LUKE! What the—"

"Lily. What a coincidence." I smiled with relief.

"What are you doing here?" she asked through gritted teeth.

"Can we go somewhere else and talk so we're not in the way of people?"

She grabbed me by the arm and pulled me over to the side. "Again. What are you doing here?"

"I came to talk to you."

"You flew all the way to New York to talk to me?"

"Yes, and you're going to damn well listen to me too!"

"Not right now, I'm not. I have something to do," she snapped.

"Whatever you're doing, I'm doing it with you. You shouldn't be walking around this city by yourself."

She looked at me as she cocked her head. "It's my life, and I'll do what I want. You are not my keeper and cannot tell me what to do. Who the hell do you think you are, Luke Matthews?"

"I'm the guy in love with you and needs you to listen. That's who I am."

Her sad but angry eyes stared into mine momentarily and then looked away. "I am not talking about this here, and I'm not talking about this now."

She turned around and started to walk away. I followed behind.

∽

LILY

I couldn't believe Luke was here in New York City. I was so pissed off at him, but then again, I wasn't, if that made any sense. I reached the hotel, and he followed me inside.

"Why are you following me? I'm going to my room, and you're not coming."

"It just so happens that I'm going to my room too."

I stopped in the middle of the lobby. "You're staying here?" I asked.

"Yes." He smiled.

"Do you realize how expensive this place is?"

"Yes."

"You can't afford that."

"You don't worry about what I can and can't afford." He smiled.

"Go home, Luke," I said as I stepped onto the elevator.

"Nah, I'll stay in New York for a while."

I pushed the button to my floor and asked Luke which floor he was on.

"Same," he replied.

"You're on floor twenty-two?"

"Yep. I sure am."

I stepped out and walked to my room when the elevator doors opened. I looked over at Luke, who stopped at the door next to mine.

"No. No. No. That is not your room!"

He smiled as he inserted the card into the lock and opened the door. "Is this a coincidence, or maybe something else?"

"FUCK!"

"Watch your mouth, babe." He winked and walked inside his room, shutting the door behind him.

I couldn't believe this, I thought as I walked into the room. I threw my purse on the bed and paced the floor before grabbing a chocolate-covered strawberry and shoving it into my mouth. I grabbed my phone from my purse and called Dr. Blakely.

"Dr. Blakely's office. How can I help you?"

"Regina, it's Lily Gilmore. I need to speak to Dr. Blakely."

"Would you like to make an appointment?"

"I can't since I'm in New York. But, if she has a moment, I need to speak to her."

"She's in with a patient right now. I'll give her your message."

"Thank you, Regina. Please tell her that it's very important."

I sat down on the bed, tapping my foot on the floor. "Call, call, call," I said as I stared at my phone. Why was this so hard? Why couldn't I make my own decision? Wait. I did. I decided to cease and desist. Okay, not in the form of a letter, but verbally. Why did his coming here have the profound effect of a smidge of happiness on me? Why did I suddenly feel comfort knowing that he was right next door? It was like we were back in California. My phone rang.

"Dr. Blakely, thank God you called."

"Lily, what's wrong? My secretary said you were in New York."

"I had to go to New York for work. Luke flew in this morning. He said he wanted to talk."

"He flew all the way to New York to talk to you?"

"Yes. What do I do? My head tells me to talk to him, but my heart is shaking in the corner and telling me no."

"First, you need to calm down and take a deep, cleansing breath. It's inevitable, Lily. You need to talk to him. We've discussed this already. It's no longer an option, and it seems to me that no matter where you go, he'll always be behind you, waiting for that talk. You're stronger than you give yourself credit for, Lily, and you need to act like an adult and do the right thing."

I gulped because I knew everything she said was true. I knew it before I called her, but I needed to hear her say it.

"Thank you, Dr. Blakely."

"Baby steps, Lily. Baby steps."

I hung up, grabbed my purse, and banged on his door.

"You do realize that this is a quiet hotel, right?"

"Don't be like that with me," I said as I gave him an evil look and walked into his room.

I heard him chuckle.

"This is how this situation is going to work. I need an assistant for the photo shoots, and since you're here, you will help me. After we're finished with work, then I will listen to what you have to say, but until then, and only then, there will be no talk of such."

"Your terms, eh?" he asked.

"Yep. My terms. You game?"

"Sure. I'm game."

"Okay." I nodded. "Now, I need to go to Central Park. Are you coming?"

"I'm right behind you, but I have one question. Have you eaten yet?"

"I had a muffin," I replied.

"A muffin isn't a meal. So let's grab some lunch before heading to Central Park."

"I pay for my own," I said.

"Deal."

We walked until we saw Rumours Bar and Grill. As soon as we stepped inside, we were taken to a booth. Luke told me he had to use the bathroom and he'd be right back. I watched him walk away and couldn't help but stare at his fine ass – the one I was missing badly, and I wasn't the only one staring at him. The waiter came over to take our drink order, so I ordered Luke a beer and a margarita for myself.

"I ordered you a beer since you weren't here," I said.

"Thank you." He smiled as he picked up his menu. "What are you going to order?"

"I think I might get the Chicken BLT Wrap."

"That sounds good. I'm looking at the Prime Rib French Dip."

"Oh, that sounds delicious too. Shit, now I don't know what to get." My head was starting to hurt.

He looked at me and flashed his sexy smile. "Why don't you order what you were going to? I'll order the French dip, and we can share it."

We used to do that all the time. He would order one thing. I'd order something else, and then we'd split it. I didn't know if we should do that or not. Things between us were awkward and not normal, but what the hell? I wanted to try that French dip.

"Okay."

After setting our drinks in front of us, the waiter took our order. The place was hopping and crowded with people. It was your typical bar with big screen TVs lining the walls and different sports games for everyone. Once my eyes finished scanning the place, they caught the attention of Luke, who was staring at me.

"Why are you staring at me?"

Suddenly, he held out his hand. "Hi, I'm Luke Matthews, and you are?"

I narrowed my eyes at him as I cocked my head, and a half smile fell across my lips. I stuck out my hand and placed it in his.

"I'm Lily Gilmore."

"It's nice to meet you, Lily Gilmore."

Our hands were still locked when the waiter brought our food. His touch, which I'd craved, was comforting, and I found myself having a hard time letting go.

Chapter Twenty-Nine

LUKE

    I was starting over and reintroducing ourselves. I let go of her hand as soon as the waiter set down my plate in front of me. Her half smile and the look on her face was a start—hopefully, the start of a new beginning for both of us. I picked up half of my sandwich and handed it to her. She picked up half of hers, and we exchanged.

    "Thank you, Miss Gilmore."

    "Thank you, Mr. Matthews."

    "Why don't you tell me a little about what I'll be doing as your assistant?"

    She explained about lighting and handing her different cameras and lenses. Just as long as I got to be with her, I didn't care what I did. As we were eating, her phone beeped with a message from Brynn. She quickly typed a message back and then looked at me.

    "How are you now with Brynn and Hunter? Please don't get mad at me for bringing it up."

    "I found that the universe works in mysterious ways. I met Hunter so he could get together with my sister, if that makes sense. They were meant to be together, and I see that now."

    "As in fate?" I asked.

She looked down as she dipped her French fry in ketchup. "Yeah. Maybe."

There was still a hint of pain in her response. "So then all is good with you and them?"

I was trying to understand how she might or might not forgive me.

"Things are okay, but they will never return to how they used to be. I think the thing for me is how they kept it from me, how I almost married him, and how they would have still went on together behind my back. That will always be in the forefront of my mind."

Progress. She was talking to me the way she used to. She could have told me it was none of my business, but instead, she spoke about it, which made me happy. We finished eating, and we paid our own bill. I would have to respect her wishes if I wanted a second chance with her. I got up from the booth and waited for her to leave before leaving the restaurant. As soon as she slid out of her seat, I placed my hand on the small of her back. We walked to Central Park and took in the beauty it had to offer. Lily had brought her camera and started taking pictures.

"Lily, look! It's the Central Park Zoo. Let's go," I excitedly said as I grabbed her hand without thinking about it. "Sorry," I said as I looked down and let go of her hand. "I guess I got overly excited."

She didn't say a word. She just smiled. We each bought our own ticket and headed straight to the penguin exhibit. As we stood and watched them, the smile on Lily's face never left. She loved the penguins just as much as I did. Our next stop was the snow leopard.

"Look at how beautiful they are," she said as she took their pictures. "Did you know that their teeth are over four inches long?" she asked as she looked at me.

"No, I didn't know that. I would hate to get caught in a mouth like that."

"I love their coloring. Did you know their colors are so they can camouflage themselves in the mountains?"

"No," I said as I arched one eyebrow. "Are you a snow leopard expert and just never told me?"

She laughed. "No. I was obsessed with them one time when I

was a child and I wanted a baby snow leopard as a pet. My dad told me to do a lot of research and write a paper on the facts about them, and he'd consider it. Let's just say that he was high when he said that and then denied he'd ever said it when he was sober."

"That was really shitty."

"Yeah, well, he was sometimes a shitty father."

She walked away from the snow leopards and went over to look at the lemurs.

"Look! It's King Julian!" She smiled.

"Is there anything special I should know about them?"

She laughed. "No. I never wanted one, but look at how cute they are. I may have to reconsider."

I looked around and noticed a stand that sold stuffed animals. I told Lily I needed to find a restroom and would be right back. I made my way to the stand I noticed earlier selling snow leopard stuffed animals. I purchased one and then found Lily taking pictures of the red pandas.

"I found something," I said.

"Really? What?"

I handed her the baby snow leopard with a smile. "He asked me if I knew your name because he wanted to go home with you."

She took the stuffed animal from my hands. "Luke," she said as she looked down.

"Now you have the baby snow leopard you always wanted. I thought since you did all that research, you deserved one."

"Thank you," she said, holding it up to her face and smiling.

∼

Lily

Happy. That was how I felt at the moment. He caught me off guard, and I didn't know what to do.

"Are you okay?" he asked.

"I just have a headache. Come on. Let's go see the other animals."

I really wasn't feeling well, and after we looked at all the animals, we hailed a cab and took it back to the hotel. Luke put his hand on my forehead.

"Lily, you're burning up. I think you may have a fever."

"I don't think I have a fever. I'm just really tired. I think I'm still jet-lagged."

"You have a fever."

When we reached the hotel, Luke told me to go to my room and that he'd pick up some Motrin from the gift shop. I did as he asked because I didn't have the strength to argue with him. My headache was getting worse by the second. When I opened the door, I threw my purse on the floor, kicked off my shoes, threw myself on the bed, and closed my eyes. A few moments later, Luke knocked on the door. I took every bit of strength to get up and answer it.

"Come on. Let's get you into bed, Lily. Do you want to change first?"

I nodded as I lay down across the comforter. "A pair of shorts and a tank top are in the top drawer."

He handed them to me, and I went to the bathroom to change. When I was done, Luke had the covers pulled back, and I climbed in, laying my head on the soft pillow. He took the thermometer he purchased from the lobby shop and put it under my tongue.

"Keep it under there." He smiled as he gave me the snow leopard.

After a few minutes, the thermometer beeped, and he took it from my mouth.

"Ouch. It's 102. I told you that you had a fever." He opened the Motrin bottle and handed me a bottle of water.

I took the little orange pills and chased them down with water. I couldn't believe that I was sick. I was never sick. This had to be the worst timing. I clutched my snow leopard tightly to my chest as Luke pulled the covers up over me.

"Get some rest," he said as he lightly touched my head.

I just wanted to sleep. Thank God the photo shoot was the day after tomorrow. Hopefully, I'd be better by then. I remembered drifting off into a deep sleep, but at the same time, I felt restless because I had a dream about Luke and me. It was a dream where we were having sex, and it was nothing short of incredible until I looked up and saw Callie staring down at us. My eyes flew open, and I sat straight up and fell back down. Luke was sitting on the couch and instantly came to my side.

"Are you okay?"

"Why are you still here?" I asked sleepily. "And, yeah, I just had a nightmare. It's probably the fever."

He went into the bathroom, wet a washcloth, and placed it across my forehead. "Feeling any better?"

"No," I replied as I looked at him. "You don't have to stay here. You can go. I appreciate everything you've already done."

"I came to New York to be with you, Lily, and you're sick. There's no way I'm leaving you when you're like this. Do you want to know what the best part is?"

"What?"

"You don't have the strength to argue with me." He smiled.

"You're right," I said as I closed my eyes and fell back asleep.

Once again, I woke up and looked over at Luke, lying across the couch, sleeping. I had to pee, so I climbed out of bed and went to the bathroom. My body felt like it had been hit by a train, with every muscle and joint in agony. As I was in the bathroom, there was a knock on the door.

"You okay in there, Lily?" Luke asked.

"Yeah," I said as I flushed the toilet.

I walked out of the bathroom, and Luke was standing there with the bottle of Motrin in his hands.

"You need to take a couple more."

"How long have I been sleeping?" I asked as I climbed back into bed.

"Five hours."

"I want to take a bath."

"I'll start one for you, and then I have something I have to do, but I'll be back."

I nodded, and after he started the water, I removed my shirt. He looked at me with hunger in his eyes. I wasn't even thinking straight and shouldn't have done that in front of him.

"Is it okay if I take your room key?"

"Yeah. It's fine."

"Okay. I'm leaving, but I'll be back. Be careful in the bathtub. I won't be gone long."

I gave him a half smile, and he left the room. Stripping out of the rest of my clothes, I climbed into the relaxing tub and closed my eyes.

Chapter Thirty

LUKE

    Seeing her sick like that really upset me. I'd never known Lily to be sick unless you count the nights she got drunk and was hanging over the toilet vomiting while I held back her hair. I remembered seeing a deli earlier when Lily and I walked down the street. As I stepped through the door, I could smell the aroma of chicken soup with a mix of pastrami.

    "Can I help you?" the girl behind the counter asked.

    "I'd like to order a bowl of chicken noodle soup, a corned beef sandwich, and a tuna salad sandwich with lettuce and tomato."

    "Coming right up, sir." She smiled.

    Once my order was ready, I stopped into a party store before returning to the hotel. I picked up a few bottles of water and a few bottles of Coke. I needed to make sure Lily stayed hydrated. Lily walked out of the bathroom with her robe on when I opened the door.

    "What did you get?" she asked as she slipped her feet into the complimentary slippers and climbed back into bed, sitting up against the headboard.

    I set the brown bags on the table and pulled out her soup and sandwich. "I brought you some chicken noodle soup and a sandwich. You need to eat."

"I'm not hungry."

"You don't need to eat the sandwich now, but the soup, you do," I said, handing it to her with a spoon. "I also picked up bottles of water and coke. It's way cheaper than what the hotel charges."

"Good thinking." She smiled.

I took my sandwich and sat down on the couch. Lily looked at me, and I was surprised at what she said next.

"You can sit on the bed. You don't need to sit all the way over there."

"Are you sure?"

"Yeah," she replied as she patted the bed.

I took my sandwich and sat up next to her.

"I want to thank you for taking care of me. This really would have sucked if I was alone."

I wanted to kiss her so badly, but I couldn't. One, she was sick, and two, she wasn't ready. I could still sense the hesitance in her.

"You're welcome. You know that I'll always take care of you."

"Luke, don't," she said as she looked down.

"We're going to talk, Lily. Not tonight or tomorrow, but we'll talk, and you better be ready."

~

LILY

I told Luke to go to his room and get some sleep. I didn't want him to stay in my room all night and sleep on the couch. He paid a lot of money for his room, and I wanted to make sure he was comfortable.

"Are you going to be okay?" he asked.

"I'll be fine. I'm already feeling a little bit better, thanks to you. Plus, I have Leo to keep me company."

"Who's Leo?" he asked with a confused look.

I held up the snow leopard and smiled.

"Ah, so that's his name. I'm taking your room key in case you need me in the middle of the night."

"That's fine. If I need anything, I'll text you. I promise."

He leaned over and kissed my head. "Sorry. It's a habit. Feel better and sleep well," he said as he got up from the bed and left the room. When the door shut, I regretted telling him to leave. I felt alone. I pulled out my phone and called Giselle to see how Isabella was doing. They were bringing her home from the hospital today.

"Lily. How are you?" she answered.

"Sick. Can you believe it?"

"Oh no. Flu?"

"I don't know. I have a fever, and I'm tired and achy."

"Make sure to stay hydrated."

"Luke is making sure of that."

"So lover boy found you?"

"Yep. He sure did."

"Are you being nice?"

I rolled my eyes. "Yes. He's taking such good care of me, and it hurts," I said as a tear fell down my face.

"Why does it hurt? He loves you, and you love him. Stop fighting it, Lily. Damn. I love you, but you are being dumb about this."

"You don't understand, Giselle. I'm doing this for him."

"What? What the hell are you talking about?"

"Listen, I called to find out how Isabella is doing."

"She's fine. Now back to what you're doing for Luke."

"I have to go. I'm not feeling good. I'll call you later." Click.

I woke up the following day to the smell of coffee and Luke sitting on the edge of my bed with his hand across my forehead. I opened one eye.

"What are you doing?"

"Checking to see if you still have a fever."

"Do I?"

"It doesn't feel like it, but we better take your temperature," he said as he stuck the thermometer under my tongue. "I brought you breakfast. I ordered room service for us and had it delivered to my room so you wouldn't be disturbed. I brought it over."

The thermometer beeped, and Luke smiled as he read it. "99.5. I would say you're getting better."

I sat up with ease. My body didn't ache as bad as yesterday, and my headache seemed to have disappeared. Luke set the tray on my lap and climbed beside me with his. I took a sip of coffee, and it was so delicious. As I lifted the silver lid from the plate, I took in the aroma of bacon and eggs. I looked over at Luke and smiled.

"Good choice, Mr. Matthews."

"Did you sleep well?" he asked.

"I think so. I don't remember waking up at all."

"That's good. I think you're on the mend. You probably had some twelve- or twenty-four-hour bug."

I sat there and ate my eggs as a sudden thought came to mind. I turned and looked at him.

"Who's running the bar?"

He laughed. "Is that what you're thinking about?"

"For some strange reason, it just hit me."

"Maddie, Candi, and my parents are holding down the fort."

"You mentioned that Cody quit. May I ask why?" I said as I spread the strawberry jam across a piece of toast.

"She was hitting on me, and I had to put a stop to it. I guess she felt that she couldn't work for me anymore."

"You said you were over me, yet you showed up here."

"I said many things I didn't mean, Lily."

We were interrupted by the ringing sound of my phone. I reached over and grabbed it from the nightstand.

"Hey, Adalynn."

"Hi, Lily. I have bad news. The photoshoot has to be rescheduled for next month."

"What? Why?"

"The damn designer didn't get the complete outfits done in time. Something about his sick mother. I don't know. Anyway, he was supposed to have overnighted them yesterday at the hotel, but how could he if he didn't finish them up? He was afraid to call me to tell me he was running behind."

"That's too bad."

"Tell me about it. But you stay the rest of the week and enjoy New York. Please do me a favor and scout out some different locations for the shoot. You're creative, and I know you'll find something amazing."

"Thanks, Adalynn. I'll talk to you soon." I hung up and sighed.

"What was that about?" Luke asked.

"The photo shoot isn't happening now until next month. She told me to stay the rest of the week and scout out some locations."

"That's too bad," he said.

"Yeah. But on the bright side, I get to come back. Isn't that right, Leo?" I said as I kissed my snow leopard's face.

Chapter Thirty-One

LUKE

We finished eating breakfast, and I took the trays to the table. I happened to look out the window and noticed it was raining.

"It's raining."

"Rain? What's that?" Lily laughed.

"Yeah, no kidding. It's been quite a while since California has seen some."

Now that the photo shoot was canceled, I wondered if it was the right time for our talk. I really needed to do this because I was desperate for her. Even though things between us the past day had been amazing, we needed to talk. I walked over to the bed and grabbed her hand. She knew exactly what I was doing because she had a look of fear in her eyes.

"Babe, we need to talk, and we need to do it now."

She took in a sharp breath and pulled her hand away. "I know."

"That night was a shock for both of us, and I'm not proud of how I handled myself. I should never have walked out on you, and I'm so sorry. I want to erase that night and start over."

"You never should have left me." She started to cry. "You should have stayed, and we could have talked about it. I was just as shocked as you, and you didn't love me enough to stay. You walked out on me like everyone else in my life!" she yelled as she pointed her finger at me.

"Lily, I'm so sorry. You also need to understand what seeing that picture meant and what I felt. The things going through my head. To think that we'd actually had a conversation before you moved to Santa Monica, and that we looked into each other's eyes before we even knew each other's names is extraordinary. Lily, you were meant to be in my life, starting from the day you walked over to my table."

∼

Lily

Oh God. I couldn't do this. I didn't know what to say. My throat felt like it was closing. He was broken right now, but he would heal. When he didn't have to see me anymore, he'd heal. I started to shake, and my breathing became constricted. I threw on a pair of yoga pants and a sweatshirt.

"Lily, what are you doing?"

"I can't do this."

"What do you mean?" he yelled.

I threw open my suitcase and dug for my tennis shoes. I forced my feet into them as quickly as possible when I found them and grabbed my purse.

"I'm sorry, Luke. I promise you'll be okay," I cried as I flew out of the hotel room.

The elevator doors were open because a young couple had just stepped on. My face was soaked in tears, and my nose was running. The pretty brunette looked at me and handed me a tissue.

"Thanks," I cried.

The doors opened, and I ran. I ran through the lobby and out onto the soaking wet streets of New York City. I could see Central Park. He'll be okay. He'll be okay, I kept chanting over and over again. I figured if I said it enough, I would believe it in time. The rain was pouring from the sky, and I was soaked, as were the people leaving the park and trying to seek shelter.

"Lily!" I heard Luke yell. "You can't do this. You can't just walk away from me. I love you, and I refuse to live without you."

I stopped in the middle of the grass. "You don't understand!" I screamed as I turned around and looked at him. He was soaked, looking at me like a lost soul.

"Make me understand because I don't know who the hell you've become. I love you, and I know damn well you love me. You're still in love with me, right?"

I turned away and closed my eyes. If I told him no, I'd be lying because I loved him more than life.

"Lily, answer me!" he yelled as he approached me. He grabbed my arms. "Are you still in love with me?"

I broke out of his grip. "Yes. Yes, I love you, and I am in love with you. But it's too late. We can't ever be together. We can't go back to how things used to be."

"Why? What the hell is your problem?"

I wiped the rain from my forehead as I stood there soaking wet, crying and shaking, not only from the cold but from my own fears.

"Make me understand," he cried.

"I gave you the tickets. You had a great time, a time you didn't think would be your last with her. You were broken, so broken after her death, and then I came along and put you back together. You didn't know that I was the girl who gave you the tickets. I didn't even know I was the girl. I didn't remember you. How could I? I was in my own turmoil of my fucked up life, and when I saw you and Callie holding hands and smiling at that table, I knew you were the perfect couple, and I wanted something good to come out of the hell I was trying to climb out of. But instead, my hell turned into your hell, and I will never forgive myself for that. Every time you look at me, you'll be reminded I was the one. It will always be in the back of your mind that I was responsible for Callie's death, especially when you see or hear something that reminds you of her. I can't live the rest of my life causing you any more pain. Don't you get it? I caused you pain before we even met."

He stood there, crying as he stared at me. "You're wrong, babe. I don't blame you. I'm so sorry that I even said that. I didn't mean it.

I was in shock. You don't cause me pain, and I don't think about that when I look at you. All I see when I look at you is my soulmate and my best friend. The girl that rescued me and fell in love with me. The girl who I love so damn much that I would give up my life for. Lily, please don't do this to us. Please don't do this to me. You stand there and talk about causing me pain. The only pain you'll cause me is if you walk away from me."

I stepped closer to him and placed my hand on his cheek. "I can't. You'll move on and find someone who will love you just as much as I do. I'm doing this for you. You have to understand that."

"No! I will never understand your reasoning. Congratulations, Lily, you just caused me the worst pain imaginable. Have a great life," he said as he turned around and walked away.

As I watched him, I fell to my knees, sobbing and wanting to run after him. What was I doing? Did I even know anymore? I couldn't think or see straight as I made my way out of Central Park. I was walking down the streets, dazed and confused and crying. He said he'd give up his life for me, but he didn't understand that I was doing that for him. I was giving up my life for him.

After walking for what seemed like hours, a man called out to me.

"You're welcome to use my umbrella, miss."

I looked over in between the two buildings and saw a homeless man seeking shelter under a large overhang. He was sitting on the ground, looking up at me. His clothes were tattered and worn. He wore a tan coat and had the hood covering his head. I could see the dirt spots on his face and fingers. He was older, I would say, in his fifties. I stopped because this man who looked like he had nothing had offered me his umbrella.

"Thank you," I said as I took it from him and sat on the cold, wet ground.

"You look pretty beaten up. I haven't seen you around here before."

"I'm not from here. I live in California."

"Ah, California. I was there once. It's a beautiful place but holds many bad memories for me. The name's Philip." He smiled.

"I'm Lily," I said as I held out my hand.

He looked at me strangely, unsure, then slowly placed his hand in mine and shook it. "You don't mind shaking hands with a homeless man?"

"No. You may be homeless, but you're still a person."

He looked away. "That's probably the nicest thing anyone has said to me in a very long time. It's nice to meet you, Lily."

The rain started to slow down, and I was so cold. My problems seemed far and few compared to Philip's.

"I saw a little diner around the corner. Are you hungry? I really need some coffee."

"That's sweet of you, Lily, but you don't want to be seen with a homeless man. I'm fine."

"You offered me the use of your umbrella, and I want to thank you. So come on, Philip, let's sit in the diner, have some coffee, something to eat, and dry off."

"You're serious, aren't you?" he asked.

"Yeah. I very serious." I smiled.

"Well, if you insist. Who am I to turn down such a generous offer from a beautiful girl?"

We both stood up and walked around the corner. When we stepped into the diner, and I told the hostess we would like a booth, she gave me a strange look and showed us to the only available booth.

"Excuse me, miss. Are you okay?"

"I'm fine," I replied, looking at her strangely.

"I'm sorry," she said as she walked away.

I looked at Philip, and he laughed. "People are strange. Just ignore her."

Chapter Thirty-Two

LUKE

 I went back to the hotel and stepped into the hot shower as soon as I got to my room. I placed my hands against the smooth, tiled wall and cried. I completely broke down. My head was spinning and reeling with all kinds of emotions. How could she do this to us? She said she still loved me, yet we couldn't be together. She was wrong. Dead wrong! I would never look at her and think of Callie. She made her decision, and there was nothing that I could do to change it. I tried, and I couldn't do it anymore. When I returned to California, I was moving out of the apartment building. I couldn't be near her. She was so fucking worried about me feeling pain every time I looked at her. Well, she was right. Now, I would because I loved her, and it hurt way too much to look at her and know that I couldn't have her.

 After I finished my shower, I looked up flights back home. The next flight out of New York was at nine o'clock tonight. FUCK! I needed something earlier, but I was out of luck. I put on some dry clothes and lay down on the bed. I replayed our conversation over and over again until I fell asleep.

Lily

"Order anything as much as you want," I told Philip.

"If you'll excuse me, Lily, I'm going to use the restroom and clean myself up a little."

I smiled as he got up from the booth. The waitress came by and poured coffee into both of our cups. A few moments later, Philip returned to the table, looking better. He had washed his face and hands, making himself look cleaner. He sat down, and when he sipped his coffee, he closed his eyes as if it was the best thing he'd ever tasted.

"The aroma of coffee always gets me. I love it."

"Me too."

There was something about Philip that reminded me of my father. I couldn't exactly put my finger on it, but something about him comforted me.

"When I first saw you, you looked like you had been crying. Would you like to talk about what happened?"

"Not really," I replied.

"Sometimes talking to a complete stranger is more therapeutic than talking to a friend or someone who knows you. They seem to tell you what you want to hear."

I smiled at him as I took a sip of my coffee. The waitress walked over and placed our food in front of us. As we ate, I told him everything, starting from my wedding day. He sat there and intently listened to me as I told him all about Luke, but he never spoke a word. He just listened, and now it was his turn.

"So why are you homeless?" I asked.

"Getting right down to the nitty gritty, I see." He smiled.

"Sorry," I said as I looked down. "You said that California held many bad memories for you."

He took in a deep breath. "I had it all once. A high-paying job, a beautiful wife, two beautiful children, a dog, and the house with the white picket fence, until my wife was killed in a car accident three years ago."

"I'm so sorry," I said.

"We were having a dinner party that evening, and she had asked me if I would stop on the way home from the office and pick up some extra bottles of wine. I had a crazy and bad day, and I forgot. When I got home, I wasn't in the best of moods, and I wasn't looking forward to having people over. Elise asked me where the wine was, and I told her I'd had a bad day and forgot to pick some up. She told me to go back out and buy some. After saying a few choice words to her, I said I would after I showered and changed. She could sense the irritation in my voice, so she told me to forget it. She grabbed the keys from the counter and went herself.

After I showered and dressed, she still wasn't home. An hour and a half had passed, and I started to worry. Her cell phone went straight to voicemail every time I called. Our dinner guests were scheduled to arrive in an hour, and it wasn't like Elise to be gone so long. That was when I climbed into my vehicle and drove to the party store, where we got all our liquor. As I was close, I noticed a long back-up of cars. She would have called to let me know if she was in that lineup. I sat there for fifteen minutes without moving until I got out of my car and saw flashing red lights up ahead. I walked in between the vehicles to get a closer look. It looked like an accident happened. My heart stopped beating when I saw a car resembling Elise's completely smashed. I asked God to please not let it be her, but when I got closer, I looked at the license plate, and it was her car. I looked next to the car and saw someone covered in a white sheet. As I started screaming her name, two police officers ran up to me and held me back. They said that she was already dead when they got there. Apparently, she was going through a green light, and a semi-truck driver didn't realize the light was red on his side, and he just went through and smashed into her."

A tear fell down his cheek as several fell down mine. I reached over and grabbed his hand. "I am so sorry that happened to you. That wasn't your fault."

He looked down as he continued eating. "That was as much my fault as it was the truck driver's. If I had never forgotten to get the wine on the way home or argued with her about it, she wouldn't have gone, and she'd still be here today."

I was in complete shock by his story. "Philip. That was not your fault. We can spend a lifetime doing the 'what ifs,' which won't change anything."

"Just like Callie's accident?" he asked.

I instantly changed the subject. "What about your children? Where are they?"

"My mom is taking care of them."

"I'm sorry to ask this, but how could you just leave your kids like that after they lost their mother?"

He gently smiled at me as he placed his hand on mine. "I was a constant reminder of their mother's death. They overheard us arguing that day. They heard the things she was saying to me. The way she called me lazy and selfish and never thought about anybody but myself. They told me flat out that she would still be alive if I had only done what she had asked, and they were right. I told my mom I was going on a trip to look after the kids. That was three years ago, and I never looked back," he said as he stared at me. "Every time I looked into my children's eyes, I would see the blame. It was too much to handle, so I had to spare them."

I sat there and was at a loss for words. "So you gave up everything? Why?"

"Because, my dear, I gave up on me. I lost all my self-worth, dignity, and clarity. I realize now that I was a fool and I was wrong. Nothing's really as it seems. Your perception is the one thing that pixels the truth. I didn't cause my wife's death, just like you didn't cause Callie's, and I can guarantee that Luke won't ever look at you and see you as the woman who was responsible. I just wish that I could be with my children again and make them understand."

"You can. It's not too late," I said as I squeezed his hand.

"It is. For me, at least." He smiled.

"No. No, it's not. We can call your children right now. You can talk to them, and I'll send you home. You can fly back to California with me. What's your mom's number? I can call her for you, and you can talk to your children."

He rattled off his mother's phone number as I punched it into my phone. As it rang, he exited the booth and placed his hand on my shoulder.

"Take what I've told you today and rebuild your relationship. Clear your mind and see the truth for what it really is, not what you think it is. Second chances are always the best in life, Lily." He smiled.

Philip turned, walked through the diner, and out the door. Before I could stop him, I heard an older woman's voice on the other end of the phone.

"Hello," she answered.

"Hi, my name is Lily Gilmore, and I'm calling about your son, Philip."

"Yes. How can I help you?"

"He's in New York, and we just had a long conversation and—"

"Excuse me. Is this some kind of a joke? My son, Philip, passed away a year ago from pneumonia."

My jaw dropped, and I sat there silently, looking at the door.

"I'm so sorry. Maybe I have the wrong number. I'm so sorry." Click.

What the fuck just happened? The waitress came by and placed her hand on my arm.

"Are you okay, sweetie? You look like you've just seen a ghost."

"That man that was sitting here with me for the last four hours."

"What man, sweetie?"

"What do you mean 'what man'? You served him food."

"No. You've been the only one sitting here for the last four hours. Do you need me to call someone for you?"

I heard his voice in my head as I stared straight ahead at where he sat. "Clear your mind and see the truth for what it really is, not what you think it is."

"I'm fine. I'm just really tired. Here," I said as I pulled out my money and handed it to her. "Keep the change. I need to go."

"Thank you, sweetie. Take care of yourself," she yelled as I quickly left the diner.

Chapter Thirty-Three

LUKE

As I sat on the edge of the bed with my feet planted firmly on the floor, I sighed as I cupped my face in my hands. I picked up my phone, and there were no messages. I shook my head as I got up and threw my things in the suitcase. I had slept too long and needed to get to the airport.

After quickly scanning the room and making sure I had everything, I went down to the lobby and checked out. I couldn't get out of here fast enough. The valet hailed a cab for me and told the driver to take me to the airport. Since I still had a little bit of time, I decided to get something to eat before heading to my gate. I pulled my phone from my pocket and dialed Sam.

"Hey, bro. Gretchen and I were talking about you and Lily. How are the two of you? Getting along, I hope."

"It's over for good, man. She decided it, not me."

"Luke, I'm sorry. I'm going to put you on speaker so Gretchen can hear."

"Luke, what the fuck happened? What did she say to you?" Gretchen asked.

"She said that if we were together, I would be reminded of

Callie every time I looked at her. She said that she caused me enough pain in my life, and she couldn't do it anymore." My eyes started to fill with tears.

"She's an idiot!" Gretchen yelled. "What the hell is the matter with her and her fucked up way of thinking? That's what she meant that night at Charley's birthday party. I told her you're so in love with her, and she said you only think you are."

I shook my head as I took a bite of my pizza. This was unreal to me.

"I'm at the airport now. My flight will be boarding soon. I'll talk to you guys later."

"Take care, Luke, and we're on your side," Sam said.

I finished my pizza and then headed to my gate. I really thought that we'd be flying home together. I was dead wrong. My phone had ten percent battery left, so I turned it off and put it back in my pocket. Sitting in the chair, I noticed the couple sitting across from me. They were smiling, holding hands, and sharing small kisses. I couldn't sit there, so I moved to the other side and sat in the corner.

⁓

LILY

Shit. I didn't really know where I was. When I walked here from Central Park, I was in such a daze of confusion that I didn't pay attention. I hailed a cab and told him to step on it to The Plaza Hotel. He looked at me strangely until I held out a twenty-dollar bill.

"It's a matter of life and death. I need to get there NOW!"

"Sure thing, lady."

He pulled out into traffic. Weaving in and out, slamming on the brakes, and almost getting me killed a few times. He pulled up to the hotel, and the valet opened the door. I paid my fare and ran into the hotel, pressing the button on the elevator numerous times. The doors finally opened, and I rode it up to my floor, with a few stops on the way. I pushed my way through the crowd of people on the elevator when the doors opened and went right to Luke's room. I knocked on the door and then called his name. No answer. I knocked again. No answer. I BANGED on it. No answer. I pulled my phone from my purse and dialed his number. It went straight to voicemail. SHIT.

I got out my room key, went inside, changed into different clothes, and went down to the front desk.

"Can I help you, miss?"

"I'm trying to get a hold of Luke Matthews in room 2212, and he's not answering, and I'm worried."

"Mr. Matthews already checked out."

"Oh." My heart sank. "That's right. He said something about going home earlier than planned. He was going home, right?"

"I don't know, miss. He didn't say."

"Right. Thank you."

I turned around, and my eyes filled with tears. What was I going to do now? I tried to call him again, and it went straight to voicemail.

As I walked outside the hotel, I asked the valet about Luke and showed him his picture. He told me he took a cab to the airport about an hour ago. I thanked him as I hopped in a cab and told the driver to take me to the airport. I searched flights out of LaGuardia, and the only flight that Luke would have been on was the nine o'clock flight. I looked at my watch. I still had time. I could make it.

"Excuse me, but you need to drive faster," I told the cab driver.

"Ma'am, this is New York. I'm doing the best I can."

We finally reached the airport, and I ran to security and was instantly stopped.

"Boarding pass, please."

"I'm not flying out. I need to go and get my boyfriend. I need to tell him how much I love him and that I made a terrible mistake."

He looked at me with irritation. "You aren't getting through security if you don't have a boarding pass."

"Have you ever been in love?" I asked.

"No," he said as he made me turn around and pointed to the ticket counter.

"I can see why," I mumbled as I stood in line.

I was running out of time. I needed to get to the front of the line to buy a ticket and try to stop Luke. I couldn't let him get on that plane. I walked up front to the next person in line. A young man. A very cute young man.

"Excuse me. I don't have time to stand in line. I need to get to my boyfriend before he boards his plane. Can I please have your spot in line?"

"Sorry, lady, but I'm in a hurry too."

I flashed a fifty-dollar bill at him. "Still in a hurry?"

"One more person won't make a difference," he said as he took the money from my hand and motioned for me to get in front of him. I looked back at him.

"I want you to know that your cuteness factor just went out the window."

"Next," the man at the counter said.

"I need a ticket."

"To where?"

"I don't care where. Just give me a ticket!"

He looked at me and narrowed his eyes. "You don't know where you're going?"

"Fine. Give me a ticket for the next flight out to LAX."

"Okay. That flight leaves at one a.m."

"Wait. Don't you have a nine o'clock flight?"

"Yes, but that's sold out."

I sighed. "Fine, give me the one o'clock. Just hurry," I said as I handed him my I.D. and credit card.

"Here you go. Do you have any bags to check?"

"No. I don't," I said as I grabbed the ticket and ran to security.

"I see you're going on a trip." The security officer smiled.

I shot him a look as I waited to go through. It was all moving quickly, but his plane was boarding right now. I took off my shoes, threw them in the bin, got scanned, and grabbed them as I stood and looked at the monitor to find out which gate he was at. Once I found out, I looked at the signs and, oh shit, I had to run. Of course, his gate would be at the other end. I ran through the airport, pushing people, saying excuse me and almost tripping over someone's cane. I would tell Luke I was wrong and beg him for forgiveness. Why was I so stupid? How was I so stupid? I didn't have time to analyze my stupidity as I finally reached his gate, and the doors shut. I ran up to the desk.

"I need to get on that plane."

"I'm sorry, miss, but it's too late. It's closed."

"No, no. You don't understand. My life is hanging by a thread, and the answer to that is on that plane. I need to get on that plane," I said with a shaky voice as I showed her my boarding pass.

She looked at me and raised her eyebrow. "Your ticket isn't even for this flight. Do you need us to call someone for you?"

Why does everyone keep asking me that?

"No. I'm sorry," I replied, looking down and slowly walking away.

I went to the window and looked at the plane as the tears started falling. I wasn't feeling well, and it was the overwhelming sickness that I might never be with him again.

Chapter Thirty-Four

LILY

I sat down in the chair for a moment to compose myself. Everything that had happened today was strange. I couldn't wrap my head around it. Did I even want to? I took in a deep breath and got up from the chair. I started to walk away when I heard my name from a distance.

"Lily?"

I stopped momentarily and turned around to find Luke standing a few feet before me. I ran to him and threw my arms around him as tightly as possible.

"Oh my God, I'm so sorry for everything. Why are you here? You were on the plane!"

He looked confused but happy at the same time. "We have to switch planes. This one was having mechanical issues. Do you believe it?"

"Yes. After today, I do believe it. I believe everything, including you. I'm so sorry, Luke. Please forgive me. I love you so much, and I can't lose you."

He grabbed my face and smashed his lips against mine.

"Lily, you don't know how happy I am to hear you say that."

"Yes, I do. I love you."

"I love you too, babe. God, I can't believe this." He smiled as he picked me up and spun me around. "What happened? Why did you change your mind?"

"We can talk about that later. Let's go back to the hotel. We have so much to catch up on."

"We sure do, babe. We sure do."

∽

Luke

We couldn't keep our hands off of each other. She felt warm again. She fumbled in her purse for the keycard as I had her up against the door, passionately kissing her. She handed me the card, and I inserted it as the green light flashed, and I turned the knob.

"Wait," I said as I broke our kiss.

I held the door open with my foot, picked her up, and carried her inside. She smiled as her arms were wrapped around my neck.

"Babe, I want to make love to you so bad. But we have to take your temperature first."

"What?!" she exclaimed.

"You feel hot."

She sighed as I sat her down on the bed. "Fine," she said as she stuck the thermometer in her mouth. It beeped. She looked at it and then at me.

"It's 100.5, and I don't care because we already mixed saliva, so you're going to get it anyway." She smiled as she pulled me down on top of her.

"I didn't say I wouldn't make love to you. I was saying you felt warm."

My lips trailed her neck as she fumbled with the button on my jeans. Once she managed to get them unbuttoned, she unzipped the zipper and stuck her hand down the front of my pants. I moaned.

"You have no idea how much I've missed this," she gasped.

"Kind of like I missed these." I smiled as my hand grabbed her breast.

Her hand was stroking me up and down, and I felt like I was already going to come. I stood up, removed my shoes, and stripped off my clothes. Lily sat up and did the same, except for her bra. She left that on and smiled at me. She knew how much I loved to take it off of her. I climbed on the bed behind her as she sat straight up. My tongue made tiny circles around her shoulders and upper back as my hands unhooked her bra. I reached in front of her and lightly took hold of both her breasts, kneading them and pinching her hard nipples. Her moans increased as she placed her hands on mine, guiding my hands around her breasts.

"God, I love you, Lily."

"I love you, Luke."

She turned around to face me and sat up on her knees. My hand found its way in between her legs as my fingers plunged inside her, and my thumb slowly rubbed her clit. She arched her back and started making the "ah" sounds as she ran her fingers through my hair.

"You're so wet. I think you need to be wetter, though," I said as I brought my mouth down to her. My tongue softly circling her swollen area was arousing her even more. She began to thrust her hips as my tongue dipped inside of her and played around.

"Oh God, Luke. Baby, what are you doing to me?" she asked with bated breath.

"Making you come," I whispered as my tongue circled her clit and my fingers went inside her. I brought her to the edge and smiled as she released herself on me.

She pushed me back and climbed on top, but not before sucking me off for a few minutes. Her mouth wrapped around my cock was the hottest thing to me. I loved watching her. She brought her lips to mine and gently climbed on top of me. I was so hard and more than ready to be inside of her. She lowered herself onto me and began slowly moving. Looking at her entire naked body making love to me was amazing. Our lips were locked tight as I thrust myself inside her. We both gasped as I nipped her bottom lip. She broke our kiss, and her lips traveled from my chin down to my nipples. She licked each one before sitting up and moving her hips in a circular motion. I couldn't get enough of her. She felt so good.

"Lily, you feel amazing."

"So do you. You're so hard," she said as she leaned back and placed her hands on my legs.

I grabbed a hold of her hips and moved her back and forth on my cock. She was swelling and getting ready to have orgasm number two.

"Lily, I'm going to come."

"Me too!" she yelled.

She sat straight up and rode me faster as her legs tightened at my side, and we both came at the same time, calling out each other's names. She collapsed on top of me and hugged me tight. Our hearts beat rapidly together as our breathing began to slow. My hands traveled softly up and down her naked back. It felt so good to have her body near mine again.

"You need to take some Motrin," I whispered in her ear.

She let out a laugh as she rolled off of me. "Really, Luke?"

"Yeah, babe. Really." I winked.

Chapter Thirty-Five

LILY

I took some Motrin, like Luke said, and got up from the bed.
"Where are you going?" he asked.
"To get the room service menu. I'm starving." I smiled.
"Me too."
Luke climbed under the covers, and I climbed next to him as we looked over the menu.
"What time is it?" I asked.
He glanced over at the clock. It's eleven-thirty."
"Oh, well, we need to look at the overnight dining menu."
"I think I want the burger."
"Me too." I smiled as I kissed his lips.
After I placed our order, I snuggled against Luke's chest as he stroked my hair.
"Lily, what made you change your mind about us?"
I slowly closed my eyes. Did I tell him? Did I lie because I didn't want him to think I was crazy?
"If I tell you, then you'll think I'm crazy, and I mean certifiably legit crazy."
He chuckled as he kissed my head. "I would never think that."

I sat up, took a deep breath, and told him about Philip. "And as I was calling his mom, he got up from his seat, and I'll never forget what he said to me."

"What did he say, babe?"

"He said, 'Take what I've told you today and rebuild your relationship. Clear your mind and see the truth for what it really is, not what you think it is. Second chances are always the best in life.' Then he walked away, and when his mom answered, she told me that he had died a year ago of pneumonia."

"Are you serious? Lily, that's an amazing story."

"You don't think I'm crazy?"

"No, I don't. Think of all the events that happened involving us. Hunter and Brynn, the tickets, the accident, you moving in next door, our friends hooking up and getting together, you meeting Philip, and my plane having mechanical problems." He smiled. "Think about it, Lily. We were meant to be together, probably since the day we were born. I think we are the true meaning of soul mates."

He was right. If you put everything together like a puzzle, everything fit neatly together. Every event we endured, and every person crossing our paths played a significant role in our lives. Once you link everything together, it all made sense. Room service arrived, and I quickly put on my robe as Luke pulled on his jeans and opened the door. The man wheeled the cart in and set up the table, and Luke tipped him before he left. We ate our burgers, talked, laughed, and made love two more times before going to sleep.

∼

Luke

Waking up with Lily wrapped up in my arms was something I missed so badly. I placed my hand across her forehead. She felt a little warm, but not as warm as last night.

"Are you checking me for a fever again?" she mumbled.

"Yes," I said as I pressed my lips against her forehead.

"What do your lips say?"

"They say I love you."

A smile graced her face as she opened her eyes and looked at me.

"And I love you."

"Why don't we shower, get dressed, grab breakfast, and then go for a walk? I have someplace I want to take you."

"You forgot something."

"What?" I asked in confusion.

"You forgot to say that we had to make love."

"Believe me, babe, I didn't forget that."

We climbed out of bed, showered, made love, dressed, and then headed downstairs to eat. Once we finished breakfast, I took Lily's hand and headed towards the place I couldn't wait to take her to. Once we stepped outside, I stopped and looked at her.

"If you're feeling up to it, we can walk. It'll take about fourteen minutes to get there. If you'd rather cab it, we can do that. It's up to you, babe."

"I want to walk. It's a nice day out, and we can explore the city."

We walked and did a lot of window shopping. Lily was so happy, and so was I. My phone beeped with a text message from Sam.

"Dude, I thought you were getting in last night."

"Sorry, I forgot to tell you that the flight was rescheduled due to mechanical problems."

"When are you flying out?"

"I'll let you know."

We were coming up to the store I wanted to take Lily to, so I started to slow down. She looked at me.

"Why are you slowing down?"

"This is the store I wanted to go into with you."

She looked up and then at me. "Luke, this is Tiffany's."

I smiled as I led her inside. "Why are we here?" she asked.

"Lily," I said as I took hold of both her hands. "When I lost you, my world ended. My heart stopped beating, and I felt like I was dead. You are the most important thing in my life and my world. I would die for you. I never want to lose you again, and I want to spend the rest of my life with you. You're my soul mate, and I love you so damn much. Will you marry me, Lily Gilmore?"

A tear fell from her eye as she brought her shaking hand to her mouth. "Yes. Yes. Of course, I'll marry you, Luke." She smiled as she wrapped her arms around me.

I picked her up and twirled her around as the customers and employees clapped and whistled for us.

"Let's pick out your ring. I wanted us to pick one out together."

"What did I ever do to deserve someone like you?" she asked as she kissed me.

Chapter Thirty-Six

LILY

All the rings were stunning, but I found one that Luke and I both loved. When I tried it on, we both knew right away that it was the one because it fit perfectly, just like we did. I was the happiest person in the world and couldn't wait to tell everyone we were getting married.

"I have an idea. Let's send a mass video telling everyone we're engaged," I said.

"That's a great idea. Who's going to take it, though?"

"We'll find someone in Central Park. Let's do it there." I smiled.

Luke loved the idea, and we walked to Central Park. We walked over to the fountain and saw a young girl sitting alone.

"Excuse me? Would you mind taking a video of us?"

"Not at all." She smiled.

I set the phone to video mode, and Luke and I took our place in front of the fountain.

"Go," the young girl said.

"Hi, friends and family." I waved.

"Hey, everyone." Luke waved.

"We're sending you this video because we're going to stay in

The Upside of Love

New York for a while longer. We have some news we wanted to share with you. I love this man so much!" I said as I pointed to Luke.

"And I love this woman so much!" he said as he pointed to me.

"And guess what? We're getting married!" we both said at the same time as I held up my hand with my ring on it.

"We love you all, and we'll be home soon! Bye." I waved.

"Bye." Luke waved.

"Oh my God, that is so awesome!" the young girl said as she handed me my phone. "Congrats, you two!"

"Thank you." I grinned.

She walked away, and we sent the video to our family and friends. We sat on a bench by the fountain, and Luke took hold of my hand and brought it to his lips.

"There are two sides of love: the upside and the downside. We've experienced both sides, and I never want to see the downside again. From here on out, babe, this is what the upside of love is. Us. Together forever. Loving each other no matter what life throws our way."

I brushed my lips against his. "You are the upside of love, Luke Matthews."

It wasn't long before our little moment was interrupted by both phones blowing up. We looked at each other and laughed as we turned them off and spent the rest of the week exploring New York and making up for lost time.

~

Two weeks later

"Give me my goddaughter." I smiled as Giselle and Lucky strolled into the bar.

"She's not just your goddaughter, don't forget." Gretchen smiled as she leaned down and kissed Isabella's head.

"I know that, but I will be her favorite godmother." I winked.

Gretchen laughed and put her arm around me. "I'm so excited

to watch the boys play. It seems like it's been forever. What song are they doing?" Gretchen asked.

"I don't know. Luke wouldn't tell me. I tried to threaten him with no sex, but all he had to do was smile, and I was on top of him."

"I am so happy for both of you. I knew you'd come to your senses, eventually. You said you'd tell us what happened to make you change your mind," Giselle said.

"I will, but not tonight. It's a long story."

Luke's dad took over Cody's position part-time, and I couldn't have been happier. Luke and I both agreed to wait about a year before getting married. I wanted to ensure that my career and the studio were off the ground and running, and Luke wanted to ensure things stayed calm at the bar. Neither of us was going anywhere, and we wanted time to plan the perfect wedding. I told Luke he was in charge since I'd done it once before. He laughed and said that he'd gladly accept the challenge.

Charley was so happy about the wedding that she wouldn't stop talking about it at Annie and Tom's house the other night. Lucky officially moved into Giselle's house, and they became an exclusive couple. Gretchen hadn't known this yet, but Sam bought her a ring and would propose to her on her birthday next month. Maddie and Adam were in love, and Charley told us that her dad had started staying the night. As for my sister and Hunter. They're getting married in a couple of months, and Luke and I are attending the wedding. According to him, we must celebrate the couple that brought us together.

Luke walked over and kissed Isabella on the cheek. "You're turning me on holding that baby." He winked.

I smiled as he walked to the stage. The bar was packed, and more people had come when they heard that Luke's band was playing. Luke picked up his guitar and winked at me as he started to play "Don't Fear the Reaper."

"Oh, I love this song," Gretchen said as she began dancing to it. "I always wondered what it was about."

"It's about eternal love." I smiled as I walked toward the front of the stage and watched the love of my life sing to me.

This was, without a doubt, the upside of love, and I loved every second of it.

I hope you enjoyed the conclusion of Luke and Lily's story!

I invite you to join my Sandi's Romance Readers Facebook Group, where we talk about books, romance, and more! Join the fun!

Newsletter
Website
Facebook
Instagram
TikTok
Bookbub
Goodreads
Follow Me On Amazon

More Sizzling Romance

Looking for more romance reads about billionaires, second chances, and sports? Check out my other romance novels and escape to another world and from the daily grind of life – one book at a time.

Series:

Forever Series:
Forever Black (Forever, Book 1)
Forever You (Forever, Book 2)
Forever Us (Forever, Book 3)
Being Julia (Forever, Book 4)
Collin (Forever, Book 5)
A Forever Family (Forever, Book 6)

Wyatt Brothers Series:
Love, Lust & A Millionaire (Wyatt Brothers, Book 1)
Love, Lust & Liam (Wyatt Brothers, Book 2)

A Millionaire's Love Series:
Lie Next to Me (A Millionaire's Love, Book 1)

More Sizzling Romance

When I Lie with You (A Millionaire's Love, Book 2)

Happened Series:
Then You Happened (Happened Series, Book 1)
Then We Happened (Happened Series, Book 2)

Redemption Series:
Carter Grayson (Redemption Series, Book 1)
Chase Calloway (Redemption Series, Book 2)
Jamieson Finn (Redemption Series, Book 3)
Damien Prescott (Redemption Series, Book 4)

Interview Series:
The Interview: New York & Los Angeles Part 1
The Interview: New York & Los Angeles Part 2

Love Series:
Love In Between (Love Series, Book 1)
The Upside of Love (Love Series, Book 2)

Wolfe Brothers Series:
Elijah Wolfe (Wolfe Brothers, Book 1)
Nathan Wolfe (Wolfe Brothers, Book 2)
Mason Wolfe (Wolfe Brothers, Book 3)

Kind Brothers Series:
One of a Kind (Kind Brothers Series, Book 1)
Two of a Kind (Kind Brothers Series, Book 2)
Three of a Kind (Kind Brothers Series, Book 3)
Four of a Kind (Kind Brothers Series, Book 4)
Five of a Kind (Kind Brothers Series, Book 5)
The Kind Brothers (Kind Brothers Series, Book 6)
Six of a Kind (Kind Brothers Series, Book 7)
Seven of a Kind (Kind Brothers Series, Book 8)
Eight of a Kind (Kind Brothers Series, Book 9)
Nine of a Kind (Kind Brothers Series, Book 10)

More Sizzling Romance

A Kind Wedding: Jackson & Georgia (Kind Brothers Series, Book 11)
A Kind Wedding: Conner & Charlotte (Kind Brothers Series, Book 12)
A Kind Wedding: Nathan & Sofia (Kind Brothers Series, Book 13)
A Kind Wedding: Christian & Charleigh (Kind Brothers Series, Book 14)
Ten of a Kind (Kind Brothers Series, Book 15)
Eleven of a Kind (Kind Brothers Series, Book 16)
Twelve of a Kind (Kind Brothers Series, Book 17)
Thirteen of a Kind (Kind Brothers Series, Book 18)
Fourteen of a Kind (Kind Brothers Series, Book 19)

One Night Series:
One Night In London
One Night In Paris

Broken Hearts Series:
Unspoken
A Beautiful Sight

Baby Drama Series:
Baby Drama
Baby Drama II
Baby Drama III

Harbor Falls Series:
Love In Harbor Falls
Only You

Standalone Books

The Billionaire's Christmas Baby
His Proposed Deal
The Secret He Holds
The Seduction of Alex Parker

More Sizzling Romance

Something About Lorelei
The Exception
Corporate Assets
The Negotiation
Defense
The Con Artist
#Delete
Behind His Lies
Perfectly You
The Escort
The Ring
The Donor
Rewind
Remembering You
When I'm With You
LOGAN (A Hockey Romance)
The Merger
The Property Brokers
Unwrapping Romance: A Single Dad Holiday Romance

Made in the USA
Columbia, SC
09 March 2025